Carter's Boys

Charles Beagley

First published 2018

Publishing Partner: Accentia Design

Cover design artwork, typesetting and prepared for publication by: Accentia Design. www.accentia.com.au
Cover photo: William Hellman, USN SEAL (Ret), Courtesy of STIDD Systems, Inc., Greenport, NY USA, Copyright 2010.

A Cataloguing-in-Publication record is available from the National Library of Australia.

ISBN: 978-0-6480070-8-1 (Paperback)
ISBN: 978-0-6480070-9-8 (ePub)

Dedicated to Jonathan and Lydia
for your patience and care.
With all my love.

CHAPTER 1

In the cold early morning mist that shrouded the canal, Richard Briar's old setter was nowhere in sight. The mist clung to the ground in a thick layer deep enough to cover Max, except for his wagging tail that made little impression on the swirling surface.

"Max... Max... heel boy, where are you?" Richard called out.

Usually Max was content following his master along the cycle path on their regular 6:00 am walk, satisfied with the scents lingering on the dew-laden grass verge separating the path from the incline down to the Grand Union Canal. However, this morning was different. Richard felt an overwhelming foreboding: a sense that his walk was not as it should be.

"Max... damn you, where are you?" he shouted again, coughing as the damp vapour clung to his chest; striking deep into his lungs.

Max's occasional yap punctuated the echo of his lone voice somewhere in the dense mist. As old as he was, his latent sniffer-instincts had more than likely locked onto the scent of some nocturnal creature on the lower ground. His barks were becoming more frequent and louder, as Richard approached the ancient wooden lock ahead.

It was an awkward contraption, allowing a vessel travelling up stream to transfer to the higher level beyond the opposite gate.

In the cold early morning mist that shrouded the canal, Richard Briar's old setter was nowhere in sight. It clung to the ground in a thick layer deep enough to cover Max, except for his wagging tail that made little impression on the swirling surface.

He decided to move down to the towpath alongside the canal where Max appeared to be, by the echo of his barks resounding off the nearby water. Watching his footing, as he traversed diagonally down the crude wooden steps from one level to the other, Richard noticed with surprise how high the water was this morning.

This disturbed him. He had never experienced such a level in this short stretch of water between the Uxbridge locks before, or the knowledge of Max swimming should he miss his footing, until the suspense was broken by his shrill bark resounding again; closer this time, just in front by the dark ominous shape of the lock's wooden structure.

As Richard slowly approached the mammoth twelve-inch square lock balance beam, used to push open the equally monumental lock doors he became aware of another sound, one he had missed earlier: that of water cascading close by.

All these realisations came together suddenly. Framed in one instant, one concentrated window of time: the large blue granite buttresses supporting the lock mechanism formed an angular structure protecting the immediate area of the towpath, allowing no mist to intrude and capturing all within like a clear window.

Richard Briar stood fixed, as if not part of the scene: more as a spectator. The large black beam split his field of vision horizontally, while Max was sitting quietly without looking around on his arrival; yet aware that his master was close by. His pointer instinct fixed on the naked body of a man staked out, violently crucified on the beam.

His head was hanging low on his chest, his arms stretched

out either side, held in place by large nails through his hands. His muscular shoulders strained in raised ridges, bulging under the full weight of his torso dangling freely over the canal. His skinned bloody feet, bound in fence wire, disappeared just below the stone edging of the towpath.

Although his athletic body was lacerated with countless minor cuts, the major wound responsible for all the blood that streaked in an arc across the flags in front of Max had to be the gaping hole left where his severed genitals once were.

Richard suspected the beam and its occupant had been pushed forward to allow his legs to hang free over the water, causing the lock doors to part slightly, releasing the water that had built up behind them, explaining the cascading sound he heard, and an explanation why the water level was so high.

Richard suddenly realised the magnitude of the horrific scene. He had to do something before the early morning rush of pedestrians that used the path as a short cut between the nearby estate and the town on the other side of the park.

There was a waterways phone on the stone buttress and he dialled the emergency number. It was a garbled message, and he had to repeat himself more than once, as he stuttered in shock. A cold voice told him the police were on their way.

By the time Inspector Jack Hammond and Sergeant Brian Binstead arrived at the crime scene the doctor and forensic were already there. They did not look happy. The seasoned detective mumbled something his sergeant did not hear as he stepped out of the car.

"Remind me, Sergeant why you called me out of my warm bed at this time?"

"You have to be present on a murder, Boss."

"How can you be sure it's a murder?"

"Oh I'm sure, Boss."

Before they headed for the group at the crime scene Inspector Hammond took hold of his sergeant's shoulder.

"I must admit I was still half asleep to hear what you said, Sergeant... remind me."

"We just got an urgent call for assistance," he replied.

"And what's this emergency then?. Inspector Hammond continued.

Sergeant Binstead reached into his pocket for his notebook.

"A man walking his dog found a naked body in the canal... well over the canal... I think. The operator was very confused."

"Over the canal?"

The Sergeant passed his notebook to the Inspector.

"What's this crucified nonsense?"

"That's what she said, Boss... crucified. I got her to read it back to me."

"Good heavens, what's this place coming to?" he exclaimed, still perusing the sergeant's unbelievable scrawl.

The mist had almost dissipated when the Sergeant headed first towards the steps leading down to the canal.

"Watch your step, Boss," he said, warning the Inspector of the slippery grass.

Everything was much clearer now that the mist had lifted, and as they traversed the same rough wooden steps Richard Briar had taken, they too experienced the horror of the scene before them. They would not forget this one in a hurry.

"My god, what lunatic was let loose here?" the Inspector remarked.

Doctor Jessop turned to see who had arrived. He too found the scene particularly traumatic, especially since he also was not at his best this morning.

"What do you think, doc?" the Inspector called out to the

middle-aged medic kneeling by the body. "I must say you got here quickly."

"Don't you people ever say good morning?"

"Good morning, doc," the Sergeant said, raising a laugh.

"Well it isn't a good morning, Sergeant," doctor Jessop grunted. "This was my day off, and I was looking forward to a day of fishing at the reservoir," he stated curtly, continuing to measure the excessively large patch of blood that had soaked into the stone surface, spreading outwards like blotting paper, looking like a sinister Arabian crescent.

The Inspector had regained his composure. Dead bodies left him cold.

"So why are you here?" he said.

"My Locum's got a cold... on my day off."

"Isn't that the truth these. Anyway... what about my question"

"What question?" he had lost track. "Oh yes, I won't really know until I get him down, but by the looks of his injuries and the amount of blood scattered around these flags, I'd say he bled to death."

The Inspector stepped cautiously to one side, not wanting any on his shoes.

"Boss," the Sergeant interrupted. "I've just been talking to Mr Briar; he's been here since six. Can he go home. I've taken his statement."

"Just hold on, Sergeant, I want a quick word."

"What about me?" the doctor asked.

"Sergeant... what are those forensic doing?"

"They're working on the towpath, Boss."

The Inspector stepped sideways around the blood.

"Then get them down here so that the doc can take the body away. And cover him up for Christ sake, he looks obscene."

As the Inspector climbed the steps to the higher level, he noticed Richard Briar posed a miserable sight in his running suit, crouching on a seat above the lock by the cycle track. As young as he was, he appeared to have aged from the experience. Still shaking, and taking what comfort he could from his faithful dog's head on his lap.

"Sorry you had to wait, Mr Briar, I'm Detective Inspector Hammond," he showed him his warrant card, for what good it did, and sat down beside him. "I know the Sergeant has already taken your statement, but I'd just like to get your first impressions leading up to when you found the body, while it's still fresh in your mind. By tomorrow it'll be long gone."

He looked at the Inspector with open, questioning eyes. "Oh it won't... I'll remember that scene forever," he replied, gripping his forehead. "I'll never forget that moment when I broke through the mist; you should have been there, it was like opening a window."

"What was, Mr Briar?"

"This big black beam, with him crucified on it... dangling over the canal."

"It was you who said he was crucified then?"

"Yes... didn't you see him. His hands nailed to that cross."

"But he wasn't on a cross, Mr Briar."

"Yes he was. A cross in the biblical times didn't mean what it does today. It was usually just a straight piece of timber nailed on top of a pole."

"You know about these things then?"

"Yes... I'm a teacher at the local High School."

"I see, and you run here every morning at six?"

"Yes... thereabouts. Why did he do that to him?"

"Do what, Mr Briar"

"You know... that with his... cut his genitals off."

"I don't know. I expect we shall find out in due course."

The Inspector noticed he was going into shock.

"Mr Briar, we're almost there... you're doing extremely well. What made you leave your normal route. Assuming you stick to the cycle path in the morning."

He had to think for a moment, "Oh... Max here," he stroked the head on his lap fondly. "He doesn't usually run off like that, always staying to heel. But this morning he picked up a trail back there on the path, and disappeared into the mist following it"

"This trail... where was that?" he asked, the Inspector sensed his first clue.

"Up there by that chestnut," Briar hesitated to regain his place. "It was low this morning, the mist that is, almost on top of the water... so you couldn't see a thing, except for that isolated little area by the buttress. Anyway I could hear Max barking, and I realised by the echo he must be on the towpath. I was so frightened, I didn't know if he could swim or not, it would be so easy to lose your footing and fall into the canal when it's misty."

He paused for a moment, looking into the distance, licking his lips as if he were thirsty: a sure sign he was going into shock.

"Just take your time, Mr Briar, easy does it," the Inspector assured him.

"Then I saw Max by the stone buttress, there was no mist, it was like a window," he repeated, passing his hand across from left to right. "Max was just sitting there, he knew something wasn't right. He was looking up at the black balance beam with him hanging there... and all the time the sound of water pouring."

"What was that about the water?"

"From the lock, they were partly open... the doors I mean."

"I'm sorry, I don't follow you?"

"The beam had been pushed out just enough for him to hang over the canal, which meant the big doors had opened a little, letting the water out."

"How was it doing that?"

The Inspector's ignorance irritated Richard Briar.

"You obviously know nothing about locks, Inspector," Briar said. "The canal on each side of this double-lock is at different levels."

"I understand that much, Mr Briar."

"Well the water in between is at the same level as the side opened last. This morning it happened to be the high side, so a vessel must have passed up stream last."

"I see what you're getting at... thank you,"

The Inspector had a vision of a small boat passing through the lock, stopping off on the other side with the body, and carrying on up the canal. This was yet another clue if they could calculate when this happened; and at what time the lock opened.

Suddenly he remembered the doctor was about to pull the victim in, he quickly jumped up. "Stop... don't close the doors anymore," he shouted down to them.

"No, Inspector," Briar cried, "They have to or you'll lose the level."

"Okay, thanks, Mr Briar, just wait here and I'll get the doctor to have a look at you, and then we'll get you home."

"I'm all right... really," he replied, swaying dizzily.

The Inspector stumbled down the incline as he called for the sergeant.

"Get them to go over the end of the beam extra carefully; Mr Briar says the killer must have pushed him out over the canal, that's why the water's escaping."

"What water, Boss?"

The Inspector realised it was now silent: the cascade had stopped when they pulled him in over the flags. He was on his knees, with his feet tucked up behind him. A constable was removing the wire with wire-cutters under the watchful eye of the doctor, who was also attempting to examine a strange mark on his neck.

"You could have completed your forensic before bringing him in."

"Okay, Boss... look," he took him closer to the beam end. There was a semi-circular track of grooves cut into the flags below the end of the beam to stop their feet slipping when they pushed the heavy beam in either direction. "It's too heavy to move from the end, you have to get behind it this side to push it forward."

"Good... then get them on to it, I want every splinter checked."

"What's with the water, Boss?"

"Well you've closed the lock now, so it's stopped running. Mr Briar said something about the water level getting too low."

The Sergeant slapped his side in frustration.

"Yes, Boss, I remember now. You have to change the level of the water between the locks to equalise the level when you pass through."

"Yes, well I had that lesson from Mr Briar. But the interesting thing is, Sergeant; he said the last vessel through must have been going up stream, as the lock was full, so when the killer pushed our victim out he inadvertently started the water flowing down stream again. Now if we measure the depth it is against what it should be, we'd have a good idea what time the killer crucified him. And what time this unknown vessel was here."

"Are you suggesting the victim was brought here by boat?"

"It's possible... at least we know a boat was here sometime in the early hours. And that gives us either a suspect or a witness, so get on with it."

"Wouldn't it be better to wait for the doc to give us the time of death?"

"Sergeant... time of death and the time the killer left the scene could be two different things. We want to know who was around at that time. And another clue Mr Briar let out was, Max caught the scent of something up by that chestnut tree."

The Sergeant was busily making notes of all the things the Inspector wanted. "Boss... how am I going to get all this information?"

"I don't know, Sergeant; do some detection. There must be an authority that controls the canal network and who uses it."

The Inspector turned back to where the doctor was finishing. "Any answers for me yet, doc?"

"Well I can tell you this; he didn't bleed to death as I first thought."

"Then how did he die?"

The doctor pulled the zipper back on the black body bag revealing a man in his late fifties, made worse by his bloated face, which he did not pick up earlier while in the position he was with his head lolled on his chest. The doctor pointed to the continuous plum coloured line around his neck, the unmistakable impression of a thin cord, and as the Inspector studied the bruise, the doctor bent down and retrieved something from his bag.

"Here's your culprit," he passed the Inspector a plastic bag containing a necklace of animal sinew, carrying a single ornament: a wooden pawn.

"It's a Garrotte isn't it?" The Inspector commented.

"Yes, Inspector: a thin ligature with a knot in it, or in this case, a wooden pawn. You place the loop over the victim's head with the pawn over his windpipe, with your arms crossed, and then pull them apart and 'Bobs your uncle'. And it's all over very quickly, in the hands of an expert."

"And would you say this was done by an expert?"

"Oh yes, very much so... very professional."

"What I can't understand, doc, is why do this here. It must have taken some time to cut him up like that."

"He didn't," he answered, standing up again to face the Inspector. "On closer inspection, I found that the blood on the majority of wounds had dried; only the genital area was fresh."

"So he was only brought here to finish him off... is that what you're saying?"

"And to make a statement, I suspect."

"A statement?"

"Well as I see it, and this is only until I've made a more thorough examination, the victim was tortured over a long period of time."

"Wouldn't his screams have drawn some attention?" the Inspector interrupted.

"Look here," he pointed to the sticky tape marks around his mouth. "He was obviously gagged, and at the appropriate time driven to this spot, nailed to the beam, his genitals removed and garrotted. By the way have you found them yet?"

"I don't think so; they're probably at the bottom of the canal, feeding the catfish." The Inspector stepped back to allow the ambulance men to take the body away. "Still... he would have been quite a handful to get up onto that beam."

"As I removed the Garrotte, I smelt a faint trace of Chloroform, which suggests he was probably unconscious when he was transported to this spot. The beam is too low to stand him up against, which I agree, would have been difficult, but the scrapes on his knees suggest he was knelt in front first... then each arm taped to the beam."

"Taped to the beam?"

"Yes," the doctor pointed to the faint traces of plaster on the dark wood.

The Inspector squatted down to check.

"They correspond with marks on his wrists," the doctor continued, "although there's no sign of any tape about. He must have waited for him to recover, nailed his hands in place, and then removed the tape. Once he was sure he was fully awake in this kneeling position, he probably did his bit with the knife, and then garrotted him."

"Well that sounds more plausible doc, anything else?"

The doctor started closing the bag to leave.

"Just that his mouth was taped up as well, probably for some time; the discolouration either side was darker than his arms."

Inspector Hammond glanced down at the notebook in his hand, quickly scanning the hurried notations he had made during Dr Jessop's brief report. He pointed the pencil at him. "So you're suggesting he was tortured somewhere else then brought here to be crucified?"

"Exactly... well can I see to Mr Briar before he becomes my next patient?"

"Yes, doc... sorry about that. Oh by the way," Inspector Hammond called out as the doctor began to make his way up the steps. "What about time of death?"

"That's a difficult one. Naked body, exposed to the early morning mist. I'd say at a guess, sometime between midnight and three. It was a full moon last night, so our maniac would have had plenty of light. I'll have a better idea after the autopsy."

As they had disturbed the tranquillity of this idyllic haven, so they left it. The ambulance drove off with the unfortunate individual of their investigation; for as yet no identification had been possible, Doctor Jessop was attending to the distraught Richard Briar before taking him home and the forensic team still had work to do; especially since. Inspector Hammond had issued his latest input.

Sergeant Binstead walked over to the Inspector, "What now, Boss?"

"What time is it," he said checking his watch. "8:15 am... that's not bad. We'll get back now and set this thing up. Who knows, we might even find out who this poor wretch is... did I ask you to check Missing Persons?"

CHAPTER 2

Other than the early mist at the crime scene, it remained dry and overcast but who was noticing under the gruesome experience. No sooner had they arrived back at the Uxbridge station, the heavens opened.

The Inspector was first through the doors, shaking the drops from his coat and mopping his head with a hanky, to a chorus of 'April Showers' from his old friend the Desk Sergeant behind the counter.

"I keep telling you to take your umbrella with you, Jack," he said.

"It's all right for you lot stuck in a warm office all day."

"Each to his own, Jack."

The Inspector walked up to the counter, "Anything for me, George?"

"Not a sausage... it's your lucky day."

"You wouldn't say that if you had the morning I've had."

The Desk Sergeant changed his expression, "No... I heard."

Inspector Hammond nodded his head and turned to join the others heading for the CID room then stopped and caught Sergeant Binstead's arm.

"What happened to that new Constable. We haven't lost him have we?"

"No, Boss... I sent him off to the Water Board to check on that water level. I thought it could give him some experience, and keep him out of your hair for a while."

"Now that's what I call good thinking, Sergeant."

"Shall I set-up the incident board with what we have already, Boss?"

"Yes, Sergeant, but first run our John Doe through the Missing Persons file on the computer. You never know, someone could have called in."

"Isn't it a bit early for him to be missing, Boss?

"It was something the doctor said to me before he left: Something about the killer taking his time torturing our man, and the wounds on his chest being older. That adds up to him being out of circulation for some time."

The Sergeant turned to leave, "I'll get onto it straight away."

On entering the squad room, the Inspector could sense the familiar buzz of excitement always generated at the start of a new case. Everyone was busy going through the routine stages of establishing the why, where and when.

Standing watching the activity, he had to admit, the adrenalin was rushing through his old arteries just the same as it always did. His mind was buzzing with all the things he wanted to achieve. Yet his thoughts always returned to an idea that had become uppermost in his mind lately: that of whether the next case would be his last, the one that would earn him that long overdue promotion of Superintendent.

"I hope you lot aren't neglecting the old cases," he shouted, returning to reality. "If they're finished, make sure they're tied up nice and clean. If they're not, then you should be working on them, not getting carried away with a case that's hardly established yet."

The Sergeant entered the room and followed the Inspector into his office.

"These are the missing person reports you wanted, Boss."

"Have you had a look at them yet?"

"No, Boss, I just picked them up."

"Okay leave them with me. Have you heard from D.C. Forbes yet?"

"No, Boss, as I said, I sent him down to the Water Board to see a Mr Carpenter. By the conversation I had with the man, he could be all day."

"Good, that'll keep him busy for a while."

"Shall I call the brief now, Boss?"

"No... not yet, I'd like to know what we're dealing with first. Let's see what develops later in the day. In the meantime see when forensic are going to have something for us."

The Inspector spent the rest of the morning going through the missing person reports. No mean task, being twelve A4 computer printouts; each one containing twenty names and corresponding information. He started by eliminating the obvious: women, men under the age of fifty and ethnic cultures, reducing the list substantially, but he still had thirty-two possibilities to scrutinise.

To reduce his list further, he crossed off bald men, men who were known drifters and men with distinguishing identification marks that did not fit his victim. By lunchtime, he had narrowed the field down to thirteen.

"How's it going, Boss?" the Sergeant asked, sauntering into his office with mugs of tea for both of them.

The Inspector looked up at his eager Sergeant. His young enthusiasm reminded him of what he was like when he was a young sergeant. Then again, he had a mop of blonde wavy hair, while his was already thinning at an alarming rate.

"Great... I could kill one of those," the Inspector said, pushing all the discarded sheets over to him. "All of those are out; I'm down to thirteen possibilities. Let's get the files up here and check the mug shots, assuming we do have pictures."

"Usually we ask for pictures, Boss... I'll check."

He turned back as he was going through the door.

"Oh by the way, D.C. Forbes is back, Boss and forensic say they should have some preliminary guidelines this afternoon."

"Guidelines. I thought they were state of the art. Okay, send Forbes in."

A thin, energetic looking young Constable with a bush of ginger hair leant presumptuously against the Inspector's doorway, "You wanted to see me, Boss?"

The Inspector smiled to himself. He could give him a rollicking for taking things for granted, but that would only stifle the most important asset a young detective could have; his audacity. On the other hand, he could learn a lesson or two.

"Right, Constable, tell me you've got something interesting for me."

"Well I had some problems getting hold of this Mr Carpenter, Boss; he was inspecting some sewer in the town. But I eventually found him, and drove him out to the lock explaining what we wanted to know about the difference in the water level."

"And?" the Inspector looked impatient with the Constable's detail. He wanted to get on with it, not know the man's itinerary.

"He wanted to know what all the fuss was about, it was nothing for him to tell us what time those gates or doors were open. He just took the Sergeant's figures, did a bit of number crunching, and hey presto."

"Never mind about hey presto, Constable, and I'm not interested in how he arrived at the answer, or your difficulties in finding him. All I asked is did he know what time the lock doors were opened?"

"Yes, Boss... 1:30 am. Thereabouts."

"How thereabouts?"

"Oh, give or take ten minutes," replied D.C. Forbes, slightly deflated.

"Excellent, Constable. Now if you want to work for me, you'll have to learn all that's important is the final conclusion, unless I think detail is pertinent to our case."

"Yes, Boss, I'll remember that and I'll congratulate or roast you just the same."

"Yes, Boss"

"Good. Now take that information and give it to the Sergeant, he'll show you where it goes on the general incident board."

He finished off his tea just as the Sergeant was returning with the files.

"Right, Boss, thirteen files with pictures," the Sergeant said entering his office.

"Split them into two piles and we'll go through them now"

"What about lunch, Boss"

They were in the habit of going round to the local. It was a small pub in the next street, run by Babs: a middle-aged widow, who at one time was a raving beauty according to the photographs decorating the walls. Of all her regulars, Jack Hammond was her favourite.

The Inspector glanced at his watch.

"We'll grab something on the way, Sergeant. I want to have an identity by the end of today, and a relative I.D. by tomorrow. Then, with the cause of death, the time, and the victim's name, we should be in good shape for the briefing."

"What's the hurry, Boss... this is only our first day?"

"I told you, Sergeant, when I brief the squad tomorrow I want them to have as much info as possible, I've got a funny feeling about this one."

The superiors looked upon Jack Hammond as a skilled man, too valuable at street level to rise above his station. His only chance of promotion to increase his retirement package was through commendation: Solving an important case, as he had done with all his other promotions. This had the hallmarks of such a case. Therefore, he had to get it right, and to do that he had to start right. Get off on the right foot, or forever be out of step.

By twelve thirty, they had the manila files sorted into three groups: the first group was no good by the fact that the picture bore no resemblance at all to the Polaroid they took of the victim's bloated features in the body bag.

The second group, was debatable, but the Inspector felt their twenty-four hour missing period too short, remembering the doctor's comment on the killer taking his time torturing his victim; which left them with the third pile, five in all, good possibilities, with long enough time before being reported missing and near enough to break for lunch.

Inspector Hammond and the Sergeant spent most of the early afternoon in what looked like developing into a fruitless exercise. Of the five possibilities, when they double-checked they found two had returned, their partners forgetting to inform the police. Two others, still missing, turned out dead ends; the photographs brought in were of them at a younger age. Finally, the last one looked promising until the wife admitted she could not be certain, due to the victim's bloated condition.

"Did you read his file, Boss?" the Sergeant remarked casually.

"Of course I did... why?"

"Well I noticed when she mentioned her husband's medication for heart trouble, that he recently had a bypass. I don't remember our man having a scar on his chest, or any other major surgery, come to that."

The Inspector was not pleased.

"You're right, he didn't."

Walking back, the Inspector kept thinking of the group of files that could have matched their man, if it had not been for the lack of time to accomplish the gruesome task. 'Unless', he thought, 'one of them hadn't been missed until later'.

His first action on returning to his office was to reassess the second group of files, quickly displaying the four missing reports at the top of his desk, each photograph underneath. With the victim's picture centrally on his blotter, he rested his chin on his clasped hands and studied the group as a whole; looking for a way to reduce their number.

"Hard at it again I see, Boss," the Sergeant commented as he entered with another mug of tea. The Inspector did not answer. "Tea, Boss?" he said again.

"What. Oh, yes thanks, Sergeant."

"Which ones are those?" he said, trying to capture his attention.

"The ones I discarded because the time frame was wrong."

Sergeant Binstead parked himself in the chair in front of the desk. According to his training he should have questioned the Inspector for narrowing his search horizon too early, instead of following a procedure of sort and eliminate until the pattern of evidence dictated a more concentrated effort.

"So why look at them again?"

"Well after our fiasco with the last lot, I wondered if I had been a little hasty at discarding these just because they were only reported a few days ago."

"You said yourself, Boss the killer had spent some time with his victim."

The Inspector sipped his tea and pondered his reply.

"Yes I know, and that's still true, according to the doctor. But what if a person reported someone missing, but didn't know when they went missing."

"I see what you're getting at, Boss: Someone like a landlady or daily help."

"Exactly. Or a relative who only visits now and then."

"Yes... so anyone with a wife wouldn't count."

"You're right," the Inspector said, glancing up at the box indicating relationship. One card stood out a mile: it read, Brother, and his address was different. He nudged the card out of its place towards the Sergeant, "Give him a ring," he said.

He checked the card and dialled the number. It seemed to ring for ages and just as he decided to replace the phone, someone answered.

"Mr Lonergan?" the Sergeant questioned, looking up at the Inspector.

"Speaking," the voice replied.

"I hope I didn't disturb you, I thought no one was in."

"I wasn't able to get to the phone straight away, what can I do for you?"

"This is Detective Sergeant Binstead, Mr Lonergan. You reported your brother was missing..." he paused to check the card again, "Terry Lonergan, missing two days ago."

"Yes... have you any news for me?"

"I'd like to call in to see you; would this afternoon be all right?"

"Have you found him?"

"We don't know, Mr Lonergan, we'd like to show you a photograph."

"Has something happened to him, he's had an accident, hasn't he?"

"We don't know yet, it would be better if we talked to you."

"Oh very well, this afternoon will be fine."

The Sergeant replaced the receiver. "He said he'd see us this afternoon."

"Fine, let's go then. Where is he?"

"Over the other side of town, Boss, about three quarters of an hour."

"Good, if this is our man, we should tie things up by tonight.

Then I can call in on the doctor for his report on my way in tomorrow, ready for our briefing."

The afternoon traffic was kind to them, arriving at Mr Lonergan's in only half an hour, but having less success in getting him to answer the door. Like the strange phone call, there was no immediate response. The Inspector started to make his way around to the back, and was almost through the gate, when the Sergeant called him.

"We've got some activity here, Boss," he said, hearing someone removing the door chain, and the Chub unlocked.

There was an answer to the problem when Mr Lonergan confronted them in a wheelchair. He looked worried and moved backwards to allow them space to enter.

"Sorry about the delay; as you can see I have some difficulty moving about."

They both embarrassingly mumbled that it was no problem, and was sorry they had not realised, moving hesitantly into the lounge.

"Can I get you anything to drink?" he asked following them.

It had been a long day, and they were tempted to say yes when he stopped by the drinks trolley. His hand was already on the whisky when the Sergeant made a suggestion.

"If you tell me where the tea things are I don't mind making us all a pot."

"I have to be well organised, or I'd be wheeling myself back and forth all day. You'll find everything on a tray in the kitchen. All you need do is boil the kettle and get another two cups out of the cupboard next to the cooker," he said.

Lonergan watched with interest as the Inspector occupied himself, studying what appeared to be a man's home. He was looking for signs of their victim: a picture of the brothers together, or better still, a close-up of him on his own.

He was obviously the younger of the brothers. In his early forties, blonde straight hair, lean face. Intelligent looking, with a similar upper body shape to the victim, although what he could see of the lower half looked wasted. The astute man in the chair spoke first, he looked annoyed, agitated.

"I gather you're the Inspector and our tea maker is a DS?"

"I'm Inspector Hammond yes, and it's Sergeant Binstead in the kitchen. You appear familiar with police formalities."

"Not really... I was an Army Adjutant some years ago, and I had frequent encounters with the civilian police when they locked up our wayward soldiers."

Being in the Army would explain his bearing.

"I see... that makes sense," the Inspector replied.

"I can see you're finding it difficult to open the subject regarding my brother's disappearance. Is it that bad?" Lonergan said.

"Firstly we have to establish that it is your brother we're inquiring about, Sir, before any assumptions are made, so let's not jump the gun."

The Sergeant returned with the tray, and placed it on a nearby coffee table. After taking a sip of tea, the Inspector reached into the manila folder and handed the picture of the victim to Mr Lonergan. As expected, his immediate reaction was one of horror, revulsion, followed by a more concentrated examination. His other hand slowly reached for his lower lip, and his shoulders began to hunch.

"What do you think, Mr Lonergan?" the Inspector asked.

He suddenly realised he had dropped his guard, stiffening and returning to his self-assured pretence, "That's Terry," he said straight out, still scrutinising the picture.

"Now take your time, Mr Lonergan, be sure," the Inspector urged, surprised he was able to make such a quick identification of anyone looking like that.

"Oh I'm sure," he said again, looking closer at the photograph. "That crescent shaped scar above his eyebrow, I'll never forget it. I gave it to him with a cricket bat when I was only nine," he continued staring at the picture. "Why is his face so bloated?"

"I'd like you to formerly identify the body before we go into any details."

"So he is dead then?"

"Well this man certainly is, Sir... I'm afraid."

Len Lonergan suddenly looked as if a wall had fallen on him. He had that look everyone first has when hearing their loved one or close friend was dead. That look of finality, of the fact that they were unable to tell the person how they felt while they were alive. The Inspector's instinctive sense, that there was something between this man and his brother that they never settled, intrigued him.

Suspiciously ranking the man in the chair as one of his first suspects, the fact that he was a cripple had not entered his reckoning. For the meantime, he had to get this man to identify the victim, although he was not sure of his fitness.

"May I suggest we call for you tomorrow morning?" the Inspector said.

"Can I see him now... why wait?"

"Are you sure that would be wise under the circumstances?"

"Are they going to get any better?" he cried.

"No, Sir," the Inspector acknowledged. "Sergeant, make the call please."

"You can use my phone if you wish, it's in the hall."

While they waited, the Inspector asked the question that caused them to take so long before they found the right missing person.

"The doctor tells us he suspects your brother has been missing some time, yet you only reported him missing two days ago?"

"My brother doesn't live with me. We... didn't get on. I was ringing him since last weekend, with no answer, so I asked a neighbour to call in on him. He found half a dozen bottles of milk on the step, so he was naturally suspicious."

"Do you have a key?"

"Yes," he swung around in his chair so that he could reach into a draw in his sideboard, then rummaged for a moment and passed it over. "Here you are."

The Inspector slipped the key into the small pocket in his trouser waistband.

"Thank you," the Inspector said. "We will have to get forensics in to examine your brother's house. I'll return it as soon as we're finished."

"Have it as long as you like, Inspector."

The Sergeant returned to the lounge, nodding his head to the Inspector then smiled nervously at Mr Lonergan.

"Well it looks as if everything's okay, Sir, if you're really sure you want to see him today, I would advise though, leaving it till tomorrow."

"No... let's get it over with; I'll just change if you don't mind."

"Certainly, Sir; take your time."

He wheeled himself away leaving them standing, feeling uneasy, not knowing what to say. Things had suddenly come to a climax, at least as far as knowing who the victim was and how he died. Now all they had to do was find where this atrocity took place, and the killer responsible.

While they waited for Len Lonergan to prepare himself the Sergeant told the Inspector what the doctor really said. "He hoped it would be tomorrow after the autopsy," he said. "The body's not looking too good at present."

"I bet it's not," the Inspector remarked, listening at the door.

"They're trying to clean him up as best they can."

The Inspector reached over to the piano, taking a photograph of two men either side of an attractive young girl. One looked much older.

"Notice anything?"

"You mean the cracker between them?"

"No... no wheelchair."

"Oh yes... I reckon there's a story there, Boss."

"One I shall be pursuing, Sergeant."

The morgue was never a good place to visit at the best of times, but under the circumstances, it was even worse. Mr Lonergan though, appeared to be bearing up very well; better than the Inspector had expected. Except it was not the doctor.

"Gentlemen, we're ready now," the doctor's locum called out, suddenly realising the trolley with the victim on was going to be too high. "And are we the relative, Sir?"

Lonergan looked up at him scornfully, obviously not a man to be taken lightly. "Yes... we are," he snapped.

"Very good, Sir," the locum replied.

Under normal circumstances, the relative would stand by the glass to identify the body. However, realising the situation the locum opened the door to the small anti-chamber and ushered him inside.

"If you would position yourself at this end please, Sir," he said politely, rearranging the trolley so his chair would fit alongside,

Len Lonergan had maintained a cold personality, but now, as the locum wound down the trolley to a lower level; he appeared to soften. He nodded when he was ready, and the locum pulled back the green sheet to below his brother's chin, avoiding the marks on his neck and chest. Lonergan sucked in a deep breath.

"My God, what happened to him. Who could have done this?" he cried.

"Is it your brother, Sir?" the Inspector calmly asked.

Lonergan moved closer. He hesitated for a moment, then lifting his arm above the trolley; he reached out to touch his brother's forehead. Then he slowly passed his finger over the raised crescent scar above his eyebrow. Satisfied, he suddenly clenched his fingers into a fist and quickly withdrew his arm back to where it was on his lap. They could see he was desperately fighting back his tears.

"Yes it's Terry all right; recognisable even in this state."

The Inspector nodded at the locum to cover him again, then wheeled Lonergan out into a small waiting room that did not smell of death and carbolic.

"I'm sorry you had to go through that, but unfortunately it was a necessary formality. You're quite sure this is your brother, Mr Terry Lonergan?"

"Yes I am... I said I was. What happened to him?"

"He was murdered sometime in the early hours of this morning," Inspector Hammond hesitantly replied, while Sergeant Binstead stood to one side with his note book, ready to take down every emotion, every twitch; every syllable the brother uttered.

The Inspector was a stickler for detail. When forming a profile of a suspect, he learnt more from their reaction to a question than the answer itself.

"Murdered... how?"

"It's too early in the investigation to divulge any details, Mr Lonergan."

"But it must have been a brutal death," he continued.

"Please, Mr Lonergan, let us do our job. You will know all the gruesome details soon enough. I would have preferred you did not see him in this state... but you did."

"Why would someone do such a thing?"

"That was to be my first question to you."

"I have no idea... as I said, we didn't communicate very often."

"This was obviously an attack of vengeance. Was he having any problems with anyone the last time you spoke to him?"

"Not to my knowledge: although I'd probably be the last one to know. Big brother was always the macho one. Did you know he was a commando during the war. And everyone had to know it. He still kept up his training, as you will see when you visit his place. It's full of memorabilia."

"We need to build up a picture of your brother's activities over the past weeks: anything you can remember that may help."

"I'll do my best, Inspector, but I don't think I'll be much help."

The Sergeant broke his silence, appalled by the man's lack of kinship.

"I would have thought you might want to help us get his killer."

"I do... but as I've already said, we weren't close. He had a different life apart from me that I knew nothing of. You'll find out more from one of his Army pals."

"Army pals" the Inspector questioned.

"Of course you wouldn't know. He was a career man until recently."

"That's very interesting," the Inspector commented. "How do we contact these people... or is that too much for you to remember also?"

Lonergan chose not to answer that remark, saying instead: "I have no idea. I'm sure he has an address book in the house somewhere... Can I go home now?"

"Yes of course, it's been a shock for you," the Inspector replied. "Will you be all right on your own? Can we contact any relatives for you?"

"That won't be necessary thank you. I can do that myself."

After they returned Lonergan to his home, they continued on to Terry Lonergan's house, further out of the city towards the open country.

The property was very secluded, totally cut off from the main route on an unmade side-road that serviced a couple of farms. On their way, they called for forensics thinking this may be as far as they need to look for their torture scene.

The house was a single storey sprawling group of misplaced boxes, surrounded by a collection of other buildings that made up the property. Regardless of the land it covered, they sensed the original dwelling was a much smaller stone cottage that occupied the central area. It was easy to see Lonergan had added the extensions on at random, sprouting forth at will, making little sense architecturally, until they entered the house.

Once inside the mystery soon became clear. From the main hall, a labyrinth of separate rooms sprang off in different directions regardless of the function of the original rooms. The add-ons were a gymnasium in one, a games room in another and a trophy room to their right. It soon became evident that Terry Lonergan was a man of impulse, giving way to his passions first, at the expense of practicality.

The Inspector guessed this man had spent the greater part of his life following rules and procedures until something happened; something so terrible that it made him question the perfect order of his life; something that may possibly have eventually led to his death, under such bizarre circumstances.

"Good grief look at this place," the Sergeant exclaimed, as he entered the larger of the rooms, expecting it to be the lounge, only to find a shrine to World War 2. "There's enough armament here to start a war; I wonder if it's all registered?"

"I doubt it," the Inspector said, following him.

Each wall appeared to have its own place in this man's career: weapons on one, maps and campaign paraphernalia on the next and photographs on another. The fourth was pristine, being the one with the large window and the door in the corner.

The Inspector returned his attention to the wall of photographs. He was curious, not because the scenes were familiar, but because the poses intrigued him. They reminded him of his own intimate wartime pictures from Korea.

Then his eyes focused on a group photo in the middle.

"Look at this, Sergeant. The old squad photo."

"What's so particular about this one, Boss?"

"I think every man in the forces would have one of these: The day they got the squad or regiment together for a group photograph. This lot even gave themselves a name by the look of it," he pointed to the bottom margin. "Carter's Boys. I wonder who Carter was."

They spent the next hour going from room to room, checking the occasional draw, and trying not to disturb anything until forensics had started. They arrived only a few moments ago, it was getting late, and the sun was now low on the horizon. The Inspector stood by the window overlooking the open fields to the west; he could not remember when he last saw the sun so large, and such a deep shade of Vermillion.

He could see this man was obsessed with keeping himself fit. He had every imaginable piece of equipment in his gymnasium: 'an ideal place for torturing anyone', the Inspector thought. Yet the polished wooden floors put paid to that idea: Too difficult to remove any bloodstains.

"Take care to get in around all those mountings," he ordered one of the forensic team who was kneeling on the floor next to him. "He could have hung him up here, and used a sheet to catch the blood," he pointed into the build-up of grime where the chrome base plate to a weight-press machine was screwed to the floor.

Outdoors again, the Inspector was also keen to see inside some of the outbuildings: another source of hiding anyone, with high sturdy beams capable of hanging a victim from. The Inspector was also interested in the abundance of straw, sacks of seed and a beautiful set of tyre tracks that were quite recent by the looks of them.

"There's not much we can do here, Boss until forensic are finished, and that's likely to be in the small hours of the morning. So how about us heading home, we can make an early start tomorrow?. The Sergeant suggested.

"All right, Sergeant, you can have an early night tonight," he said.

"Early night, it's seven-fifteen, Boss."

"When you pick me up in the morning, you can drop me off at the doctors, then come on here and get stuck into this place. I want to know everything we can about this man, there's a clue somewhere to our killer, and I intend finding it before this trail goes cold."

"What's the hurry, Boss? We haven't even had our briefing yet."

"I want everything perfect this time."

"Who said it has to be perfect, Boss?"

"I do damn it... do you realise this may well be my last big case; my last chance of promotion before I retire. This one's got to be perfect."

"Sorry, Boss... that possibility hadn't occurred to me. I only know this case doesn't add up. We're missing something, and you know it. You haven't stopped rubbing your neck, and in my book that always means trouble.

CHAPTER 3

Doctor Jessop was already in pathology when the inspector arrived at the Morgue. He appeared agitated, trying to catch up with what his locum had done on his day off, and was surprised to find a relative had already identified the body.

He took a few moments to catch up on his locum's report, nodding his head this way and that, in what the Inspector guessed was a sign of approval. Then he looked up and returned to the first page, "Okay... first, as I suggested, the cause of death was by the garrotte. The sinew hanging round his neck with the pawn on it was the culprit. It's been returned to your forensic people for tracing I gather... if that is possible. By the way, did you know it had a letter 'S' on its bottom?"

"I didn't get much opportunity to examine it, if you remember."

"No... you didn't. In isolation it's meaningless," the doctor commented.

"You don't think we have a chance?"

"No not really, this man was very clever. He chose a common wooden pawn, which you could pick up at any Woolworth's, and the sinew from any game-knackers yard. Come to that he may even be a hunter himself."

"Surely there wouldn't be many of those about?"

"Probably not, but I wouldn't like the job of tracking one

down. Anyway, I was right in thinking the wounds on his body were inflicted at a different time. The tests on the congealed blood put the earliest around four days ago.”

“As long as that?” The Inspector interrupted.

“Yes… and the latest about two. Any luck with the level of water in the lock?”

“Yes. The Water Board says the lock doors opened about 1:30 am.”

“That’ll be about right,” he said, turning the page. “One thing though that may help you; and we’ve sent samples through to forensics. Embedded in some of the dried blood were pollen seeds, most definitely picked up in the country.”

“He couldn’t have picked them up on the way or from the vehicle he was in”

“No, definitely not… as I said the wounds had dried over. They had to have entered the wound while it was still wet. My guess is you’re looking for a barn.”

“Thanks, that’s great news,” the Inspector acknowledged, knowing what he knew about Lonergan’s house and its outbuildings.

“Also he used different weapons. My assistant was quite clever here; he saw a linear continuity in some of the strokes. The killer jabbed the blade tip into one side making an elongated wedge-like cut, much like a cuneiform stroke, then dragged the heel down on another area further on making a straight cut.”

“You said two weapons.”

“I did… as for the removal of his genitals… have you found them by the way”

“No, we’re still checking the canal.”

“Pity, they would confirm our analysis. Not to worry… he used a much shorter knife here, probably because of the position he was in, the killer couldn’t get a one stroke slice, but had to draw the blade back a bit then finish it off with a second thrust.”

“So we’re looking for a sword and small knife?”

He continued scanning the report, "Ah yes, he was most definitely transported in an open vehicle, say a pick-up. We found traces of oil, paint and clay marks on his back and rear, similar to the ridges on the floor of these types of vehicles. My guess is the killer dragged him feet first off the back. We think he sustained a gash behind his left ear when this happened, which contains similar substances. As we thought, the grazes on his knees correspond with being in a kneeling position," he flipped over the page. "Nothing on the nail wounds, probably your people can shed some light there... that's about it. There's a lot of technical stuff forensics will be interested in, otherwise I can't help you anymore," he folded up the wad of papers and placed them in an envelope."

"No connection to a boat?"

"Most definitely not; you can rule that out.

"So we're looking for a utility vehicle: Either an open truck with a tailgate, or one of those delivery vans, that was used previously to transport something connected to the country: earth, straw, that sort of thing."

"You have it, Inspector."

Looking pleased with himself, Inspector Hammond took the envelope and made his way out. Dr Jessop, or more rightly his assistant, had pretty well confirmed most of his earlier assumptions: particularly those to do with Terry Lonergan's property.

"That's much better than I expected doc... thanks."

"Good... I'm glad someone's happy."

The Inspector had arranged for the nearest squad car to pick him up and take him out to Terry Lonergan's house where the Sergeant was. However, the driver told him the Super was chasing him, and wanted him back at the station.

"Very well, take me back," he said.

Meanwhile, on the Lonergan property, Sergeant Binstead was in the process of emptying another draw, amazed at this man's capacity for correspondence. A quick glance soon revealed he was heavily into the area of promotion: his own promotion. His political aspirations appeared to embrace more than just the local council, some recent correspondence hinted at government itself.

"By the Inspector's taking a long time at the morgue," DC Forbes commented, setting down a mug of tea on Terry Lonergan's sideboard."

"I reckon the Super's caught up with him," the Sergeant said. "There was a call out for him earlier, so I don't think we'll see him for a while."

The constable grinned, removed his jacket and parked himself in a nearby chair. "That's good, we can have a rest."

"Don't let him hear you say that. When he does show up, he'll want to see some results from your day's labour, or you better have a good excuse."

"Yeah, I guessed he was a slave driver," he said, standing up again.

"He is, but that's not what it's all about. On a case like this, or any really, the trail goes cold very quickly, and if no headway's made or any leads created within the first couple of days... watch out. The last twenty-four hours is all about setting up the basics so that his first brief can be a good one."

"Even my Water Board information?"

"Yes... it fixes a time-frame for the alibis. But in this case, it also gives us a window of time, which we can canvas the neighbourhood for unusual incidents, like strangers in the area or unfamiliar vehicles that were parked too long in one spot."

"I see, now I understand why he was so persistent."

"Umm, this is interesting," Sergeant Binstead mused, coming across a photo album, about three inches thick, bound in crocodile skin. Dated and categorised in a flowery hand on a gilt-edged label inside the first leaf.

Apart from the usual baby, school and family pictures, which took up only a small introductory section of the volume, the right hand side displayed a group of different coloured tabs covering his military activities, categorised into campaigns.

"What's that, Sergeant?"

"By all accounts, our Mr Lonergan was quite a hero. He looks as if he was involved in almost every sector of the war."

"Which war was that?"

"The Second World War, of course. Look at this, France, Italy, Crete, Malta, North Africa and here's another section on the Pacific."

"Hell... he got about a bit. Usually most soldiers stay in one place."

"And here, he's even got stuff on Malaya and Korea."

"Surely he was too old by then?"

"Well he was, but it's all here. He must have been an adviser or something. I remember his brother telling us about him being a commando; probably he was one of those who went in first to clear the beaches."

"Maybe he was a mercenary."

"I doubt it," the Sergeant said, closing the album. "His brother said he was always boasting. Mercenaries usually keep quiet about their activities: especially if you want to get into politics. And they don't end up high ranking officers either"

"No you're right... I wasn't thinking."

The Sergeant carefully placed the heavy album in the carton amongst all the other interesting papers he had collected. The Inspector was going to be in for some very familiar reading, he thought. This was his era.

Inspector Hammond looked less than happy when he entered the station.

"He found you then I see," the Desk Sergeant called out.

The Inspector grunted and continued down the corridor.

"Ah, Jack, come in and sit down," the Super called out through his open door; left open especially to catch him.

"Thanks, Sir, is it urgent?"

"Why is it, Jack, that you and I can never just have a quiet talk?"

"I think we both know why, Sir. You're too busy with all your economy drives, and I'm too busy catching crims."

"Suggesting I'm not?" the Super said, looking up from his desk.

"I didn't say that, Sir,"

"No, but you thought it."

"Actually, Sir, I'm probably the only one in this station that thinks officers of your level do play an important role in the running of the police force. Someone has to see to all the paperwork and the raising of funds to keep us going."

"I'm glad to hear that, Jack... just as old reprobates like you are just as essential in the fight against crime."

"Exactly, Sir, but you didn't call me in to discuss our work roles."

"Err... no, I didn't," he said hesitantly, fidgeting as he did when he was uncomfortable with something. "The Commissioner is interested in your case."

"I've hardly started, Sir."

"I know... but the brother of the victim rang the mayor, and so on."

The Inspector was surprised, "Why should he do that?"

"Well he's upset, Jack, wouldn't you be?"

"Yes, Sir, but people don't start ringing the Mayor until things go wrong; this is only the start of our second day."

The Superintendent nervously shuffled again.

"It appears, Jack, your neutered victim was one of our leading citizens."

"How high was he?"

"The head of the Masonic Lodge; local Councillor, entrepreneur... you name it. Apparently, he was a very busy man when it came to the local affairs of Uxbridge and according to the Mayor, he looked a good candidate for our next MP."

"So he may well have had many enemies... that's interesting."

"That's beside the point, Jack, the brother has powerful friends too, and he feels we're not doing enough."

"That's because I delved a little too deeply into his relationship with his brother. He became very upset, and most uncooperative. I think my suggestion that we would be returning to question him further after I saw his brother's house, shook him a bit. Maybe he has something to hide?"

"Well don't upset him anymore. In fact... leave him out of this."

"Are you suggesting I overlook a possible suspect, Sir?"

"No of course not. But how on earth could you possibly term him as a suspect. He's in a wheelchair for God's sake," the Inspector had struck a raw nerve.

"Does that preclude him from organising his brother's murder?"

"Jack, the idea's preposterous. I'd like you to play a low profile on this, unless you're absolutely certain of your facts."

"Very good, Sir... was there anything else?"

"No, Jack... that's all," he said, then stopped him at the door. "Jack... don't fight me on this one, it's too important. If it gets out of hand, I can't protect you."

"Thank you, Sir, that lets me know where I stand."

He closed the door behind him, hesitated for a moment, pondering on which way he should go, then turned on his heels back towards his office. He rang Terry Lonergan's home, telling the Sergeant he had been detained, and to collect as much of the paperwork as he could and return to the station. This episode with the Super had rattled him.

Shortly after lunch, large cardboard boxes began appearing on the incident room table next to the Inspector's office. At first, he did not take much notice, until a constable arrived with another, followed by Sergeant Binstead and Constable Forbes also carrying more boxes.

He got up from his desk and went to the door, "Hold on," he called out, "where have you two been. It's gone lunch time"

"Sorry, Boss," the Sergeant said, following him back inside and sitting down, out of breath. "Bring in the rest Constable, there's a good fella," he continued.

"Well, I'm waiting for an answer," the Inspector prompted.

"Boss... look at this lot, we couldn't sort through this in an hour."

"Did you have to bring his entire house back with you?"

"Oh, Boss this is nothing to what he's got stashed away. I only brought the interesting stuff," he disappeared outside, reached into one of the boxes and retrieved the large album, then returned, and slammed it down on the Inspector's desk. "Like this for instance, it should interest you."

The Inspector flicked through the black leaves, filled with photographs that were of no particular interest to him at that time, until, as the Sergeant had indicated earlier, his attention fell on the segments covering the war.

"Very interesting... I suppose you managed to stop off at the local pub for some lunch and a drink or two on your way back?"

"We didn't, Boss, cross my heart. His fridge was quite full; it was a shame to let it all go to waste, so we had lunch there."

The Constable struggled in with the last of the boxes.

"Sorry, Boss... It's not as if he was going to need it anymore."

"And where did you get all these boxes. They look brand new."

"In one of the outhouses, there were stacks of them, folded flat."

"What on earth would he want with brand new cardboard boxes?"

"I don't know, Boss, Constable Forbes found them."

The Inspector called the Constable into his office. He looked at the Sergeant's face hoping to catch a glimmer of what the Inspector wanted.

"Where did you find these cardboard boxes, Constable," the Inspector asked.

"I found them in the main barn, Boss. I thought at the time it was a bit strange at first. Out of place, you might say."

"Why strange?"

"Well, Boss... they were at the side, neatly stacked in two piles, as if they had just been off-loaded; next to those tyre tracks."

"I see. And why should that be strange, Constable?"

The Constable suddenly felt he had made more of this than he should, "Well I wouldn't have put brand new cartons on top of all that muck. I don't know what he wanted them for, but they wouldn't be much use where they were."

The Inspector sat silent for a moment, running over what he had just heard.

"Very good, Constable. It's not apparent yet what significance these boxes have, but I like the fact that you suspected them. Carry on."

He left the room looking much happier, even if a little puzzled.

The Inspector turned to the Sergeant, "Have you any idea why this man should need all these new boxes?"

"No, Boss... to be honest I didn't give them a thought. I suppose he could be moving. I know the removers dropped a lot of cartons like this off at my house."

"Yes but those cartons usually have things printed on them, like, 'This way up', 'Fragile', and the company name."

"True, Boss... true."

"Sergeant... hasn't it dawned on you that the significance of these cartons, lying in a neat pile in the barn, as the Constable so precisely described, right next to the tyre tracks, could simply be because they were removed from a van to make room for a body?"

The Sergeant looked aghast, "Christ, Boss... you're right, sorry I missed it."

"What am I going to do with you, Sergeant?" he said, flabbergasted. "Well you'd better check them for any fingerprints that could connect them to Lonergan first, just in case you're idea about him moving was right.

"Okay, Boss"

"At the same time, get forensics to check them out for other prints. Who knows, we might get lucky and get some off that don't belong to you two."

Inspector Hammond now had more than enough to proceed with his briefing. After carefully breaking down the main aspects of the case, which he wanted everyone to be aware of as a benchmark to their investigations; he spent the last hour identifying the key issues. By now, the group were getting restless: keen to get started.

"Okay you lot... settle down. We're not finished yet," he shouted.

"Sorry, Boss... I thought you were finished," someone shouted back.

"Well I haven't, and this is the most important part, so you'd better listen carefully if you want to stay on this team. I've got pressure from the top brass."

He went over to the white board where he had scribbled in three headings. Method, Opportunity and Motive. He picked up one of the marker pens as if he was about to make more entries but simply used it as a pointer.

"Right, pay particular attention to these three areas when you start sifting through all this stuff the Sergeant has kindly gathered for you. First, Method, it's certain our man was tortured somewhere other than the crime scene, possibly on the victims own property. I want evidence to prove that, if not find out where. Forensics is looking at the samples of organic material dropped from the van, which should narrow down your search area.

"We also know he was transported to the site by the canal in a pick-up or van. I want that vehicle, it must be somewhere... someone must have seen it. Check any tyre tracks at the victims place and see if they match with the ones we found in the park by the towpath. The killer used two weapons to mutilate the victim: a sword like blade and a short knife. Forensic is checking the victim's collection of wartime weapons; we may have some luck there. Thankfully, we have the garrotte... check out the pawn, it could be vital.

"Next... Opportunity. We know we have this window of time between 12:00 and 3:00 am. Everyone isn't in bed at that time, so I want both sides of the canal entrances door to door canvassed for any suspicious people moving about and unknown vehicles; especially pick-ups. All we need is a lead on anything fitting our scenario. It could simply be a registration number, and don't forget the remote area where he lived, only a couple of hobby farms nearby, but they may have seen or heard something.

"Finally... Motive, the worst possible scenario; yet it could be our best. Just think about it, this is no ordinary killing. It took careful planning. He executed him with precision. The killer was calm and collected when he mutilated this man, but he made three mistakes that we know of. One, the tyre tracks in the soft ground after an early morning mist. Two, the trail of old rubbish his vehicle left when he dropped the rear flap down; and three... sneaker footprints in the soft earth alongside the towpath."

Inspector Hammond looked round at the intent faces.

"Now I know this isn't much, but if he made these errors, there's a possibility he made more; so look for them, because they're sure as life not going to jump out and bite you. Somewhere, amongst these papers is the reason why this maniac did what he did... I'm sure of it. So go through them with a fine tooth comb... look for a possible motive, vendetta, or payback for something in the past, anything that would give us a lead."

"Excuse me, Boss," a Constable called out.

"Yes, speak up."

"What if this man just likes to kill people like this, for no reason?"

"Good question. I've come across such people, and they're the devil's own to catch. Every time, Constable... even the most insane killer, didn't just go out and immediately do what he did. If they did, our job would be much easier, because someone would see them. No... motive or no motive, every move was planned. He picked his victim and watched his every move. That very sequence will be his undoing."

The Inspector paused to catch his breath.

"Well if there are no more questions, let's have you. Make your notes, and then we'll have a meeting first thing in the morning to hear what leads you want to follow up."

He noticed the Sergeant hovering about in the background; he obviously wanted to see him. The Inspector waved his arm, beckoning him into his office. The Sergeant nodded.

"Tell me you found something interesting, Sergeant... a key, anything."

"Not much, Boss," the Sergeant looked very nervous, "nothing out of the ordinary on Len Lonergan. A few traffic offences, travels abroad a lot, went to University, did his National Service and married young... his wife died in a car accident, which left him a paraplegic; other than that, he's quite average."

Inspector Hammond stopped him from continuing, his hand poised in the air while he thought, "Go back to the accident,

Sergeant. Does it say who was responsible?"

The Sergeant read the paper again until he reached that part, and a surprised look came across his face. He looked back at the Inspector, "The driver of the vehicle was none other than Terry Lonergan, Boss"

"I see," Inspector Hammond said, as if it was no surprise to him. "Very interesting, Sergeant. So Terry Lonergan not only killed his brother's wife, he was also responsible for him being a paraplegic."

"So it would appear, Boss."

"Wouldn't you agree that constitutes a good motive for murder, Sergeant?"

"None better, Boss; if he got someone to help him."

"Chalk that one up on the board, Sergeant... now what about the victim?"

"As for Terry Lonergan, he's been a busy man, Boss. He was a professional soldier most of his adult life. He retired as a highly decorated Colonel, and returned to his hometown a hero as a result. He became a Councillor, with a term as Mayor... and consequently was on the board of the local packaging company."

"Did you get a chance to cross reference the M.O.?"

"Yes I did, Boss," he looked noticeably hesitant.

"And?" the Inspector emphasised, impatiently.

The Sergeant looked nervous, "You're not going to like this, Boss."

"Oh... and why not?"

"I couldn't get into the programme; all I got was an SCI flag." He waited for the outburst.

"Oh bloody hell. Tell me it was a mistake. You typed in the wrong code... please."

The Inspector could see by the look on the Sergeant's face that he had not. "I knew it; the moment I saw that man hanging there, I got that old feeling. Even in my briefing, I found myself referring all the time to a clever well-planned killing. This man had a pattern. Look for the routine. Damn, I almost found myself saying serial killer."

"Sorry, Boss I tried to get around it, but it just kept flashing."

The Inspector suddenly looked resolved, accepting it was no good fighting these people; they were too powerful. To succeed in what they had to do, they had to take control, regardless of any career's they may destroy on the way.

"Okay, Sergeant, alert everyone to wind down. They have probably dispatched their henchmen already. I suppose I'd better inform the Super," he said, still looking devastated. "Christ, Sergeant, things were just beginning to shape up, I was looking forward to this one."

"Me too, Boss. Can we stay involved somehow, and follow up the leads we've already started?"

"Do you want to do all that work, so they can get the glory?"

"I suppose not, Boss."

"When was the last time we had a run-in with these people?"

"Oh it was a while ago now, Boss. It was when we uncovered all those old notes on the building site... remember. In that buried cellar from the previous house."

"That's right. God that was a laugh, turned out to be some of Hitler's funny money. He planned to flood England with it to ruin our economy. Silly bugger, it was ruined already by the war," they laughed.

Inspector Hammond did not finish the conversation with his Sergeant, he just walked off, deeply involved in his own thoughts, heading in the direction of the Chief Superintendent's office. Lonergan was about to be scrutinised by the SCI.

"What was all that about, Sergeant?" the inquisitive DC Forbes asked, standing close by. "Did I hear right. We're not going on with the case."

"You heard right, Constable."

"What's this SCI?"

"Didn't they teach you anything at the Academy. If you get a SCI flag on a national records file in the computer, it stops you from going any further. It's a block on the file, and you need an authorised password to open it."

"Well what does it mean?"

"It means the Special Criminal Investigation Branch has taken over the case, because it's either a serial killing that involves other cases, it's to do with national security, or high ranking people are involved, and so on. Nothing is sacrosanct with these people."

"Sounds a bit heavy handed to me."

Sergeant Binstead laughed as he started to collect the files together.

"Heavy handed... Listen, Constable, if they come in on the scene, you immediately take one step backwards, keep a good firm hold of your balls, and never ask any questions."

"Right, Sergeant, I'll remember that."

CHAPTER 4

An excited female constable on duty at one of the national records computers rang her superior on discovering the triggered SCI alert on the Uxbridge CID network. Superintendent Simon Stone had been waiting for this moment for some time, evident by his excited outburst on hearing the news. Middle aged or not, he was still fit enough to draw attention to his energetic dash through the office, with his not so fit, second in command, Inspector Mark Fraser following behind.

"Let's see, Constable," the Superintendent cried out. A sight he had been counting the days to see. He grabbed the operator's hand and kissed it. "I knew it... I knew it. Let's hope this is the break we're looking for."

They had three bodies, from three different counties, each one identically mutilated, without a scrap of evidence to prove the same hand killed them all. Yet Superintendent Stone knew only one man did this, and it was driving him mad.

For months, he had waited for the killer to strike again, or another sloppy CID to overlook the importance of the SCI. Who knows how many more were out there. The only thing that kept him sane was the thought that another would present itself on his screen, and this one could be that break he was looking for.

He slapped the top of the monitor, as much to say, 'I have you now you bastard', and turned to his assistant Mark for some sign of equal excitement.

He showed only his usual cold acknowledgement of the situation.

"We'll have to get out there straight away, Boss," the Inspector prompted, "before the yokels tamper too much with the crime scene. You know what happened with the others, and heaven knows what these local forensic have missed... or like that last lot, messed up."

"Yes, Mark, I know. Let's just hope Uxbridge has done a good job. Who's running the show there now?" he asked aloud for any comment.

"DCS Chomley, Boss, the girl at the computer replied.

"No I mean in charge of the case."

She roamed the screen clicking on different boxes, looking for the appropriate information until she found the signatory to the records retrieval, "Ah... a Sergeant Binstead opened the file... and his superior is... Inspector Jack Hammond."

"My goodness," Stone murmured softly. "It can't be."

"Someone you know, Boss?" the Inspector asked.

The Superintendent shook his head and re-examined the screen in the event the girl had misread the name. She had not. It was Inspector Jack Hammond.

"Well I'll be damned, talk about turning up skeletons. If it's who I think it is, I started in the Academy with him. If it's the Jack Hammond I know, we're home and dry. He'll have everything all nice a ship-shape."

"He's good is he, Boss?" Fraser said with a smirk

"You'd find it hard to match him anywhere else. That's how good he is. I followed his career for a while in the early days, once we got out of uniform. A smile crossed his face: one of pleasant memories.

"Why didn't you stay together then, Boss?"

"I don't know... he was better than me, so I used him as a

yardstick; something you should take heed of, Inspector."

"It's different now, Sir. You need qualifications to get on"

"If you want to end up behind a desk; but out there... doing the real stuff... you need experience and a sixth sense."

"Then how come he's still only an Inspector, when you're a Superintendent?"

"That's something I shall have to find out, although knowing Jack Hammond, and his aversion to organisation; I'm not surprised."

The dark haired young Inspector was keen to make his name before he was much older, like his Boss had, although he would have to slim down if he was going to stand the pace he had set for himself.

Superintendent Stone on the other hand never had that problem. He returned to his office leaving the Inspector to sort out the details before taking over his old friend's case, still thinking about his own ability to control his weight.

Coincidentally it was with Jack Hammond and his days at the Academy that proved to be too high-pressured to put on any weight, and over the years, he has never changed. A little older perhaps, greying at the temples, certainly a much better dresser than those times, he thought, looking at himself in the large plate glass window of his office in the New Scotland Yard building. That finely trimmed moustache he had developed since that time, looking closer at his reflection. There was another reflection now, a bigger one, it was the Inspector, bringing his mind back to his weight; Superintendent Stone spun round, looking embarrassed.

"Oh, Mark, I didn't hear you come in."

"I could arrange for a full length mirror, if you want, Boss?" he joked.

"No thanks, I was just thinking of my days with Jack at the Academy, and how we must have changed since then."

"We can't stay young forever, Boss."

"No, Inspector, but we can do something about our weight."

"Sorry, Sir. I know you told me to get down to the gym more often, but I don't seem to be able to find the time."

"You can find the time to go out to eat, so do it; and now."

"Yes, Boss," he said.

"What was it you wanted anyway?"

"I wondered if you wanted me to drive you over to Uxbridge this afternoon."

"Inspector, there's such a thing as protocol to be observed. We can't just barge in and say we're taking over your case. There are pleasantries to be taken into account."

"Very good, Boss, I'll just get on with what I was doing."

"You do that, Inspector. I'll let you know when you can get the knives out."

Superintendent Stone managed to catch the Chief Super of Uxbridge in before he left to attend another of his many community functions. He got the impression over the phone that the man was least interested until he told him the reason for his call; then the Chief Super became uncannily attentive.

Stone explained the on-going cases he was already working on, directing his attention to the obvious serial killer ramifications, while DCS Chomley appeared to be more concerned with the ramifications within his CID squad.

Stone also mentioned his old connection with Inspector Hammond, and that there may be some embarrassment there when the case was removed to the Yard. That he would dearly wish to avoid out of respect for an old Academician, and hoped the Chief Super would soften the way prior to him arriving tomorrow morning.

"Everything all right, Boss," he heard someone say.

"Inspector I'm strongly considering tying a bell to your neck.

You always appear when I least expect it... What is it?"

"Do you want me to go into the Uxbridge files?"

"What did I say. We do nothing until I've spoken to Inspector Hammond."

"I just thought I could get ahead of your meeting tomorrow."

"I don't wish to discuss it, Inspector, I think you should make yourself scarce for the rest of the day, and ponder on the saying, 'stepping over the line.'"

Stone was beginning to regret his past acquaintance. This man of lesser rank was beginning to get under his skin; beginning to sour his initial excitement of the prospect of new evidence; beginning to undermine his confidence; and worst of all he knew Inspector Fraser was astute enough to realise that. He had to face Jack Hammond alone tomorrow, and bury the skeletons that had been haunting him all these years.

The following morning Inspector Hammond arrived to find the Chief Super was requesting his attendance. He had been expecting this since their discussion the previous day, and saw no reason in delaying the inevitable.

"By heavens, Jack... that must be the shortest period between me asking to see you and you actually getting here," the Chief Super started.

"Is that so, Sir?" the Inspector replied calmly.

"What no delaying investigations?"

"No, Sir, none of those today, in fact my crystal ball tells me I might not have any of those problems again in the near future."

"What makes you say that?"

"You mean this isn't one of those, 'Toe the line or resign', meetings?"

"Of course it isn't, Jack, what's got into you?"

"Well we are going to discuss my case being taken away from me aren't we?"

"Jack, you must be the most infuriating man I know."

"I gather you've had contact with the SCI since our discussion yesterday?"

"Yes," the Chief Super hesitated, fumbling with his diary. "They're coming in about eleven. I've authorised them to take whatever material they need, with a brief on what you have so far on the Uxbridge incident."

"Presumably you want me to do that."

"It's up to you, Jack, but I think it would be better coming from you."

"I have no problem with that, Sir, as long as they don't expect me to do their job for them. I can't abide people who steal other's glory."

"I think you'll find, Jack, they have a lot more right to this case than you do, and certainly more background on this killer. They have three others after all."

"Three. So this is a serial killing after all... I suspected as much. This man has been busy... it would be interesting to see those files."

"Superintendent Stone did say you would be able to see what he had."

"Stone?" the Inspector repeated.

"Yes, he says you might know him."

"I wonder if it's the same Stone I went to the Academy with. No it can't be, the one I knew wasn't very bright; he couldn't have lasted this long."

"I doubt if it's this Stone then, he's a Superintendent."

"Then it definitely isn't," the Inspector replied, but still wondered. The Stone he knew was an astute fellow, if low on concentration; he was still capable of working anything out one way or another. No one expected him to pass out of the Academy. Yet he did.

"Well, Jack, whoever it is, for once in your life be tactful... please."

"I'll attempt to do that, Sir. Is that all?"

The Chief Superintendent looked blank, "Yes... for now."

When he returned to the squad room the Inspector walked into a mass of expectant faces, even confiding in only one was too many it seemed.

"So it's official, Boss?" the Sergeant commented, looking at the Inspector's face when he returned from the Super's office. He was standing by the Telex machine receiving a bundle of papers still coming through.

"The official hand-over is at eleven, so get everything boxed up, and I mean everything, they'll be through here like a dose of salts."

"These as well, Boss?" he said, waving the papers in his hand.

"What are they?" the Inspector grabbed them, looking at the top document.

"I thought I'd have a look at his military record. Look at that lot."

"I don't want to; it's not our concern any more. Shred them."

"But, Boss... won't they want them?"

"If they want to know about his military record, let them do what you did."

The Inspector disappeared into his office, slamming the door behind him. The Sergeant told everyone to get everything packed up, while he began shredding Terry Lonergan's extensive career in the Army.

The Inspector sat at his desk staring at the open leaves of the victim's photographic album; it was still open at the section covering his war exploits. It brought back memories; not of this war, he was too young, but Korea. His experiences, as horrific as they were, were not a patch on this. His drifting thoughts were brought to an abrupt halt by the ringing phone, it was the Chief Super; his guests had arrived. He snapped the album shut, snatched it up from the desk, and tossed it into one of the open boxes as he passed.

Psyching himself up before he entered the Chief Super's office, he prepared himself to absorb the immediate surroundings, to know whether or not this man was his old friend; the last thing he wanted was to be put in a position of surprise. He wanted to look nonchalant, as if this was not concerning him.

As much as he prepared himself, the instant snap shot of time, was not what he expected: the Chief Super was half standing at his desk, arm outstretched about to introduce him to an overweight scruffy character who couldn't possibly be Stone, he was too young, and an older man he didn't recognise either. Could this polished, well dressed, dandy of a man be the Stone he knew. He struggled to remember his face.

"Ah, Inspector this is... .

"Jack. Is that you, Jack Hammond," the smart man interrupted.

"Stone? Not the Stone I knew at the Academy," the Inspector replied, moving towards him, still not recognising him.

"Yes... the same old rat bag. How are you?"

"Stone... sorry, Sir. I didn't recognise you, you've changed so much."

"I hope for the better, and don't call me, Sir for Christ sake."

There was an uncomfortable pause, as the two men slowly come to terms with their meeting, leaving the other two feeling out of place.

"You two obviously need to catch up with each other," the Chief Super said, when he finally got a word in; the other man remained silent, overawed.

"Oh sorry, Sir," Stone said. It's such a surprise seeing Jack after all this time." he was still shaking his hand vigorously.

"That's all right. Why don't you take them into your office, Jack, catch up with old times, and sort out what has to be done with this case."

"Fine, Sir, that's a good idea," the Inspector answered reassuringly, ushering them out of the Super's office, waiting for the delayed reaction of the other man.

A sudden sense of relief fell over the Inspector. The embarrassment faded with his new sense of expectancy, but of what. Maybe knowing how his friend managed to rise to Superintendent would satisfy his apprehension.

"Sorry, Mark, you know how it is in the excitement. Jack... this is Inspector Mark Fraser," the Inspector shook his hand, suspiciously.

"Nice to meet you at last, Sir, the Boss hasn't stopped talking about you two since he heard it was your case."

"What's with the Sir, Mark?"

"You're senior; I only became Inspector six months ago."

"That doesn't count in my book, Mark, it's Jack." Those two words: 'You're senior' said a thousand words. He must have checked his record first.

"Great," Fraser said, pretending to be satisfied.

"Now where's this squad of yours, I've heard a lot about it," Stone said.

As they made their way along the corridor, he felt pumped as they passed the lower ranks cautiously nodding, keeping their distance as if they had the plague.

"Come off it, Stone," the Inspector said, stopping in his tracks. "I can't even remember your first name."

"Why should you, I never told anyone. I liked being called Stone... remember. It sounded more like what a detective should be called."

"That's right; we used to pull your leg, 'A rolling stone and all that.' Anyway, what I was going to say," he started up again almost at his door. "You don't fool me. You must have called for all the information on me and my squad as soon as you heard. Am I right, Mark?"

Hammond shot a quick glance at Mark, catching him off

guard. He looked at his Boss; they both looked uncomfortable.

"Okay, I could never fool you like the others, Jack," Stone confessed.

Inspector Hammond introduced the pair to his squad, starting with Sergeant Binstead, who virtually took over: after all, it really was his domain. Then the Inspector and Stone settled down in his office and started to enjoy old times and a good malt from his bottom draw, while the Sergeant briefed Inspector Fraser on their progress to date.

As they passed briefly through each box, each file and photograph, a line of constables removed them to the Inspector's vehicle outside. It was evident Mark had been briefed on what to say, as well as what not to say; diplomacy was the order of the day.

Stone did not want to leave any ruffled feathers on this trip, regardless of their treatment of other jurisdictions. As far as Jack Hammond's patch was concerned, he wanted everything done by the book.

For some reason, despite Stone's higher rank, he felt insecure alongside his old colleague, as if his friend knew where to look for buried skeletons. He knew how someone with his limited education was able to fool the teachers at the Academy.

"What happened, Jack?" he said, finishing his drink.

"I don't follow."

"You should be a senior Superintendent by now."

"Oh... I blotted too many copy-books."

"That sounds like the Jack I used to know; you always were a rebel."

"I seem to remember you were a collaborator... a good one at that."

"I collaborate with a different level of people these days."

Stone saw his Inspector hovering in the doorway, the dirty deed had been done, there was no need to prolong the agony any longer; it was time to go.

"Well, Jack it's been great talking to you, but my Boss is going to want a report before he goes tonight, I'm sure you understand."

"Oh... I understand all right," the Inspector said, with an obvious double meaning.

"Now I meant what I said. I want you to come round to my patch where I can fill you in on this butcher, and how your case fits into the overall picture."

"Will tomorrow be soon enough," he replied, surprising Stone.

"Err... well... yes, why not. Definitely, you're on. What time?"

"Oh I'll give you time to have your morning tea, say ten o'clock?"

"Fine. Well I'll see you then."

The Inspector stood at his window watching them in the car park, arranging the last of the boxes, and a short altercation with his assistant. He continued watching them all the way out as they drove off, not so much for them, but more for what they were carrying.

"That's it, Boss," Sergeant Binstead said, standing with a mug of tea.

The Inspector took it from him and turned back to the window. Then turned back with a determined look on his face.

"Well you and I are going to Scotland Yard in the morning to find out all about this case; on Superintendent Stone's invitation. Who knows we may find a way of getting some of that glory shit to stick to us after all."

"So you're still going, Boss?"

"I'm not going to let that upstart steal my thunder.

"Is he really the Stone you went to the Academy with?"

"I hate to admit it, but yes he is."

The welcome mat and VIP treatment was still working for them when they arrived on Superintendent Stone's patch. The much-coveted Scotland Yard turned out to be little different from the Uxbridge CID, only much bigger.

The whirlwind tour of all the departments turned out to be no more than Stone being late. His first bad mark as far as the Inspector was concerned.

"Oh, Jack, sorry to keep you waiting," he said, hand outstretched.

"That's all right, Sir, we were well looked after."

"I told you, Jack, it's Stone," he shook his hand and turned to the Sergeant to shake his. "It's, Sergeant Binstead isn't it. Welcome to the SCI or in case you didn't know; Special Criminal Investigations."

"Thank you, Sir," he replied, without telling him he did.

Superintendent Stone made no excuse for being late, he appeared to be flustered and they made straight for the Incident Room. On a rough count, there must have been about fifty desks in three rows, with people busily checking files, working at computers or simply huddled together in conversation.

What caught the Inspector's eye was the enormous white-board running the full length of one wall, with female constables making entries with marker pens in various colours, reminiscent of the war days when they plotted the incoming German bombers.

"Well, Jack, this is our operation so far," he proudly pointed to the board that was still occupying the Sergeant's jealous attention.

They had split it into eight sections with black tape. Three of which were full of photographs, diagrams and the notes the girls were continually adding; each headed with a name. The fourth was blank like the remainder except it too had a name; Terry Lonergan. The Inspector walked over to the space.

Stone moved up beside him, "Yes, that's your man, Jack, we're just about to build in the evidence you've come up with so far."

Inspector Hammond slowly walked along the line of names: John Hebden, Mark Guldon, James McCulloch, then turned and retraced his path back to Terry Lonergan's virgin panel, nodding at the young girl adding his particulars.

"What common denominator links all these to a serial killer?" he said.

"Everything. Usually at first were lucky to make a couple of M.O. similarities but with this case just about everything mirrors the others. For instance, they were all tortured over a long period. The killer moved their bodies to another site, using a structure to crucify his victims. Death by strangulation with a Garrotte was the main M.O., all carrying a pawn with a letter on its base. I was anxious to know what yours was, an 'S'. We now have the beginnings of a word: 'MOUS.'"

"Did they all lose their… ?" the Inspector glanced at the young female constable."

She looked at him and smiled.

"Yes, Jack… they were all mutilated in that way," he shook his head and smiled. His remark had no effect on her.

The Inspector coughed and continued, "MOUS… how did you arrive at that?"

"Look, Jack… everything about these cases points to a pattern. The man is following some form of re-enactment or pictorial vengeance. Either way there's a significant reason for these letters, and the pawns… which could stand for something other than a chess piece."

"Or a 'Foot Soldier,'" Sergeant Binstead interrupted.

They both turned to the Sergeant, who until now had remained silent.

"Foot Soldier? Stone repeated, as if the Sergeant had spoken out of turn.

"Yes, Sir… it's in the dictionary. A pawn could be a Foot Soldier."

The Inspector could see the Superintendent's surprise.

"He's a crossword fanatic, always picking useless information out of the dictionary when he thinks it applies," the Inspector remarked.

"No... that's great," said Stone, scribbling into a section of the board at one end, named 'Hunches.'" That could lead somewhere."

He made his way back to them pointing to the large letter in the corner of each section, M... O... U... then he added an S to Lonergan's panel.

"Do you know," Stone hesitated, looking at the Sergeant, "There's only four eight letter words in the Oxford dictionary starting with these letters: Mousekin, Mousmees, Moussaka and Mousseux; none of which tie in with our victims yet."

"There may be more in the larger version," the Sergeant pointed out, spotting the concise volume on a nearby table, "Or have you thought of anagrams"

"Please don't make it more complex than it is, Sergeant," Stone exclaimed.

"Sorry, Sir."

"No really. I appreciate your contribution, but I'm certain this man isn't trying to be complicated, it's just that we haven't found the key yet."

"Key?" the Inspector questioned.

"Yes... we're convinced all these beautifully fitting similarities, hang on one common principle... the key that will unlock everything."

"Why the fixation on the number eight?" the Inspector asked.

"Eight?"

"Yes, eight letter words... eight segments to your work plan," the Inspector said, pointing to the five empty panels, including his own.

Superintendent Stone looked back at the board.

"Ah... yes, I see. Well as I said, assuming this follows a defined pattern, and the pawns play an important role in his logic... then it goes to follow, there are only eight pawns in a chess set, therefore eight letters for eight victims."

"That's a long shot, isn't it?" the Inspector commented.

"Jack… one of the reasons this task force was set up was because cases like this need a new approach. The old way doesn't work anymore. In most cases, we're dealing with psychos or twisted minds, and we need people who know how these lunatics think. That means we have to turn to psychiatrists, human behaviour specialists, even clairvoyants."

"Clairvoyants?" the Inspector remarked.

"Yes, even people who can tell you the killers profile from the touch of a hair, or even by looking at the victim's picture is enough."

"I don't know, Stone, it's all above me."

"Don't get me wrong, Jack. There's a place for your nose and investigating skills."

The Inspector laughed, "Not by the look of this lot."

"No really, Jack, I can see already, the groundwork you've done on forensics and tying this in with a rural torture site, will add enormously to our profile so far. I'm certain we're on the right track with this," he paused, looking at the Sergeant again. "And yes, Sergeant, you may well be right with the letters.

"I've spent sleepless nights pondering that very possibility. Thinking my 'MOU' may be in the middle of a word. Then I said to myself, 'This man is making a special effort to draw our attention to himself and the message he is leaving with these crimes'; and what better way than a name building up letter by letter."

Belonging to the old school, the Inspector was still sceptical. Yet he was not about to cast water on his old friend's creativity, by mentioning that the remaining victims may not necessarily fit neatly at the end of his chosen eight.

"Have you considered you may be dealing with a religious fanatic: someone reeking damnation on evil doers such as my high flier. His motive might well be as simple as crucifying them like the robbers alongside Christ?"

"Jack we've done all the profiles and asked all the questions. Besides, the first victim, James McCulloch, was a loser. He never took advantage or harmed anyone."

"Well it was just an idea."

"But that's it, Jack, that's what we're all about. We're sifting through these people's lives looking for that common denominator... and when we do find it, we'll have him."

"I hope so... I hope he isn't playing us all for suckers. All this analysing, profiling and psychiatric stuff is all very well, but it should only be used to verify the evidence."

Stone could see he had to be diplomatic.

"I'm one hundred per cent behind that, Jack, but with serial killers you've got to get into their heads. We can't keep waiting for another murder... we have to jump ahead... anticipate his next move."

"Well that's hardly my concern any more, is it, Sir."

"What did I say about calling me, Sir. It sounds like you're pushing a wedge between us, Jack. I thought we could renew our friendship."

"That's fine... Stone, but there's a gap there regardless."

"Maybe so, Jack... but I intend changing that, I want you to be kept informed on any new developments, and I want you to continue digging into your end"

"Why the special treatment?" the Inspector asked suspiciously.

"I owe you one, Jack... that's why"

"You haven't even opened half the boxes yet, so how can you make that out?"

"No not that, from when we started together. Don't you remember. The night before our Academy exams... we were all going for a drink to wind down. Stone noticed the Sergeant's ears prick up. "Err... Sergeant, would you mind helping Mark break open the boxes and probably you could fill him in on their contents; if that's all right with you, Jack?"

"Sure... good idea," he nodded to the Sergeant.

Sergeant Binstead knew when he was not wanted.

"Where was I?" Stone muttered.

"You were about to tell me about that night; and I do remember."

"Good, well you had all decided we should wind down... have a drink."

"And you suddenly changed your mind, or should I say character, and decided to stay in the room and swat."

Stone shook his head and started laughing, then stopped and cleared his throat.

"That's right, and I remember you saying, 'It's too late now, if you didn't know it all by now, you could forget passing'... remember?"

"Yes... painfully.

"And I was wrong, it did work, you passed."

"The truth is, Jack; I took a gamble that night... the biggest one in my life. I didn't know a thing on operational techniques, so I stayed back to study your notes, thinking if anyone knew, you would."

"You what?" the Inspector was horrified.

"Sorry, Jack. I knew I didn't have a chance otherwise."

"You did take a gamble, bigger than you thought," Jack spluttered.

"Why's that?"

"That was my weakest subject, probably why I'm still an Inspector."

They both laughed: the funny side helped to nullify the deed.

"We both know why you're still an Inspector, Jack; you're frightened to death of paperwork and driving a desk."

"You're right, but I still wanted promotion. How did you manage to do it?"

Superintendent Stone led him into his office, sat him down and offered him a drink.

"Would you like one?" Stone asked.

"No thanks, still on duty and all that. I was just admiring all the finery. You must have pressed all the right buttons to get this lot."

"A bit of a fluke really. Oh, don't get me wrong, like you, I'd been struggling for years on Inspector's pay, stuck in a tiny office with my grandiose ideas... you know me. Then one day the Commissioner came round with his latest fad; a psychologist. I got interested in the statistics he was giving us on unsolved murders throughout the country.

"His idea was that they stayed unsolved because there was no motive or local evidence to link with any known criminal, whom, he implied, invariably pointed to a serial killing. He said, 'if all these unsolved murders were entered into a computer programme, set-up to identify common denominators, rather than criminal records, we would surprisingly find that a good percentage could be linked together.' Everyone thought this idea was interesting, but too hard to implement."

Then Stone's eyes lit up, he had that impish look about him that immediately struck a chord with the Inspector's memory of him. 'This was the real Stone, the one always lurking inside.' Jack thought.

"Except for Inspector Stone," Jack said.

"How did you guess. I saw this as my opportunity to move myself up into that elite sector. So I did my research... persuaded a charming young female constable to put my report together... "

"How did you wangle that?" the Inspector interrupted.

Stone laughed, "A week of posh diners that nearly sent me broke, and then I presented it to my Super for the attention of the Commissioner... making sure he knew I had been inspired by his lecture of course."

"Which was given the immediate go ahead?"

"Not quite... but almost. You see I identified in my report that such an elite force had to have complete autonomy, as we would be up against other jurisdictions, treading on a lot of Inspector's toes... such as your own. This meant I had to be at least a Superintendent, and my immediate assistant's, Inspectors."

Inspector Hammond laughed at the audacity of the man, but envied him also.

"And he went for it?"

"Eventually. So you see, Jack, 'By hook or by crook'."

"You don't fool me. As soon as I learnt of your take over, I checked up on you. You've got a good record, and your team is handpicked with excellent reputations."

"I put that down to the new technology available today that most CID's are unaware of... without the ability to solve crimes. I'm not knocking good detective work. What your people have done so far with your case amazes me. Such insight... take the Foot Soldier as a point in question."

"Since you mention that, when I was looking at the names on your board, John sounded very familiar. Not like when you think you know someone... but more like when you came across it somewhere recently," the Inspector said.

"Go on, I'm fascinated," Stone said, with a sense of excitement.

"I've seen that name written down, and only recently."

The Inspector got up and walked back out into the large room towards the board, with Stone following. He stood studying the name; it was the last before his victim.

Then walking over to the table where the Sergeant and Inspector Fraser were arranging the remnants of the boxes into piles, he paused scanning the mass of paper and plastic bags, then moved to the other end, spotting what he wanted: It was Terry Lonergan's photographic album.

He picked it up and turned to the military section; carefully examining the snapshots of Terry and his comrades. The

Superintendent, not familiar with this evidence yet, was becoming more intrigued by the minute.

"There you are; I knew I was right," the Inspector called out jabbing his finger at a picture of three soldiers sitting on the front of a tank. Under each man, he scribbled a name. The first read, Steve, which meant nothing, the second, simply me, and the last, John.

"My God, Jack," Stone exclaimed, grabbing the book in disbelief, "It's all coming together isn't it, see this is what I meant about a key; I prayed the next one would give us a break. The Superintendent impatiently searched to associate his victims with names in the album, becoming engrossed in pictures.

Inspector Hammond decided to leave him to it, he had pointed the way; the rest was up to him. On reaching the door, he paused and turned back on hearing his name.

"Oh, Jack... Should this trail lead back to Uxbridge; it'll be your cop."

The Inspector looked at him blankly, as if it were of little consolation.

Back at the car the Inspector looked up at the men watching them from the window, just as he had done yesterday; no words needed to pass between them.

"There's one sad man, Mark," the Superintendent reflected.

"Oh yes, Boss... How's that?"

"His type lives for the resolution of their cases; one more notch on their belt; that much nearer to promotion."

"Well he'll have to chalk this one up to experience, Sir."

"I guess he will."

CHAPTER 5

A cleaner noisily entering the room suddenly disturbed Superintendent Stone. She jumped at the sight of his reclining silhouette in a plush chair, framed by the grey dawn light breaking through the large window alongside his desk.

"Oh sorry, Sir," she said, and hurriedly clutched her vacuum cleaner and left.

Startled, he half turned to see what the commotion was, but it was too late to explain his presence. He had spent most of the night examining the contents of four folders still spread out across his desk, along with the album Inspector Hammond had given him earlier: the catalyst to his night's ordeal.

The folders contained the abridged lives of the four victims; the earlier three of no substance, ordinary, without cause as to the reason why they should have died the way they did; the latter was the Uxbridge crucifixion; the key, he was sure of that.

He placed his hand on the open album. The photographs felt cold with the night's chill still on them, thinking of this man's life unfolding before him as he went back and forth over the snapshots. Sorting their order in his mind, delving into the motive why Terry Lonergan kept such a meticulous record of this group's activities during the war.

Picking up the list he had compiled of all the names of

Lonergan's wartime comrades for the umpteenth time, he digested all fourteen names, four of which he had added the surnames to and underlined the victims; they were the link he was looking for.

Four separate victims of violence, connected to each other by one common denominator: the Army, and possibly four others on this list were destined for the same fate, if he was not able to unlock this puzzle quickly.

"It is you, Boss," Mark called out, and then switched on the lights.

"Switch them off, it's too much," Stone shouted.

"I thought it might be you when I came in and overheard one of the chars complaining she couldn't clean your office. "I gather you've been here all night"

"So it seems," he replied, stretching. "I started on this album Inspector Hammond gave me, and one thing led to another."

"It usually does, Boss"

Stone looked at his watch, "What are you doing here at six thirty?" he said, getting up and switching on his percolator.

"I knew you would want an early start on the fourth victim, and I couldn't sleep anyway thinking about him... so I decided to come in early."

"Good... because after going through this lot last night, I've decided to jump the briefing and go straight to the next stage with Mary Carson"

"Do you think we've got enough for her, Boss?"

"Oh yes... more than enough. What I need now is a second opinion, and a reasonable assurance that this key I think we have is worth following up. I'd hate to think all the research it's going to take would lead us up a blind alley"

The percolator began bubbling and Stone poured a coffee for himself, at the same time gesturing to the Inspector who picked up a cup and rubbed it with a tea towel.

"You mean the Army angle, Boss?" he said.

"That's exactly what I mean."

Stone filled the Inspector's cup, and moved back to his desk to pick up the list and pass it to him; at the same time noticing that same condescending look his Inspector had yesterday. He realised he had an immediate dislike for the man who provided them with the missing link they were looking for.

"Fourteen soldiers," Stone started. "The underlined ones are our victims... so how's that for a coincidence; if there ever was one?"

"Are you sure of Inspector Hammond's evidence, Boss?" Mark replied, scanning the list, pretending his previous remark had no connection.

"It's the best lead we have."

"He's a glutton for punishment, Boss. You take his case off him, and then he hands the thing to you on a platter."

"Not quite Mark, there's a long way to go before we can say that."

Mark turned towards the door, blowing on his coffee. He indicated that he might as well make a start before the others arrive, and walked back into the squad room without any further comment, leaving Stone pondering on his next move.

"And don't forget, Mark," he called out. "Give Mary a call... and see if she can come in straight away. Tempt her with the idea that we've broken the case... I want to get this thing moving as quickly as possible... It's been too long without any activity."

"Right, Boss, why don't you go home for a few hours, we won't have everything ready here until at least eleven."

"Yes, I may just do that," he called back, stroking the growth on his chin, and then raising his shirted arm high enough to smell his own stale odour. "Yes... I think I will, before Mary gets here. Give me a buzz when you have a time for her."

Mary was a strange personality. Three subjects occupied most of her time. Namely, she lectured at Bartholomew's hospital in Human Behaviour and Psychology. Then there was her private practice in helping people with mental disorders. In addition, she worked with the police as a profiler: one who forms a detailed character of the suspect, and guides the police investigation through her analysis of the motivation and performance of the crime.

To some she had a split personality. On the one hand, she was a scientist of sorts, on the other an attractive tease. Neither observation could be further from the truth. She was a private person, doing several jobs that she excelled at; the rest was mere conjecture.

"This is absolutely marvellous, Mark. It's what we've been looking for," Mary Carson said excitedly on her arrival, after her examination of the new evidence, which the constables were in the process of adding to the fourth panel.

"The Super's going crazy about it also; I don't quite see it myself."

She swung round from the board and stared at him.

"You must be blind, Mark if you don't see the significance of this new evidence. At least we have a link now between these men, which proves the murders are by the same killer. At the same time... it confirms this was part of a serial ritual."

"You mean with these pawns."

"That's right, and the fact that he's leaving us clues, which means he's goading us into solving this thing before he kills again."

"You're assuming there will be others," he said sceptically.

He was uncertain of the Superintendent's trust in this type of procedure. Although not distrustful of her as a person; to the contrary, he was enamoured by her personality. It was what she stood for that disturbed him.

To his mind, she better served her abilities delving into the distorted manifestations of manic-depressives, not involving herself in the science of criminal investigation. This prejudice clouded his judgement, dulling his sense of the possibility that he was wrong, and she was able to see below the surface of her subject: finding the true character.

She turned to him, sensing confusion. "Oh I'm sure of it, Mark... In fact there may be others we don't even know about yet."

"The Super has made up a list of possible candidates," he handed it to her, tolerating her comments. "He says the other four are on there somewhere. That's if you follow his connection between the number of pawns in chess, and the victims."

She turned to him, "You're not happy with this, are you, Mark?"

"Not entirely. I prefer the evidence to lead the way."

"But, Mark... that's the whole point of the SCI. These type of cases can't be solved in the traditional way... they're too bizarre."

"Well... let's see what you make of this last one... it's different"

She studied the draft list prepared by Stone the night before. She recognised his oblique writing, and the broad down strokes of his designer calligraphic pen, straying slightly now and then: the sign of a tired hand. She also recognised the four names underlined with a red marker, leaving ten others, some he had obviously considered, by the tiny dots alongside where his pen had pondered.

"This is fantastic, I'm glad you managed to catch me before I left. I can see these underlined names are ours, how did he get them?"

He looked up and smiled, "You can ask him yourself, he's just walked in."

Stone had made the effort to go home, not to grab some sleep, as he should have done, but to shave and shower, pick out his best white shirt with the faintest blue line and painstakingly select the tie he knew Mary liked; the maroon silk with gold pin-points. He then chose his gunmetal pinstriped suit; all so that he could make an impression on Mary Carson; the other problem that was preoccupying his thoughts lately.

"Mary... good morning, how good of you to come on such short notice," he said, greeting her from the other side of the room. Then making contact with his usual embrace, and kiss on the cheek: His Dunhill after-shave captured her senses.

"Simon... I see we're looking our usual immaculate self and I like that new after-shave. It is new. I haven't smelt it before."

"Yes it is, bought especially for you and you're looking as beautiful as ever."

"If you continue like that I'm going to lose interest in this case and suggest we go somewhere private," she said, playing his game.

No one was amused, least of all Mark. They played this game every time they met. It was as if the more public their suggestions to each other became, the less they risked a more serious relationship. Mary Carson continually reminding the Superintendent, and anyone else listening, of her strict 'No mixing pleasure with work', rule.

"Did you get that, Mark. You're my witness," he jested.

The Inspector winced with embarrassment when he turned away to flirt with her again. He was not as eloquent as these two when it came to sexual bantering, although he secretly fancied her himself, something else to be jealous about.

He watched them as they teased each other, observing her body language as she talked to Stone. She was not conscious of being thirty-nine. She still had a good firm body, always wearing clinging clothes with knee length skirts to show off her legs.

Her face showed maturity in a graceful way, lightly made up, framed by her shiny black hair. Mark was beginning to learn he had feelings he should keep to himself. Buried with his ridiculous notion that he did not want Hammond's input to develop, or if he was honest with himself, he did not want the Superintendent to succeed.

"Simon, you have to tell me how you made this dramatic

discovery, and how you came up with this list?"

"Well my love, as much as I adore impressing you with my brilliance, I must admit our breakthrough was entirely due to this other murder on an old friends patch."

"I can see that, but what's that got to do with it"

He broke away from her to look at the board, which was now complete.

"He's brilliant... the way he and his team put this case together in so short a time, just falling straight into our profile, as if he was looking for this angle from the start. Although in reality we really have his nose to thank."

"His nose?"

"Yes... he's got the best nose for a clue I know of."

"I thought you hadn't seen him for years, Boss," Mark interrupted.

"I was referring to my memory of him. Also the research I did on some of his past cases... quite brilliant; the way he intuitively took a particular line with the evidence."

Mary could sense the introduction of this Jack Hammond had thickened the waters. She turned her attention to the board again, returning to her serious role. Flirting was only a pastime to her, an inherent feminine need. The unknown turned her on.

Reading the emotions of others from scraps of evidence was the aphrodisiac that Stone longed to possess. He watched her become high on the energy of evil: the side of her personality that made her good at her job as a profiler.

"Well we could certainly do with a nose like that," she said. "When I see him I'll give him a big kiss. In the meantime let's see what we have... it looks exciting."

As quickly as that, everything returned to normal. It was as if they were two different people: totally cold and professional. The sexual stimulant they needed was over.

"As you can see we've made a link between these men and

the Army," Stone started, presenting her with the album opened at the section containing the named photographs. "There," he pointed. "Each of our victims."

"Yes I see, pity they're only Christian names," she said, studying the different snapshots. "Do you get the impression he's the head honcho".

"I did, straight away. He has that set in his body, always up in front. Always finding himself a position slightly nearer the camera, or higher than the others."

"Yes... I see what you mean," she agreed. "Is there anything on their Army records to qualify that?" she glanced over at Mark.

"We're processing their records now," he said, at the same time reaching for a bundle of files he had put to one side for them.

"God... it would be interesting to know what the connection was. I mean the real connection, not just that they were in the Army together," she said, still looking at the album. "What about their homes, anything there?"

Stone reached for the main diary where all the notes were.

"That's the strange thing," he remarked thoughtfully. "As you know, until this latest victim, we had absolutely no idea there was a military connection at all."

"Maybe you didn't go back far enough," she said.

"Well I didn't think of going back forty years, if that's what you mean. My initial reaction was that these murders were spontaneous, not some long term issue."

"Well let's not jump the gun just yet... let's check the records now that we've been alerted to them, and go from there," Mary said.

"Nonetheless, Mary," Stone emphatically continued. "Do you agree or not that the Army aspect needs further investigation?"

She turned and faced him suspiciously.

"Simon... how many times recently have we been down this path. I am not about to jump on your bandwagon just because you have found your first bit of real evidence to link these murders together. You said yourself... this one had too many clues, whereas the others had none. Doesn't that make you cautious?"

"When you put it like that, I have to agree; but it's so obvious."

"I know, Simon, and I share your enthusiasm... I really do. But someone has to keep a level head here. This is the first time there's been a direction to follow. I just don't think we should rush into it until we're sure," she looked at his disappointment. "All the same... I must admit I can't ignore the Army connection."

"I'm glad we agree on something," he said, half-heartedly.

"I do... if that makes you happy but we must first determine whether these murders relate to something that happened in the past, or merely to them as a group."

"I don't follow your thinking."

"Well... you're looking for a reason to delve into their past thinking it originates there, when the connection between these men could be something as simple as them belonging to the same club... or maybe some army reserve unit."

Stone turned his attention back to the board and pondered.

"Okay, Mary let's leave it at that at present," he conceded. "How would you like to handle it. It's you're show at the moment."

"That's very nice of you... I think the best way would be if Mark reads out the Army files, since they've arrived, you Simon do the case study and forensic, and I'll do the pathology... okay. Does that make sense to you?"

"Sounds good to me, how about you, Mark?" Stone said.

Mark nodded his approval, then stopping a passing female constable, "Right, Jenson, stop what you're doing and grab a pad... you can be our scribe."

Mary Carson picked up the pile of pathology reports and started sorting them into the same order as they were on the board. She glanced up to check.

"Right," she started, "Victim one, James McCulloch: Sixty-two years old. Found in Thorne Mill, Norfolk, by a side road off the A1064, nailed to one of the blades... ”

“Sails,” Stone prompted.

“Sails?”

“Yes... they’re called windmill sails... we must be correct.”

“Oh very well... nailed to one of the Sails.”

“Sorry.” Stone said, “We only got the first one after the second one.”

“Yes I remember the second one, that’s when you called me in. It was Mark Guldon,” she confirmed. “Anyway, what’s next with McCulloch?”

“He was a very prosaic man. Never married, did not appear to socialise much, no clubs or memberships. Worked as a cook in the local take-away, no long-term work habit or abode. He appeared to drift about a lot. No one knew anything about him, except he was inclined to blow his top now and then... usually losing him his job: a police record for much the same reasons; small stuff... no charges.”

Mary turned to Mark, “Anything on his Army record”

“Joined up in 1940 at twenty one, made a Rifleman, Cook. Served in France, Belgium, Germany, Italy, and North Africa... oh, he was one of those taken off the beaches at Dunkirk. That’s it, no more after ‘42.”

“No charges, commendations, anything?” she remarked.

“No... nothing,” Mark replied, rechecking the file.

“Okay Next, Victim number two, Mark Guldon: Sixty-one years old. Found much the same as the other... nailed to a carcass-splitting trestle in an abandoned knackers’ yard in Birmingham; again many distinct sets of mutilation wounds.”

“Yes I remember,” Stone said. “It was only a matter of hours before their Inspector decided this was no ordinary murder, and called us in... that’s when we linked with the first.”

"Anything about his life?" she continued.

"It's beginning to look like these men had something against women, or at least marrying them," Stone continued. "Guldon, I believe, lived with his mother until she died two years ago... staying in the same house. It appears he had little influence on the house. Her things dominated everywhere, except in his room and the wooden garage where he tinkered on with an old Austin Cambridge."

It was getting monotonous; Mark automatically picked up from there, and continued with an equally standard service report.

"Joined the Army in 1940 at twenty as a Rifleman, Driver; Served in exactly the same places as McCulloch, at the same time... and no charges or anything and his file was closed in 1942 also."

"Hold on," Mary jumped in. "What do you mean closed, wasn't he demobbed, pensioned out or something?"

Mark rechecked, at the same time glancing at the others.

"No... the document just ends. The last date 1942, they're all the same."

"That's strange," Stone commented. "I remember when I was demobbed from Korea. My record stated the date, time and everything, for the paymaster's benefit"

"Exactly," she agreed, "Mark, did we get any records from the paymaster?"

"No... should we."

"Well I think we should, what do you think, Simon?"

"I agree. Arrange it, Mark will you"

"Okay,"he made a note then continued. "One thing that just struck me was, if all these reports place everyone in the Second World War, in particular, Europe and North Africa, why do some of the pictures in the album refer to Korea, Vietnam and the pacific?"

There was a momentary silence, while the significance of his statement sunk in, and then they both went for the album to check.

"You're right, Mark," Stone acknowledged.

Mary continued his sentence with, "You know what this means. These records are false. They've been fabricated to cover something up."

"Yes but they didn't do a good job of it, they're all the same"

"Well they've been good enough for forty years," she said.

Stone had to admit, "So what about John Hebden and Terry Lonergan"

Mark opened them both and placed them alongside the others on the bench, "They're the same, Boss," he replied.

Mary paced back and forth before speaking again.

"All right, let's take it read that the military records have been faked for some reason. We do know however, there are subtle differences. So let's concentrate on those for a moment. Who's next?" she said, "Victim three, John Hebden: Fifty-nine years old. He was found early in the morning nailed to a Water Wheel in Wetherby, Yorkshire."

Stone looked back at the board.

"Have you noticed how all these crime scenes are always old wooden edifices, Lock Balance Beam, Windmill, Water Wheel, and what was the other. Oh yes, the Splitting Trestle," Stone pointed out.

"Yes, and his pathology was just the same, no point of even reading it. His pawn had the letter 'U' on it," Mary commented. "I see you're placing a big letter on each panel… that's a good idea; it'll jog peoples grey cells. They may even come up with a name."

"Have you considered it may not be a word at all, but an acronym?" Mark said. "Each letter may have a specific meaning to do with each victim, what his crime was; if that's what all this is about… or even where he was killed," Mary commented.

"I went through that phase, and checked into all those things and more, without finding anything that made a connection," Stone said. "To be frank with you I think it could turn out to be anything. I even gave the problem to ciphers and they just said the same."

"But we now have four, Boss," Mark reminded.

"Then... I only had three," Stone corrected.

"Okay boys, I get the drift. We can leave that problem for now." Superintendent Stone's noticeable frustration was annoying her.

"Isn't it strange that no one saw anything when he was crucifying his victim. I mean to drag him to the crucifix. Nail him in position. Cut his genitals off and finally stand back and enjoy his deed... or the agony he was putting his victim through... not to mention the time it must have taken to strangle him."

"I know, Mary," Stone acknowledged, passing her as he went to the board, studying the pictures again. "Hammond pointed something else out to us, which was missed on the others. His victim was chloroformed. He suggested it was probably to get him from the previous torture place to the death scene; which means he may have had to wait for him to come round before he continued."

Mary thought about what Stone had just said for a moment, joining him as he studied the photographs. The similarities in each case proved to be her main interest.

"Why do this to these men?" Mary said at last.

Stone noticed the pictures that had her attention, "Removing their genitals?"

"Yes... do you think this was a homosexual act?"

"I doubt it," Stone said in their defence. "Lonergan was a commando".

"And commandos can't be homosexuals?"

"You know what I mean."

"Then maybe they raped this person's sister, or mother, if it was during the war, and he's seeking retribution."

"I would say that's more likely, but it doesn't sit right with me."

"Come on, Simon, there were plenty of women raped during the war."

"That wasn't what I meant," Stone said, turning away from the board. "If you read the files on these men, especially the last one, you would understand that they were men with only one purpose; the designated target."

"Maybe you're right. It will reveal itself soon enough."

"Inspector Hammond seems to think so," Stone pointed out.

"I think it would be a good idea to get this man in on our side; don't you?" she said, glancing at him for a reaction.

"I'm ahead of you on that one, Mary," Stone boasted. "I invited him to continue with his case at his end, and join us whenever we wanted his advice."

"Good... who's next, Mark?" she said.

"Here we are... John Hebden. Enlisted at 18 as a Rifleman, Clerk. Exactly the same theatres of war as the others. Oh here's something new, he was promoted to Sergeant in 1941, gives no reason though, just says Sergeant Operations 1941, and blank after 1942."

"Well we're certainly establishing another common denominator," Mary said, peering over Stone's shoulder. "But why?"

"Let's just carry on shall we, try and get the total picture," Stone said.

"Okay, now we have the newest victim, and the one who appears to have given us our breakthrough," Mary said, turning once more to the board. "Why did it do that, what's the thing that changed?"

"I had a good discussion with Hammond on this one. It's the one that led us to the Army connection..."

"That's right," she interrupted. "I'm sorry, Simon. Carry on".

"His house was full of memorabilia. It may pay us to give it a visit and check his album, which gave us the names of the fourteen soldiers with him. His campaign medals, don't tally with the records, but are similar to the photographs."

"He's certainly the best victim," she mused. "And the only one to continue his obsession as a professional soldier. Most of his details appear to be the same. I think we should follow this lead in..." she checked the board, "Uxbridge."

"It's already in hand," Stone said.

Mary picked up the last file again.

"Now we don't really need to go into all this stuff, we've covered the important points, so what about his Army record. Are we going to be lucky there as well?"

"I suppose it depends on what you mean by lucky. Yes his file is different, but not in the way we would have liked," Stone answered, twisting his face over the folder, and getting a puzzled look back from Mary.

"What is that supposed to mean."

"Well you be the judge. He started in 1940 like the rest, at the same age as Hebden, 18. Again as a Rifleman, Clerk. Exactly the same campaigns, but this time it's different. His record includes three promotions, two non-commissioned: Corporal, Sergeant, then in 1941 he suddenly got a field commission to Lieutenant."

"That is interesting. It provides a link with what Hammond said about him being a leader. Maybe they all suffered for something he did?

"I don't know," Stone continued. "But the rest is the same as the others; his file stops dead in 1942 also"

"So here we have the open indication that in some way he was still connected with the Army right through to 1965. Making him a professional soldier, although hinting it was in an instructive capacity... but what happened to those missing years?" Mary pointed out.

She took the report out of Stone's hand and studied it, looking for something that may not be there. She then gestured for the other papers: the ones referring to his later years.

"What are you looking for?" Stone questioned.

"Did you notice that these two groups of papers are totally different... they don't continue. They look like they've been taken from another file."

"Show me," he said.

"Look," she said, pointing to the form headings. "You would think, since he was a professional soldier, in for the term, that they would correspond... but they don't. It's as if he finished with the Army in 1942 like the others... then started again afresh"

Stone checked the papers more carefully. There had never been a need before. He examined them more closely, having knowledge of such things from his own service experience. "There's something funny going on here," he said.

"What... have you found something?" she asked.

"These can't be separate records," he pointed out to her. "They both have the same serial number."

"So they do. Is that possible?"

"It's not only possible... it proves Terry Lonergan was using the same ID card all the time. Regardless of this hole in time, he was still using his card."

"And according to this, all his promotions ended in 1942." she said.

"Exactly, and that would tie in with what Jack Hammond found out. Lonergan was a professional soldier that retired around the late sixties, suddenly becoming a businessman with big connections in commerce and local government."

"How do you suddenly get influential friends after spending most of your adult life in the Army. Was it through his brother?" Mary continued.

"It doesn't say, although I don't think so. Hammond made it

quite clear there was a rift between them... although he didn't know why."

Mary Carson turned back to the board again, outstretched her arms as if to embrace the whole thing, and then flapped them back onto her ample thighs with a resounding slap.

"Well, Simon, I have to agree with you, the Army connection is most definitely the one you put your money on. Everything keeps revolving around this area. It reeks of skulduggery, and when you have that ingredient mixed with murder; then it's pretty certain the two go together in some way. And it all stems from what happened in 1942."

"Finally, we have a single path to follow," Stone said.

She continued her analysis of the scribbled notes on the board. "You know, Simon... the more I study these four victims, the more I can now see the pathways radiating away from them to a shadowy hole at the end which we need to fill.

"Terry Lonergan is the key to all this, maybe not the precursor, but certainly a major player; he's the one that led us to the Army connection, which we must follow back into the past; 1942 is our second pathway, something happened then that changed all these men's lives, and is the answer to why their files were falsified. The pawns are significant too, and the manor of the execution; find those connections and everything will start unravelling."

"I'm glad you came to that conclusion, Mary, you'll write us up a profile won't you... and as quickly as you can, before we lose this momentum."

"I'll do it tonight; I won't get a wink of sleep until I do," she kissed him on the cheek. "By the way, what would you have done if I'd said something different?"

"You don't want me to answer that do you?"

CHAPTER 6

Two days had passed and the trail was getting cold. Stone was spending hours going over the documentation originally formulated by Inspector Hammond's team, with very little if any input from his own. Mary Carson's report and profile of the killer only reinforced his own theories, with no real added input to stimulate another course of inquiry; which heaven knows, he desperately needed at this moment. All he had was a revised version of Inspector Hammond's original hunches.

He tried to clear his mind and think back to the euphoria of this new victim, the new leads, the Army connection. 'Why was it all falling apart?' he thought. 'Had he lost the impetus of those first few hours?. He realised he was in fact deflated by the block on his only new lead, the one he was positive would give him that quantum leap he was looking for; the Army connection, and in particular, what happened in 1942.

All communication with the Ministry led to dead-ends; deliberately fabricated he was sure: if only he could prove it. What he needed was some way to get around the reason why they falsified the records.

In Stone's 1942 fixation, he had come up with the notion that they had got themselves involved in something that had to be covered up, and the idea was driving everything else out of his mind. He knew he would not be satisfied until he had visited the house.

Stone decided it was time he called upon his old friend's infallible nose. He invited him to a return visit to Lonergan's home where they could examine this man's life and attempt to find out what happened back in 1942.

He surprised the Inspector when he called. It had been over a week since hearing anything, and the Inspector was beginning to think the superintendent's invitation to be part of this investigation, was proving to be as he first suspected; all crap. Stone arranged to meet him at the house at two o'clock.

Inspector Hammond still had the phone in his hand, looking studiously out of the window when Sergeant Binstead waltzed in with a pile of reports; it was the end of another quarter once again.

"What's up, Boss? You look as if Mr Lonergan was ringing you again."

"Don't mention that name, Sergeant, he's driving me crazy," he said, putting the phone down, realising Stone had hung up.

"Just pass him on to Superintendent Stone, Boss."

"I have, but it doesn't make any difference. I'll just have to go and see him and put things straight. But not now, I've got other fish to fry."

"The call, Boss?"

"Yes... it was Stone, he's in trouble."

"I didn't expect him to cry for help so soon."

"He didn't actually say it in so many words, but I know him; he's in trouble."

"You're not going to help him, are you, Boss?"

"What can I do, Sergeant; I promised the Super I would support him if he needed it. And if I don't, he'll just order me to, and we don't want that do we"

"No, Boss. When are we having the pleasure of his company,

and that miserable Inspector. What was his name… oh yes, Fraser."

"There's no we, Sergeant. He wants me to meet him at Lonergan's house."

"Okay, Boss, but please make him grovel."

The Inspector suddenly realised Binstead was standing with a pile of folders up to his chin. "Oh what have you got there, Sergeant?."

"Sorry, Boss… it's that time again"

"Well I suppose you'd better put them alongside the others."

Mark spotted Stone as he was about to drive off. He was suspicious, and ran to his car.

"Where are you going, Boss?" he called out.

"I'm going out to the Lonergan house to get this thing rolling again."

"Do you want me to drive you?"

"No that's all right, Mark thanks. This is going to be a quiet little outing with Inspector Hammond. Who knows, I might even squeeze something more out of him."

"I could read these new notes I put together for you on the… "

It was too late. Stone sped out of the car park, turned left at the shiny New Scotland Yard sign, and out into the busy traffic.

When he arrived at Lonergan's he hoped the car parked outside belonged to Inspector Hammond, he had no desire to meet anyone else, such as the brother, who had been threatening him. He was relieved to find Hammond in the lounge, with his back to him, examining the fine array of well-maintained weapons on the far wall.

"Oh, Jack there you are. How are you?" he called out jovially. Hammond turned towards him, hand outstretched.

"Glad to see you're still as punctual as ever."

"Sorry, Jack, got caught up with my Boss, you know how it is."

"Oh I know how it is, Stone," he replied suspiciously. "So what's so important that you need me to hold your hand while you're looking over the place?"

Stone laughed, "I just wanted to see if I could get the feel of what's going on."

"So... that over, what do you really want, is it Sir or Stone?"

"You know there's no rank between us, Jack, not at this level anyway. Besides you know me too well for that, I can't fool you, can I?" he joked, shaking his hand. At that moment, they attempted to take the measure of each other.

"Well you know what they say," Hammond replied, still holding onto his hand. "Once a wheeler and dealer, always... "

"Okay, Jack, cards on the table."

He knew full well, Hammond had his number, and the only way he was going to get what he wanted, was to be up front with him; well almost.

"The case came to a grinding halt yesterday, Jack," he started pacing the floor between the window and the decorated wall where Hammond was, a sure sign of nervousness he thought. "We opted for the Army link, but got stonewalled by Military Records."

"What does that mean," Hammond asked, watching him pass by again, remembering that he had asked Sergeant Binstead to shred theirs, so he was working blind.

"Stonewalled. You know, as in being led up the garden path."

"Hold on, just stop burning a hole in the carpet for a minute and tell me what you're on about; I didn't see any records"

"Of course you didn't, sorry," Stone said, walking over to him. "Each report was identical, and I mean a copy, as if the same person had typed each one. They all served in the same theatres of war, the same duration, and the same end to their reports... 1942. You note I didn't say demob time, because there was no entry to the effect that any of them had left, just 1942, and nothing else."

"What about our fella... Lonergan. He was supposed to be a professional soldier."

"His report started exactly the same as the others, and ended in 1942 also, except he did have a number of other reports following the original in 1945, which didn't appear to be part of those. More like a further record after the end of the war."

"I see" Hammond said, walking over to the window. He looked out across the tranquil scene of the garden, although he was not thinking about flowers at the time. "And you think these records have been falsified?" he continued, still gazing out over the verdant expanse of the late Terry Lonergan's immaculate lawn.

"Well doesn't it smell like that to you?"

Hammond turned back, walked over to the sideboard, lifted up a cut glass decanter and removing the glistening cap, sniffed its contents.

"It seems to me like one of two possibilities," he started, gesturing with the decanter while taking a glass from the tray.

"Why not" Stone accepted.

Hammond poured two stiff scotches, walked back to where Stone had planted himself in a chair next to the coffee table, and joined him.

"Usually the authorities falsify records because they want to cover up an incident, and the best way of doing that is to muddy the waters. Or they need to give new identities to people in covert operations," he sipped his malt. "Either way, they can make life very difficult for people like us."

"Then how are we able to run a check on their records?"

"Did you corroborate their authenticity?"

"No... I don't think we did".

"That's what they bank on, who's going to check if your social security number is correct or not".

"So what do we do then"

Hammond glanced at Stone suspiciously.

"Ah... so now we find out the real reason you asked me here."

Stone gulped down his drink, went over to the decanter again, poured himself another, and walked back to the Inspector with the decanter. The Inspector shook his head and placed his hand over his glass. He did not intend to be this man's lap dog, sorting out his problems every time he ran up against a brick wall.

"Look, Jack, I did intend looking over the place again, who knows I could have found something, a new lead, I don't know. And yes, I did intend pumping you, you're well known for your hunches, you know."

"So you've checked up on me have you?"

"I never do anything blind, you should know that," he shook the decanter.

"No thanks... and I'd watch that stuff if you want a clear head."

Stone nodded as he returned it to the sideboard. The weapons on the wall caught his attention, just as they had done the Inspector. He gestured to them saying:

"This man's got to have more history than they want us to know. But how do we find out?" he swung back to Hammond's casual gaze. "I even asked the brother, but he was no help, totally useless."

"Use your contacts," Hammond said.

"What contacts"

"You were in the Army, weren't you. You must have formed some relationships with other sections of the establishment at some time. If I remember you were pretty good at that, and you always said, 'It wasn't what you know, but who you know'... or was I mistaken?"

"No, you're right, but I was no more than a private during my whole term in Korea. All I got involved with was transport and supplies."

"That sounds about right"

"It didn't do me much good though, not like you I'm sure, in the MP's."

"So you know about that as well, do you?"

"It was easy enough to pull your records at the same time as the others."

"Was that on your initiative, or Fraser's?"

"It's all the same difference."

Inspector Hammond was beginning to get a little tired of all this tiptoeing around the real issue; they would be here all day and still get nowhere at this rate.

"Okay, Stone, so you finally got to the point. You know I was in the Military Police and you think I know someone who could help you."

"Well do you".

"As a matter of fact I do, but whether or not he'll oblige I couldn't say, it' been a while since I last spoke to him."

"What about finding out now."

"God man... I'd hate to be in Inspector Fraser's shoes."

"Oh I don't know... he has a pretty good life."

"Have you asked him lately?"

"Just make the call," he said sharply, picking up the phone.

Hammond grabbed the phone and stuffed it under his chin while he checked his diary for the number. Dialling in the digits, he relaxed back in his chair and waited.

"Oh yes... good afternoon, is Stephen Monagal there?" he said.

Stone waited impatiently while the Hammond's eyes fluttered listening to the other end, it seemed interminable.

"It's Jack Hammond... would you do that please... thank you," he looked at Stone with an upward movement of his head, covering the mouthpiece with his hand.

"Their looking for him, I gather it's a big complex," he explained.

"Are they paging him?" Stone asked.

Hammond was still listening to the noises on the other end.

"I think so..." he started, "Yes Stephen Monagal... that's right," he covered the phone again. "They've found him, I think"

"Thank goodness for that," Stone sighed.

"Stephen, is that you?"

"Of course it is, Jack, who else would it be?" he replied.

"I wasn't sure there, I must have been all round your building."

"That's rubbish, I think they do it just to get a fix on you and monitor your call," he let out a raucous laugh on the other end.

"We're not being bugged are we?" Hammond asked.

"Why, are you going to be devious, Jack?"

"You lot are all the same, answer a question with a question."

"Sorry, Jack, and no we're not being monitored. This is a secure line."

"Thank goodness for that, because I am going to be devious."

"Fire away, but I warn you I'm covered by the Secrets Act."

"Well are you breaking any secrets by telling me if you're still in Special Ops?" he said winking at Stone, who was trying to get as close to the phone as he could.

"Yes I am, but I can't tell you anymore."

"That's okay; I don't want to know anything about your activities. I just want some advice on a problem I have."

"Well tell me what it is, and I'll tell you if I can help you."

Hammond explained the situation as succinctly as he could, endeavouring to point out their suspicions of the records being tampered with. He also stressed the importance of them being able to get more information on these people, as there was a killer at large, undoubtedly trying to do the very same thing. He had already killed four, with a possibility of four more to go.

"I understand where you're coming from, Jack, and I agree with your suspicions, but there's not much I can do about it," he answered.

"I know that, Stephen, I'm not asking you to get involved, but can't you just point us in some direction. Or someone who might be able to help."

There was a pause on the other end while Stephen thought.

"Okay... 1942 is the key factor. Cast your mind back; there was a lot going on in different campaigns, and it's easy to come up with a scenario to fit your problem."

"Such as?" Hammond questioned.

"Well... for instance. Say, in 1942 a group of specialists were put together to perform a particular task which was so secret very few knew of it. During the performance of that task, something went wrong, or someone died, and a relative is on a trail of vengeance against the others. He paused for some response."

"A bit thin isn't it?" Hammond commented, expecting better of him.

Stephen pondered on his own rule of non-involvement, and then relented.

"Do you have a pen and paper handy?"

"I have someone nearby who can act as a stenographer... why? Hammond said, as Stone fumbled for his notepad, giving Hammond a desperate look.

Stephen told him about a group of units that acted as handlers for special operations: selecting the right people for the right job, deploying munitions for the operation and so on. He also pointed out that these people may not be in the service anymore; or they may even be dead. He was dipping deep into his memory now.

When Hammond was ready, Stephen began telling him the different units and the names of certain operatives specially trained for the role he previously mentioned.

"That's it, Jack, I can't give you any more... I shouldn't have given you that."

"I'm much obliged, Stephen... and no one will know."

"I hope not, Jack... must go... all the best."

"You bet... cheers."

The phone went dead and Hammond looked at Stone, "Did you get that?"

Stone finished scribbling the last name down, "Sure did. I certainly hope this lot gives us something to work on. That's if Mark can read my writing."

Inspector Hammond shook his head in exasperation. If he were honest with himself, he would have to admit he wanted this case, and he was prepared to do whatever it takes. But he was not about to let Stone know that.

CHAPTER 7

The following morning Inspector Fraser stopped as he noticed the Superintendent sitting quietly in his office, studying the list Stephen Monagal had given them.

"How did yesterday go, Boss?

"Very tight lipped," he said. "God I hate dealing with these Special Operations people. Everything's got to be all this need to know stuff.

Mark looked surprised at the Superintendent's answer; the case had taken on a new dimension that he had no knowledge of, "What Special Operations people?"

"Oh sorry, Mark, you have no idea. I didn't know myself until we got there and then Inspector Hammond phoned this Army pal called Stephen."

"Phoned who? Was this at Lonergan's?"

"Didn't you get my message?"

"No I didn't. Then I wouldn't... I went to the canal site to get a feel for the area. I'm not familiar with that district, and since we haven't heard anything about their canvassing yet, I thought I'd see for myself... he was one of those was he."

"Very much so."

"How did Inspector Hammond know him?"

"I gather they go back to his time in the Military Police."

"A policeman through and through."

"So it seems. Anyway, I understand Hammond had a lot of contact with the Army Specials, I don't know why."

"So what did you get out of him?"

"Apart from some advice and supposition, this list of people who may be able to help us with our Army records problem," he passed it over.

"It's big enough," Mark commented.

"I think you'll find a lot of dead wood in there, so first order of the day is to get those names checked out. See if they're still living, where they now reside, if they are, and in what capacity... retired or whatever, you know the drill."

"Yes, Boss, I'll get onto it right away. Oh by the way, Mary called."

"Thanks, and get that smirk off you face."

Stone relaxed back into his chair looking at the mundane part of his work scattered across his desk, guessing there was a good day's hard grind there. He also contemplated whether to ring Mary now or get stuck in, 'no,' he thought. 'Let's see what she wants and then get stuck in. He picked up the phone and dialled her number.

"Mary... how are you, I understand you were trying to get me yesterday."

"Yes I was. It wasn't important really; I just wanted to know if you had got any further with the military scenario?"

"That's what I was doing yesterday. After drawing a blank with records, I decided to contact Jack Hammond again."

"The bright Inspector. I told you he would be useful."

"Yes well... I did just that, and he phoned an old Army buddy of his in Special Operations. The case is developing nicely."

"Oh my... Special Operations. Was he able to tell you what you wanted?"

He swung round in his chair until he was facing the city

towards the Thames. The sun was behind casting a long shadow over the streets below, forming a chasm of nothing below the fourth floor. It was an eerie sight at this time each day.

"In a manner of speaking," he said, almost losing the gist of their conversation. "He supplied us with a list of possible contacts."

"Great, so we move forward a bit more then," she said, more relaxed.

"We'll see; Mark's checking them out now."

"Don't forget, if you want me to vet any of them, I'm available."

"I intend to invite you along on the interviews if we arrange any."

"That's good; I'll look forward to that. So I'll hear from you. Bye."

"Bye, Mary, speak to you soon."

He continued gazing across to the spires of the Houses of Parliament and further over towards Westminster Cathedral, losing all track of time, until he realised she had hung up. He swung back and replaced the phone.

That out of the way, he still had the mess on his desk to clear. What he wanted now was another distraction, but the squad room was quiet. Inspector Fraser had everyone occupied checking his list. There were no dramas for him to sort out.

Meanwhile, the Chief Super called out from his open door as Inspector Hammond passed.

"Got a moment, Jack?"

"Yes. Sir, what's the problem?" he replied, entering his office.

"No real problem, Jack, I just wanted to know if everything went off smoothly with the transfer."

"Yes, Sir, all went well," he stated, hoping that would satisfy him.

"I understand you were out with Stone yesterday."

"You don't miss much do you, Sir"

"Well I am paid to keep my finger on the pulse, Jack."

The Inspector wondered why it always seemed to be his.

"Stone ran into a problem with Army records and as I had

some contacts from my Military Police days, I volunteered to help out. We did say we would continue to give help if needed, didn't we, Sir?"

"Oh yes, of course. No that's fine, Jack, glad to see you're prepared to do that much. No hard feelings and all that?"

"The important thing, Sir is that we catch this bastard, by whatever means."

"Most definitely, we have to do that at all costs," he shuffled; there was something else on his mind, no doubt the main purpose of calling Jack in.

"Was that all, Sir?"

"Err... there was one thing, Jack."

"Sir?"

"Have you heard anything more from Lonergan's brother?"

"Regularly, Sir, it's becoming a joke. I've told him we're not on the case anymore, even given him Superintendent Stone's number, but he won't listen."

"Yes... he's been onto me again, complaining."

"What's his problem, Sir?"

The Chief Superintendent squirmed in his seat.

"I don't know, Jack, but as I said, he has some powerful friends and they're on my back to do something; he's getting them all uptight and this SCI investigation isn't helping any. I thought once we got rid of it that would be the end of that."

"I told Mr Lonergan, Sir, when their flag came up, that there was no chance of shaking them loose."

The Chief Superintendent shuffled with his blotter again.

"It's not that I want to shake anyone loose, Jack. I just want the inquiries to be concentrated on the important areas; not a bunch of bureaucrats."

"You said that, Sir, not me."

"You know what I mean, Jack"

"I do, Sir... okay, I'll go out and see him again, see if I can't dissuade him from pestering you lot. In the meantime I suggest you contact Superintendent Stone and ask if he can have a word with the Commissioner, apparently, he's in with these people."

"Sorry, Jack, stirring up the Commissioner and his friends isn't good for the station."

"Sir... I shall never understand politics, thank goodness."

"Thanks again, Jack; I'll let you get on."

Sergeant Binstead was waiting for the Inspector as he entered the squad room.

"I see the old man grabbed you again on your way in this morning, Boss, anything life threatening?" he asked.

The Inspector's future was constantly on the Sergeant's mind these days, since his only chance of promotion greatly depended on when the Inspector retired. Once he passed his exam, that thought began to take on greater than usual proportions.

"He was just nosy about what I was doing yesterday, and letting me know our pest Len Lonergan has been after the Commissioner again."

"Oh yeah, I forgot to tell you about that. He rang yesterday. When I told him you were out all day, he said he hoped you were on his brother's case."

"What did you tell him?"

"Just that you didn't confide in me, and I would give you his message."

"With answers like that Sergeant you'll make Inspector in no time."

"Hold on, Boss, I've only just started looking at my Inspector' papers."

"Is that so... I shall have to keep my eye on you, won't I. Good Sergeants are hard to come by these days"

"I can't stay a Sergeant all my life, Boss."

"I know you can't... I'm only kidding. In fact I've been meaning to say something to you about your future for a while, someone's got to take over when I retire, and I'd much prefer it to be you."

"That won't be for ages yet, Boss, you've got plenty on your plate."

"Yes, you're right, I'll have to go out and see Lonergan now, get it over with once and for all. The Inspector stood up; gazed through the open Venetian blinds out into the squad room where everyone was busy on other cases, this one forgotten and buried.

"I think he's trying to draw attention to himself, Boss."

The Inspector turned back to his desk, reached into his top drawer, and took out his diary. He flicked through the pages he had started on the case to see what Lonergan said about the accident that left him a quadriplegic.

"Or draw our attention away from him," the Inspector mused.

"How come, Boss?"

He placed the small book in his inside pocket and made to leave.

"I don't know, Sergeant. But I'm going to find out."

It was a pleasant day; the Inspector's mind was drifting as he drove through the open country, thinking how he was going to approach Lonergan with his suspicion. However, this new development had interesting possibilities, and filled him with that feeling he got when he was about to go in for the kill. He did feel sorry for the man though; it had to be difficult for him: tied to a wheelchair all day.

While others coped with their disability, he had turned in on himself.

He pulled up outside the small cottage, and spotted Lonergan in the front garden pruning his roses. Lonergan saw the Inspector and turned his chair to face him at the gate, looking just as sour.

"So, Inspector you finally decided to answer my calls," he said, sharply.

"Mr Lonergan, I told you last week this was no longer my case. Your brother's death was a serial killing, and as such, Superintendent Stone of the SCI has taken it over."

"Remind me again what that means."

"I haven't come to play games with you, my time is too valuable."

"Then humour me, after all I am a taxpayer."

He spun round on his wheelchair and headed for the rear of the house, Inspector Hammond had no alternative but to follow. When he reached him, he was stationary beside a table and chairs by the French windows. He gestured to a pitcher of lemonade.

"Thank you" the Inspector said politely, "Shall I pour you one."

"Yes please."

"As I was saying, I can no longer supply you with information on this case, but for your better humour, SCI stands for Special Criminal Investigations."

"Thank you, Inspector," he replied, picking up the glass. "So what were you doing yesterday if you weren't still on the case?"

"That's none of your business."

"It's just that I saw you at my brother's house with that Superintendent."

"Why didn't you come in?"

"I wasn't ready. Besides I don't go in that house if I can help it."

"Why not. He was your brother."

"I've already told you my brother and I stopped speaking."

Although the case was not his, and he had no right to question a man who he still considered a suspect, despite the Chief Super's instruction, he felt this was the right time; that special time when the balance of power appeared to be on his side.

"I think, Mr Lonergan, all this pestering the Commissioner is a smokescreen."

"What do you mean?" He said indignantly, still pumped up.

"I think you had good reason to want your brother dead.

Regardless of people telling me that a man in a wheelchair couldn't possibly be responsible."

"You should listen to them, Inspector."

"I listen to my hunches, Mr Lonergan and you don't smell right. You smell of guilt. You smell of jealousy. You smell of a petty man who's been made a... "

"Go on say it... Cripple."

"I was looking for a kinder word."

"It doesn't matter how kind the word is, Inspector... I'm still a cripple."

"You didn't let me finish. I was going to say... wants his revenge."

He looked devastated. The Inspector had found his flaw.

"That's not true," his voice wavered. The Inspector could sense he had touched a raw nerve. Lonergan no longer looked him in the eye.

"Because your brother was driving the car you were injured in, you wanted him dead. You wanted him to pay for killing your wife and leaving you in this degrading situation."

Lonergan was surprised; he spun round and frantically wheeled himself off down the lawn behind the house, then stopped and paused for a moment.

The Inspector followed, "You envied him, his popularity, while you sat in that contraption in his shadow."

"How did you know about that?"

"I am a policeman; we do have records of accidents you know."

"Yes well, he shouldn't have been driving so fast."

"I understand you were egging him on, it was in your brother's statement."

"I don't want to discuss it anymore, but I do want to know what's happening about catching his killer."

This constant urge to find the killer of a brother he hated puzzled the Inspector, it was out of character with the pretence he was conjuring.

"Why should it matter to you, you obviously hated your brother. His death, I would think was poetic justice for what he had done to you and your wife."

Lonergan suddenly broke down in tears; his head dropped to his chest and in turn, his upper body collapsed on his lap. The Inspector moved forward and raised him upright again. Holding him firmly by the shoulders, the Inspector looked into his red eyes. Lonergan could barely look him in the face.

The Inspector continued holding him; following the move of his face from side to side, finally fixing him, stare for stare. There was something else in his eyes, the reason he was averting their contact. Where the Inspector looked for fury, satisfying vengeance, he saw a plea for mercy. Everything suddenly became clear.

"You were driving, weren't you?" the Inspector said.

Lonergan did not answer immediately. He sat staring out across the fields to his right, his eyes fixed on the horizon, as if the whole episode was flashing before him again, as it must have done many times before.

"Yes," he replied, almost with relief. "Yes, I was driving. I didn't have a licence so my brother said he was behind the wheel."

"But if your legs were badly damaged..." the Inspector started.

"Oh we were thrown from the car; it was an open sports car. My injuries were caused by my impact with a stone country wall; there was nothing in the car to say otherwise."

"Why didn't you speak up?"

"Don't you remember. My wife died. She unfortunately went through the windscreen... died of a massive brain haemorrhage," he continued sobbing. It was coming from deep down, his chest was heaving uncontrollably. "I was too much of a coward."

"You mean you allowed your brother to bear that burden all this time?"

"That's the way he wanted it," he said, regaining his composure. "He said he was trained to accept such responsibility... he had other deaths on his conscience. One more wouldn't make any difference."

"I can't believe you went ahead with this because of your wife's death."

He suddenly regained his composure and stared back at the Inspector.

"If I was driving, I wouldn't have been able to claim as much as I did against his insurance. I had nothing else to live on."

"I see... that puts things in a totally different light."

"I suppose you're going to be a policeman now and arrest me for fraud?"

The Inspector laughed, to Lonergan's surprise. "Arrest you for fraud... I was about to arrest you for murder. I'm not interested in what petty things you've done, or reporting you. I suspect you are your own punishment. I just want you off my back, and my superiors. I won't hear any more of this... do you understand?"

"Yes... I just want to find out who killed my brother."

He turned away again.

"So do we all. But this isn't just some local incident; it goes back into his past. Something happened when he was in the army. Not just to him... but to eight others, and someone is making it pay-back time; he's killed four now."

Lonergan looked terrible; his head bent forward in his hands.

"Oh my god I'm a selfish bastard," he wept. "I'm so full of guilt; I've forgotten my brother's actually dead. Who the hell cares who killed him, it won't bring him back. I tried so many times to make my peace with him. It's too late now."

The Inspector placed his hand on his shoulder, "I can't help you with your personal problems, but it's good that you realise the truth of the matter. If it's of any consequence to you, I promise I shall keep a close watch on the SCI people, and make sure this tragedy is settled one way or another; as quickly as possible."

Lonergan looked up at him, wiping his eyes, and for once actually smiling. He turned his wheelchair around to where the Inspector was making ready to leave.

"Thank you, Inspector; you've helped me a great deal. I suppose my pestering was a cry for someone to put me in my place, and you saw that, I'm grateful."

"You're lucky I didn't arrest you."

"I know... as far as my other problem, I shall have to clear my conscience on that. When I feel ready I shall turn myself in... to you I hope. I promise I won't ring your superiors again or use my brother's important friends," he continued, bracing himself against the back of his chair, trying to look less pathetic than he was. "Will you call now and then. Just to say hello and give me any news you may have," he said, shaking the Inspector's hand and following him out to his car.

Inspector Hammond left him with one more passing word.

"Don't worry, we'll get this man; he's going to pay."

As the Inspector drove away, he glanced into his rear view mirror at the pathetic man in a wheelchair sitting by the gate. He sincerely hoped he would find himself again. Maybe one day, like his brother, he will find his place in society.

The names Stephen Monagal supplied comprised of fifteen Army personnel dealing with Army Records in one way or another; presumably covering the period in question. What made this group most significant was the fact that they were retired and no longer subject to Army regulations. Superintendent Stone was gambling that someone amongst this group would make sense of the bogus files that were giving them trouble.

He did not underestimate the deviousness of the bureaucracy. If they had taken the trouble to falsify government records, they certainly would have included the Army records in their scheme also. His hope, based on Inspector Hammond's discussion with his friend, was to depend more on the memories of these men rather than the chance that they may know of other records; maybe the original documents.

Late in the day, the results of their many phone calls were beginning to take shape. Stone walked out into the incident room.

"Well... how are we doing, Mark?" Stone asked for the umpteenth time.

"It depends on whether or not you're a percentages man, Boss," he replied.

"And what is that supposed to mean for Christ sake?" he said.

"Well out of the fifteen names, only three are attainable," he said cautiously.

"After a whole morning's work, you only manage to find three," Stone snapped loudly, causing everyone to look up.

Inspector Fraser was in his usual pedantic phase.

"No, Boss, I said attainable. We found them all, even though some had changed their address, and in one case was living in another accommodation."

"You'd better explain."

Inspector Fraser moved over to his desk and picked up a sheet of paper: "Five are dead. Four went abroad. Two are in sanatoriums with terminal illnesses. One refuses to say anything about his work... I think he should be in a mental home also, and, as I just said, three are leading a normal retirement."

"They weren't told anything?"

"No, Boss, it was the usual non-committal inquiry."

"Then what's this about one refusing to talk about his work?"

"Oh him, the paranoid; he saw through the ruse straight away. The only way I could get him to talk at all was to tell him what

I really wanted. He thought I was someone from 'Big Brother', trying to manipulate his freedom."

Stone waved his hand at him impatiently, urging him to get on.

"Yes all right, I see your point. Any details on them?"

"Ah yes. Fred Butler lives here in London; Slough in fact... out on the M4."

"I know where it is," Stone interrupted, "funnily it's just below Uxbridge."

"Yes, Boss... anyway he's a widower, retired Army Records man. Owns his own semi, and does part time work for the Salvation Army."

Stone laughed, "Can't keep away from the Army can he. Okay, who's next?"

"Reg Clitheroe. Again, he's retired Army Records, living at Lyme Regis in Dorset. He works part time in his son-in-laws garage."

"They're scattered about a bit. I suppose the last one's in Scotland?"

"Not quite, Boss, but far enough. He's in Wieldsea near Bristol. His name's David Cantrell, this one could be interesting. He's retired Special Operations Records."

Stone rolled his eyes and rubbed the back of his neck. "You can be sure he won't say much if he's like Stephen Monagal... it's ingrained into them."

"Well he's not listed here as working."

Stone studied the list, and then walked over to the map of England on the far wall, reaching up and stabbing each location with a pin he grabbed from the side.

"Okay... we haven't got time to race around the country as a group, so let's split this one up. I'll take Cantrell, you visit Clitheroe, and you can brief Constable Freeman on Butler... and don't forget, we must concentrate on unravelling these records, or at least find a more direct source on what links these victims together; is that understood?"

Mark looked interested at last, gathering the papers together.

"Right, Boss. We'll get on to it straight away," he paused, turning back to Stone. "Oh by the way, Boss, when are you going to Bristol?"

"I'll set off after lunch, stop off overnight and get an early start in the morning."

"If Freeman interviews his contact this afternoon, why not wait to find out if he gets the answers you want... might save us both a long journey for nothing."

"No, I want all three properly investigated. I don't trust any of these people any further than I can throw them. I'd rather make my own decisions on the information we get, with as many comparisons as possible."

"Okay, Boss, I'll tell Freeman, and that we will possibly see you tomorrow."

Stone returned to his office and started tidying his desk.

While Inspector Fraser was heading South-West on the M3 to Lyme Regis, and Superintendent Stone West on the M4 towards Wieldsea, DC Freeman was drawing up alongside a typical suburban semi in Arlott Grove, Slough. Saddled with a car that had a blue light on the roof he drew the attention of the next-door neighbour: a middle-aged portly woman sporting gardening gloves, a long floral housecoat and large sunglasses.

Whilst under the pretence of clipping her hedge, she nosily edged her way towards the constable entering the gate of number 26, "Is it Mr Butler you're after. If so, he's with the Salvation Army in the afternoons," she enlightened him.

"Have you any idea where that may be?" he asked, walking round to her front gate to meet her face to face.

"Oh yes, luv'... they 'ave a place on the estate. Has a relative died?"

"No nothing like that, Mrs... "

"Mrs Barrington," she told him.

"Right... Mrs Barrington. We just want some information... that's all."

"Well you'll find him there 'til around four," she muttered, as she continued with her clipping; no longer interested.

"Sorry to be a pest, Mrs Barrington, where would that be?"

"The Estate? I can see you're not local?"

"No... I'm from the Met."

That was different; now she was interested. "Oh... up from the city are yah? Well if you continue the way you were going to the roundabout, go round to the far side, then take a left... it'll lead you right into the estate; you can ask from then on," she returned to her hedge muttering excitedly. "Up from the Met, are we?"

"Thank you, Mrs Barrington," he replied, and set off.

Her directions were good, and before long, he was asking someone where the Salvation Army was. As it turned out, he was almost outside, just two buildings up around the back of a large clothing factory, to an open warehouse.

On entering, he could see it was a clearing station for the household goods donated for further distribution, where they were sorted, repaired if needed, and made ready for delivery to other destinations. There must have been at least fifty workers, with the activity concentrating on a white haired man in the familiar black and maroon uniform, shouting orders and ticking his clipboard.

"Can I help you officer?" the man said, as DC Freeman approached.

"How did you know I was a policeman?" he said.

"I'm afraid the blue light is a dead give-away young man."

"I'm, DC Freeman Sir," he said, holding out his warrant card. "Do you have a Mr Fred Butler working for you?"

"Oh dear, I hope Fred hasn't been doing anything naughty."

"No, Sir, I just want a word with him."

"Well he's here somewhere, but I'm not sure where. Let me see now," he said raising his stature slightly on his toes as he surveyed the large open area of the warehouse. "Are yes... there he is," he pointed. "He's over by those big cardboard boxes; the man with the dark brown trilby and mustard coloured overall."

DC Freeman caught sight of him, "And your name is?"

"It's, Major Felby," he laughed for some reason. "Anytime... here's my card, maybe you could show it around your station; every bit helps you know."

"Thanks, I will."

The Constable approached the man with tufts of white hair jutting out from under a battered brown trilby. He looked in his late sixties, yet showed great agility as he manhandled the pieces of furniture destined for the needy.

"Mr Butler?" the Constable called out.

The man raised his head with a questioning look on his face.

"Who wants him?" he answered.

"I'm DC Freeman, Mr Butler; I'd like a few words if you can spare the time."

"Police aye... what do the police want with me?" he replied, putting the coffee table he was holding down and walking over to him.

"Nothing serious, Sir; just a few questions you may be able to help me with."

Butler reached into his waistcoat and checked the time on his old pocket watch, then returned it to its pocket, and looked up at the young man.

"It's my tea break, so you can buy me a cuppa."

They walked around the corner to the canteen belonging to the clothing firm. The Sergeant bought two mugs of tea and an

Eccles cake for the old man, who had already found them a table by the window away from the other workers.

It was amazing how people preferred talking to the police in private, regardless of whether they were in uniform or not.

"They let you use this place do they?" the Constable asked, sugaring his tea.

"Oh yeah, well they would, we rent their warehouse off them."

"That's very benevolent of them."

"You must be joking; this lot, it costs a packet. Business is so bad in the rag trade and they make up the difference on mugs like us."

"Shame isn't it. Anyway, Mr Butler according to our information you were an Army Records clerk before you took up this noble pastime."

"That's correct... what's that got to do with the price of bread?"

"How long, Mr Butler?"

"How long. Oh dear now, let me see." He paused looking off into the distance, "Well I joined up in 1939; went the duration of the war until late '45. Got demobbed... didn't make a go of it in civvies so I signed on again in '51. Then retired on full pension... 1960 it would be," he continued in the period for a moment, stirring his tea. Then picked up his Eccles cake and looked back at the constable.

The Constable slid the folder he was carrying containing copies of the soldiers records across the table to him, and the old man removed some glasses from his top pocket. "We know these files are falsified because they're dead ends, the names are about the only thing we can rely on because we have corroborative evidence. Is there anything familiar to you in them, or any way you can give us a lead?" he said.

"Good heavens mate, I couldn't remember any of the thousands of soldiers records that passed through my hands to save my life."

"Well what about just the early war years?"

"It's got to be the same answer, these records mean nothing to me," he said.

"Look... I shouldn't really tell you this, but these men were murdered, and there are possibly others in danger... so we've got to find the rest, and quickly," the Constable emphasised, pushing the folder at the old man again.

"What do you expect me to do?"

"Look again, Mr Butler please; if you were ever involved in falsifying records, I want to know under what circumstances, and who you did it for."

"Ah... it all makes sense now. You can't get to them through normal channels."

"Something like that."

"Well I still don't think I can be much good to you, I only had three such instances in my whole career in records when I had to lift some files and put a WO. Notice on them," he saw the constable's blank look. "That's a War Office eyes only document. We had stamps for everything in those days."

"Believe me, Mr Butler... nothing's changed; so what happened then."

"Well on those occasions the CO. would come down to records with his High Command documentation: that's a lot of fancy signatures, mostly Lt Generals; and commandeer a group of men's records"

"What... you mean your files"

"Yes. They asked us to duplicate them without any history, and a WO. Notice such as these have in the corner," he pointed to the small stamp.

The Constable suddenly became curious, "Where, let me see."

He noticed the insignificant stamp in the top right hand

corner, almost as if it had been printed as part of the form; being slightly out of align gave it away, but it still had to be pointed out to him: WO-3109. The decisive factor was they all ran in sequence, 3110, 3111 and so on.

"Well I suppose that's something, but it still doesn't take me far," he said.

"What about the CO's names, would they help?" the old man said.

"Would they... why didn't you tell me about them before?"

"Well... all you seemed interested in was the actual records"

The Sergeant bought another mug of tea each and more Eccles cakes. He thought it looked good enough to try, and he recorded the CO's names Fred Butler could remember.

It was a slow process, digging up each name from his fuzzy past, "Don't rush me," he said, feeding DC Freeman each name as he recalled them. "I'll never forget those names. They came across my desk every day. Sometimes they called me direct."

Two hours later DC Freeman returned to the city. He was chuffed with himself. Old Fred had given him the three commanding officers responsible for withdrawing soldier's files for what could only be described as covert action: evident by the sequential WO numbers.

CHAPTER 8

Earlier that afternoon Superintendent Stone had checked his map. He had a hundred mile journey ahead of him, but luckily, most was going to be on the M4 motorway. According to his map it would be a carefree trip all the way until he reached the M5 heading north; where it appeared he was leaving civilisation.

As imagined, his journey was uneventful right up to the M4 – M5 junction, where he pulled into a service station for a drink and some information. It was difficult trying to get the man behind the counter to listen; all he wanted to do was add something to eat with Stone's mug of tea. He bought a meat pie and asked him again.

The man was not able to supply a phonebook to check out Cantrell's address, but he did know of a good hotel nearby. Apparently, Wieldsea was no bigger than a main high street and he could not miss the one and only pub called The Western Star.

Annoyingly, Stone had to go back onto the M4 and take the second slip road onto a small single-lane road heading for the coast. Actually, when he checked his map again, he was heading for the Severn estuary, yet the smell of the sea was very strong.

Glancing in his rear-view mirror he could still see the blue sky he left in London, but ahead of him was an ominous mass of black clouds. As he signed in at The Western Star hotel, the proprietor was talking continually about the sea fret that frequented this area.

"On business are we," he uttered, with a hint of Welsh in his accent, sounding like his standard greeting, as he examined the register, "Oh, there's interesting now Mabel," he said to the plump women behind him selecting a key, "Mr Stone here's a policeman, up from London he is."

"Front or back?" she asked, unconsciously.

"I beg your pardon," Stone replied, still hanging onto the proprietors last words, as he was having difficulty with the disjointed sentences.

"Front of hotel or back, Sir?" she said again. "Your room."

"What difference does it make?"

"Well then... we have plenty of rooms at the front... you get a lovely view of the Severn if that's what you like, but the front's always the dampest this time of year."

"I'll have one at the back then," Stone said.

She smiled back at him as she selected a key.

"The back is over the main bar which tends to get a bit noisy if you want to go to bed early, that is," she continued.

Stone looked at them scornfully; he had no time for all this local nonsense. An overnight stay was by no means long enough to learn the meaning behind the accent. On the other hand, being a police officer had its advantages.

"Then you'll just have to inform your patrons that there's a miserable old policeman upstairs, who's a stickler for licensed premises following the rules of their licence to the letter... won't you?"

They looked up at him with fear in their eyes as he made his way upstairs. The last he saw of them that night was their heads disappearing through the bar door.

"Hey... quieten down you lot, there's a copper from London just moved in upstairs," someone said, followed by an ominous silence.

He overheard, and smiled to himself.

By 8:00 am, Uxbridge was wide-awake and bustling. The officers in Inspector Hammond's squad room already had an hour under their belt, as Sergeant Binstead peered through the open Venetian blinds of the Inspector's office, watching him push pieces of paper around his crowded desk. Even though some time had passed since he lost his case.

"Are you busy, Boss," he said hesitantly.

"Do I look it?" the Inspector snapped back.

"I just saw all the paperwork on your desk, that's all."

The Inspector looked at him; knew that he meant well, but he was no help. He kept thinking about the crucified man, and all the loose ends lying unattended to. He had cleared up his suspicion that Len Lonergan had motive enough to kill him, but that quickly disappeared below the confusion that daunted this case.

He looked up, "Sorry, Sergeant, I didn't mean to chew you off. I'm not in the best of moods these days... what did you want?"

"Oh it doesn't matter, I just wondered if you were still interested?"

"Interested in what? Explain yourself."

"In the information about the van. Or should I send it to SCI?"

Inspector Hammond jumped up and grabbed the paper from his hand.

"What's this?"

"It's the address we finally run down from sightings of that old truck or van we've been looking for."

"Great, let's get down there," he said, grabbing his hat from the stand.

"I thought we weren't supposed to be on this case anymore?"

"Shut up, Sergeant, and let's go."

The information was generated from a printed flier for any

information on the vehicle description they simulated using the forensic evidence on the scene. A combination of the flier left with businesses in the area and word of mouth by the local police on the beat, brought in a number of sightings in a low rent district near the railway sidings: a street of partly derelict terraced houses. The few that were barely habitable, remembered the van outside number 16.

"Here it is Boss; it's hard to see if it's 16 or 19... what a mess."

"I'd like to know what they charge for this," the Inspector said, pushing open the graffiti spattered door with his foot and letting out the worst of trapped smells.

The day had warmed up slightly and it was not helping. They had to take out their hankies and cover their nose. From the damaged letterboxes just inside the hall, at some time the large terraced house had four apartments. They carefully entered the long hallway towards the staircase. The place was in disrepair, with pieces of plaster and peeling wallpaper strewn everywhere.

"What do you want," a gruff female voice called out.

They turned to an open door, where, on closer inspection, they saw an old woman in a rocking chair by her window. She resembled a bag of rags, with strands of yellowy-grey hair hanging down the side of her sallow skinned face. A baggy stocking straggling down one leg and the other was so full of holes they wondered why she bothered.

She half turned to see who was disturbing her, revealing a tartan scarf criss-crossing her large chest, and disappearing under her short heavy arms. The Inspector suddenly remembered what that smell was as he approached her threshold: the room was full of cats.

"What do you want?" she repeated, wiping something from her mouth.

The Sergeant stepped forward, leaving the Inspector where

he was, and presented his warrant card, "DI Hammond and DS Binstead, Uxbridge CID," he replied officially.

"Cops aye, there's nout for you 'ere, they've all moved out."

"There was a report of a blue van parked regularly outside this house."

"That'd be the Indian's, he's done a bunk," she snorted.

"Can we see his flat?" the Inspector called out across the room.

"Who's going to pay his rent then?" she asked.

"That's your problem ducky, and if you give us any trouble we'll call in the Health Department, Housing Inspectors, Town Planning... "

"Okay... okay," she interrupted and threw them a key.

They made their way up the stairs, frightened to touch anything, in case it collapsed in their hands, until they reached the top floor. As they opened the door, their first impression was one of absolute amazement.

The apartment looked like a lounge, bedroom, bathroom and smaller box-room off to one side. The occupant had turned the lounge into a workroom, with a large rickety table in the centre covered with piles of pre-cut fabric, and a sewing machine with all the paraphernalia to go with some form of garment manufacture.

What caught the Inspector's attention first was on the far side of the room. Photographs, maps and crude sketches covered the wall, much like their incident board.

On closer inspection, it became apparent that these were representing the four murders so far. Fortunately, as far as the Inspector could make out, there were no new victims, except a separate group of fragments, still attached to drawing pins.

"Take a look at this," the Inspector said to the Sergeant as he returned.

"There's been no one here for a while, Boss," he said.

"He's our boy all right. Either he's planned no more victims or he was frightened off, taking the new one's with him," the Inspector fingered the torn fragment of paper still attached to a drawing pin. There were several others.

"You're right, Boss."

"And look at this, no pictures but a plan of a large house, and a piece of road map, but of where. It's too small to see what county."

"We could narrow it down through the national directory, Boss."

"Okay, let's not do anything until forensic get here; I want them to go through this place with a fine tooth comb. Give them a call now."

"But what about Stone?... don't you think he will want his people to do this?"

"I want to present him with the evidence, if he still wants his people to look the place over, all well and good. He told me I could continue at this end."

Inspector Hammond was feeling more confident now.

"Yes, Boss... but I don't think that included doing your own work-up."

The Inspector then returned to the remnant of a road map showing a road called Walton Avenue, forking off Walton Bridge Road, running alongside a river. A plan of a large house with a red cross in a small room marked Study. A piece of blue lined note paper torn from a small pad or wire stitched diary, with notations on it in poor writing that read, Mon – 6:30 pm to 8:30 pm, Tues – 10:00 am to 12:30 pm, and so on.

After one last look around the flat the Inspector decided to have another go at the landlady; that was if he could stand the smell long enough to get anything out of her. When he arrived, the Sergeant was already asking her questions, looking frustrated, by the look of relief on his face when the Inspector walked in.

"Has she improved on her statement?" he asked, glancing at his notes.

"She says she wants a solicitor present."

Hammond looked at the old bag-of-bones and laughed.

"That's all right dear, we can take you down to the station and you can ring for your solicitor from there."

"You can't do that," she shouted at them.

"Oh yes I can," the Inspector said forcefully.

She managed a condescending look, "All right... what do you want?"

"That's better, now what's this Indian's name for starters."

She shrugged her shoulders hesitantly, "Allan Dumbleton."

"That's not an Indian name," the Sergeant stated.

"I wouldn't know about that," she snapped back.

"So this is the name he used to rent the flat off you," the Inspector said.

"I told you didn't I"

"Okay... give a full description to the Sergeant, and make sure you're more cooperative this time," the Inspector threatened, glancing at the Sergeant.

"Oh thanks, Boss... very much."

The first thing Inspector Hammond did on his return was ring Stone. But he was out of luck; the Superintendent was out running down a new lead. Inspector Hammond said nothing, other than to let him know he rang. He knew Stone would be on to him soon enough, if his news was good.

After a surprisingly excellent sleep, Stone was woken by a loud knock on his door. No sooner had he shouted enter, the door opened and the proprietor entered carrying a tray, with his wife hovering close behind peering over his shoulder.

"It's eight o'clock, Sir, thought you'd like a spot of breakfast before you start the day. Have we anything special in mind?"

"Yes... a man always needs a good meal inside him, if he's

going to have a full day ahead of him," his wife parroted, still from behind.

"I expected bed and breakfast, but not breakfast in bed," Stone said, jesting.

They both laughed nervously, as the proprietor placed the tray of sausage, bacon and eggs, toast, orange juice and a pot of hot tea on a nearby table.

"Do you know I didn't get your names last night?" Stone replied.

"Mr and Mrs Barraclough, Sir," the proprietor said, and then gesturing with his thumb, "the wife's Mabel and I'm Claud."

"You'll find we look after our guests here at The Western Star, Mr Stone, or should I call you Superintendent," she said.

"That's fine. Now if you'll excuse me."

"Oh Yes," he said, "Come on, Mabel."

Being at the back of the hotel Stone had not realised how bad the weather was until he went downstairs. Claud was pottering about at the counter while Mabel was vacuuming the dining room after breakfast.

"Going anywhere particular, Superintendent. Only the weather has turned nasty out there. It happens this time of the year... that's why we're slow then."

"I'm looking for a David Cantrell," he stated, hoping for an instant reaction.

"David Cantrell?" Claud muttered, obviously digging deep into his memory.

"I know who he's talking about," Mabel interrupted, turning off the vacuum.

"Who's that then my luv'?" he asked.

"You know then, him that's building the boat on the point."

"A boat builder?" Claud replied.

Stone's head went back and forth, as they questioned each other.

"You know, the bald man. Wears a dark blue donkey jacket and comes in once a month for a drink and a bottle of rum to take away with him."

"Oh yes, now I know who you're on about."

"I knew you'd remember," Mabel said, nudging him.

"Yes... he's coming back to me. Wears a knitted cap to keep his head warm and smokes one O' them fancy pipes."

"Is that so," Stone said, with some exasperation, "So where is this point?"

"Come on, Sir, I can show you better from outside."

Stone stepped outside. He could see it had been raining and by the look of the menacing clouds, there was a lot more to come; so he needed to get this interview over as soon as possible. Claud stepped out and turned him towards the end of the high street.

"Now carry on to the very end of the road where you'll see a left-hand turn. Take that and follow the road towards the Severn estuary... you can't miss it."

"But what about Cantrell's house?" Stone blustered.

"You can't miss that either; it's the only one."

"Thanks a lot," Stone said, getting into his car.

"You'd better be quick then," Claud shouted. "If that lot catches you out there you'll know it all right. It looks like a real storm's brewing."

"Thanks again," Stone shouted, and closed the window.

Stone knew he was heading towards open water. The sky opened up, albeit dark and foreboding and the country around him became flatter. The road narrowed with the occasional flood sign and there was an overpowering smell of seaweed.

The further he continued the land became flatter and the Severn expanded, the horizon disappeared and he felt like all that was between him and the grey depths was the small chalky ribbon he was following. If he did not find the Cantrell cottage soon, he felt he would disappear into oblivion.

CHAPTER 9

Stone stopped when he saw a sign pointing right to Northwick. Claud said it was the last cottage, so he continued at a slow speed until he saw a mixture of white and dark green rectangles up ahead through the condensation on his windscreen: it was in fact a white cottage with a large dark green timbered building alongside.

He found it difficult to find somewhere to park. Piles of timber occupied every flat space, stacked as they were cut from the trunk, with thin strips as spacers between the planks to facilitate their weathering.

"You'll be all right there on the road, unless you're trying to turn round," a voice called out from a blaze of bright yellow light on the side of the cottage.

"Well if you're David Cantrell I don't want to turn round," Stone replied.

A door opened wider in the front of the cottage, and a heavyset man stepped out. He was certainly in touch with the season; wearing a thick grey and white dashed woollen jumper, heavy black trousers tucked into wellingtons, with the white tops of his socks turned down over them. Smoke was drifting from the old briar in his warn and gnarled hand as he greeted Stone; beckoning him out of the car.

"And who might I ask has come out on a day like this to see me?" he called out from under the porch that was protecting him from the fret that was now turning to icy rain, as Stone looked up at him from his half open window.

"Superintendent Stone from the London Met."

"Damned if I know what the Met wants with me, but you'd better come on in before it arrives," he said in a slow drawl. Time was important in this part of the country, more so since 'It' was about to arrive: whatever 'It' was.

Stone dashed from his car as the heavens opened and entered the warm, inviting timber interior. By the look of it, Cantrell appeared obsessed with wood, what with the enormous stockpile outside, the wooden building that towered above the cottage, and the overpowering presence about him.

"So what brings you all this way to see an old recluse like me?" he said, pressing down the dying tobacco embers in his pipe, and relighting it.

Stone trusted the face he had only caught sight of a few moments ago. It was a face of contentment. He envied his serenity; something he would have to discover the secret of before he left, but for now, he had to continue with his business: that of establishing that Cantrell had been a records clerk in the Army.

After Cantrell made him a hot drink he decided to tell him the whole story, emphasising the fact that to save the remaining men, they desperately needed to track them down before the killer did; assuming the killer's delay in following through with his plan was due to him having as much difficulty in finding them as he was.

"I sympathise with your predicament, Superintendent, but I really don't see how I can help you; it's been many years and thousands of names, and none important enough to warrant a place in my memory."

This was not what Stone wanted to hear. He had to find some way of stimulating his grey cells. 'What would Mary do under the circumstances?' he thought. He hoped his life as a recluse had not destroyed all recollection of the outside world.

"Mr Cantrell, you said something odd to me outside, about something arriving."

Cantrell eased himself up from his seat and went over to the small window, beckoning Stone to follow. "That's what I was referring to," he gestured with his pipe. "I was watching it coming over the horizon when you arrived," he pointed to the heavy black ridge hanging just above the bright line on the horizon, spreading out to infinity either side.

They both watched in silence. Other than the icy rain, now quite heavy, the scene before them was not dramatic, yet Stone felt something he had not felt since his days in Korea, when he watched the undergrowth on the hill opposite their positions begin to writhe and slowly move forward, as if possessed by some evil force. The evil he knew to be the enemy. Yet this black seething mass rolling across the surface of the Severn before them had no face, yet still possessed that same pervading presence of evil.

"What time do you reckon it'll hit?" Stone questioned.

"You don't expect to get back tonight do you?" he said, laughing.

"Well... I did intend interviewing you and then heading back to London," he replied naively. "Are you saying I should leave now?"

"You'd get half way round the point when it hit, and that's not a place I'd like to be," he said, poking his pipe at him as a teacher would when making a point.

Stone checked his watch, it was only ten, "I have plenty of time... how long will this thing last? An hour... two hours?"

"This lot is coming from the Atlantic, made worse as it's funnelled up the mouth of the Severn. It could blow itself out in an hour or go on all day."

"All day," Stone let out.

Cantrell chuckled to himself as if he knew something.

"I've been here nine years, and I've never experienced anything as bad as this. You... " the phone rang, breaking his sentence. He picked it up, "Cantrell... Yes... oh hello... yes he's here now... I doubt it... is it. Then that settles it, if it gets worse he can stay with me. Okay thanks, I'll ring you later, if I can."

"What's up?. Stone asked, now warming himself by the fire.

"That was Barraclough," he said, putting the phone back, "he wanted to know if you arrived all right before the blow... seemingly it's causing havoc in Wieldsea."

"Is that so. What was that about staying here?"

"The storm doesn't look like abating yet, and even if it did, Barraclough says the road's out. So you'll just have to stay here tonight," he explained.

"That's very good of you. When did he say the road would be fixed?"

"He didn't, that's why I'm going to ring him later."

Stone thought this would be a good opportunity to take him back to when he worked in Army Records. He started by showing interest in the plans strewn across a large trestle table on the back wall, alongside a marvellous model of what he perceived to be the Ketch Cantrell was building.

"Tell me," Stone began, picking up a compass, "how does one who's spent years in Army Records become a boat builder. Or is it something you've come back to?" he said, sitting down at the table.

"The nearest I ever got to building a boat, was one of those plastic galleon things... The Santa Maria it was, I think."

"But this is a phenomenal skill?"

"Which I found out to my frustration," Cantrell said with a laugh.

"So how did you start?"

"When I left the Army in 1970, I was so drained of mental

stimulus, through sheer boredom; I decided I had to do something totally new and challenging."

He messed on with his pipe before continuing.

"I had my demob money so I thought I'd buy a business. But after going around for twelve months looking at all the 'Get rich' schemes, I realised that wasn't what I was looking for. So I decided to leave it and go back home for a while, do a bit of travelling about; you know, get back to basics."

"Yes I do, I did the very same thing myself when I returned from Korea.

"I was lost, until I visited Wieldsea and wandered down the point where I came across this old family boat yard. It had not made a boat in years, the old man's workers left him long ago. He invited me in, much as I did you today, you could see he'd lost interest. These were his plans, his model, and outside, not covered like now, the keel of this grand ship. I knew he would never finish it, and so did he, so I made him an offer. Without thinking... it just came out on the spur of the moment."

"What was that?"

"I'd pay all his debts. Look after him till he passed on, if he showed me how to finish his ship. He lived for another three years, taught me all I know."

"That's a great story, although I don't know much about ships."

"Yes... I'm pleased with her so far. At least the hull's finished."

"And when do you think you'll finish the rest?"

"Well there's still a big job ahead, fitting her out that is. Then there's the rigging, although I know a man who'll do that for me; for a price. Who knows, probably someone will come along and offer to finish it for me, just as I did."

"I tell you what," Stone jested, "You try and remember what I want and when I retire, I'll come back and either ask you for a sail in her or make you that offer; how's that?" he said with a broad smile.

"You're on," Cantrell agreed.

They continued talking for the rest of the morning, with a break for cold meat, cheese and onions. Once again he managed to draw the conversation back to Cantrell's Army days; this time, knowing his memory of the many records he had dealt with was vague at best, he aimed his questions at the unusual, anything or anyone that was out of the normal routine; something at least that might have lodged in his memory.

"I see what you're driving at, Superintendent," he said, filling his pipe again from a miniature rum-cask. "You need to identify these remaining men."

"That's why we're sticking our necks out, gambling on the possibility that they were all in the same group during the war, part of some special operation." Stone thrust the files of the four men and their identical war activities back in front of him. "I've come to the conclusion it would be easier to find the operation, than the men?"

"You're quite right of course, although it would still be a tall order," he puffed studiously at his old burnt down pipe, then pointing it at Stone, "What you're talking about is very deep stuff, I don't know if any of it still exists. Oh... I don't mean covert operations; they'll always be with us under some guise or other."

"So what are we talking about?"

He looked off across the room, "Private stuff."

"But isn't that what it's all about?"

"Good heavens no. All top brass at one time or another have wanted to get around protocol, regulations, call it what you like, for the good of the public interest; or simply to cover up their own blunders. And they didn't want to be seen using one of the authorised Special Operations groups... that was too dangerous; too many spies watching each other; too easy for anyone to get something on record for the future. What you have to understand," he jabbed his pipe at the papers. "These Commanders were political pariahs. They were way ahead of the mission. They were thinking of where they'd be after the war."

"So what did they do?"

"They formed their own, 'Need to know' units. And that practise went right to the top; to Winston himself. In fact I wouldn't put it passed him being the instigator."

"Churchill?"

"Yes. He always said, hearsay of course, I never met him personally... 'If you want something known, and quickly, tell the Secret Service. Otherwise do it yourself'. And that's why they hatched their own little schemes."

"But that would need some expert to organise them; surely?"

"General Whitehouse," Cantrell confirmed knowledgeably. "He was the Army's man in the War Room; he could organise absolutely anything."

"Hold on," Stone uttered, becoming suspicious. "If this was so hush-hush, even from the Secret Service, how come a lowly records clerk knew about it?"

"I was coming to that," he replied confidently. "I wasn't always a lowly records clerk, as you say. In '41, and I don't know any of the details so don't ask me, General Whitehouse was put in charge of Records. We wondered why at first because he was a member of Churchill's War Room staff, as a tactical adviser, and that was general knowledge: No big secret. Anyway, early in '41 the War Office put all their records clerks through three weeks of gruelling tests. They went into all sorts of stuff: supposedly in the interests of changing our rating levels and dividing us into teams dealing with different information. It was then, when we'd been organised into smaller groups, no more than ten or so, that we met the General and found out what the training was really all about."

"Go on," Stone urged, when he paused to light up again. This was just starting to get interesting: This was what Stone wanted to hear.

"Well... it appears they weren't reorganising after all. The tests were to sift out an elite group of records experts... one group for each service, solely dedicated to searching for the personnel required for these particular covert operations."

"Which was?"

"Top secret behind the lines stuff."

"Oh I see... so what you're saying is, you helped form operations that even the normal Special Operations didn't know about?"

"Exactly. Only the immediate participants and first level organisers knew. And to answer your original question... the records you suspected of being tampered with, probably weren't. They were just the basic stereotype service record without any history, because there wasn't any. Those men just disappeared until they were killed, taken prisoner or demobbed."

"It all makes sense now. So all I've got to do is find this General Whitehouse, assuming he kept records?"

"Oh yes, most definitely. He always covered his arse did the General. Unfortunately he died in 1974."

The Superintendent's shoulders sank as he scratched through the General's name, "Oh that's great, so what was the point of telling me if the man's dead."

"Because, Superintendent, if you weren't so impatient... I was about to tell you that the General's chief organiser, the one I had most contact with: General Peter Carter, is still alive and kicking somewhere in Somerset."

"How do you know that. It's been forty years."

"Well coincidences of coincidences, for your information, Peter Carter launched his memoirs last year... inviting all those who were still left of the 'Records undercover operation', as he called us, to his book signing. To celebrate the occasion and give us each a signed copy of his book."

He placed his pipe on the hearth, levered himself up on one hand, and went over to the bookcase. He knew exactly where it was; withdrawing a shiny black covered volume, and brought it back to where Stone was lounging by the fire.

Stone studied the cover for a moment, the large red question mark was quite impressive, with 'General Peter Carter' above, and 'Carter's Boys' below in generous letters. "You could have shown me this at the beginning," he said, "It may have saved us time."

"I doubt it, his book covers behind the scenes decisions and the action his group took, and others like them, which played a determining role in the final outcome of the war; not so much how this was actually achieved. I'm afraid it's all still very secret... even if most of the participants who made these decisions are now dead. Let's face it; today they'd probably get a court martial for their actions. Instead, their memories have been left intact, as ingenuous men who stopped Hitler invading this country of ours."

The Superintendent suddenly realised that this book probably brought about the reason why these murders occurred now, instead of forty years ago. It either rekindled old grudges or furnished the murderer with information he needed to find these men.

"So you were saying you met this man recently. How do I get in touch with him and possibly any of his team?"

Cantrell leant forward and flipped the cover over. Penned across the right hand corner of the flyleaf was his name and address.

"One thing I forgot to tell you was I became the group leader of my section, which meant we spent a good deal of time together going over the profiles and the serviceman's special talents. We had a lot to talk about last year, but not enough time. So he invited me down to his place, hence the address.”

“Did you go?”

“No I didn’t. I regret that… there was a lot left unsaid.”

“And you still say, after being so close to him, that none of these names mean anything to you?”

“Not a thing, really. They were just numbers to me, qualifications on a piece of paper. In most cases I didn’t even see a photo of the man I was selecting.”

“Things unsaid aye,” Stone mused, remembering his own time in Korea, even though he managed to keep away from the front line most of the time.”

“Yes,” he answered simply. Then realising the unbearable drone they had been shouting over for the past hour or so had subsided. He went over to the window. Stone followed and looked over his shoulder through the small window.

“Still looks bad,” Stone commented, watching the rain ricocheting off the woodpile outside. “At least your timber still looks intact.”

Cantrell scanned the sky, which still appeared dark and menacing.

“No it’s all over now, just dumping its load as it passes over.”

“Over. How can you say that?… look at it out there.

“It’s the wind that’s the killer… and that’s blown itself out by the looks of it.” He glanced at the clock on the mantelpiece, it was now 3:45 pm. “I’ll give them a ring and find out about the road. You may still get back to London yet.”

Meanwhile, Inspector Fraser was beginning to get a bit worried; he had seen the news on the television showing the damage to Wieldsea and neighbouring resorts, caused by gales whipping up the Severn at speeds of up to 120 mph. He rang the local police, who were surprised, and a little upset that they hadn’t been informed that there was a Superintendent on their patch;

not knowing where he was.

They eventually found out he was stranded out on the point, in a boat-builder's cottage, but okay. They gave him Cantrell's number.

"Well the line must be okay, it's engaged," he said to Constable Freeman sitting close by. "I'll try again shortly."

"Probably he's trying to ring us," he replied.

"Maybe. I wonder what he's managed to find out from this Cantrell fella."

"He'll be pleased to learn I've got some more names," the Constable said.

"He'll be delighted if you could add some address's to them," Fraser answered in a curt manner, deflating the Constables ego.

"Well it was forty years ago, Boss, people move about in that time."

"If you want to find out what he expects, I suggest you wait and see."

"I'll go and have another look?" he replied, with a worried expression.

Stone was still hypnotically watching the rain when Cantrell finished his call. He put the phone down and walked back to the window.

"Well it won't be open till tomorrow. It appears, as fast as they shift the mud and stones, the rain brings down another lot. They'll have to wait for it to clear."

"Then I'm afraid it looks like you're going to be stuck with me overnight."

"I wouldn't worry about that, Superintendent, you've been good company; in fact I'll be sorry to see you go."

"Funny enough so will I, it's been an experience. And stop calling me Superintendent, call me Stone; everyone else does."

"Right... and you can call me Cantrell," he laughed. "We sound like a couple of explorers... Stone and Cantrell."

"If your ship was ready we could sail to Greenland, I've always wanted to do that.

"Not in my two-master I'm afraid."

"Oh dear, never mind."

At that point the phone rang, Cantrell instinctively glanced out of the window as he picked it up, it had stopped raining; maybe they managed to clear the road.

"Yes... yes he's here... hold on I'll get him for you," he beckoned to Stone, holding the phone out to him, "It's for you; an Inspector Fraser."

Superintendent Stone almost felt himself hesitating, as if the mention of the name Fraser was a link with that other world he had no wish to return to. In that world he thought he had achieved his goal; only a step away from control of his destiny.

He looked back at the man contentedly smoking his pipe and realised something he had never considered. In this world, it all meant nothing.

CHAPTER 10

Whether by years of manipulating his way out of difficult situations or the look on Cantrell's face, Stone snapped out of his daydream and became a boring police Superintendent again.

"Boss... is that you?" the Inspector called out, the line was very bad.

"Yes... I'll be stuck here till tomorrow... the roads out."

"I heard, I've been onto the local cop shop, they told me all about the trouble."

"I wish you hadn't done that, I didn't ring the local Super to inform him I was coming into his territory. I bet he was a bit upset?"

"He was, Boss, sorry. But how was I supposed to find you?"

"Okay... it's done now. I'll just have to call in on him before I leave. How did you get on with those names?"

The Inspector reached for his notes.

"I bombed out I'm afraid, Boss, my man was most uncooperative. I tried to get him to think back but he wasn't having any. I didn't pursue it."

"Don't worry about it, how did Freeman do?"

"Very well actually, he got three names of CO's in charge of special units during that period; he's checking them out now."

"Great... is a General Peter Carter on his list"

"I'll see, Boss," the Inspector clicked his fingers at the

Constable, "The list."

He rushed over with it, "Is that the, Boss, did you tell... "

Inspector Fraser waved him off, to be quiet. "Here it is, Boss, and yes Carter's on it, what does that mean?"

"I think it means we've got our man Mark, tell Freeman he's done a good job, and that I've got Carter's address."

"Does that mean we can forget the other two?"

"No... for heaven's sake. Carter may turn out to be a fizzer, get the information on the others just in case. Oh and ring this number and make an appointment." He gave him the number from Cantrell's book.

"What time, Boss?"

"That's a point," he paused to think, "Well I won't get out of this place till tomorrow morning sometime, then I've got to drive back... say the next day."

"Okay, Boss, watch yourself. I understand things are still rough up there."

As Stone replaced the phone, he thanked Cantrell, who pointed out to him that his new-found relaxed state was short lived. Stone questioned his meaning, and he told him how he had become a human being again for a while.

When Stone returned to his office the following day, he found it had turned into a war zone. As well as the intermittent phone calls and Inspector Fraser constantly questioning him about aspects of the Wieldsea interview, he was unable to get his paperwork in order until mid-afternoon. It was then that he came across Inspector Hammond's phone message.

The Inspector undoubtedly did not intend to allow Hammond any further foothold into this case. On reading its apparent urgency, Stone shouted his name.

"Yes, Boss," he replied, leaning into his office.

"What's this note saying Inspector Hammond has some new urgent information?"

He looked around guiltily and walked into the office.

"Oh yes... sorry, Boss he called while you were away. Wouldn't tell me what it was all about; couldn't have been that important"

"I'll be the judge of that. You could have told me when we were on the phone yesterday. We've lost a whole day now."

The Inspector could not understand Stone's constant reliance on this man.

"Sorry, Boss, you were giving me so many things to do, it just slipped my mind," he was not fooling anyone. The guilt on his face was plain to see.

Stone dismissed him gruffly, pausing a moment before picking up the phone. He suspected Mark was jealous of his old friend, they were the same rank, but he did not expect it to cloud his judgement. When he finally got through, Hammond was out on a case, some three hours later, in the early evening, Hammond returned his call.

"Stone, you're finally back then," Hammond said, opening the conversation.

"Yes, Jack, sorry I took so long to get back to you, Mark forgot to tell me you called," he said, with a nonchalant easiness in his voice.

"I suspected as much."

"You won't believe this bit of luck, Jack, I actually found the man who was responsible for putting our group together," after realising what he had just said, he had second thoughts, "Well the group we think they're part of... that is."

"That's terrific, congratulations."

"Oh it was all due to your contact; it was his list that led to this man."

"So what did he have to say?" Hammond continued, knowing Stone was dying to tell him; he could feel the excitement down the phone.

Stone pulled his notes across the desk to refresh his memory.

"Actually I haven't seen him yet, I've got an appointment to interview him tomorrow... Say, why don't you come along?"

"Do you want me too. I won't be cramping your style?"

"Don't be silly... I want intuitive advice on this trip, not 'By the book' hand-outs."

"Then you're on, I look forward to it, what time?"

"We're going to Somerset, so get here early. By the way you didn't tell me what your urgent news was."

Stone's enthusiasm had overshadowed Hammond's discovery and the impact he wanted had gone. The forensic report was still to come, so it could wait for the time being.

"Oh it'll keep till tomorrow, see you then."

"I look forward to it, Jack," Stone replied smugly.

Inspector Hammond had actually broken his own rule. He had withheld vital information from a superior. Coupled with the new evidence forensics had found pointing to the Indian, described by the old woman, they were losing valuable time in not issuing an alert to all districts. Hammond still had his hand on the receiver, contemplating whether he should phone Stone back. He decided the deed was done.

The following morning Inspector Hammond made an early start, cheerfully feeling this was going to be his day. He had spent a fearful night weighing up his remaining time in the force against the idea of stealing Stone's thunder, and decided, after several attempts at bringing himself to call him, to take the chance, and to hell with it.

Stone and Mary Carson were already studying the new implications of the revised white board when Hammond arrived. Stone turned expectantly as he entered the room. There was an overwhelming sense of electricity in the air, like two cocks preening themselves before the fight. Mary noticed this and turned.

Hammond spotted Mary and was stunned.

"Jack, great to see you again," Stone said, shaking his hand, and then leading him over towards the attentive woman by the board. "This is Mary Carson, my Human Behaviour Adviser; she'll be coming with us today."

Hammond jumped his greeting with Stone, totally wrapped with this attractive woman he was about to make contact with. "Hello, Mary, I'm very pleased to meet you at last. Superintendent Stone has told me so much about you; I feel I know you already, although I'm afraid my budget won't stretch to a Human Behaviour specialist... mores the pity."

"For you, Jack, I might consider waving my fee, I was so impressed with your earlier work on this case, and the profile was absolutely fantastic," she replied, giving him her smouldering look, while they held hands. "By the way, I can call you, Jack can't I. I'm so fed up with all these DS's and DI''s; first names are much better, don't you think?"

"I agree, Jack's just fine."

"When you two have finished, I'd like to know what is more important than us going out to see the very man who possibly organised the operations of our eight mystery men," Stone said, aiming his remark towards Hammond.

Hammond walked deliberately towards the board while the others watched; including Mark, hovering in the background, not at all happy that he may be stealing their thunder. "As important as it is that we fill these four blank remaining places, if indeed we are talking about eight men, and identifying their whereabouts to stop this maniac killing again; what would you say if I could name the killer now, with all the evidence to prove it?"

They were all speechless. No one said a word, just stared at him disbelievingly. Here they were about to embark on a further investigation that hopefully would provide another vital change in the profile of this case, and Hammond says he has solved it.

"What?" Stone grunted. "What do you mean you know the killer's name? I was under the impression you were no longer on this case." Stone blurted out, struck by the realisation that his case was about to be pulled out from under him. He glanced over towards Mark who was unmistakably showing signs of, 'I told you so. Mary, on the other hand, simply parked her bottom on the corner of the trestle table in front of the board, looking somewhat turned on by the events that were about to unfold.

Hammond placed the briefcase he was carrying on the table and opened it. He removed the folder handed to him that morning. It contained a match with fingerprints taken from two of the crime scenes; an identical footprint to that found by the canal, plus the all-important landlady's statement identifying the suspect as one Allan Dumbleton. It was one of the names in Lonergan's album.

"You should have left the crime scene for my people, Jack," Stone remarked, showing his disappointment.

"What do you think I am," the crime scene is still intact and under guard, and these are only copies, as you will see if you look closer," he said, spreading the contents on the table. "I was continuing with my own investigation relating to the missing vehicle, and we found it. I called you immediately, but you were out according to Mark here," the Inspector shuffled his feet looking uncomfortable.

"When I couldn't get any response, I deemed it more important to get the crime scene covered forensically first, and worry about protocol later. We do belong to the same force by the way," Hammond took a deep breath. "Besides, if you saw the place; if you saw that fat, dirty, money grubbing old woman, just about to clear his place out because he owed her rent, you would have done the same; she was about to destroy everything."

"Bravo," Mary exclaimed, then averted her eyes from Stone's frown.

Stone started going through the papers, mumbling something about the name not being Asian, as he turned the wrath of his disappointment in not being part of this exciting discovery onto Mark, who had been studying the same paper for some time. It was quite evident he held him mainly responsible for this fiasco, in not getting on top of this when Hammond first rang.

"Get all this lot sorted out and I want a team out there today," he shouted.

"And, Jack, I'd like to know why you continued with this when you were told not to."

"Before you 'tar and feather' me, Superintendent, I didn't continue with this as you suggest. If you remember, my task force had already been set in motion, with standard procedures such as handing out fliers and notifying the local Bobbies on the beat. I decided to leave those things in progress since you told me to keep things moving in Uxbridge, in the event something might turn up, on our patch.

"I still don't know why you didn't press Mark," he continued.

"Right, Superintendent, you can have complete control."

Inspector Hammond snatched up his briefcase and made for the door.

"Now where are you going?" Stone called out.

"I'm doing as you suggest, Sir. I'm going back to my patch in Uxbridge."

"Come on boys," Mary jumped in before Stone could reply, "At the end of the day what does it all mean. Look how far we've come." she turned to Stone. "Are you going to let this source of experience go so easily?"

"Jack... come back, I'm sorry," he called out.

The Inspector was almost out of the door when he stopped.

"I'm sorry to, but I can't work under these restraints."

Mary called out, "Jack... at least finish the information you have."

"How do you know there's more?" he said, slowly walking back.

"Jack... according to this he left in a big enough hurry, or why else would he leave all this evidence, unless he wanted us to catch him," she pondered.

"I thought about that," he replied. "I could only conclude he saw the police activity in the area, or heard they were looking for his van, and panicked. Then took his opportunity and grabbed only that which pertained to the future."

"Now why would you say that?" Stone questioned.

"I don't know; it's just a feeling I have. When I was going around the place, everything applied to what had been, nothing of what was to be... except," he paused and went through the photographs taken of the wall containing the pictures of the victims. "Look here, this large area over to the right with drawing pins in it."

"Yes. That could be just a dumping ground," Mary said, looking more closely.

"No I don't think so. Look how the drawing pins are in groups of four, as if they had held a piece of paper by each corner. If you look closer, you'll see a small fragment of paper still attached to one. No I think our man snatched whatever was pinned up there."

"Yes... I can see it now," she said.

Stone checked the photograph himself, agreeing also.

"And there's this scrap of map he forgot, which again could be a lead to the future; it doesn't tie in with any of the other evidence," he pointed to it. "As you can see it's quite ambiguous, it could mean anything, but the fact that it was here at all is significant in itself."

Mary turned the photograph this way and that, trying to read the names in what looked like a forked road with a river running above it, and scribbled numbers underneath. "The upper road is, Walton Bridge Road, and the lower one is, Walton Avenue. There's no name on the river," she said. "Someone's marked a small square above Walton Bridge Road, maybe that's his next target, and these numbers; maybe telephone numbers?" she wasn't sure.

"No, I've already tried every combination," Hammond said, "3303358 must stand for something else."

"Hold on," Stone interrupted, grabbing the photograph and reaching for his notebook, "That looks familiar."

He flicked through the pages covering his discussions with Cantrell, and then he stopped and paused when he found what he was looking for.

"Oh my god," he exclaimed.

"What's up?" Mary asked.

"Would you believe the address we're going to today, is 14 Walton Bridge Road, Taunton, Somerset. This is General Carter's residence."

"Not so fast, Stone," Hammond said, holding his arm, "This map has been there for some time, so if he intended to kill this General Carter, wouldn't he be dead by now?"

"You're right; he must have some other reason for wanting his address."

"What if our killer's doing the same thing we are," Mary suggested; which should have been obvious. "I mean, the gap in time between the first four victims, and the rest could simply be because he doesn't know where they are."

"Of course, you're right, Mary," the Inspector agreed. "If he had all the addresses at the start, there would have been more victims than four for us to contend with by now. This Indian's just ahead of us, but not as knowledgeable as we thought."

Mark tried to enter the conversation by mentioning what Stone had said about the gap in time that they could not fathom out, "Remember, Boss, you said the General called all the team together in London to his book signing."

Stone looked up from his notes, remembering his time with Cantrell, "Yes that's right. Cantrell said it was the first time they had all been together since the war. I said, 'that would stir memories up a bit. Then I realised that meeting was probably the catalyst we were looking for that started all this, the dates of the murders certainly fit in with that date."

"They do," said Mark, "I checked them out this morning. The first murder was reported about a month after the meeting, and then the others followed at regular intervals."

"So he must have obtained the first four addresses quite easily from the meeting," Mary commented, "Which means he must have been there, maybe one of the men himself."

"But Jack said he was an Indian," Stone replied.

"No, the old woman said that. I questioned the English sounding name."

Stone clasped his head in despair, "You see how ambiguous everything can become without proper eye witnesses. We have a killer that looks like an Indian, but has an English name," he was trying to dampen Hammond's achievement. "Didn't you get anything to corroborate her statement? That could indicate he was from India?"

"You see what I mean, Sir," Hammond rasped.

Stone burst out laughing, the first signs of him relaxing since Hammond had arrived, "Oh, Jack, you're precious. On one hand you're telling me you had to forge ahead before the crime scene became contaminated, then on the other you say you couldn't go too far until you told me." He brushed the tears from his eyes and returned to his notes; something was still on his mind. "Anyway, Jack you needn't worry about those numbers," he assured. He had checked the road map that evening before he left Wieldsea to see where the General lived in Somerset, so that they could get a good start the next day, "3303358 you said?"

"That's right."

"Well it means M3, A303, A358... the route from London."

"There's also this other list, indicating days of the week and times," Inspector Hammond pointed out as he retrieved it from the folder.

"Maybe train times to Somerset?" Mary volunteered.

"It's obviously a timetable of some kind," Stone commented, putting his notebook away. "Maybe we'll make more sense of it at the General's."

"Well I hope you manage to sort things out," Hammond said, turning away.

"Oh come on, Jack," Stone said, catching his arm. "The case is more important than our problems. We need to catch this villain."

They agreed to put their differences to one side until they had visited the General; there was no point in arguing about who was right or what evidence was prudent to their new direction in this case. One thing they did agree on however: they would not get there at all, if they continued arguing about it.

They made good time towards Somerset, even though Stone referred to the narrow roads and the fact that on his previous trip, he was half way across the country by now. They decided to break their journey at Ilminster for lunch, before turning onto the A358.

They arrived at 14 Walton Bridge Road, as agreed with Mrs

Carter, just after lunch. She had arranged this time with Stone as a point of courtesy, as the General was in the last stages of Multiple Sclerosis, and meal times were especially embarrassing for him. His mind was still quite sharp and agile, however, he found it difficult moving about.

"Good afternoon, Mrs Carter," Stone said, greeting the thin, smartly dressed elderly woman opening the door to her home and ushering them in. "I'm Superintendent Stone... my assistant spoke with you on the phone about my visit to see your husband, and this is Mary Carson, a specialist in human behaviour, and of course Inspector Hammond."

"Ah... do come in, he's expecting you all," she replied. Leading them forward across the thickly carpeted hall, she paused a moment. "My husband is so excited about your interview, as explained by your assistant; he doesn't get much opportunity to talk about the past; his good years, as he calls them. But I must ask you to try and keep him calm, he soon gets tired these days."

"I understand, Mrs Carter, we'll watch it. We desperately need his input."

Their home was as he would have expected of a retired General: a large mock Tudor around the late 1800's, one of the first built in this area, so Mrs Carter was proud to inform them; it was evident that she was the one responsible for the building's renovation.

She furnished the interior in complimentary pieces: mostly Jacobean antiques, on polished dark wooden floors with the odd square of Persian and Axminster carpet.

Fine brocade highlighted the overall dark wood, complimenting the rich paintings adorning the rough plastered walls.

Mrs Carter, who appeared to be leading them towards the rear of the house, was perfectly in tune with her surroundings. She wore a fine tweed dress, held at her waist by a polished leather belt, with a patterned silk scarf loosely held in place by a beautiful silver and amethyst Scottish brooch.

She led them to a pair of large French-doors, and stood holding one open, beckoning them to enter what looked like a glass conservatory. At the far end was a white haired man in a heavily padded chair, hunched over a lower than normal table overlooking the garden. His back was towards them, making it difficult for him to turn and greet his guests when his wife called out to him from the doorway.

"I'll make a nice pot of tea," she said, motioning his guests to a position where he could see them.

"Ah... Superintendent Stone?" he questioned looking up, not knowing who to greet, one hand gripping the edge of the table whilst the other lay quivering on the tartan rug that covered his legs.

Stone took his limp hand and shook it, "How do you do, Sir," he said. "This is Mary Carson and Inspector Hammond."

"Hello," he reciprocated looking at them, but fixing his attention on Mary.

"You're not a policewoman then?" he stated.

"No, General... I advise the police on criminal profiles."

He smiled at her, his eyes still able to enjoy an attractive woman.

"Oh that sounds highly technical," he said, then turning his gaze to Inspector Hammond. "And are you the assistant my wife spoke to?"

"No, Sir, I'm the investigating officer who found the last victim."

"You'll have to excuse me, Inspector, I don't really know what all this is about, other than it could involve my boys," then before the Inspector could answer, he changed the subject abruptly. "By the way, does being a policeman mean you're good at puzzles?"

They noticed he was sitting in front of a very large puzzle.

"It doesn't naturally follow, Sir, but in fact I do myself have a passion for puzzles."

"Yes... it's a good one, over a thousand pieces. It's a picture of the 'Western Front' you know, not that I was in it, but the detail is brilliant... except for this piece, it's been driving me mad trying to find where it belongs."

Hammond took the piece from him as he pushed it about with his inept fingertips, attempting to pick it up and placed it at the top left hand corner outside the puzzle.

"There you are, Sir, that's where it belongs."

The General looked at him with amazement, "But that's not in the puzzle."

"No, Sir. But I always put the pieces I can't find an immediate place for up there in plain view. That way I can get on with the puzzle without worrying about them. Sooner or later it becomes evident where those pieces belong."

"Well I never," the General said. "That's brilliant... how simple, yet so obvious. I can see you must be an astute investigator."

Mrs Carter broke the digression from their original purpose, by entering with the tea. After serving everyone, she made an excuse to be elsewhere, as the General explained his physical limitations whilst sipping from a mug covered by a lid with a spout.

Stone soon began to outline the connection between himself and the men in Lonergan's album, the assumption that only eight of these men were actually involved, because of the significance of the pawns left with each body.

The General listened ardently without a word, even when Stone had obviously finished he said nothing. He simply stared at the group with glazed eyes, as if Stone's summary had triggered long lost memories of those young men under his command.

He showed no reaction to what had happened as a result of something that had taken place back then, until Hammond interrupted his silence, then he looked up at him; This time as if he did not recognise him.

"General... the other day we came across a flat in Uxbridge

which we think was occupied by the killer. He gave the name of Allan Dumbleton, who you will see is one of the men on our list, and in Lonergan's photographs; at least he's the only man with the Christian name Alan."

"That surprises me," he remarked, shaking his finger at the picture in the file that had engrossed him. "Everyone called him Chessman," he continued.

"Chessman?" Stone exclaimed, "Then it all fits. The pawns, I knew they were significant. They had to have something to do with chess."

"That's not possible," said the General, "He didn't come back from that last mission. I don't know what happened, but everything changed after that."

"That can't be possible," Stone exclaimed.

"Sorry, Stone, I must interrupt," Hammond said. "General, I said this man was identified as Allan Dumbleton, what I also should have said was, his landlady described him as being an Indian, as having olive skin."

"Then that wasn't Chessman, all my operatives were British."

It became apparent to Stone, as undoubtedly it must have to the others, if Dumbleton was in fact this 'Chessman' who did not return from their last mission, then who was Hammond's Indian... and where on earth did he fit into all this?

"General," Mary spoke for the first time, "Why Chessman?"

He hesitated, appearing more interested in her face than the question.

"Because he always carried a miniature set with him, never went anywhere without it. When he went on a mission, he would leave all his personal belongings behind, but not his chess-set. He was only allowed to carry it because it was so ordinary and wouldn't lead anyone to us if he were caught."

"Have you any thoughts on the significance of these letters

marked on the pawns... M.O.U.S.?" she questioned, showing him a photograph.

"Oh yes indeed, I recognised them straight away. It was the code name of the last operation, when we lost Chessman: MOUSTACHE, it was."

"How can you remember that one, you must have had hundreds?" Stone asked.

"Ah... well it was a very special one," he replied.

His eyes glistened when he said that. His jaw line became firm, as if he were issuing orders again, thinning his face and drawing his sagging jowls closer to his neck, even showing a slight twitch in his own moustache.

"I'm sorry, General, but Moustache has nine letters," Mary continued.

His eyes became bright: darting in her direction. She had touched a trigger, "I'm aware of that young lady, in fact I pointed that out myself when it was first suggested to me. As it turned out, I was the 'E'; it had to be, you see. He made a mistake, and quick witted as he was, he made good of it."

"Who did, General?" Mary said; she was playing her skill. She was moving him gently back into the past, without him realising. Stone caught on, leaving her to take over. Hammond had not seen her at work before; in fact, he had no idea what her role in the investigation was, other than Stone had told him earlier, until he witnessed her ability to manipulate people under stress.

"Winston Churchill of course. He wasn't good at spelling you see, he always had his communications edited before they went out."

The name caught everyone by surprise.

"You mean you actually met Winston Churchill?" she continued, while he noticeably drifted back down the long road from the present into the past somewhere.

"I did... It was the most auspicious experience I've ever had."

He always referred to that meeting when he returned to that period. A period his wife so noticeably warned them he was taking more often these days.

Lapsing into the past was a natural development of his condition or the consequence of his medication. Either way, he was spending less time in the present, and more back there with his boys. 'Carter's Boys'.

CHAPTER 11

The General began to explain; not in retrospect, but in present tense, as if he were back in the past reliving every moment once again. As he did so, his tremor slowly settled, and he began to look normal again; he had moved to a time before his affliction.

The War Rooms were claustrophobic, not designed to accommodate the number of people scurrying about from one meeting to another. However, the increasing number of raids on central London by the Luftwaffe only frustrated the dilemma, intensifying the War Office personnel, constantly passing through the skilled concentration of High Command beneath the unsuspecting city of London.

General Peter Carter spent many hours waiting outside Churchill's War Room, although at the time he was only an Adjutant to Battalion Commander General Whitehouse. He never became accustomed, like some, to the continuous sound of distant voices, and hard as he tried, it was impossible to make any sense of the annoying chatter.

Like the 'Whispering Gallery' of St. Paul's Cathedral, ghostly-disembodied murmurs of secret trysts echoed through the chambers: creeping into his head and taking over his concentration completely.

He became familiar with the hard bench seat outside: a

remnant of many years in the house, stuffed with the barest of horsehair, sporting the familiar red Moroccan leather covering and the gold coat of arms of government. Scarred with cigarette burns and discoloured scuffs marking the passage of many sittings, its lack of comfort no deterrent against sleeping parliamentarians.

Peter Carter glanced at the stony face of the corporal on guard outside the steel blast-doors. Their eyes met, like two strangers standing on a deserted railway platform, shuffling their feet, fearful that the other might suddenly speak.

The Corporal noticed the Adjutant was picking at the brass studs on the bench between his legs, "Funny you should choose that spot to sit, Sir," he remarked.

His short ambiguous statement was so unexpected Peter jumped, dropping one of his files on the floor. He took the opportunity, while picking it up, to check if the corporal was speaking to someone else. He was not, so he straightened up and faced him as an officer of higher rank would.

"I beg your pardon, Corporal?"

"That very spot, Sir," he nodded, "They say Lloyd George sat there, when he was on the back-bench, that is."

"Oh... is that so; very interesting," Peter said, shuffling slightly, as if it had any significance. The corporal said no more, and continued staring at the wall opposite him, as if the interlude had never happened.

On that particular day in 1942, Adjutant Peter Carter also continued what he was doing, patiently clutching his rolled up maps and binders containing battle orders and strategies, when one of the heavy doors opened opposite and the hatless, white haired General Whitehouse poked his head out.

He was Peter's immediate superior: a fifty-four year old Sandhurst regular of the First World War. He continued in the intervening years as a commander, chosen to join Churchill's group of advisors in the War Room. He headed a team of experts like Peter to help him and other officers formulate their strategies of the war.

The General's appearance triggered the corporal to stand to attention suddenly, clashing his heels together with a loud crack that resonated throughout the corridors. Adjutant Carter stood up to attention also, an instinctive response, as best he could without losing control of his armful.

"Sir," he shouted, holding out his documents, expecting the General to ask for something as he usually did before disappearing back into the inner sanctum.

"No, Carter, he wants you," he responded.

Carter was overwhelmed, only uttering a feeble reply of, "Me, Sir?"

"Yes man... you. Come along, and be quick about it."

A sense of terror suddenly gripped him. It was general knowledge around the ministry that Churchill frowned upon anyone that could not stand toe to toe with him in a debate: his favourite pastime. "But, Sir I'm not prepared."

"It appears he is about to brief us on Singapore, and he wants you present."

"But he doesn't know me, Sir."

"Not you personally man... it's your expertise he wants. Now come on... we mustn't keep him waiting."

The General's last statement was even more baffling. Peter's recent expertise centred on North Africa: Rommel's territory, he knew nothing of Asia, least of all the little known island of Singapore.

This was the first time he had entered the room where the fate of the world rested. By the array of braided caps and swagger sticks on a table in the corner, he knew at a glance he was joining the company of giants: Generals, Admirals, Air vice Marshals, more top brass than he had ever seen gathered in one group before.

They had gathered around a map of Europe spread out across a large plotting table. Large regional maps of the war fronts decorated the walls, with coloured pins and arrows indicating the present positions of the warring factions.

The General led Carter to a huddled group in one corner, where Churchill was relaxing on an old leather couch, puffing on one of his enormous cigars, with a grey trail of ash down his lapel, looking just as he had expected him to in real life.

"Sir, this is my Adjutant, Sub Lieutenant Peter Carter," the General said.

His moist eyes looked up at him; he looked tired yet had a mischievous boyish expression on his ruddy face, as if he was in a state of constant exhilaration: the decisions of war certainly suited him.

Removing the wet cigar from his mouth, he immediately spoke to Peter with his familiar slurred diction, "Do you carry that lot around with you all the time, Lieutenant?"

"No, Sir... I just thought they might be needed."

"You remind me of one of my old tutors at Harrow; he constantly carried volumes and rolled up papers under his arms. No one ever found out what he did with them; but he did present a scholarly figure," he continued, looking him in the eye. He took another puff of his cigar. "Do you refer to text books or are you a thinker?"

Peter was nervously aware that he would be intently judged by every word, and subsequently every reply, leaving him no room for second thoughts or come to that, the precious thinking time Churchill referred to. The General nodded slightly; he had an honest wisdom in his face Peter respected. He was used to dealing with people like Churchill.

"I like to imagine I'm a thinker, Sir."

"Only imagine. You mean you don't get the opportunity?"

he chuckled.

"I wouldn't say that, Sir... it's a question of being in the right place at the right time," Peter said, beginning to come to terms with Churchill's banter.

"I see," Churchill said, still thinking, still puffing, still weighing up the Adjutant. He continued, "I understand from General Whitehouse, that you're an expert on strategy, and plan most of his campaigns?" he continued without allowing time for an answer. "We have a problem, or should I say, I have a problem. Which, although dictated by events in Europe, still poses an important decision, given the limited time and resources available to us."

Churchill had assembled his chiefs of staff to brief them on the serious development in Singapore. He awkwardly lifted himself from the couch, with some assistance, "Thank you General," he said, inviting him and the others to accompany him to the map of the Pacific Region on the far wall, pointing in particular, to the British held island of Singapore and the peninsular of Malaya above.

"Gentlemen... On January 15th, 1942 the British held lines on the mainland were breached by the Japanese, forcing our men to retreat back to the Singapore Garrison in the south of the island.

Lt General A.E. Percival had totally misjudged the situation, concentrating his forces in the south; anticipating an attack from the sea.

Churchill sat down again, "Continue, General, will you."

The General reached up and pulled down an enlarged map of Singapore Island itself, showing the main defences and the garrison prior to this date. Peter, unfamiliar with this part of the world, immediately compared it with the Isle of White where he grew up. Its shape, close proximity to the mainland, even the disposition of arterial roads was uncannily similar. The General picked up a pointer and began his debrief of the ensuing battle while Churchill reached for a glass of whisky sitting on a small table close by.

"On February 8th, the Japanese crossed the Causeway and landed on the landward side of the Island, a circumstance Percival did not calculate; he had not accounted for the ingenuity of the Japanese. As we understand, they mounted their attack on bicycles through the dense jungle, hence surprising our forces. He had prepared for a naval bombardment and subsequent amphibian landings. On February 15th, after some savage close-quarter fighting in the areas of the Causeway crossing, the water plant and airport, the Japanese repelled all attempts to stop them, making any following drawn out resistance impossible."

Churchill stood up again and continued, painting a grim picture, softening his audience to accept the outcome. He was a master of disinformation: boasting he never interfered with his commanders' tactics, preferring the expert on the spot to make his own decisions. Yet, it was commonly known to intelligence officers such as Peter, that he flooded the communications with constant dispatches to the same commanders issuing his support and a few well-chosen suggestions; leaving them in no doubt as to his overall views on the strategy for the progress of the war on any given front.

"It would seem gentlemen that Singapore has all but capitulated. The unfortunate decision has been made for the British and allied contingent of some 70,000 to 100,000 troops under the command of Lt General A.E. Percival to unconditionally surrender."

There was a unanimous outburst of: 'God, Christ, and good heavens', which quickly returned to a profound silence, seeing Churchill had not finished; he did not take kindly to being interrupted. He continued with the communiqué.

Then Churchill looked up and peered over the spectacles resting on the end of his nose. The previous show of emotion, which he expected instead at this juncture in his announcement, was not forthcoming. The Chiefs of Staff, so often ready to state their services point of view, were speechless. Peter was amazed at the impact this news had on them; looking as if the 'Death Nell' of the war with Japan had sounded.

Churchill was astute in his use of paraphrase.

"Sir... with all due respect, I don't understand," Peter said aiming his remark at Churchill rather than the General. "You quote my expertise as if you require my advice, yet I'm informed of the imminent tragedy to befall Singapore, when there is no time to avert the outcome, or I imagine the inclination to."

"That's uncalled for, Carter," snapped the General.

"No, General, he's quite right," Churchill said calmly, coming to his defence. "The secrecy in this room Adjutant is such that sometimes circumstances have to be taken on trust. You are quite right in that we have neither the time nor inclination, as you so tactfully put it, to do anything to save these poor souls. However, the code breakers at the Bletchley Park Cipher School have advised me, that Lt General Percival has a book containing the Japanese codes for that area. Code JN 25."

"I'm familiar with that code, Sir," Carter acknowledged.

"Good," Churchill exclaimed with a snort of satisfaction. "Although it doesn't appear to have helped him I might add." he turned to Carter with his hand still spanning the islands of the Coral Sea. "What I want from you is your considered opinion on the value of this document, and the viability of mounting a mission to rescue said package from the Japanese."

"Am I to take it, Sir that this package is all you intend to rescue?"

"If you say the mission is viable."

"If their surrender is as imminent as you say, I would have

thought the package you refer to would be in Japanese hands before we get there," Carter questioned.

"I have it on good authority that the code book is always kept in a secret place in General Percival's H.Q. And unless the Japanese are informed of its whereabouts, or the building is destroyed, it is quite safe," General Whitehouse advised.

"In that case, Sir, I would say the book has to be recovered. It would take months, if at all, to gather such information again, and when this offensive to regain the area from the Japanese is mounted, those codes would be vital to its success."

Churchill glanced at the General knowingly, without divulging anything further on their ultimate agenda, before he returned his attention to Carter.

"And you say we can launch such a mission?" he asked, looking back at the map.

"I see no reason why not" Carter replied confidently.

Churchill's manner changed, "With the utmost security. You understand it must never be known we rescued a book before all those men."

"As a matter of interest, Sir," Carter said, "how many are we actually talking about?"

"I already gave an initial estimate, which should suffice."

"Yes, Sir... that's fine. It was only my insatiable appetite for detail."

He chuckled, "I like that Adjutant. Just the answer I would have given under the circumstances. Your curiosity deserves feeding," he fumbled with some papers on the map table in front of him and retrieved another communiqué. "According to this we shall lose approximately 33,000 British troops, 17,000 Australians and 50,000 Asians," he gave his audience that discerning look again across his spectacles, "Yes gentlemen; no mean number. I know what you are thinking: 'What could we do with all those men in Europe?. I've asked myself the same question a number of times. But when it comes down to it, it's as simple as being in the wrong place at the wrong time. That's what war is all about gentlemen, picking the right place at the right time."

"Thank you, Sir, I understand perfectly, and in answer to your question, I would only need a limited number."

"How many?"

"Eight, Sir."

"Eight... why only eight?"

"Time and secrecy, Sir."

"What would be the time constraints?" the General asked.

"I have such a team in Aden on R and R... a week at the most."

Churchill appeared impressed with Carter's immediate grasp of the situation, at the same time elevated by the excitement of coming events.

"I know you have to plan your procedure, but for an old desk jockey, have you any ideas on how you will get there?" he said, lighting up again.

"Sir, you would be surprised how many pre-planned routes, transfer points, and refuelling stations we have set up for just such occasions, simply waiting to be activated."

"Excellent," he blurted out, rolling the wet cigar around his mouth.

"They will fly out to an island just below Sumatra," Carter excused himself as he moved amongst the officers to the Pacific map, and pointed to a tiny island. "It's called Cocos Island, where the Australians have an MTB base for cruising around the islands gathering information. From there a couple of boats can sneak through the Sunda Strait, here, under dark and weave their way up the Sumatran shoreline to one of the islands off Singapore," he moved over to the close-up map and pointed to the largest of the small islands spreading out below Singapore. "Blakang Mati. We can't risk being any closer with the noisy MTB's or the Japanese would hear us; they're bound to have gun boats down there."

"How will they get to the garrison then. It looks a good few miles from this Blakang Mati to me," the General interrupted.

"That's something I've got to go away and think about, Sir."

"Well I wish you well then, the whole mission is going to hang on that."

"I'm aware of that, Sir. I already have one idea, but it all depends on what happened to this item in Aden."

"Can't you elaborate on that, Carter?" the General questioned, knowing Churchill hated being kept out of the picture.

"Well it's a shot in the dark, Sir, nothing may come of it"

Churchill shot him a short meaningful glance.

"We will not hold you responsible, Adjutant, and if it's a few strings you need us to pull," Churchill assured him.

"It's not that, Sir, you see the last time I was there, in Aden that is, I came across a couple of Italian 'Chariots'. They would convert nicely for what I have in mind; it's just finding the bloody things again."

"What's a Chariot, assuming we're not talking about the historical Roman type?" Churchill asked, laughing; infecting everyone else.

"No, Sir... it's a manned torpedo. The Italians used them with success when the war started. They used them with great effect to carry a large load of explosives to the unsuspecting target, then slipping away after attaching the lethal cargo to the ship."

"How do they ride them?"

"They have two seats, and they're able to be steered."

"But you have eight men."

"That's what I meant about converting. Removing the 700 lbs. of explosive will allow another two men to ride it."

"And these will do what you want?"

"Oh yes, Sir, admirably. They'll be able to leave the MTB's

safely hidden on the other side of the nearby island, while they proceed under water to Keppel Harbour and the Garrison. They can then leave the Chariots submerged until they return."

"Well it all sounds very admirable," Churchill said, looking up at the General again with his usual broad grin when he was satisfied, and nodding his approval. Then with his customary sweep of the other services, they nodded likewise. "Done," he continued. "I want detailed plans and ETA's in four hours."

"We'll start immediately, Sir," General Whitehouse said.

Adjutant Carter nodded his acceptance.

With his hands behind his back, Churchill turned and began pacing in the small area behind the map table, "Now all we need is a password."

He took a deep puff on his cigar, letting the blue grey smoke out slowly, drifting in a spiral up to the extractor fan above, as his agile mind searched for an appropriate code name.

"Shall I get the code book, Sir?" the General asked.

"No, General, we don't want a standard code for such an operation."

They all hung on his word, expectantly.

"MOUSTACHE... Yes, MOUSTACHE he said. Then writing the letters out on his note pad, but noticeably missing off the 'E' from the end, "a letter for each man," he said, examining the pad at arm's length. "Yes... from under their noses, gentlemen." They all agreed, and laughed at his brilliance.

"But there are nine letters in Moustache, Sir, you missed the 'E' off the end," Carter corrected, and then shrank back on realising his gaffe.

"Is that so, Adjutant," Churchill replied, followed by an ominous silence, and then cheerfully he continued. "The 'E' is silent is it not. Not part of the main body so to speak. However, a vitally important element, without which, the ending would destroy the whole essence of the word. Consequently, I choose

you as the silent 'E'. The Executive of 'Moustache', who I trust will secure me the perfect ending I am looking for in Singapore."
"You'll have to excuse Carter, Sir," the General interrupted. "He's inclined to forget his place at times."
Churchill smiled and sucked on his cigar.
"Never mind, General, I think we were all guilty of that," he said, returning his focus on Carter, this time more seriously, which began to frighten him. "So I missed the 'E' off the end did I. Then we'll just have to put it right, won't we?"
"If you say so, Sir, I'm sorry I drew your attention to it."
"Are but, Adjutant, that's what I expect you to do. You see I can be expected to make mistakes, and I've made a few in my time, probably that's why I became Prime Minister." He chuckled and coughed a bit, the others hesitated at first then joined in, except Adjutant Carter; he was feeling the brunt of his astute humour.
"I'm sitting in the big chair, so I can be excused… but you can't, so you're entitled to question anything that doesn't appear right to you. So, as I said, we'll just have to make you the 'E', won't we Carter. How about Operations Commander Lieutenant Peter Carter, would that make up the nine letters?"
Peter Carter was flabbergasted, but Churchill could be like that, just as he was capable of sending 100,000 soldiers to their possible certain death under the Japanese.

CHAPTER 12

Everyone had become so engrossed in the General's past adventures, they did not realise he had finished. He beckoned for a drink and Mary obliged, expecting him to continue, but he did not. By his expression, he was still back there.

"General, are you going to tell us what happened next?" Mary asked.

His eyes focused on her again, "What was that dear?" he mumbled.

"The rest of the story, what happened?" she repeated.

"Ah yes, Operation Moustache," he uttered loudly.

The success of this hastily contrived mission depended on selecting the right team, and Carter knew just the men to achieve this. They were a newly formed group: the SOE (Special Operations Executive). Put together as highly trained subversive specialists or 'Irregular Forces', as some would term them, engaged in clandestine operations.

Officially, they listed under 'unconventional warfare', familiar with activities behind enemy lines: collecting intelligence and making as much of a nuisance as possible. They were on a well-earned R and R in Aden after several months in the North African desert, booby-trapping fuel dumps and sabotaging

Rommel's supplies.

Commander Carter wasted no time in catching the earliest flight to Aden, which turned out to be a delivery of Mosquito's. He had to be strapped into the bomb aimer's position, which would get him there faster than any other flight available.

After sending a message to Lieutenant Terry Lonergan, the Operations Lieutenant, to ready his men for another engagement, it was no surprise to see the full group waiting for him by the runway with RAF transport when the Mosquito squadron touched down. R and R was a constant thought for these men when in action, it retained their sanity, but once languishing at base they soon became bored, itching for the next mission; that feeling of living on the edge was like an addiction that had to be satisfied.

Commander Carter almost strangled himself as he fell out of the belly of the Mosquito, when Terry Lonergan opened the hatch under the plane. Luckily he was able to unbuckle the strap he was caught up in quickly as the hatch, that was partly supporting his weight, dropped away, averting a tragedy before the mission had started.

"Take it easy, Sir; we don't want to lose you before you even touch ground."

"Thanks for that, I much prefer a seat before a hammock."

"Anyway it's good to see you, Sir," Lieutenant Lonergan said, shaking his hand and grabbing his hold-all."

"Yes... I haven't had time to catch my breath yet. Would you believe, two days ago I was in a meeting to decide this lot."

"We heard about your promotion, congratulations."

"Thanks, Churchill's persuasion ploy."

"So you're taking over from the General then?"

"Not entirely... just this one at present, it's my idea, so I've got to carry it out. I wish I was going with you though; I've had so little time to work on it."

"With due respect, Sir, you're the strategist, we're the ones that have to make it work; whatever diabolical mess you've got us into this time."

They arrived at the beaten up old RAF truck, where the others, a motley bunch of misfits, certainly not looking like the highly trained soldiers they were, dressed in their Bedouin robes, were waiting eagerly for the usual round of greetings and congratulations.

Then Carter climbed into the front cab alongside Terry Lonergan while the others loaded themselves into the back. "I guess you're right," he said sadly, as they moved off with the sound of wrenching gears and puffs of black smoke.

"Where to this time, Sir," Lonergan questioned, "Northern Desert or South?"

"I'll tell you when I get cleaned up," he stalled, sounding more secretive than usual, noticing Lonergan's tension.

The last operation against Rommel's Afrika Corps' fuel dumps was a particularly bad operation, one the R and R in Aden had not yet fully erased. He glanced at the grave faces of the others in the back through the rear mirror, hoping his loyal friend could find eight good men for this mission.

Regardless of their constant questioning; their inability to remember his new rank; their laughing and joking with him as if he were still the Adjutant and the General their CO, he would not divulge the purpose of their new mission. Instead, as the evening drew to a close, he called Lieutenant Lonergan to one side, escorted him out into the cool Arabian night for a stroll across the deserted airstrip and a private unofficial conversation.

As they sauntered along the tarmac, Carter, forgetting how hot it was here during the day and nearly losing his boot to one of the sticky patches of melted tar, still had difficulty in finding the words to tell Terry they may not return from this mission.

"Have you heard about Singapore?" he started.

"Just what we hear on the grapevine from incoming radio chatter, it's under siege I gather," they stopped and sat on a nearby mobile generator.

"You're right. In fact, as we speak Percival has probably already surrendered."

"But he must have at least 80,000 men, why surrender?"

"It's a 100,000 actually, and I can't say... it's on a need to know basis but he was ordered to; a case of expediency."

"So what's this got to do with us?" Terry Lonergan asked, looking across at his old friend the new Commander, "It has, hasn't it."

"Yes... you're going there."

"Going there?" he shouted, then lowered his voice, realising how sound travels at night in the desert, "What do you mean exactly?"

"There's a valuable book of Japanese codes hidden in Percival's HQ, which we must have if we are to launch an offensive against the Japanese."

"What's the point now?"

"The point is: it will shorten the war in the Pacific when the time comes. Otherwise, if they find out we have this information; they'll change all their codes."

"So what does it matter what they do, it's all finished anyway," Lonergan grunted.

Commander Carter was surprised at his attitude. Usually he was first in line, like all the team, that was why he picked them for the job.

"Terry... do you know how long it took to get those codes?"

"Well they didn't help that lot in Singapore did they, so how good are they?"

"Oh don't be a bloody fool man... you, above all should know how dirty it is. You and your men have been a band of mercenaries running wild around North Africa for the past two years, so don't start being pious with me now. Besides, I have orders too, and from a much greater height than you have."

"Yes I know, sorry, Sir," he kicked his boot into the soft sand beside the crumbling tarmac to vent his anger. "So what do you want us to do?"

"This mission is so vital, it has to be on a 'Need to know' basis only, so I want you to select seven men capable of getting into the Singapore HQ under the Jap's noses, get the book and out again without them knowing. Oh... and they all must have their aqua rating."

"You do intend telling me why later, I suppose."

"I'll tell you at 0:800 in the morning," Carter paused, and smiled at him. "By the way, you do have yours I hope."

"Well I did, before Africa; we haven't had any need for it in the desert."

"Then you'll just have to brush up on your technique in the Cocos won't you," he said, standing up and making a move back to the billet.

"What about the Cocos?" Lonergan called out as quietly as he could.

"All I can say at this stage is, that's where this mission is going to start... okay. So for the meantime I want you to concentrate on selecting your best seven men."

On entering the Nissen hut Carter found his eight special operations soldiers were silently waiting stony faced, void of the merriment from the night before. As he walked down the narrow aisle towards the briefing dais, Lonergan gave out a 'SHUN', and they all stood to attention presenting him with the customary salute.

That set the mood for the day; they were no longer individuals. They were now a singular fighting unit once again; obedient specialists awaiting their orders. Commander Carter wasted no time reflecting on their change, but accepted it and joined the charade, with that gnawing feeling in the pit of his stomach, that this may well be their last mission.

"At ease men," he ordered, and then turned to address Lonergan, who was standing to one side. "Have you advised your team, Lieutenant?"

"Yes, Sir: as much as we discussed."

"Very good," Commander Carter said, pinning his main chart of the Pacific region onto the board behind him. Their eyes suddenly opened wide.

"This is your theatre of action gentlemen," he stabbed his stick at the tip of the Malaysian peninsular, "and this is the target... the Singapore Garrison."

There was a murmur from the group, quickly stifled by Lonergan.

"Yes... I know what you're thinking; Singapore has fallen to the Japanese. I'm not going to give you any details, except to say, they won't be getting any help. You're not going in to reconnoitre a rescue expedition for any future landings. You're going in to recover an important code book"

At that point, the air filled with more than just murmurs, until Lieutenant Lonergan once again brought his men back in line.

Commander Carter was annoyed at the lack of discipline. These men had been involved in missions before that relied on their iron will to go about their business.

"Anyone that feels he is not suitable for this mission, leave the room now," he said firmly, perusing the ranks with a steely gaze.

Silence fell over them. No one wanted to leave and be seen not fit to serve his country. Satisfied that was the end of it, the Commander continued. "I don't want to know what you think about all those thousands of men taken prisoner... we can't do anything to help them. But we can help thousands of others by getting that codebook, and allowing the allies to eavesdrop on the Japanese plans in the Pacific.

"Question, Sir?" Lieutenant Lonergan spoke out.

"Yes, Lieutenant."

"How long do you estimate we've got before they're secure in the area?"

"None really, the island is a fortification already, they've just taken over. I estimate we have at least a week before they secure the waters around the island. They have to organise between 70,000 and 100,000 prisoners. They have to repair the damage to communications, which I understand was quite extensive. This is where the prisoners will come in, and if I know our chaps, they'll sabotage and delay things as long as they can."

Lieutenant Lonergan continued his questions. "That doesn't give us much time, it's a long way, Sir," he said, "How are we going to land on the island without them knowing?"

"Gather round and I'll show you," he said. "0:800 you leave Aden in a PBY Catalina for the Cocos, where the Australians have an MTB base. At this moment, two submersibles are being converted to carry four men each, a PBY delivered them yesterday, and the other MTB is being fully armed as an escort."

"Excuse me, Sir," Sergeant Hebden interrupted.

"Yes, Sergeant?"

"Who's going to sail these Submersibles, Sir, if that's the right word?"

"I wouldn't know if you sail them or drive them, Sergeant. Oh, don't worry they're quite easy to manoeuvre, they're just a couple of torpedo's with seats."

Carter showed then a picture of the normal two-man machine.

"Looking at this, Sir, it looks as if it'll sink like a brick, so how do we submerge and come back up again? Hebden continued.

"There's a simple mechanism of releasing ballast and pointing the thing down, anyway I've allowed four hours at the MTB base to practise; that should be enough. Then you can decide who is going to be the pilot in each case. Once you set off from the Cocos, it will be a high speed run to Sumatra, arriving by nightfall, I don't know the timing here... the Australians will have all that under control. They say there are no Japanese in that area at present, so they can do some fast running right through the gap between Sumatra and Java... here, at the Sunda Strait bringing you out at the tip of Bangka Island.

"This will be your turning point, hugging the Sumatran coast line until you get in amongst the hundreds of islands all the way up to Singapore. This is where you may have to take it easy; the Jap's could have a gunboat or two nosing around. You can leave yourself in the Aussie's hands though, they know this area backwards; they patrol it once a week. I estimate you should be off Singapore sometime during the following evening."

"What do we do while we're resting up during the first day?" Lonergan asked.

"What do you normally do. Check your weapons and practice. The MTB's will drop you off behind Blakang Mati Island so you can make a submerged run to Keppel Harbour, where you can leave the Chariots and your gear on the bottom and make your move on the headquarters. And remember, you must be off the island before dawn."

"Where is the code book?" Lonergan asked.

"I was coming to that. Once in the main building, the General's office is the one at the far end. Look for a large Colonial desk," he showed them a sketch. "On the sitting side you will see the usual four small draws either side, and this large bowed one in the middle below the top. It's supported with an inch and a half strip of wood, embossed with the egg and dart pattern. Pressing the last egg and pulling the rail simultaneously, will allow a tray to be withdrawn from under the top. I am told this tray is full of sensitive books, you want the black one with the red spine, no other."

He looked at the group, expecting them to comment, but they said nothing.

"This book must be brought back at all costs, if anyone is injured they must not jeopardise this mission, is that quite clear?"

There was silence; they knew what he expected of them.

He took the maps and charts down, and handed them to Lieutenant Lonergan, as he drew him to one side, "These must not leave your hands."

"No, Sir" he confirmed, taking them and their responsibility.

"You understood what I meant by not jeopardising the mission?"

"Yes, Sir, probably more than you do. Every man knows he will be sacrificed for the good of the mission, they don't have to be reminded."

Commander Carter looked apprehensive.

"Okay, I'll see you and your men at 0:800 tomorrow for final briefing," he grabbed Lonergan's arm, "I'm available if you want me. God knows I won't sleep."

"By the way, Sir, what's the password for this one?"

"Oh yes I nearly forgot, although it's in your orders with the other sensitive material. It's MOUSTACHE. It's Churchill's choice if you don't like it.

"No, Sir, it's quite clever actually."

Carter suddenly realised, regardless of the fact that he had planned the mission; he had nothing to do with it. The Lieutenant made that obvious, even if he did not say so. It was their show now; they were the ones leaving in the morning.

The sun was already beginning to heat up the runway. The surface was shimmering below the wings of the Catalina flying boat; making ghosts of the men readying her for her flight. He stood there watching the silhouettes as everyone assembled waiting for the final word to go, along with his final reminder.

"Now remember, the MTB's will hide up while you're on the mission. The small beacon you have must not be activated until you're back behind the island, only then will the boats respond and even then only to your password."

Without any further ado, the group lined up in single file, carrying their large holdalls over their shoulders. In their full combat gear, they boarded the truck that was to take them out to their waiting flight: to an unknown destiny.

General Carter looked tired, obviously finished, by the length of his pause. His wife had returned earlier without interruption, knowing that disturbing him during these phases could be worse than just allowing him to finish.

"I must ask you to finish now," she eventually said to his guests.

"It's all right, dear," he said, my story has ended."

"Can you give us no information about the mission itself?. Stone urged, causing sharp glances from the others.

"I cannot," he said wearily. "When they returned, their mission a success I should add, I was informed it was at the cost of one team member, Chessman, and one Australian MTB with all its crew."

"And it ended there?" Stone said. "No investigation to find out what happened?"

"Oh there was an investigation all right, but it amounted to nothing. Each man, for whatever reason, had decided to be silent. Something happened all right, and it destroyed the group, they never worked together again."

Stone continued to ask questions.

"These remaining men, do you know where they are. We must contact them before this maniac strikes again."

"Yes, I've managed to keep in touch with occasional reunions, do you mind, dear," he said to his wife who had already moved over to the bookcase, to the lower shelves where they could see two rows of old green notebooks.

Hammond recognised them immediately. The same type he used at school.

Mrs Carter appeared puzzled, as she ran her hand back and forth along the books. Then she stopped, she finally found what she was looking for. "That's strange, dear," she said. "You haven't had the master book out have you?" she asked, walking back to the table.

"No, dear, it's always in the same place."

"Well it wasn't this time, someone's moved it."

Hammond remembered the copy he had taken of the curious scribbling of the weekly times, realising immediately what they now meant.

"Good heavens," he exclaimed, taking his notebook out and turning to the appropriate page. "Do these times mean anything to you, Mrs Carter," he passed his notebook to her.

She studied the notations for a while, and then gasped with sudden awareness.

"Of course... these are the times I take my husband to his therapist, the library and the local barracks, where they allow him to watch training."

"Are you suggesting what I think you are, Jack?" Stone questioned.

"Mrs Carter has just confirmed that our killer was here."

"Oh, dear," she exclaimed.

"That's all right, Mrs Carter; it's not your husband he wants."

"Are you sure?" she said shakily.

"Yes... quite sure. He must have watched your movements until he found the best time to enter the house when it would be empty, it was information he wanted."

"Is that so significant?" Mrs Carter asked.

"Oh yes," Hammond answered most positively. "The fact that he didn't take the book with him indicates he didn't want anyone to know he had seen it."

"So he's ahead of us again," Stone said, examining the book, noting down the addresses, including Chessman's; regardless of the assumption that he was dead.

"Maybe he' not ahead of us," Mary said. "If you remember, his profile indicates that he moves into the area of his victim, and then meticulously plans his operation. This should allow us enough time to contact each one before he's ready."

"How on earth did he find me after all this time," the General said. "He appears to have had the advantage of knowing things we didn't from the beginning. I could understand if it was Chessman, but it isn't; so who is it."

No one had an immediate answer for the General; his questioning eyes searched theirs one by one. It was evident this invasion of his privacy had affected him.

"What I did back then is history and I have to live with the consequences. One man's life was insignificant compared with the thousands we must have saved later when the allies fought back in the Pacific. My only concern is that someone is taking retribution for that man. Please... don't let this maniac turn what was a successful operation into a catastrophe. He must be stopped."

Mrs Carter moved round to the back of his chair.

"I'm sure the officers know what they're doing, dear. They have the boys' addresses now, so we must let them get on... time is of the essence."

She saw them back to the front door, feeling it necessary to accompany them to the car: her emotions too much for her to hide. "I want to thank you all for what you did back there for my husband, this illness of his hasn't been easy, made worse by his fixation that this is some form of heavenly retribution. But your explanations and assurances have made him happier in himself, I know that much. I think the next few months will go over easier now, and I thank you for that. And if you can give him some idea of the remaining three's security, it would mean so much to him."

Back in the car Stone did not attempt to start it; he was still back in the past wondering what happened to the general's boys when they took off in the Catalina flying boat to the Cocos island.

"Well are we going then?" Hammond asked.

"Err... yes. Right," Stone said, and turned the key.

CHAPTER 13

As Stone entered the lift the following morning with Mark, he suddenly decided to read the latest entry in his notebook, "Ralph Collins, Steve Farney and Martin Drake, those are the last three alive."

"What about the fourth one Boss?"

"Believe it or not, he was my main suspect, but apparently he's dead. His nickname was 'Chessman', it all fitted so neatly."

"Who said he's dead, Boss," Mark questioned, holding open the doors after the lift stopped on their floor. "I mean... did anyone actually see him die. Was it official?"

"No, but the special operations team said he was killed, so someone must have, he certainly didn't come back with them." Mark had sown a seed of doubt in Stone's mind. He sensed this mystery had something to do with them leaving him; maybe he did not die at all. Then what did this Indian have to do with it, using his name, he pondered.

Stone's first duties were to get his notes typed up; verify the addresses the General gave him of the remaining three; arrange interviews as quickly as possible, as well as warning them of the danger they were in and setting up around-the-clock surveillance, before he began analysing his own doubts on who the killer really was.

When Stone caught up to Mark, he was adding the new names to the white board. He had no order yet, or a letter to identify them.

"It looks much better than it did yesterday," Stone called out as he entered the room. "Even if it doesn't mean much, it looks like we're progressing."

"But we are progressing, Boss," Mark said, stepping down after his addition to the last panel and taking a further look.

"Why the question-mark?"

"Well who knows, I might be putting the killer's name up there."

"I tell you what's missing," Stone pointed out.

"What's that?" Mark said admiring his work.

"The rest of the code name, what else."

"So it's a code name is it?"

"Yes... Moustache."

"I saw that in the dictionary, but it has nine letters."

"There's a tale attached to that, which I haven't time to tell you, just complete the board and leave off the last letter 'E. You can find out when you read my notes."

Stone was more obsessed with the idea that Chessman was his suspect, somewhere there had to be an answer. It buzzed around in his head, making him lose concentration as he left the squad room for his office. There was no way he was going to get anything done in this state; he had to visit the killer's last accommodation and find out what the landlady really meant by, 'an Indian'. He glanced at his watch. It was almost lunchtime.

He decided to have a quick bite at the local pub first, and then off to Uxbridge.

"I'm off out to lunch and then on to the house in Uxbridge, is it still under surveillance?" he called out.

"Yes, there's a constable on duty; do you want me to come?"

"You're welcome to join me for lunch, but then I need you back here."

"Something personal?"

"No, I just want to get the feel of the place. See why she called him an Indian and see this board Jack Hammond kept talking about."

"Well an Indian's an Indian, Boss."

Stone stomped out of his office, and for some peculiar reason, ran down the stairs, instead of using the lift as he usually did. He felt somehow that the exercise might clear his head, even rid him of his frustration.

As Superintendent Stone made his way across the city out towards Uxbridge, he had difficulty with the muffled voice on the other end of the phone, "Jack... is that you?. "Yes... who's that?"

"It's Stone... I didn't recognise your voice first off."

"Oh... sorry about that, I was biting into an Eccles cake. What can I do for you. You sound in a hurry, and what's all that noise. It sounds like traffic."

"It is," Stone shouted back. "I had my radio patched through to your phone, and I'm in the middle of the worst traffic on my way over to the house by the yards. I thought you might like to come, we can have a chat."

"You mean you've got a problem, and you want to bounce your ideas off me. I thought that's what Mary was for?"

"No actually I wanted to reprimand you, and thought the scene of your skulduggery would be the best place."

"You what?"

"Seriously, Jack, you know me better than that. Come if you want." He abruptly shut Jack off at that point. Stone knew Jack's curiosity in this case was too much to resist an invitation to revisit the house.

Hammond grabbed his lunch and left; he did not intend to allow Stone to get to the old woman first. Leaving her alone with him for five minutes and he would have her saying anything to suit his purpose.

"I'm off to see what Stone's up to on our patch with the old landlady," he told the Sergeant as he passed through.

"Hold on, Boss, what if the Super asks where you are?"

"Don't tell him anything; say I'm following up a lead."

"He's going to catch you one day, Boss," the Sergeant said, laughing.

"What can he say; I am following up a lead."

He was determined to get to the old crone before Stone did, confident in the fact that he knew her place was much easier to get to from his side of town.

As soon as he entered the derelict area by the railway yards, its oppressive atmosphere overwhelmed him. The Council had torn down complete blocks, and noisy yellow machines scooped up the last memories of this once vibrant community.

"I see you're back then," the scruffy old woman shouted."

Hammond was just getting out of his car when he spotted her cranking her arthritic frame into sight above the battered hedge. She was retrieving her milk from the doorstep, her filthy toes sticking out of her stockings through the holes in her tattered slippers.

"Now don't be like that. Just think what sort of a day it would be like without us handsome men visiting you," he said sarcastically, winking at the bored looking constable in the small blue and white parked in front of him.

"Oh yes," she exclaimed, chuckling to herself, as she disappeared inside.

"How long do we have to watch this place, Sir?" the Constable questioned.

"Hard to say, Constable, you need to ask Superintendent Stone, it's his case now," he answered, and turned as another car drew up behind his. "Speak of the devil, here he is now."

"I thought you may be here first," Stone said, shutting his car door.

"Actually our landlady was outside, and she wasn't very impressed, so I was chatting with your constable, waiting for you to have the pleasure of softening her up," Hammond said, smiling at the constable again.

Stone allowed Hammond to enter the derelict building first.

"You should have worn an old suit, or brought some overalls with you," Hammond commented sarcastically as he knocked on her door.

"I didn't expect it to be like this... it's filthy."

"Go away you lot," came the reply.

"Come on now, you don't want me to warn you again," Hammond shouted.

The door opened a fraction and she peered out, enough to send a whiff of putrid air in Stone's direction, almost making him choke, "I said clear off."

"She's a fiery old bitch," Stone commented, still clutching his hanky.

"I heard that," she retorted.

Then through the small gap she watched Hammond take out a box of matches, strike one and drop it on the broken lino tiled floor, then another, and yet another. The years of wax polish engrained into the lino soon caught alight.

She became horrified. "What do you think you're doing, you'll set the place on fire," she cried, opening the door wider.

"Then I'll just have to call the fire brigade," he replied, looking at Stone.

Stone was surprised, but realised what his game was and joined in with the act.

"What do you think a few hoses would do to this place?" He said.

"What about my cats?" she screamed.

"Give them a good wash, that's for sure," Stone said.

She returned to her favourite chair by the window. "All right...

what do you want?"

Hammond stubbed out the small fire that had started in the hall with his foot. "Actually it's Superintendent Stone here who wants to talk to you, so pay attention and answer him like a good girl."

"Oh I rate a celebrity do I then?" she said.

"Your statement says this lodger was an Indian, and yet he has an English name."

"That's right, Superintendent, they all do. Most of them were born here."

Stone could see she was going to be difficult.

"What makes you so sure he was Indian?" he said.

"Because he had long black hair tied back in a ponytail, and coffee coloured skin."

"That could describe anyone," Stone shouted.

"Okay," Hammond said. "Let's leave her for now and go upstairs."

"That's a good idea," Stone said.

He pushed the door open, as they stooped under the black and yellow police security tape and entered the undisturbed domain of the killer. All that was recognisable of another's presence was the fingerprint dust that pervaded everywhere.

"Wasn't this room locked up?" Stone questioned him as he followed.

"Come on man, one puff and the door will fall off its hinges."

"I suppose you're right, but it doesn't make for a tight crime scene."

"Nothing about this case is tight, Stone."

"It has to be Chessman, everything points to him; he was the one obsessed with Chess; he would have the best motive if they left him behind to face the Japs."

Hammond swung him round, before he wandered away.

"Hold on... where did the General's testimony say he was left behind alive. The SOE briefing said Chessman died. You're just changing things again to suit your own theory. You need hard facts to make a U-turn like that."

"But, Jack, the facts as they are don't fit."

"Exactly… that's what you're meant to think. This man is clever. He finds out about Chessman's death, takes on his identity, and goes about killing off the bastards, for whatever reason, making us think it was because they left him behind."

"Or equally, it's as I say, and it is Chessman, disguising himself as an Indian. All he needs is a wig and some makeup."

"Haven't you overlooked the age difference?" Hammond said, "Chessman has to be at least in his late fifties. Our Indian sounds more in his twenties."

"I said he was made up, that could make a difference."

Hammond remained silent for a moment; there was some truth in what Stone said; regardless of the fact that deep down he knew Stone was determined to make this fit his own criteria. There was merit in both scenarios.

"Okay, let's just say you're right, what on earth has he been doing for thirty odd years, it's a bit late to start feeling vengeful."

"That's the one aspect in all this that has me worried."

"Have you done anything about our three new names yet?"

"Mark is checking on their addresses now."

Stone turned his attention back to the pictures on the wall.

"Did you pick up on these photos, Jack?" he said.

"You mean their similarity?"

"Yes, that as well, but I was really thinking of the lack of passion in them."

Inspector Hammond studied the pictures again. It must have been the umpteenth time he had done so, especially since he had a full set copied for his own examination, and this was the first time he really looked at them.

Stone was right, they were no more than post mortem

photographs; devoid of any attempt to capture the essence of the moment, or hint at the emotion the photographer was feeling at the time. It was as if someone not associated with the victims took them.

Hammond walked away from the wall and turned to face Stone, "Do you realise you've just upset the whole applecart."

"What does that mean?"

"It means one of us is going to have to go over every report again."

"Don't be daft... what's so dramatic about a few photographs?"

"For once man, listen to your experience. That little voice in your head told you something was wrong with these pictures. Instead of trying to fabricate leads, listen to your hunches; for once you're thinking like a detective.

They spent the next hour or so going over the scene where they found the abundance of evidence, another thing that worried them; it was all too easy.

Was the clever butcher drawing them into his web, or was he the bumbling maniac Stone would like everyone to think. Either way, Stone's inner warning system had also noticed this very important clue, or flaw in an elaborate ruse to throw them off the scent.

Mark spotted Stone in his office, "Oh your back, Boss, I didn't see you come in."

"I'm preoccupied."

"Sorry, Boss, I just thought you looked a bit... "

"A bit what?"

"Never mind I'll get on with what I was doing."

"Oh no you don't, bring me up to date on our new names. Have you made any contact yet... set-up any appointments?"

Mark disappeared for a moment, returning with his notebook,

and entering the office hesitantly, he looked awkward.

"What's wrong?" Stone asked sharply.

"I was just wondering what that smell was, Boss, can you smell it?"

"I should do, I haven't been able to get it out of my nostrils since I was in that hovel in Uxbridge. That woman should be reported."

"Oh sorry, Boss, I didn't realise it was you."

"For Christ sake get on with it man, then I can get home and change," he checked his watch. "Good heavens, is it that time already?"

"Would you rather I left it till tomorrow?"

"No... get on with it."

"Well we managed to find them all at the addresses the General gave us, but as usual they're all scattered about a bit."

Stone fidgeted with a box of tissues in his bottom draw.

"That appears to be what this case is all about," Stone snapped. "Why our killer couldn't be like Jack the Ripper, and select all his victims in London, I don't know."

"Anyway, Boss," Mark continued, not wanting to get into whatever was really bothering the Superintendent: "Ralph Collins, sixty-three years old, runs a pub in Hackney. He's not that far off... we can see him first. Then there's Martin Drake, sixty-four, retired Major. Why didn't we pick that up, he obviously didn't leave in '42."

"Nothing about this case is what it appears; you should know that by now."

"Well he lives in Harrogate, Yorkshire, so that'll be a day away. And finally, Steve Farney, fifty-nine but not all there; I doubt if we'll get any change from him."

"Why's that. What do you mean, not all there?"

"He's in a nursing home in Folkestone."

"That's great, that's all we need to add spice to the pot. Okay, it's Collins tomorrow and this Major Drake the next day. Now I'm off, and don't you dare comment on that," Stone said crossly, as he stood up from his seat. "Oh and, get in touch with Mary and see what her situation is like, we don't want to make any arrangements, only to find she's engaged."

"Right, Boss," Mark said, finishing his notes. "Oh and... what happened with the old woman. Did you have any luck with the Indian?"

"I'm no further forward, if that's what you mean. In fact, I want to have a look at all those photographs Inspector Hammond gave us again; there's something funny about them."

"What was that, Boss?"

Stone glared at him, and as he moved around his desk to leave Constable Freeman walked over to the office door with an envelope in his hand.

"Here are those print-outs you wanted, Boss," he said, handing them through the doorway as he passed, "What's that funny smell?"

"Out," Stone shouted, "before I put you both back on the beat."

CHAPTER 14

Fresh from a hot bath and straight into his towelling bathrobe, Stone felt like a new man. His experience with the old woman's stench had taught him a lesson: always be prepared; Jack Hammond said as much. Clear of the putrid smell at last, he needed a stiff drink.

Stone immediately made his way to the drinks cabinet in the corner and poured himself his usual two-fingers of whisky, and paused for thought, then added another two.

He moved around to the couch in front of the fire, stacked a few cushions at one end, and eased himself into them with a sigh of satisfaction; he was in the comfort of his own home, he felt clean again and he had a good whisky. He absorbed the ten-year old malt aroma, took two quick gulps, winced and placed the glass down.

Usually by now he would be feeling relaxed, but he was still tense with the memory of that old woman's hovel. He sniffed each hand in turn, but nothing except the pleasant fragrance of his Dunhill cologne.

A good book could do that, and he cast his eyes towards the small bookcase. He spotted his briefcase and the photographs came to mind. He rolled off the couch, retrieved the briefcase, opened it to take out the file and spotted General Carter's book.

Back on the couch and another couple of swigs inside him, Stone took the weight of the heavy tomb of seven hundred and eighty-eight pages in his hand.

The black cover with the bright red question mark impressed him, as it had done in Cantrell's cottage, and the title suddenly made more sense. Carter's Boys had no immediate meaning then, as most titles were created simply to capture attention. Now, knowing a lot more than he did then, he realised this book was an epitaph to all those soldiers who anonymously sacrificed their lives for world peace.

As Stone flicked through the initial acknowledgements, he almost passed the Introduction. It was the first line that caught his attention, the words Cain and Abel, and he was so intrigued he had to read on.

It was a short introduction, just three-quarters of a page. It dealt with glory and heroes, those who sacrificed their lives for others. He was touched, and as he read on he also realised these particular men were very special to Carter. They had a bond that could not be broken; they were in fact Carter's Boys.

Then he came across what he was looking for, chapter twenty-three: The Fall of Singapore: Operation Moustache. It was uncanny. The first lines echoed the story General Carter told them about the day he sat on a hard bench outside Churchill's war room and he suddenly became excited.

Stone reached down for his drink, the glass was empty. He pushed the book to one side, jumped up to fill his glass; this time four fingers, and then hesitated, before grabbing the bottle and returning to the couch. He wanted nothing to distract him from finding out what happened after the plane left Aden. Then he pondered for the moment, and flicking through how many pages covered this section, he wondering how the General could have written about the mission if he was not part of it. Then he recalled what he said about making the reports he received more interesting, by writing them as if he were actually there.

Settled again, he hastily reached the part where Carter was standing on a deserted airstrip in Aden, waving to his boys taking off on their journey to the Cocos.

It was 8:00 am. February 28 1942. It was unusually cold at that time in the morning, something to do with the extreme temperatures at this time of the year, and yesterday was one of the highest. The sun was still very low when the eight men climbed into the Catalina flying boat at the RAF base in Aden. They felt it strange calling it that, when it was standing on wheels on the tarmac. The inside was very cold to the touch. Condensation ran down everywhere on the metal interior, and everyone was grumbling, except Chessman.

As usual, he had settled down quickly, buckled himself in, and pulled out his infernal chess set to continue the game he had started earlier. The two giant engines were kick-started from a mobile generator below the wing. It almost shook the plane to pieces until the pilot adjusted the revs, then the anticipation kicked in.

Once both powerful engines were at taxiing speed there was a sudden lightness as the whole craft lifted on its tyres. As the ground crew pulled the chocks clear and the green light flashed, warning everyone to buckle up, the ungainly amphibian careered down the makeshift runway and lifted clumsily into the sky.

It skewed sideways over the sea for a short distance then headed eastwards across the Gulf of Aden towards the Indian Ocean. They were pinned back in their seats as the engines throttled forward to maximum power, lifting the PBY into a higher altitude, out of the reach of stray enemy fighters. The Catalina was an easy target, no real armament to speak of, especially when used as a carrier for personnel and the supplies they needed.

Once the plane reached its cruising altitude, everyone became relaxed, yet insular: each man coming to terms with his own demons, and attending to his gear as a means of occupying his mind. The flight was uneventful, except for a break about noon when they opened the packed rations; it was then when they saw the pilot for the first time. He was looking for Lieutenant Lonergan, smiling and nodding at everyone as he passed.

"Everything okay with you chaps?" he said in a matter-of-fact way.

They all greeted the red haired man in his heavy lambskin jacket, as he moved down the plane towards where the Lieutenant sat by himself.

"How are we doing old man... all set?" he said.

"This is the boring bit, will it be long now?" Lonergan replied.

"We should be touching down in about two hours," he said, leaning across the metal seat in front, watching Lonergan counting his ammunition clips.

After a few moments he stood up, as much as anyone could in a Catalina, with both hands gripping the seat in front, as the plane banked into its last heading. Turning back down the plane, he began his announcement.

"This is going to be a sea landing chaps... if you haven't done one before, I'm warning you it'll be a bit bumpy. A green light will go on to tell you to make ready, then I want you to buckle up again and brace yourselves on the seat in front of you. Put your head under your arms if you like."

Before carrying out his instructions, they all had to see the island: the team's starting point. The small atoll called Cocos, with its meagre contingent of Australian forces with their MTB's, was to be their way into the Java Sea and the Indonesian islands, and on to their ultimate destination, Singapore.

The island looked so tiny, it was a wonder they ever found it, a pinpoint of green surrounded by a white halo of coral sand; like a sentinel, keeping a watchful eye on the Sunda Strait: the gateway to the Indian Ocean, should the Japanese choose to threaten the Antipodes. As the PBY literally dropped out of the sky onto the blue water below, the pilot's use of Bette Davis's famous expression: 'Hold onto your seats, we're in for a bumpy ride', was if anything, an understatement.

The only consolation, if any, was the expert handling of the Australian MTB that raced out to pick them up, bringing them back to terra-firma first and then going back for their supplies, and maybe their stomachs, if they could find them.

They spent the rest of the day transferring the supplies to the MTB, while the Aussies familiarised them with the island, a debriefing with the Lieutenant and a few unusual beers with both MTB crews.

The overwhelming fact of the evening was, these carefree Aussies were about to embark on a trip through dangerous waters placing their lives at risk, without once asking what the eight were doing in their part of the world.

The following morning they spent hilariously trying out the two Chariots, which took a bit of getting used to, but provided them with an episode that gave light relief from whatever lay ahead. Most of the team, not particularly fond of water sports, likened the Chariot to a rolling log. It was top heavy without its 700 lb. explosive ballast: something they did not account for in the conversion.

The Aussie crew tried time after time to find a way to mount the beast without it rolling over. It was their first experience of these contraptions also, until finally one had the bright idea of holding onto the rear end with his legs apart to stabilize it, while the first man climbed on. Once they mastered the procedure, they then had another problem: one of the contraptions decided it was not going to leave the bottom, forcing the crew to abandon it and swim to the surface.

The Aussie divers came to the rescue once again, by going down and adjusting the ballast valve until finally everything was okay. When the other craft surfaced after completing its trials, Sergeant Hebden, at the helm, was the first to associate the experience with a submarine left stranded on the bottom.

"Thank goodness they would be on the outside should anything like that happen again," he said, squeezing the water out of his nostrils.

Everyone was relieved, especially Lieutenant Lonergan; they had to be off Sumatra by nightfall, and that was no mean task. The time had arrived. They assembled on the small jetty with the two MTB crews; waiting for the command as they always did on such operations, knowing full well, once they were on their way, the snakes in their stomachs would soon dissipate.

"Okay you lot," Lieutenant Lonergan shouted out, calling them to order. "In a moment we'll board the MTB, and you'll go immediately to the stations allotted to you yesterday. From this point on until we reach our destination, you will take your orders from Lieutenant Bradley and his officers on anything to do with shipboard discipline," he bellowed at eight stoic individuals about to find their sea legs.

They all shouted back in the affirmative.

"Right lead out you lot, and let's get this show on the road."

Once on board they found the craft a tight squeeze for eight men and its crew, despite them gutting the boat of its torpedoes and heavy armaments, which left the defence of the operation solely to the sister MTB.

Those who expected a dramatic departure the moment their gear was stowed were in for a surprise. It seemed an eternity, slung in the makeshift hammocks meant for the deadly torpedoes, listening to the squeaky rubber plimsolls of the Aussies scrambling about on deck, before they heard the deep growling retort of the giant engines.

Like the Catalina, the torque began to drag the light frame askew in the water as the small plywood boat taxied away from the jetty and headed out towards deep water on their journey to the Sumatran coast. The waters were treacherously shallow in places, and according to the MTB crew, it would get much worse passed the Sundra Strait.

As soon as they found good water, they opened the throttles and the powerful horsepower of the Merlin engines roared into life, sending the boat and its armed shadow, skipping across the surface at a phenomenal speed.

It was breath-taking for those on deck who had never experienced such a craft before, but devastating for those below with no point of reference, who experienced a sudden need to vomit, as the G's forced their stomach into their chest.

They called the phenomenon, cresting: when the light craft skipped from the top of one wave, before falling into the trough of the other. If the uninitiated could stand the pace, it would be fast enough to bring them off the Sundra Strait gap between Sumatra and Java within five hours. In the meantime, the boat was awash with paper bags.

The light was uncanny, when they arrived: hardly one thing or the other. They coasted until nightfall, and watched the orange sun begin its decent into the horizon; soon it would be dusk and they would be able to start their journey along the dangerous Sumatran coastline.

While the two boats eased their way in amongst the shoreline undergrowth, waiting for dusk, the crew busied themselves checking the engines after the long high-speed run, in readiness for the next leg. The eight-man team crawled up top and collapsed on deck in the stifling humidity, unable to do little more than re-check their gear and defend themselves against the giant mosquitoes that had suddenly descended upon them.

That night everyone sat on deck watching the eerie shoreline for life, native or otherwise, imagining all forms of danger. They rubbed their eyes constantly to focus on what they thought was out there, whilst being bombarded with all sorts of sounds from Sumatra's nocturnal creatures; playing out their nightly roles in this vast ecosystem.

Hardly noticeable, the boats turned left, slipping between the mainland and Bangka Island and reducing speed so that a lone sailor could swing the lead and test the depth below them, listening intently to the noises of things scuttling away from the water's edge, as the boats passed close to the shore.

Everything was looking good, as the MTB's gently passed the island and back out into open water where the speed was slowly increased, and to the relief of everyone, the humidity began to fall as they moved further out away from the shoreline.

"Make the most of it, mates," an Aussie sailor commented as he passed, "we'll be off the islands soon, and that means slowing down again."

"Thanks for that," the Lieutenant said, attending to the lumps that were beginning to rise on his neck and arms.

The MTB crew appeared to be immune to the biting monsters of the night, whereas Lonergan's men could do nothing to stop them, regardless of the repellent they were busy sloshing all over their bodies.

He was right; within the hour, the boats slowed down to a crawl, as masses of jagged peaks appeared silhouetted against the previously flat horizon. The boats spent what was left of the dark hours winding their way cautiously through the western edge of countless tiny islands, sprinkled randomly like pebbles all the way to Singapore. It was slow going, and the humidity was becoming unbearable for the newcomers struggling to find sleep in their hammocks below deck, until they told them of the sweet spot on the prow of the boat.

A small triangular area caught the light breeze coming off the spray cast up above the bow as the boat cut through the water. No one knew how long it took to succumb to sleep, other than waking abruptly in the twilight hours wondering what was wrong.

That day turned out to be the worst they had ever experienced. When dawn arrived, they found each boat tied up in a cove on one of the small, uninhabited islands, not much more than a mini-jungle right down to the water's edge that was more rock than sand.

They helped camouflage the boats with palm leaves, then moved inland to hide and find shade. It was now back to at least eighty per cent humidity, which after the dry heat of the African desert was intolerable.

The Lieutenant had given orders for them to off-load one of the chariots so that the men could occupy their time by catching up on valuable practice, at the same time cooling down in the shaded waters of a small lagoon.

"What's the point," Private Collins mumbled.

Being a demolitions expert, he saw no reason. He was more concerned about running down the battery that would be their only lifeline when they had to return.

Lieutenant Bradley made a point of explaining the batteries they were using were not the ones set aside for the mission. Bereft of further excuses, Collins had to admit this was really all about the fact that he hated the water, and never was any good at aqua diving; always sucking in when he should be blowing out.

The next landfall was to be Blakang Mati Island, where the final approach to the Singapore Garrison using the chariots would take place. Lieutenant Lonergan called a meeting with Lieutenant Bradley in the cramped galley of the MTB in the late afternoon.

The operatives chatted amongst themselves until the two men arrived.

"Okay… Lieutenant Bradley is going to run through this last leg, and give you his opinion on our mission status should things run to plan."

"Thanks, Lieutenant," he said, unfolding a chart and spreading it out across the small dining table. "This is the situation. We've had a better than expected run up the Sumatran coast, here," he pointed, "up through the island chain, where I expected to see some native activity that may have slowed us down. What I mean by that is: we are not sure who is with the Japs or us now, so I was concerned there may be some radio traffic to a possible gunboat in the area. We know there is definitely one and possibly two in this region. They are moving in fast now… you just made it. I would say that by this time next week they would have boats in amongst most of these islands. However, there's been no traffic anywhere in the immediate vicinity so far, which is a good sign.

He hesitated, as the men hung on every word. What he was not about to speculate on was, the situation on their return journey.

"Just because there's no radio traffic, Sir, does that mean the Japs aren't there?" Private Guldon interrupted. "Couldn't they just be waiting for us?"

There was a nodding of heads and mumbles around the table.

"That is a possibility," the Lieutenant answered, "but we have to assume they haven't arrived yet, knowing, as we do, that these waters were free of Japanese ships prior to the fall of Singapore. We've been patrolling this area for over a year now and we haven't come across any yet."

"Then what was that about one, or possibly two gunboats?" Collins said.

"Information supplied from spotters. We have several hidden out amongst the islands off Singapore, and we had two reports of gunboats leaving Singapore and moving into the islands, nothing nearer than that."

"How fast can they travel?" McCulloch questioned.

"Stop!" Lieutenant Lonergan shouted. "This is not a question time. The Lieutenant has kindly agreed to bring you up-to-date on the situation, not listen to your concerns. Put any future questions through me."

They averted their eyes.

"Right lads, where was I... oh yes. This also means I've managed to get you quicker through the islands than I planned, and if we set off in the next half hour continuing at our previous speed, I should be able to land you behind the target island by 20:30 tonight, which is here," he pointed to the last island below Singapore. "With the prevailing currents in this area, I estimate you'll reach the Garrison by approximately 22:00, under water. I don't know how long you require for your mission, but if you wish to return to the boat during darkness, you'll have to be back on your chariots by 03:30."

"That's ample time," said John Hebden, who was the operations controller. "I think we'll need some leeway on both underwater journeys quite frankly."

"Yes, I agree," Lieutenant Lonergan said. "Also, I'd like to know how reliable these beacons are when we return."

"Well we haven't had any problems with them so far. However, I did point out to one of your drivers... " he paused looking at Mark for his name.

"Private Guldon, Sir," he prompted.

"That's right Private Guldon, sorry. If you remember, I showed you the release mechanism for the rescue buoy on the chariot."

"That's right, Sir. It sends a small orange float to the surface on a line, which in turn also emits a signal. How do we know if it's working?"

The Lieutenant stood up and stretched across to an overhead locker. Lifting the lid, he retrieved one of the small beacons and sat down again.

"When you press this button, one of two lights will come on. If it's green we've picked you up, if it's red we haven't, it all works on the Sonar principle."

"Any more questions?" Lieutenant Lonergan asked.

There was no reply. Some just sat there blank faced, others began making notes on their plastic boards that they could read under water.

"Okay chaps, that looks like we're on, I'll call you at 20:30 hours."

As the boats continued on their way, Lieutenant Lonergan stressed they should get what rest they could until landfall. This was easy for some, like Guldon, Hebden and McCulloch; they could fall asleep on a railway track, as they proved many times in a sand storm. Chessman never appeared to sleep, always playing his chess game whenever he could. As for the others, they were too nervous to do anything.

Collins aimlessly wandered the limited space below deck. Drake, Farney and Lieutenant Lonergan fell into their usual routine, dismantling their weapons and rebuilding them again. A habit they all got into in the desert; the sand worked its way into every crevice, if you let it; unnecessary here, but still essential if you wanted your weapons to work when you needed them.

Superintendent Stone was suddenly aware of a change in the book's tempo. Reading ahead of himself, as he often did when anxious to learn an outcome, he realised, from here on the ending was contrived. General Carter had based his account of the journey from Aden to Singapore on the debriefing with each man, including cited quotes and the emotions of the occasion, but as soon as he asked what happened at Percival's HQ, they closed ranks and became silent: with only the codebook as proof of a successful mission.

CHAPTER 15

Mark was a little apprehensive when he picked Stone up the following morning, after his harrowing experience the previous day, and the abruptness with which he left; he was surprised to find him in such good humour, and naturally smelling a lot better.

It was 8:30 am. A bright day, and there was no more than a half hour journey ahead of them to the Queens Head in Hackney, where Ralph Collins was the tenant landlord.

"Good morning, Boss, you look in a better mood today."

Stone spread his nostrils and sniffed the air. "There you are, not a hint of that place," he replied. "Do you know it took six nasal douches last night to clear my head of that woman's foul animals, and my suit was ruined."

"I bet you parcelled it up for the cleaner's quick enough."

"No way... straight into the incinerator, everything I was wearing, all gone."

"That was a bit drastic, Boss," he commented, as he turned into the busy morning traffic, knowing the amount of money his boss spent on clothes.

"I wasn't going to let someone else smell my clothes; I couldn't look them in the face. Anyway, enough of that, did you bring this man's file. Who is it... Ralph Collins?"

"Yes, Boss… it's on the back seat, with the others if you're interested."

As Mark battled his way through the honking taxis and early morning sign language, Stone busied himself reading the thin files of the remaining men who were part of that memorable event in Singapore. What happened there was going to be the lynch-pin of this case, according to Hammond, and it was imperative that they find out what followed. Stone secretly hoped there would be a simple solution.

"Here we are, Boss, the Queens Head, Hackney."

They looked up at the balding man polishing a stained glass decoration above the Saloon door. He wanted to know who they were looking for; opening time was not for a while yet. They showed their warrant cards, and asked for the proprietor.

"You're looking at him," Collins said, throwing his chamois into the bucket. "You must be the cops that want to interview me?"

"That's right," Stone replied, somewhat surprised.

He expected Collins to be in his dotage, until he realised they were only boys back then: Carter's boys.

"Come through here then, it'll be more private."

Collins had the hint of an east-end accent, with something else Stone could not put his finger on. His years in the army probably accounted for that, spending most of the time, in his younger years, in foreign lands.

He took them into a small room off the main lounge, looking as if it was doubling between an office and a well-used bed-sit. In front of the small desk up against the back wall was a card table. He pulled out one of the four chairs around the table and gestured to them to do the same. It was apparent that he used this room for more things than just doing his books; although cramped, it evidently served its purpose.

"Mr Collins, you understood what we meant yesterday about you being in danger?"

He hesitated for a moment, and then sat down at the table, looking decidedly uncomfortable. Mark's phone call must have stirred up bad memories.

"Oh yeah, I think. It was terrible about the others; I haven't seen any of them for ages, not since the last reunion. Who is this maniac anyway?"

"Well, Mr Collins, we're not sure, that's why we need your cooperation."

"Sure... sure, anything you want, I don't want any butcher carving me up."

Stone looked at him intently, he was not sure if he was ready for the truth yet.

"But, Mr Collins, you were a 'Behind the lines' man at one time, so you should be able to handle yourself," Stone started.

"Sure, anything," he said, sweating.

"This maniac as you call him, strung your mates up, stripped them and cut them up badly. Not being satisfied with that, he nailed them up on a crucifix and cut their genitals off; all while they were still conscious, then garrotted them."

Mark looked horrified at his Boss's initial approach; Collins was shaking and sweating profusely by now.

"You're trying to frighten me aren't you... why?"

"Because, Mr Collins, that's going to happen to you if we don't catch this man, and that will only come about if you tell us the whole truth."

"You already admitted I could take care of myself, so why the scare?"

"So could your friends, and look what happened... the truth, Mr Collins."

"Okay... I get the point, Superintendent, just the truth, I promise."

"You didn't tell the truth at the inquiry after you returned from Singapore. You all stayed silent, just reporting the bare facts."

"All right!" he shouted, pressing a beer-mat onto the table they were sitting at until it snapped in half. "What do you want to know?"

Stone looked at Mark with his particular look that meant it was time for him to start taking notes. He was also aware, on his first cursory look around the room, that Collins had a copy of the General's book. It still looked pristine, just as he received it.

"Okay, Mr Collins, I notice you have the General's book, so we can take it for granted that we all know what happened on your journey from Aden to the island off Singapore. Do we agree?. Mark looked puzzled, he was not aware.

"I suppose so," Collins said, looking nervously over in the book's direction. "I haven't had a chance to read it yet, but... I trust the General to get it right."

"It doesn't matter," Stone said. "What happened during that part of the journey is immaterial; it's what happened at Percival's HQ that I'm interested in, especially the detail on why Chessman didn't return with you."

"You know his nickname then?"

"We know quite a lot, so I'll know if you're filling me full of blarney."

Collins looked at him with a blank stare, "Shall I start now?"

"Yes. But start from when you left the small island."

Like the General, Collins had to dig deep into a past he preferred to forget. Then he stood up, went over to a small bar against the wall, and brought back a bottle of whisky, three glasses and a packet of cigarettes. A large red chunky ashtray was already sitting in the middle of the table. The short interval irritated Stone.

Like most barmen, he had the knack of holding several glasses in one hand and waved them in front of their faces before setting them down on the table. They looked at each other, as if to say why not, and nodded their heads. He poured three fingers in each, placed the bottle beside his seat, and sat down.

He looked nervous; trying to recollect a time that he had gone to great lengths to bury, which surprisingly, began to take shape once he conjured the first moments.

"Whatever we'd heard about the warm balmy waters of the Pacific," he started, "was not true that night when we dropped in alongside the chariots. We had a hard time climbing into our seats. We had forgotten everything the Aussies on the Coco's base had told us about counterbalancing the vessel first."

"Keep it simple, Mr Collins," Mark said, having difficulty taking notes

"Very well," Stone said. "Carry on, Mr Collins, only a little slower please."

Collins gulped another mouthful and continued. "We were all shaking so much with the cold, even in our wet suits, that our power of thought was sluggish. Once we acclimatised, and received a round of good luck's from the crew, we checked our gear one last time before stowing it in the compartment where the explosives used to be.

"Once Private Guldon finally managed to get us down just above the white sandy bottom, and maintained a course without dragging our feet, the going became much easier. It was surprising how fast the chariots could really go, reassuring also, after giving thought to the possibility of outrunning any curious sharks."

"Sharks... at that time?" Stone said.

"Yes. They don't sleep you know."

"Oh yes, I remember... carry on."

"Right... err... we eventually arrived at the encrusted jetty supports we were told to head for. That was after the detour we had to make around a bunch of Jeeps that had been discarded by the garrison forces before the Japs arrived."

He took another drink, finishing his glass, and poured another. Mark was about to say something but Stone shook his head; he wanted to know what this man was feeling; assuming he was reliving the experience.

"It was terrible. There were corpses everywhere and broken rifles and would you believe it, furniture, crockery and artillery guns... it was horrific. Finally, we found a clear section between the supports where we pushed the chariots out of sight, switched them off and retrieved our gear. On surfacing, we found Lieutenant Lonergan had already left for his reconnoitre to establish the site of the General's headquarters, so we hid ourselves in some shrubs. Before long, he returned. He gave us a silent indication of the direction each man should take. We split up into three teams: James McCulloch, Mark Guldon and Steve Farney were on point, covering the main activities."

"Just stop there a moment," Stone interrupted him. "This is a crucial part, and I want every detail down pat. Okay, Inspector?"

"Yes, Boss."

"Now you say McCulloch, Guldon and Farney were on point."

"Yes, Superintendent," Collins agreed.

"Explain that, and their proximity to the HQ building."

"Well point means simply they were to watch everyone else's arse. We usually did that by fanning out in a broad sweep from the target in a staggered position overlapping each other, far enough away so that we could each cover a third of our radius."

"Very well... how far from the building?"

"Since the area immediately outside the small lawn surrounding the HQ was mainly rainforest, I'd say no more than fifty feet."

"So each of you had a perfect view of the building?"

"Oh yes."

"Good... continue, Mr Collins."

Collins was becoming impatient himself.

"Right," he said, "Lieutenant Lonergan, Martin Drake and John Hebden made for the headquarters; Chessman waited outside with the radio while I searched the perimeter for booby-traps, trip-wires, that sort of thing, and began preparing the explosives in the event that the mission had to be aborted, and the headquarters destroyed."

"Sorry... stop there again," Stone said, "So while the other three were in the building, Chessman was left on his own for some time?"

"I wouldn't say that, Superintendent."

He looked nervous again.

"Well you just said you went off to check for booby-traps and prepare explosives. I gather by that you meant around the building?"

"That's correct. But I wasn't away more than a few moments each time. We had to be quick... we only had a limited window. And the charges were already prepared."

"Then why say you prepared them?"

"Sorry... wrong use of words. I should have said placed them."

Ralph Collins stopped abruptly, unlike the many pauses he had made during his dissertation, this was different; he implied he had finished.

"Is that it?" Stone urged, "What happened then?"

"I didn't go inside, so I don't know."

"Well what happened when they came out?"

"Oh... well all hell let loose before that."

"So... carry on with your story."

"It must have been about ten minutes after they entered the building," he said, "Chessman was having some conversation with them on the radio, I didn't hear all of it, but it was mainly about the difficulty they were having going from room to room; apparently the doors had been nailed shut. Anyway, after a while we received a signal from McCulloch that a group of Japs were heading this way, just sauntering along.

"Chessman told the others, but they weren't ready. Then McCulloch signalled us again, saying they had turned off and were out of sight, which Chessman also relayed to the Lieutenant, who in turn instructed him to take McCulloch and have a better look at what the Japs were doing; he had to know what they were up to. They were going to be at least another five minutes." Collins caught the Inspector's puzzled expression, "I was kneeling down next to Chessman by now... I heard everything."

Collins took another drink then continued his tale.

He said, "All hell let loose. Chessman and McCulloch had moved up towards where they last saw the Jap patrol and walked straight into them. No one knew whether the Japs had seen the team and were flanking us, or just came across us by bad luck. There was only a few short bursts, ours I think... it sounded like our weapons, and a couple of single shots, and the next thing McCulloch and Chessman came crawling back... all the Japs were dead. I wondered why they were crawling, I would have been running myself, but I saw Chessman was bleeding like a pig. The noise brought out the Lieutenant's team, who had fortunately just found the codebook and were on their way back. The Lieutenant examined Chessman, and then just told everyone to go... he was finished."

Collins looked terrible.

"Hold it there for a moment, you're doing great. Catch your breath, have another drink... stretch your legs if you want," Stone said.

Collins jumped up urgently, and without a word, he left the room. They soon heard him retching. He returned, pale and gaunt, opened a small bottle of soda where the whisky was and gulped it down in one go.

"I think we'll call it a day, Mr Collins," Stone said, concerned.

Collins returned to his seat, "No you don't. I'm nearly finished anyway."

"As you wish," Stone said, relieved. "In your own time."

Collins wiped his mouth with a hanky, cleared his throat and looked as if he was trying to recall where he left off.

"The Lieutenant had just told you to leave," Mark read out.

"Ah yes... I remember. There was a commotion back up where the Japs came from; others were following. The Lieutenant ordered everyone back to the chariots, throwing the codebook to Martin and telling him to get going to the pick-up point the instant he was ready... and Private Farney was to wait with the other chariot for only five minutes, if he didn't arrive by then, Farney and myself was to follow the others.

"Farney wanted to know what was going to happen to Chessman... he was closer to him than the rest of us. He sounded upset at the thought of leaving him. The Lieutenant looked up at him. I remember the look on his face... he could have shot him there and then. He was usually such a compassionate man... always ready to put others first before himself."

"What did he do?" Stone questioned.

"He told Farney to follow orders. He said he would take care of Chessman.

As the others left, the Lieutenant knelt down beside Chessman, and undid his wetsuit to see how bad he was. All the time Chessman was begging him not to leave him for the Japs, 'Kill me, Kill me,' he kept crying out. The Lieutenant removed his radio equipment, and then reached across his body with his right hand for his automatic. He appeared to be having trouble getting it out of the holster. Then he saw me. I was hanging about on the edge of the trees to see what he was going to do. He cried out in a muffled voice, 'I told you to leave, that's an order.' I said I was on his chariot; that I would wait for him like Farney. But he obviously didn't want any witnesses."

Stone could see this last bit was difficult, "Take your time."

"I could see he meant it, the look in his eyes made me think he would shoot me too if he had to, so I left. My last sight of them was the Lieutenant pointing his gun at Chessman's head. Between there and the water I heard a shot, followed by a quick succession of other shots, rifle fire, by the sounds of it. I was back at the jetty by then. I couldn't see Farney anywhere, until I heard bubbles breaking the surface, and realised he must have gone down to get the chariot ready.

"Then the Lieutenant arrived alone. He was out of breath from running; we could hear the agitated voices of the Japs coming after us. 'Go... Go!, he screamed, they're only seconds behind. We dived into the dark water, and I started searching for my aqua gear. Then I spotted Farney sitting on the chariot with my gear, waving his arms. I stuffed the mouthpiece into my mouth first, took a deep breath, then climbed aboard just as the Lieutenant squeezed in behind me, helping me with the straps, just as a mass of white fizzy lines penetrated the surface, hitting the sand all about us.

"The bullets were still hissing through the water in front of us, when Farney manoeuvred the chariot under the jetty, then turned, and deftly worked his way through the maze of supports to the other side. We came out on the bad side that we avoided on our way in, were all the sunken Jeeps and other wreckage was, but we managed to get around them, and passed the Japs, and out into clear water.

"When we finally arrived at the rendezvous point on the other side of the small island, following our team-mates, the MTB was already waiting above, its engines slowly ticking over. We surfaced, the boat's crew lifted us onto the deck, then quickly booby-trapped the chariot and sent it back to the bottom. Collins chuckled, "I remember one of the Aussie's saying: 'they're no good now mate, so let's give the Japs a little surprise. I laughed... I remembered my own little surprise. I turned back to look in the direction of the headquarters and checked my watch. There was an enormous explosion on the horizon; I tripped the timer on my charges just before I left."

"I thought that was only in the event that you couldn't get the codebook?" Stone questioned, "... in and out without them knowing."

"That was the best scenario. But we were seen, weren't we?"

"When McCulloch and Guldon fired on the Japs?" Stone prompted.

"Right. We were blown when they did that," Collins said.

"They had little option," the Inspector spoke up.

"They had plenty of shrubs to crawl into"

There was a sudden resentment in Collins' voice.

"We're digressing gentlemen," Stone interrupted. "Can we continue?"

Collins shook his head, took another drink and started again, "Once we were all on board, the two boats picked up speed and began weaving their way back through the islands. The others had already disappeared below exhausted, leaving me on deck. I had been so preoccupied with the dangerous departure I gave little thought to Chessman, and then it hit me, forcing me to stay up top.

"When I eventually returned to the others, I stumbled into the middle of a terrible row. They were accusing the Lieutenant of leaving Chessman behind, in enemy territory. The Lieutenant on the other hand, was attempting to defend himself by telling them Chessman was dead. I stepped in and confirmed this, even though I only heard the shot fired. The group didn't survive that night; we were never the same again.”

Collins stopped once more, tears running down his cheeks.

“Take it easy,” Mark said, finishing his notes.

“That’s it. I can’t do any more... it’s too painful.”

“I understand,” Stone said, a little disappointed. But there was the other two to finish the story. “You got back all right, that’s the main thing.”

Collins laughed, “By the skin of our teeth. They were waiting for us... the Japs I mean. The little bastards blew the other boat right out of the water. But not before he sunk them both, good riddance, I say.”

“I don’t suppose you want to elaborate on that?” Stone asked.

“No way... I’m finished. You’ve messed my head up right proper with your questions. I won’t sleep for weeks now.”

Collins looked sadly at Stone and Mark closed his notebook.

“That’s it... the end,” he said, “except for that terrible homecoming. We were on deck when the MTB arrived back at the Cocos; I will never forget the looks on those men’s faces when only one boat returned.

“Well... that’s quite a story, Mr Collins,” Stone commented.

“Pity you can’t say positively that Chessman was killed,” Mark added.

“Oh come on, I saw the man kneeling over him with a gun to his head.”

“But you said yourself, you heard many shots.”

“I can tell the difference between an automatic at close range, and long distant rifle fire,” Collins was now on the defensive. “What are you trying to say?”

“All I’m implying is it’s possible that he didn’t die, therefore also possible he has returned to seek retribution for being left behind.”

“What after all this time, what’s he been doing all these years?”

“That’s what we’d like to know. And what about the pawns

around their neck? Chessman was the only one interested in chess."

"You didn't tell me they had pawns around their necks, is that why you think Chessman's still alive?"

"All right," Stone said. "I'll leave a police surveillance around the clock.

"Anyone suspicious, Collins," the Inspector continued. "Our suspect may well have. disguised himself as an Indian to put us off his track."

Collins laughed, "Here, in Hackney... you should see the place on a Saturday night. I know what I'll give him if he bothers me," he said, and looked up above the small bar at a fine example of a Samurai sword and its small sharp companion.

CHAPTER 16

The next day Mark had decided on an early start; he thought it would impress his boss if he had the Collins interview all typed up ready for him when he arrived. It took longer than he expected, and when he returned from the typing pool Stone was already sitting at his desk.

"I tell you what, Boss," he said, on entering his office, "If I hadn't taken a course in shorthand, you wouldn't have got this lot before the end of the month."

"What are you grumbling about now, Mark?" Stone replied, putting the phone down, and leaning back in his chair.

"Oh... sorry Boss, I didn't know you were on the phone," he placed the pile of typed notes from the Collins interview on his desk.

Stone flipped the corner of the pile, "He should write a book."

"That's what I was implying, Boss when I was saying..."

"Okay... okay, I get the drift. The department is grateful for night-schools."

"Was the call interesting?"

"What makes you think that?"

"Go on, Boss, I know when you're bursting to tell me something."

"Do you remember the last thing Collins said yesterday?"

The Inspector tried to clear his mind of the whole story

and think.

"Not without checking my notes, it became automatic after a while."

Stone referred to the fact that Collins was hoping the killer did come, as he glanced up at his Samurai sword on the wall.

"That's right, Boss... a fine set they were too."

"Didn't it remind you of anything?"

Mark thought for a moment, "I can't say it did, Boss."

"Come on man... think. It was in the pathology report Hammond gave us. It didn't dawn on me straight away until I was mulling over what Collins said."

"The wounds on his chest, Boss," Mark shouted.

"That's right: Long sword marks with small knife nicks."

"Yes... of course."

"Well I was just talking to forensics and they said they wanted to see Collins sword and knife. They also referred to their latest report on Lonergan's home, in particular to his collection of weapons, where he too had a Samurai, which they suggested was also a good candidate, although, apparently Hammond's forensic team ruled them out."

"Yes I remember now, it's on the board," Mark agreed.

Stone realised with that statement, he had not seen the board since he returned from Cantrell's house. A lapse he had to rectify.

"We could have questioned him about them, if you had reminded me."

"Like you, Boss, it didn't click with me. You don't suspect Collins now; do you?"

"Well he had the motive, the opportunity and it appears, possibly the weapons."

"He didn't strike me as being the type, but I suppose you have a point."

Stone's brow furrowed, "Get the Samurai set and let's have

them checked out."

"Right away, Boss. Anything else?"

Stone returned to the typed notes, "Will you do a copy of these for Mary?"

"I was just bringing them in; I thought you might be seeing her soon."

"I intend to brief her on our progress before she goes to see this... who is it."

"Steve Farney, Boss... at Folkestone."

"That's right. I think she'll be able to handle him better than us if he's not quite all there. We can make better use of our time checking up on Collins' movements during the periods in question. Rule him out altogether."

"So it's heading more the way you like it now."

"How's that?"

"Well... you've got three suspects now, the Indian, Chessman and Collins."

"Well it's better than beating our heads against a brick wall trying to fill in forty year old gaps: that's what it's all about, you know. If we could only bridge that time period with some reasonable explanation we could get on with this thing."

"Why don't I give that to Freeman as a project?"

"What do you mean?"

"Well... we desperately need a new angle, Boss. Why don't I feed what we know to him, and see if he can link them together and come up with some motives."

"Motives... have a heart, Mark; it's taking us all our time to come up with one."

"I was talking in the plural, Boss. When you think about it, we could have more than one killer here; judging by the number of different angled wounds."

Stone's mouth dropped open as he suddenly contemplated

this new possibility. For Mark it was only a casual observation, one he would have to think about before giving it any credence. He never expected Stone to take him seriously.

"Good point, Mark," he said studiously. "Look into it"

"What about Freeman, Boss?"

"Freeman"

"The forty year project."

"Ah... yes, I suppose it won't do any harm, Okay, good idea," Stone started clearing his desk before he left. "Anyway I promised Mary I'd drop this stuff off so she could go over it before tomorrow."

"All right, Boss, I don't suppose I'll see much of you today."

"We'll see, somehow I think Mary will come up with a lot more questions."

Mark smiled to himself as he went to find Freeman.

He was not far away: talking to one of the female constables working on the board. He looked as if he was more interested in her as he fed her yesterday's information.

"Constable Freeman," Mark called out on his way to the board.

"Yes, Sir," he quickly replied, turning round.

"I've got a nice little job for you."

"I hope it's not like the last one."

"Oh no," he said, "You know that we have this gap between the suspected incident in Singapore and the start of the murders."

"Yes, that's if the two are connected," Constable Freeman commented, not placing as much faith in all this vengeance from the past stuff.

"Well don't let the Super hear you say that. He's basing our whole line of investigation on something happening on the mission to Singapore. It's the only scenario that links all these men together. And we found out yesterday from Collins, that they left Chessman behind, presumably dead."

"Okay then, Sir, so what's the problem with the time gap?"

"Well for one we can't work out why the killer waited so long to start his retribution. It's that gap in time that's throwing everything out. I suggested that maybe a fresh mind on the problem might come up with something."

"Where shall I start?"

"I don't know. That would be influencing you, and would defeat the whole exercise. You're supposed to be looking at this from a fresh view-point."

"Okay, I know now what you're saying, Sir."

"Good... then get on with it, you're going to be very busy."

Stone had arranged to meet Mary at her office, but he was not ready for Mary's change of mind. When he arrived, she told him not to settle down as she had booked lunch at this quaint restaurant.

"I thought we were going through the case first."

"Oh dear me, Simon, have I upset your plans?"

"Well... I thought we could work through on the case with a few sandwiches, and then possibly make a night of it on the town."

"On the town, Simon. I'm hardly dressed for that."

"Well you could freshen up at your place first."

"I see... that's what it's all about, is it. You expected a candlelit dinner."

"We never appear to get any further than office banter."

"That's because we're both busy people, Simon. Like you, I have little time for a personal life after my day at work. You have no idea how many cases I have pushed to one side just so I can go to Folkestone tomorrow."

"I still say it's a shame you can't relax sometime, you can't be expected to be rational all the time," Stone concluded. He said his piece, so that was the end of it.

"Well for now let's just enjoy our dinner and I'll go through this heavy interview with you. I'll have to if we're going off early in the morning."

"That's just it, Mary... you'll have to go on your own."

"I see. So that's what this is all about."

"No it isn't... Mark and I have neglected the forensic evidence from the house in Uxbridge. I'm still not so sure the killer was only interested in the general's house to get the other names. I suspect he will return."

"I had that feeling too," Mary agreed.

"You see, we are on the same wave-length," Stone rasped.

"All right, I'll do my best with Farney tomorrow."

The dinner they had was Italian; in the style of small appetising dishes, ideal on this occasion, allowing them to go through Collins' story in between each course. By the time they arrived at the dessert, she was trying to understand what happened to Chessman.

"No, Mary," Stone explained. "Maybe it's lost something in the transcription from Mark's shorthand. "If you recall, General Carter said they were not to leave any wounded behind. So as Collins said, Lonergan shot Chessman."

"So you're implying that we only have Collins' word that this took place, and in fact Chessman could actually be alive," she said.

"Exactly," Stone exclaimed, finally he was getting somewhere.

"So why are we pursuing these other two men, if they were on their chariot at the time, unable to shed any further light on the situation."

"I just want to corroborate Collins' story of what happened before they left for the jetty, because if it is true, he was the only one alone with Lonergan and Chessman, and some confrontation took place about leaving him there, that gives him a motive, making him as much a suspect as anyone."

The waiter interrupted, "Shall I bring the coffee now?" he asked.

"Yes please," Mary said, looking at her watch, "Oh, look at the time, If I'm going to get an early start we'll have to leave after this."

"I was hoping we might call in at my place for drinks."

Mary laughed, "And I suppose you have everything laid out."

Stone shook his head, hoping his motives were not that obvious.

"Am I so easy to read," he said.

"I'm afraid so, Simon. But don't concern yourself, you're in good company."

By the time Stone saw Mary home, tried his technique once again and failed, he was feeling lonely on his drive back to his apartment on the other side of the city. He threw his jacket across the couch, poured himself a double whisky and reached for his briefcase. If nothing else, he could find solace in his work.

He took out the files and spread them out beside him on the couch. Each one had its own familiarity; and as he drank his whisky, he recalled each group of facts. But one file stood out amongst the others, if only by its colour: His squad room used green folders for evidence and blue for suspects. This folder was pink. It had to be one of Jack Hammond's.

His drink was finished and he decided on a refill before opening the file. He hesitated, sipping the whisky and staring at Hammond's scrawling hand at the top of the cover. It brought back memories of those early days together.

Their rivalry was not apparent at first; it was something that developed during the course of the Academy trials. Thinking about that time, in present hindsight, Stone realised it had to be Sergeant Baker that brought them together and engendered the competition.

Out of the group of fifteen recruits, he singled out Hammond and Stone. They were the brightest of the bunch and the Sergeant instinctively used them as a driving example for the others to follow. The process was so gradual, their naivety failed to notice. Then one day, Stone was suddenly aware Hammond was leaving him behind.

They were painful memories of being second to Jack all through their tests. His choice to copy Jack's final report was a big gambol, according to Jack, but his luck was with him that day. Now Jack is the one following him.

CHAPTER 17

Mary's revelation the night before changed everything. Stone had lost a vital link to what happened to Chessman, reducing whatever chance he had of corroborating Collins' statement down to the remaining operative: Major Martin Drake.

Once out of London, it was a motorway journey all the way to the Harrogate turn-off. On entering the town centre, through a massive expanse of common grassland and trees called the 'Stray', Stone turned right onto the Ripon road and left again down a shady tree lined avenue of well-established old houses that reminded him of his doctor's; in an opulent area where he lived as a boy in Middlesex.

As Stone sat taking in the surroundings before leaving the car: contemplating how the better half lived. It was hard to tell if the Major's house was trying to emulate the Tudor style, but not quite as good as the General's house. The lower section looked Gothic with an arched stone doorway and heavy black wooden door.

All the windows were of the diamond patterned leaded type surrounded by small expertly cut stones, inlaid into a rough brick exterior. The occupants must have been watching for him, as the front door squeaked open before he managed to place his foot on the polished black and white tiled porch.

"Superintendent Stone?" came the question from an elderly

woman that he took for Drake's wife, until another came to the door and opened it wider.

"It's all right, Hilda, I'll get it," the other woman said.

"How do you do," Stone said, to an attractive younger woman.

"Come in, you'll have to excuse Hilda, she's my father's housekeeper, and thinks she has to open the door all the time."

"That's okay, so you're Martin Drake's daughter?" he said in conversation.

She led him from the door across the hall to a large room. He sensed Drake lived on his own; despite the housekeeper, it was bereft of a woman's touch. His daughter said she had only moved in recently to care for him.

"Daddy... Superintendent Stone is here," she called out to the man by the fire.

He turned his greying head to face him, revealing a ruddy complexion, bifocal glasses, and a dapper grey moustache.

"Superintendent," he said, like a pronouncement. It was easy to tell he was a career Army man. "How can I be of assistance to you?" his daughter left them alone.

Stone walked over to where he was sitting, "We're making inquiries about a group of murders, Sir; serial murders in fact, which involve past soldiers you are familiar with."

"Oh sorry, Superintendent, sit down," he said looking concerned, motioning to a chair alongside him. "I've known a lot of soldiers in my career Superintendent, but none that I would say I was familiar with."

"Not even those of 'Moustache', Sir?"

"Good heavens, I haven't heard that name in years."

"I thought you might have heard it only last year at the General's reunion to launch his book of your group's escapades and others like you."

"You're very well informed, Superintendent, I shall have to

think twice before I answer any of your questions again," he laughed, Stone hoped it was a joke.

"I've already heard the very same remarks from others in your squad. I have to tell you before we go any further that four of your comrades are already dead."

"Four... Superintendent?"

"Yes, Sir: McCulloch, Guldon, Hebden and Lonergan."

"Lieutenant Lonergan... my god how awful."

"Like you he stayed in the Army and retired as a Colonel."

"Oh did he," he uttered surprised. "We didn't discuss such things at the reunion; the General preferred it that way."

"You mean you didn't want to swagger with the General. The three of you did well, whereas the others didn't."

"Is that indicating we had something to do with these murders?"

"No of course not, Sir, I'm sorry if it sounded like that. You are in no way under suspicion, in fact, as was told to you when this interview was made, you are in extreme danger, as are the other two: Collins and Farney."

"Oh dear Farney, how is he. I heard he ended up in a veteran's home with some form of mania," he asked condescendingly.

"He's in a state of mental dysfunction. So a lot depends on you, Sir."

"Oh dear... I liked Farney."

The Major was beginning to annoy Stone. He seemed to forget his place at the time of the incident, just one of the team. His promotion and the subsequent change in his lifestyle belonged to another time.

"As a matter of interest, Sir, how are you doing?"

"If by that you mean, why am I wrapped up in this rug hugging the fire. I have cancer, that's why my daughter's looking after me."

"I'm sorry to hear that, Sir... and equally sorry I had to disturb you."

"It's my lot, Superintendent... as they say. Now, how can I help you?"

"Do you have any contact with the Army anymore?"

"Not for some time now. Nor do I have with the other members of the group you mentioned. So I don't know how I can help you really."

"Let me put it this way, Major. This maniac has already killed four of your team, and there's no indication that he intends stopping there; unless we catch him first."

"Not if I can help it," he stated, taking a small automatic from his jacket pocket. "He'll have to be good to get the better of me."

"He did the others, with just the same training."

"That's what I can't understand, unless he was as skilled as them."

"That's a possibility we're looking into, although he may have had an advantage. He used chloroform to subdue his victims."

"Maybe so, Superintendent, but the killer still had to apply it. Any of our team in such a situation would instinctively react. Their training you know."

"Exactly. That's why we can't rule out the remaining team members. It's possible the killer was someone they knew; someone who was able to get close and surprise them."

"Well... as you can see, other than my gun, I couldn't attack anyone."

"I understand, Sir... just as Farney. So that just leaves Collins, who was the only one who witnessed Lonergan killing Chessman."

"Chessman? Now there was a character worthy of a mental home."

"Why would you say that?"

"Didn't you know he was a homosexual?"

"No... I didn't."

"That's why he played solo chess all the time, to keep away from his team mates; they just put him down as a fanatic. Although, after a few years it was hard to tell what he was."

"And they didn't know?"

"Well no one ever said as much, and I'm sure they would have; you know what men in close quarters are like."

"Yes I do, I was in the Army myself."

"Oh were you; War or peacetime?"

"Korea as a matter of fact."

"Ah yes... the forgotten war. I wouldn't have fancied it myself... too political."

They kept digressing. This enquiry: delving into the past was tiring Stone: Too many ghosts that kept popping up to muddy the waters.

"Major, I've had quite a bit of background on why you went to Singapore, how you got there and what happened afterwards. But there appears to be some confusion about the period between leaving the chariots below the jetty and your hasty retreat."

"Why the particular interest in the Singapore job?"

"Because we believe these murders stem from what happened to Chessman, a sort of retribution if you like. But by whom, and why has it taken so long?"

The Major placed the small gun back into his pocket under the blanket.

"I see... it was a long time ago. Some of it's a bit vague, but I won't forget that event as long as I live. I sometimes dream about it, not so much the life threatening aspect, heaven knows we lived with that all the time, but no one was happy with the idea that we were covertly going onto an island with 100,000 prisoners to find a book and then leave without doing anything to help them. And in later years, as it became apparent how many died or were abominably treated, I constantly relived that event."

"I can understand what you all must have gone through, I myself was witness to some terrible things in the Korean campaign," Stone sympathised.

"What they did with prisoners was why Chessman was

terrified when he was hit.”

“Let’s not jump things, Major; I’d like to hear the whole thing as it happened.”

“Very Well. As you said, we arrived in the dark under the jetty.”

“Sorry to interrupt you, Major,” Stone said, “Something just occurred to me, I don’t know why it should with you; it didn’t with the others.”

“What is that, Superintendent?”

“It just occurred to me; if you landed in the dark, how did everyone see what was going on. Especially the Japs coming down towards you.”

“Oh that’s easy. They chose that time because it was a full moon. Have you ever seen a full moon in the tropics, Superintendent?”

“Well I don’t consider Korea the tropics, and that’s as far as I’ve been”

“It’s big, Superintendent. We landed around 22:00, that’s ten o’clock.”

“I know my twenty-four hour clock, Major.”

The old man frowned, being used to people pandering to him.

“Sorry. Well at that time of the year, it never really got dark, only a sort of constant twilight and we were well used to seeing what they were doing at night; and the Garrison was lit up like Piccadilly Circus.”

“Well I suppose that answers that. Please continue, Major.”

“As I was saying, we removed our equipment bags from the chariots, and left our aqualungs etcetera under water, before we went to the surface. The Lieutenant had already allocated our positions; do you want those?”

“Yes please, as much detail as you can.”

“Right. The Lieutenant, Hebden and I were to go into the building. McCulloch, Farney and Guldon were on point; protecting our backs. Collins... our demolitions man, was to check the perimeter for booby traps and position explosives to destroy the HQ, while Chessman, on wireless, was to wait outside the building and monitor the communications. When we landed, everything was quiet. I think it was because the administration end of the complex was not in use at the time. From that point on nothing was said, it was all sign language, everyone going about their designated tasks, leaving the three of us trying to figure out how to get into the damned place.

"Chessman set himself up behind a convenient bush by the door whilst we entered the building. Once inside it was headlights on, and checking the plans to orientate ourselves, it was pitch black, except for the occasional sliver of moonlight creeping through the gaps of the boards on one side," he gestured for a glass of water on a nearby tray, refreshed himself and continued with his story.

"We started to really get worried when we found our bearings, the Lieutenant radioed Chessman to see how things were, telling him we were going to be longer than expected because we had run into problems: Each door had been nailed shut, so we had to remove one of the panels each time, luckily they were quite big. We had three doors to go through, and then we were there: General Percival's office and his big desk. It was at this point that the Lieutenant received a call from Chessman to say there was some Japanese activity.

"I remember discussing the possibility of us being seen, when we were given explicit instructions to get in, do our job, and get out without them knowing. The Lieutenant chuckled softly, reminding us of the mess we had made, then we realised, in any event our mission had already been blown.

"We quickly went over to the desk where the Lieutenant followed the instructions to locate the hidden book. We pulled out the secret compartment and found the book we wanted, just as Chessman called again. It appeared the Japanese soldiers had left the path leading towards the headquarters, and disappeared. He immediately told Chessman to take one of the point men and check what happened to them and radio back.

"Before we had a chance to clear up our mess and return the secret panel back to its original position, we heard gunfire. Checking the radio, we found out Chessman and McCulloch had come across the Japanese and a fight had broken out, resulting in a wounded Chessman, and all the Japanese killed. Collins and McCulloch dragged him back to the spot outside the HQ."

"Excuse me, Major," Stone stopped him. "No one seems to know what happened when Chessman and McCulloch went to check on the Japs."

The Major fidgeted with the edge of his blanket. The corner of his mouth twitched slightly, hardly noticeable, but Stone saw it and interpreted his nervousness as an untruth.

"I suppose, now Chessman is dead, it doesn't really matter anymore," he said.

"What are you implying, Major?"

"When we returned to England some time later; when Commander Carter realised the group was finished as a unit. We stopped talking to each other, and worst of all, accusations were flying everywhere. The mission was so delicate, when General Whitehouse found out about it; he ordered the whole unit to be disbanded, and those suffering with any mental problems returned to England for observation; interrogation more like it.

"I remember vocalising my objections at the time, saying I thought they were being a touch premature. Fortunately most survived the experience, except poor old Farney; he never did come to terms with Chessman's death"

"Sorry, Major, you were about to tell me what happened."

The Major laughed again, "Good heavens man so I did, sorry.

Got a bit carried away. Umm... yes, I remember now. Lieutenant Lonergan and myself were the only ones to get away with it, and were asked to interview the others as and when they were about to be released. I remember the morning quite plainly. It was a cold January morning, and I was freezing in this Army billet waiting for McColluch to be brought in for his interview."

Stone interrupted again, "Sorry, Major, the point."

"Oh yes, sorry... it's so difficult to stop drifting back. Anyway, McCulloch pleaded with me to pass him, even though it was apparent by his reports that something was still bothering him. I told him I would, only if he got this thing off his chest finally. I mean... no one cared any more. He agreed, and told me what really happened when Chessman and he went to look for the Japanese.

"Apparently he was going on all the time to Chessman about what the Japs did to their prisoners, spooking Chessman something terrible. Apparently, he knew about him being a homosexual, and was winding him up about what the Japs did to them. By then Chessman's reaction on seeing them was no surprise; he emptied his clip into them. McCulloch had dived for cover the moment it started.

"Chessman was too badly injured to contradict McCulloch when he told everyone his version of what happened. And, Superintendent, that's how it went into the record."

Stone was aghast with yet another discrepancy in the story.

"So McCulloch had been living with the idea that it was what he said to Chessman that caused all the trouble."

"Obviously, Superintendent."

"Okay, then what?"

"You think we must have stepped on an ants nest. Japanese were running towards us. The Lieutenant gave orders for all those on my chariot to get going and continue right out to the MTB. He gave me the codebook, and at the same time told those on his chariot to get down to the jetty and wait for him for five minutes, then get out of here."

"You saw nothing of what happened between the Lieutenant, Collins and Chessman?"

"No, when the Lieutenant handed me the codebook, I put it inside my wetsuit and left. He was standing by the door of the building. Chessman was on the ground, and I think Collins was leaning over him. Everything happened so quickly, they were all in different places, we all just ran back to the jetty."

"Tell me, do you remember seeing Steve Farney at the Jetty?"

"Oh... let me see... McCulloch, Guldon, Hebden were on my chariot. On the Lieutenant's, was Collins, Chessman and Farney. Now when I arrived, Farney was sitting down on the jetty and McCulloch was just dropping into the water. I asked him where the rest were and he told me they had already gone down."

"That's interesting, it contradicts what Collins said," Stone emphasised.

"So Collins lied about what happened to Chessman then," the Major stated.

"What did he tell you back on the MTB?"

"It was the Lieutenant that told us, when we missed Chessman. He just said he was dead. We knew that to mean he had finished him off. Then there was the terrible row that was aimed at the Lieutenant, Collins tried to defend him."

"That's the impression I got," Stone said. "He wouldn't offer any more."

"I'm not surprised, if you can believe what Farney told me."

"Tell me... only keep it short," Stone said, turning over another page.

"When we got back on the boat all hell erupted. Collins was being sick over the side and everyone else was arguing over what happened to Chessman. Then Farney pulled me to one side.

He said he got sick of waiting on the jetty and went back to the clearing. That's when he saw Collins shoot Chessman."

"Are you sure?"

"Well that's what he said."

"And you didn't see the others until they arrived back on the MTB?"

"I think it was the explosions that Collins set off that alerted the boat Commander; he was waiting for us. We didn't have to bother with the beacons, he was ready to go. He kept saying, 'This will bring the gunboats out,' and as soon as the others were aboard, the two boats made a dash for it. He said if they could beat the Japs through the islands before day-break, we stood a chance."

"I gather you did," Stone interrupted.

"We did eventually... well some of us. The boats pulled into a sheltered inlet as a resting place during the heat of the day. It was a relief to see nothing but open water between the far off Bangka Island, before our last run for the Sunda Strait and home. Apparently, the radioman had been monitoring some unusual chatter, which he suspected was high-speed Morse, too fast for him to pick-up. Then the Commander put a sonar mike overboard to see if anything was out there.

"I remember one of the Australian sailors told us they'd soon know if it was a gunboat or not. He said they had to leave their engines running if they were waiting for us, as it would take too long to start them up again.

"The Commander confirmed the presence of the gunboats, and the foolhardy plan to outrun them. From starting up our engines, we had three minutes to get out of range of their deadly gunfire."

"That was plenty of time, surely," Stone commented.

"It would have been, if that was the plan. But these crazy devils saw the opportunity to terminate two Japanese threats. We had no say in the matter."

"I thought the main purpose was to get the code-book back?"

"So did I... and I told the Lieutenant that but he assured us that what we were doing was no more risky than making a dash for it. Apparently, we were going to be bait. We were going to draw the gunboat out while the armed MTB hung back to torpedo it. Then once satisfied there were no others, he would follow."

"Crazy," Stone agreed. "But in hindsight you made it."

"Only just... but at a great cost."

"What does that mean?" Stone questioned.

"Everyone immediately pressed the timers on their watches. The boat then roared forward at full throttle, taking only seconds to reach top speed. You could feel the bow lifting out of the water, forcing everyone to hang onto the table supports as we began sliding backwards. Instinctively we checked our watches again, counting off the seconds, and before the three minutes were up there was an explosion off one side, an ear-popping compression that rocked the boat.

"Lying on the floor with my head pressed close to the boards, I could hear everything: the boat groaning as it zig-zagged across its own wash, the thud as it crashed back into the next trough and the underwater shock-waves each time a shell hit the water. But the last one was different, so loud everyone grasped their ears with the impact. Then the boat suddenly lurched to one side and slowed until it almost stopped. No one said anything, but we all thought that was it, we were dead meat.

"From the commotion up top, obviously that wasn't what happened. We all scrambled up the steps to the deck, and was confronted with a ball of fire in the darkness, followed by further explosions and tracer shells going off like fireworks, blazing fiery trails into the night, lighting up the other boat racing to catch up to us; bringing forth roars of cheers from their Aussie shipmates. Then suddenly a flash appeared far off to the left, a different gun flash, from another gunboat, on the other side of the island.

"It fell short, sending a huge plume of water into the air to one side of the fleeing MTB, they were the ones racing against time now; we had reached our safe distance and could do nothing but watch. There was no way we could help them; our munitions were back at base. Then they fired both their rear torpedo tubes, but it was too late, it had stopped them from using the zigzag manoeuvre that would have saved them, another flash from the distant darkness was a direct hit.

"The fragile plywood boat exploded into a thousand pieces. Seconds later, another explosion lit up the night, a posthumous reply to the gunboat's victory. Our MTB Commander didn't wait to find out if there were any more out in the darkness, and wasted no time in throttling up again to full speed."

"What a bloody waste," Stone exclaimed.

"You're right, Superintendent. There was nothing they could do for their mates now; they had given their lives so that we could escape."

The Major looked worse for the ordeal, and his eyes moistened.

Stone attempted one last question.

"What I can't understand, Major is, if these executions were meant to be retribution for leaving Chessman behind, why did the killer take so long before he acted?"

"I wouldn't have a clue, Superintendent."

Although resistant at first, the Major soon settled down and gave substance to the story Collins had told; except for two elements that put a new light on this complicated case: First, there was the revelation that Chessman was a homosexual. Stone was not sure where it fitted, but he was convinced it played an important part.

Second, Major Drake turned the tables on Collins' statement, that Lonergan killed Chessman; Stone could not get back to

London quick enough. He phoned Mark to set the wheels in motion for an arrest warrant for Collins.

CHAPTER 18

When Mark arrived the following morning, he saw Stone standing in front of the white board studying the details they added the previous day.

"Good morning, Boss," he said, walking up behind him.

Stone turned round, "Good morning, Mark. I thought I'd get an early start before we talk to Collins. You did get that warrant?"

"I did, Boss... what brought this on?"

"And did you pick up on what I told you yesterday?. Stone questioned him.

"I did... if you can believe what Farney told Drake."

"This case is getting more like quicksand every new statement we take. It's got more turns in it than a corkscrew," Stone commented, turning back to the board.

"What I'd like to know is, why did Collins lie. What did he have to gain?"

"That's what I want to find out. Which interview room did you put him in?"

"Number three, Boss. Freeman is watching him now."

Stone turned away from the board and made his way back to his office, "We'll let him stew for a while... give him an opportunity to wonder why he's here."

For some reason Stone was not ready for him, he needed

to clear his mind. He needed to know how Mary got on with Farney.

He picked up the phone and dialled her number. She answered straight away.

"Good morning, Mary," he said.

"Simon… I was expecting your call last night," she replied.

"Sorry about that. By the time I got back from Harrogate I was bushed."

"How did you get on?"

"It's too complicated to go into on the phone; I'll explain when you come in."

Mary hesitated before answering.

"I'm going to be tied up on another case for a couple of days."

"Okay… just give me the short version of how you got on."

"I didn't," she said. "Farney was too far gone for any sensible interview."

"I'm sorry you had a wasted journey. Charge us all the same. I must go Mary; I have Collins in the interview room. Ring me when you're back"

"I'll do that, Simon."

Stone replaced the receiver and paused on Mary's unusual response. He had to cast that to one side, it was time he looked in on Collins. When he did, Collins was impatiently pacing the interview room. His eyes widened, and he took on the stance of an irate member of the public.

"Ah… there you are: I'd like to know why I've been dragged down here?"

"Sit down, Mr Collins, no one's dragged you anywhere, or would you like me to arrest you here and now without an explanation?"

Stone raised his open palm towards Mark. He placed the warrant in it and Stone dropped it on the table in front of Collins.

Collins glanced at the official looking paper, "What do you

mean, arrest me?"

Stone lent forward, "You lied to us, Mr Collins."

"Who says so?" he cried out.

"I interviewed your colleague Major Drake yesterday. Among other things, he told us it was you that killed Chessman... not Lonergan."

"How does he know... he wasn't there. He went down to his chariot before us."

"Farney stayed behind. He told Drake it was you he saw leaning over Chessman, not Lonergan and you fired the fatal shot."

Collins said nothing, he just stared at them, turning all shades of red, looking as if he was about to burst. His brain was ticking over; looking for a way out.

"How can you take his word. It's hearsay... no, double hearsay."

Stone picked up the warrant, "Because his version of what happened fits what we have already. Collins went silent again, weighing up his options. "Well, Collins, are you going to sit there all day?" Stone said, waving the warrant in front of him.

"All right," he shouted, wringing his hands. "It was me... I killed Chessman."

Stone put the paper back on the table and sat back looking confident. "Why don't you tell us what really happened. Get it off your chest. You'll feel better."

"I can't get Chessman begging the Lieutenant to kill him out of my head. All the Lieutenant wanted to do was leave him... 'They'll look after him', he kept saying." Collins jumped up and started pacing again, "Why didn't he just follow orders?"

"Okay, Mr Collins, come and sit down," Stone said.

"I was going to tell them you know. But I was sick, and when I finally got down where they were all arguing, I found out the Lieutenant had taken the blame."

"That might have been all right then, but why lie to the

police now?"

"I've lived with it all this time so what the heck. I knew it would give me a motive in your eyes... I could see it on your face. So I just stuck to the story."

"So you admit you have a motive?"

"I didn't kill my mates... why would I?"

There was an embarrassing lull before Stone started again.

"I see," Stone said, picking up the warrant and leaving the table. "You're not out of it yet, Collins, so I suggest you go away and give this whole fiasco some thought. I'll need to question you again later."

"I'm free to go then?"

"Until I want to see you again."

Stone walked out of the interview room leaving Mark to finish off Collins statement. He returned to the white board and stared at his allotted segment. Mark had scribbled in the fact that Collins had killed Chessman.

"Is this a bad time, Sir?" Constable Freeman asked.

"What was that, Constable?" Stone said, turning to face him.

"I just wondered if it was a good time to tell you what I came up with."

"Run it by me, Constable, and make it brief."

Freeman opened his folder and refreshed his memory.

"Yes, Sir... I decided to go outside the box, as Inspector Fraser said."

"And... you're telling me nothing new, Constable."

He glanced at his notes, "No, Sir... but I came up with some possible reasons. One, he was in a prisoner-of-war camp. Two, he was in a civilian prison. And taking into account that he was an Indian; Three, he didn't have a passport for some years."

Stone was still back at the prisoner-of-war idea, and he liked it. "That sounds good, Constable, let me have your notes and I'll read them tonight. Very good."

Constable Freeman looked happy as he handed over his folder and stood in a daze as Stone walked back to his office.

Mark finished with Collins statement and saw Stone reading Freeman's notes.

"What do you think, Boss?" He said, knocking on the door.

Stone looked up, "I think the prison camp idea has a lot of merit, so has the civilian prison... and the passport situation. Get him to check them all out."

"He's going to need some guidance, Boss."

"Oh come on, Mark... get him to check the Military War Register, Camps and Burials. HM Prisons on long-term incarcerations and Customs and Immigration for the passport."

"You made his day, Boss... I'll get him onto it straight away."

Stone laughed as he handed Mark the folder, "Well I'm not an ogre all the time. Tell him I want all that information by tomorrow."

Surveillance has not discovered any suspicious characters at any of the remaining victim's locations, and inquiries into the new area of investigation: the Prisons, Institutions and lists of POW's, turned out to be more of a challenge than first envisaged.

At first Stone was prepared to accept Constable Freeman's suggestions for the unexplained time gap between incident and murders as a reasonable exercise to keep him occupied. However, since his suspects appeared to come and go with each new interview, the likelihood of this information bearing fruit was beginning to show more promise.

He began pushing Freeman's search for names that spanned the period towards Corporal Allan Dumbleton, alias Chessman.

Then after poring through endless lists supplied by the Ministry of Defence, the British Red Cross, Register of Prisoners of War and H.M. Prisons, a loud 'Eureka' rang out from an excited female Constable.

Her eyes were red with studying small print, her finger ends sore and cracked and her lips tasting of old dusty files; she shouted again in a trembling voice.

"I've found him, Boss... I've found Corporal Allen Dumbleton."

Mark rushed over to her desk. Stone noticed the sudden commotion.

"What's up?" he called out.

Mark paused while running his finger down the D's until he reached the name Dumbleton, Allan, underlined in red.

"I think we've found your man, Boss," he said, giving the constable a kiss on the cheek, to her surprise.

Stone rushed over and grabbed the sheet of names from the Prisoner of War Registry, reading the name underlined with its corresponding dates and location. He could hardly believe his eyes; this was the proof he was looking for: the proof that Chessman lived through the ordeal in Singapore.

He had to read it again, slowly. Dumbleton, Allan. March 1942, Camp 3, Malaya. It stood out in beautiful bold letters to him. He could see nothing else.

The Constable looked up at Stone, red faced and smiling.

"Good work everyone, especially you Constable," he complimented her, gripping her hand. "We now need to drill into this reference more deeply. I want as much detail as you can get: what this Camp 3 means, where it was in relation to Singapore and what happened to Chessman after the war ended."

"I'll get onto it straight away, Boss," Mark said.

"No. You and I are going back to see Mr Collins, and see if we can wring anything more out of him, with this new information that Chessman survived the mission. Use Freeman and what's her name, the Constable who found him; It'll be good experience for them, and a bonus.”

“Right, Boss, good idea, they’ll appreciate that.”

Whilst the Inspector was arranging that, Stone just had to ring Mary and Hammond about his latest discovery. He felt like a ‘Cheshire Cat’, twirling his chair round to face the window with his back to the squad room, hiding the expression on his face.

Mary was delighted with his news, and genuinely glad his original scenario of this case was finally beginning to fall into place, whereas Hammond’s response was somewhat less enthusiastic. Stone allowed himself the satisfaction of thinking his old friend was a little jealous, ‘Let’s face it’, he thought, ‘His scenario was quite different’.

“I thought, Jack, you of all people would have been excited that at last there was some light at the end of the tunnel.”

“All you have to do now, Stone, is prove it,” he replied.

Stone grabbed the register sheet, although Jack could not see it.

“I have. His name is there in black and white. He survived the shooting and was put in a Japanese prisoner of war camp.”

“Is that all. Do you realise how difficult that is. If he survived the camp, the American’s would have taken him to some temporary military hospital in the middle of the jungle, probably not recorded, and then onto heaven knows where.”

“Oh, thank you for your confidence,” Stone shouted, slamming the phone down. He looked up; his hand still on the phone, Mark was standing in the doorway.

“Sour grapes, Boss. He knows you’re almost there now.”

“I don’t know, Mark; he’s not like that really. If he’s critical of something you say, you can bet your life he knows you’re going to end up with egg on your face.”

“I don’t believe that, Boss, you’re right about this. I know it.”

“In the meantime let’s have another word with Collins. Is he still at his pub?”

"According to his surveillance he is."

"Good... let's go then."

It was almost twelve; the pub was beginning to fill with the lunchtime crowd making it difficult for them to spot Collins. He was huddled in a corner at the far end of the bar with a group of men. The raucous laughter drew their attention to him.

Collins spotted them coming over to him. He moved away from the group after a word and both parties converged on each other as he reached the other end of the bar.

"So... you're back again, can I get you both a drink?"

"We're on duty at the moment," Stone replied, glancing at the Inspector. "However, after our little chat, we may take you up on that; it is lunchtime."

"I thought you'd already made your minds up about me."

"Why think that, Mr Collins?" Stone said, "You know you're innocent until proved guilty. It's an on-going investigation."

"Superintendent, I admitted to killing Chessman, what more do you want?"

"Actually we came by to give you some information."

"I'm not really interested; I just want all this to go away."

"I'm afraid that's not the way life is, Mr Collins, you have to play with the cards you're dealt. Anyway, we thought you'd like to know you didn't kill Chessman."

"What do you mean I didn't kill him. The gun was close enough."

"His name has just been found on a POW list."

"Oh God... if you think telling me that has eased my conscience, you're wrong. It's worse now," Collins held his head in his hands.

Stone suddenly realised what he meant.

"I'm sorry about that, but it was our duty to let you know you didn't murder anyone, at least not by shooting them."

"You said the right thing there Superintendent, leaving him to the Japanese was as good as murdering him. He obviously didn't crack, or they would have changed the Pacific codes; but he would have gone through hell."

Stone looked hard at him, he appeared to be genuinely effected by the news; more by the fact of leaving him to the mercy of the butchers, than the possibility that this man, like his nemesis, was hunting him down.

"So, Mr Collins, it appears your role as a suspect could be shared."

"As I said before, I had nothing to do with those deaths, and if Chessman is still alive, which I very much doubt, he would be like me; too old to be able to do the sort of things you described. Besides, what happened to this Indian bloke?"

"We assumed that was a disguise, someone made up to look like an Indian."

"Yes but, didn't I hear someone say he was younger than us?"

Collins' astute grasp of the details surprised Stone, and had to admit in his zest to prove that it was Chessman, or in fact Collins; he had overlooked the age difference.

Jack Hammond was right, loose ends are inclined to come back and bite you. This new aspect threw him off guard somewhat; and he was beginning to feel embarrassed.

"Yes well there is that aspect," he clumsily excused himself. "We're developing the possibility that there may be an accomplice."

Mark looked at him oddly puzzled. Stone had made light of his previous suggestion of more than one being involved.

"So where does this leave me?" Collins said.

"For the time being, running your pub and bringing us some lunch," Stone replied, trying to add some levity to the awkward situation.

Collins took their order and vanished into the now crowded

room, leaving Stone to face the obvious questions Mark was about to throw at him.

"What's this about an accomplice, Boss?" he started.

"Well I had to say something. I mean, fancy him coming up with that."

"What... about the age difference?"

"What else."

"I thought you knew, you read Hammond's report didn't you?"

"Yes... well some of it. Okay I took a lot for granted. And before you say it; yes, I've been a bit blinkered where the Indian is concerned."

"Well the report describes him as being in his late twenties, not late fifties and sixties as this lot are," Mark pointed out.

"There you are," Stone said in his defence. "If he was involved at the beginning, he would only have been ten or so. No he has to be an accomplice."

"I suppose that's plausible, Boss, but very complicated."

They finished their lunch; Collins looking relieved when they finally left, and made their way back to the office to see if the others had faired any better. Stone had embarrassed himself, thinking the news about Chessman would flush-out a more detailed account of what really took place in those last desperate moments.

The repetitiveness of Hammond being right was frustrating Stone; the trail he set for the two young constables had in fact dragged into a marathon. It was now three days on from their earlier discovery that Chessman was alive, and all they had achieved was mountains of paper, an enormous telephone bill, and the inclusion of most of the SCI.

Stone returned to the squad room after a lengthy meeting with the number crunchers, hoping to hear some good news to brighten his day, not what was waiting for him. The expression on their faces was enough to make him want to turn back.

"Don't tell me, I can see it on your faces," he said, passing them on his way to his office, and then turning back to them. "All right... come in and give me the worst."

They followed him in and stood in a row in front of his desk, Freeman holding a bunch of papers looking as if they had chosen him to speak.

"Sir... we've got some bad news and some good news," he said.

"I see... So what's the bad news?"

"Well... we had no luck at all with the POW Registry on Chessman other than the initial information that he had in fact been listed. However, the Inspector told us what Inspector Hammond had said about the American Military Hospital."

"Yes... and? Get on with it," an irritated Stone barked.

"Well, Sir, they had a record of Camp 3, and three sets of records; Walking, Stretcher and dead. Chessman was on the last list."

"I knew it, it happens every time. We just find out he was alive, and now he is dead. So we have to rethink the whole thing through again."

"He lived three years, Sir," Constable Freeman noted feebly.

"What good is that, he should have lasted like the others."

"Sorry, Sir."

"You said there was some good news."

"Oh yes, Sir... while we were checking with the Americans, they come up with the lists of walking prisoners and stretcher cases. We ran them through the computer and finally boiled them down to twenty-three still living. They were in the same camp as Chessman."

"You've still got to track them down."

"We did that, Sir, that's the good news. One of them lives here in London."

Stone's erratic moods, brought on by the changes in the

altering specifics of this case, had swung back to a calmer state; he was contemplating what the constable had just said. They could see his mind racing through the new possibilities.

"Okay... carry on tracking down the others, I don't want to interview all of them, but we need backup in the event we don't get a satisfactory result with this one. In the meantime get onto this character and arrange a quick visit, and warn him it could be a long session. I want him prepared to tell us about Chessman."

CHAPTER 19

Jeff Wheaton was a little hazy when Mark rang him, but as soon as he mentioned camp 3 in 1942, he found it difficult to shut him up. Apparently, like most POW's, the Second World War was a subject that was never far from his thoughts.

At first, Chessman was not a name he was familiar with, but as soon as Allan Dumbleton was mentioned, he reacted with; 'Oh you mean old poofter,' which got him started. At that point, Mark had to stop him, saying he was only arranging an interview with his Superintendent.

The following morning Stone and Mark arrived at the council high-rise where Wheaton had a small flat. As expected, the lifts were out of order and they had to climb several flights of exposed concrete heavily laden with years of grime and graffiti. Unpleasant youths, who should have been at school, and the occasional suspicious look from behind tattered netting, reminded them how these people knew when a cop was on their patch.

Finally, they reached the door and knocked on the chipped paint and exposed plywood, the knocker had probably long since disappeared. They immediately heard a muffled shout, coupled with the worst bout of coughing they had heard, which seemed to go on for ages before it finished with the usual expectoration.

"I'm coming... I'm coming," the occupant repeated, more clearly.

The door opened noisily, and a man, looking much older than he probably was, greeted them with an asthmatic hello, holding out his nicotine-stained hand and squinting from the smoke swirling up from the cigarette in the corner of his mouth.

"Mr Wheaton?" Mark spoke first, before entering.

"Yeah, that's me."

"Good, this is Superintendent Stone and I'm Inspector Fraser."

"Gordon Bennett, this must be important to bring out two top cops," he said.

It was hard to tell if the inside was any better than the outside, as Wheaton rushed to clear two chairs. The room was cool, with a touch of dampness in the air and a strong smell of old cigarette butts and stale food.

The chairs looked suspicious, but they sat down after climbing those stairs.

"You'll have to excuse the place; things haven't been so good lately since they pensioned me off. I'm only sixty-three you see, so I'm not old enough for the old age pension yet, and the railway compensation isn't much. After thirty years working on their stinking trains, you'd think they'd have a bit more compassion."

Stone turned away from his critical inspection and faced him.

"I would have thought a work related illness carried a reasonable pension after that time with the railways," Stone commented.

"They got a big smart lawyer didn't they. They proved it was self-induced. Smoking caused my illness, they said, not the asbestos in their trains."

"I find that quite tragic, Mr Wheaton," Stone commented, hoping to get on. "Are you fit enough for this interview?"

"Oh yes, I've got a drink here," he reached over to the mess on the coffee table, and extracted a glass of what looked like stale beer. "So I'm all yours, how can I help. I understand you want to know about the poofter."

"Yes... but I'd prefer it if you called him Chessman," Stone emphasised. "We don't want that going into the statement, do we. We've already established he was a homosexual, so that should suffice."

"Okay, that's fine with me," he replied.

Stone glanced over towards the Inspector to see if he was ready.

"Now, Mr Wheaton, we know nothing of Chessman's POW history, so you just start where you like and in your own words tell us what you know."

Wheaton cleared his throat and took a large gulp from the glass.

"When that bloody Percival surrendered us to the Japs, we were made to clear up all the mess after the battle. We thought we were going to stay in our barracks as prisoners, but we were wrong, the blighters had other ideas.

"Sorry, Mr Wheaton," Stone interrupted, "We're only interested in Chessman."

"I know... I'm getting to him. You'll only ask me how this happened and... "

"Okay... sorry, please continue."

"Right... anyway, during the commotion we heard earlier, a wounded prisoner was captured and put in the hospital. Now we tried to get in to see him, we thought he must have been part of a recon mission to size up the situation about rescuing us... Oh did we try, but it was no good. They had him locked up and guarded."

Stone glanced at Mark trying to get everything down.

"Keep it brief, Mr Wheaton," Stone prompted. He nodded and carried on.

"So, we couldn't get in to see this mystery man, they had cleared out the whole ward, even though we desperately needed it; so he must have been someone special."

"What about the British doctor's in the hospital?" the Inspector asked.

"They were still there, but the Japs wouldn't let us see them either. Then I heard he had been taken from the hospital and they were working on him in the old guard house, again under the eyes of half a dozen Japs," he had another drink.

Mark was still curious and asked him:

"In all this time... you didn't see who they had?"

"No... not a peep. Then one day they marched us out to a mass of trucks and drove us up to the railway heading by the Causeway that separated us from the mainland." He laughed, "We knew we'd blown it up. So then, they got us onto some barges, and shipped us across to Johore Bahru on the mainland that night. They had us up at dawn and marched us all day without a break, we dropped out like flies, and as fast as we dropped, they shot us. We had to support each other until we arrived at Camp 3."

"So how long were you there before you saw Chessman?" Stone asked.

"Well it was at least three months before I tied up this puff... sorry, homosexual with the man in the hospital. I sussed he arrived here much earlier, one of the other prisoners pointed him out to me saying the Japs were giving him a particularly bad time because he was a homo: they hated them."

"You mean they didn't have any themselves?"

"I wouldn't know about that... anyway, I felt sorry for him, so I went over to him one day and introduced myself. Before long we got on about how he had been tortured and I sussed he was the mystery man back on Singapore. A little more pushing and he told me the lot, it was a good thing I wasn't a Jap stoolie. He said he came over with a group of special ops men, not what for, only that they were spotted by a patrol and he got shot."

"Did he tell you what happened then?" the Inspector

questioned, eager to hear another version of the incident outside the HQ.

"That was the funny part, he suddenly went ranting on about his mates letting him down and not doing the job properly. It must have been ten minutes."

Wheaten started coughing again, had a drink and continued.

"Not to worry, it didn't bother me then, so it doesn't now. Anyway, I got the impression, whatever they did or didn't do, they were going to pay for it, in fact I think it's what kept him going; he was in a hell of a state from what the Japs were doing to him. Old Quasimodo tortured him all the time.

"Quasimodo?"

"Yes, the camp Commandant. We couldn't pronounce his real name."

"How did he stand it?" the Inspector questioned.

"Beats me... he took more than anyone else... unless it was the chess."

"Where did he get the chess set from?" Stone asked.

"He made it, or to be more accurate, them. The Japs kept taking them away from him, and he kept making new ones. I give the man that, homo or not, he had guts. But he fooled them all about his new lover, at least until that night."

"That night?"

"Yeah... as I said we'd been in the camp a couple of years or so, when this young Malayan boy arrived, I never did find out why he was there, usually they just killed them, they never made them prisoners. He was a general odd jobber, you know, cleaning up the mess, looking after Quasimodo's dogs and so on..."

"Did he have a name?" Stone asked, for the record.

"Yeah, come to think of it he did. We always called him 'Half Pint'. The Japs killed his parents and used him and his brother as beasts of burden; pulling their gun carriages and anything else they wanted shifting."

"What happened to the brother?" the Inspector asked.

"I gather he died very quickly, or was shot by the Japs because he couldn't work anymore, then 'Half Pint' was dropped off at the camp when the troops left. Anyway, he was only about eleven or twelve," Stone glanced at Mark. "And he took a fancy to Chessman, or the game of chess. At first, all he was interested in was learning to play, then we realised they were becoming inseparable, the Malayan boy followed him everywhere like a shadow, even slept at his feet; mind you, we never knew if they did anything. The Japs noticed as well, especially Quasimodo, who was totally paranoid about Chessman having any relations with another man, to the point of having his men watch him at night; it was weird."

He took another drink.

"Do you think the Commandant was a homosexual?" Stone asked.

"I wouldn't know, he didn't try anything on with us. Then that night his guards found them together and marched them off to Quasimodo's hut for more interrogation, he must have had a sleeping problem, he occupied so many nights that way. We heard them both screaming most of the night, until Chessman was put in the oven."

"What do you mean, 'Oven,'" the Inspector questioned.

"A corrugated iron box. By mid-day it got as hot as an oven, hence the nickname."

"Then what happened?"

"About five days later the bell went one afternoon when the sun was high, and Chessman was dragged out of the oven looking almost dead, he was in a hell of a state. Quasimodo must have worked him over good that night; the marks were still showing on his naked body. Then they hauled him over to the crucifix."

"Crucifix. A real one?" Stone exclaimed.

"Oh yeah ... that was one of his favourite toys. I think he enjoyed mocking the Christians amongst us, you know, Jesus on the cross thing."

"What did he do?"

"What didn't he do more like it. You were flogged, used as target practise, oh and his favourite game was bloodletting... the thousand cuts sort of thing."

"A thousand cuts?" Stone questioned, thinking of the cuts on his victims.

"Yeah... he would nick every vein he could find until you bled to death."

"Good heavens, the bastard, he should have been brought up before the War Crimes Tribunal," the Inspector shouted out indignantly.

"He got his justice believe me, but that's another story."

Stone asked, "What was Chessman's fate."

"That was the worst," Wheaton took some time to compose himself. "I didn't have much time for the homo, but he didn't deserve that... " he took another drink.

"Take your time, now." Stone said.

Mark turned over to a fresh page and waited.

"After they dragged him out of the oven over to the crucifix in front of the whole camp, and nailed him up there for all to see, would you believe it, Quasimodo strutted back and forth swinging his Samurai about, profaning the man and vilifying him as a dirty homosexual: saying he was the most disgusting creature on earth. This went on for half an hour, with the prisoner's doctor complaining that he was contravening the Geneva Convention. He just laughed; the 'Half-Pint' couldn't stand it any longer, and made an attempt to rush forward, until we restrained him. This didn't escape the attention of Quasimodo; he didn't miss a thing."

"Did he do anything about it?" Stone questioned.

"Not then, he was enjoying his humiliation of Chessman too much. Everyone expected the bloodletting routine when he started nicking and cutting until Chessman's body was running red, but suddenly he moved closer and started shouting again. 'I will rid you of your hideous burden,' he screamed, quite out of his mind. Then, without any warning, he turned and slashed off Chessman's genitals, and threw them to his dogs. The doctor protested. He just laughed and walked back to his hut telling his goons to guard Chessman, he didn't want any of us taking him down. He was left hanging there bleeding to death, and died later that night."

"You mentioned something earlier about Quasimodo getting his in the end," Stone pointed out. This story had to have a moral to it.

"Yes... we were repatriated by the Yanks in late '44, only five months later come to that. The allied prisoners were taken to a Singapore hospital, the nationals including Chessman's friend 'Half Pint', were released to their own devices unless they needed medical treatment, and the authorities at the time immediately arrested Quasimodo and his officers, and locked them up, awaiting trial by the War Crimes Tribunal. They asked us to stay on for the trial as witness to his violations. They found him guilty and sentenced him to fifteen years. I would have executed him."

"What about Chessman's friend?"

"I never spoke to him again. I tell you this though; he was at the trial, at least watching if not participating. I saw him a couple of times and heard him shout out, 'You'll pay for this, you'll all pay for his death,' so that's why I'm not surprised in what the Inspector told me on the phone. It's him all right, only he would keep a grudge like that."

Stone and Mark were speechless. They had sat through

this man's story for over an hour, listening to his hatred of homosexuals, his coughing and wheezing. Then in his last sentence, he identified the man who was killing Carter's boys.

CHAPTER 20

Mark noticed Stone was very quiet on their way back to the city. Glancing at him when he checked the traffic he could see he was deep in thought; his usual enthusiasm after an interview absent from his vacant expression.

"Straight back to the office, Boss?" he questioned, checking again.

"What was that?" Stone replied automatically, not really listening.

"Do you want to go back to the office. Is everything all right?"

"Yes... no, I mean. Yes everything is okay, and no I don't want to go back to the office," he hesitated, as if trying to make his mind up as to what he did want. "Go to Uxbridge," he said, more decided, "Yes... Inspector Hammond's."

"Right, Boss, whatever you want."

This surprised Mark, for all they knew Inspector Hammond could be out. As he turned off to join up with the motorway to Uxbridge, he contemplated his boss' motive, and decided he wanted to rub Hammond's nose in it.

"Superintendent... Inspector," Hammond called out as he and Sergeant Binstead met them entering the lobby. "What brings you into the sticks?"

They were surprised with their luck.

"Oh... we were in the neighbourhood," Stone said. Thought you might like to be brought up to date on the case," he looked sideways at Mark, to keep quiet.

"Well the Sergeant and I were just going out to the local for some lunch."

"We'll join you," Stone continued, with Mark nodding his agreement.

They fell behind in the car park and Stone whispered;

"When you get an opportunity leave me with Hammond, and try and pump the Sergeant, I'm sure they're up to something."

"Come on you two," Hammond called out.

After the meal, Mark invited the Sergeant to a game of snooker, which he gladly accepted, warning the Inspector that he was the local lunchtime champion. Stone was finally left alone with his old friend: both suspecting the other's motives.

"So, Stone, you were going to bring me up to date."

Stone sat playing with his glass, not knowing the best way to start. "He's dead, so you can say I told you so if you wish."

"Who's dead, Stone?"

"Chessman, of course."

"You'd better explain, and I'm not going to say it."

"Well he survived for a few years in a camp, with some tyrant who didn't like homosexuals, who eventually executed him."

"Don't tell me, he crucified him just like our victims."

"You're right, and guess what. He made an association with a Malayan boy."

"How did you find all this out?"

"Through the POW Registry. They helped quite a bit actually. We eventually established a list of surviving POW's from that camp, found one lived as near as Neasden, and interviewed him this morning."

"Just passing were you," Hammond joked.

"Well... Neasden, Uxbridge, they're almost next door to each other."

"In a roundabout way, I suppose they are," they laughed, Stone was now feeling much better; glad he decided to make this detour. Their conversation became less of a contest as Stone casually glanced over Hammond's shoulder to the snooker table and wondered how Mark was getting on pumping the sergeant.

It looked like they were starting a new game as Mark positioned the spot-white and broke up the triangle of reds.

"They seem to be hitting it off okay today," Sergeant Binstead commented, putting his pint down as he prepared to take his shot.

"Yeah they do," Mark replied. Acknowledging there should be no rank difference during the game. "How's your, Boss?"

"Oh he's all right, a bit of a taskmaster at times, but he's fair enough. What about the Super?" the Sergeant asked, potting his fourth red.

"Just the same, I reckon you and I have much of a similar situation."

"Except for the rank that is, Sir," the Sergeant intimated.

"Does it embarrass you; the hierarchy I mean?"

Mark finally got a shot; there were only a few reds left.

"No," he passed it off lightly, "I expect to be there one day. I'm studying for my exams and the Inspector's helping me a lot, so it's cool... I'm okay."

"You wait till you do become an Inspector, it's all different then. More responsibility and then you'll want your own CID."

"Do you reckon you'll stay with the Super' for long?"

Mark paused as he took his shot.

"Long enough, to learn how he works. It's essential the head of a CID team has a good system like Inspector Hammond and the Super' does."

Mark has a run of luck. Three reds, but he misses the next colour.

"Well I would have thought our respective roles played a major part in that, at least I'm always trying to convince the Inspector of mine," the Sergeant commented.

"Does he take any notice?"

"Not often... sometimes."

The Sergeant finished off the reds, and moved onto the yellow, green, brown but missed the blue. Mark checks the board and decides to go out in a flourish.

"What about this case?" Mark said. "I'd think it would be difficult for him to let go so easily, without keeping his eye on things," he misses his shot.

The Sergeant pots the blue, then the pink and carries onto the black. "I think that's game, would you like another?" he said, cleverly averting the question.

Mark looked down at the empty table, suddenly aware the game had finished and realising the Sergeant was onto his tactic. "No thanks, Sergeant; I'll buy you a drink. He said, wondering if his Boss was having any better luck.

Hammond was still playing it smart, "So, Stone, now you have this Malayan's name, what do you plan to do with it?" Hammond asked.

"That's just it I haven't," he said, looking serious again.

"I thought you said you had."

"No... I said I found out Chessman had a Malayan lover."

"Actually you said a Malayan boy, not that he was his lover."

"Are you playing games with me again, Jack?"

"I'm sorry, but you can't blame me when you come down here on one pretext, and really have another: what is it?"

"The usual, I don't know why I think I can always fool you," he said.

"I see... and what have you got on him?"

"Just that his nick name was 'Half Pint'."

"Well you've got something."

"Such as?"

"His fingerprints, don't you remember, I gave you a full set."

"Yes of course, I remember. But they were useless in our records, we have nothing on him. And before you say it, neither does Interpol."

"I wasn't going to," Hammond said.

"You were going to say something; I can see it on your face."

"What I was going to say was: he may not have a record here, but what about Asia. Thirty odd years is a long time for a lad like that to go without getting into some mischief or other; then there'll be a record."

"But wouldn't Interpol cover that?"

"Not necessarily, but the military police might, especially those in Hong Kong," the Inspector took a sip of his beer, nodding over his glass.

"Why Hong Kong in particular?"

"It's a gateway. Being a British colony, every Asian displaced or on the run tries to get out by going through Hong Kong. Therefore, they have a big system set up for dealing with all those legal and illegal transients. As you know I spent some time there after Korea with the Military Police, and I tell you, those guys were on the ball."

"And you think they could have a file on our man?"

"If he passed through Hong Kong legitimately to immigrate to England, they will have a file on him... and even if he tried to break out on a boat somewhere else."

"Okay, thanks for that. So I just get in touch with them direct do I, or is there some form of protocol I should follow?"

"Normally there is, but I still keep in touch with one of their chief officers, he sometimes warns me of suspicious cargo ships bound for the Port of London."

"That's interesting. I would have thought that was the Drug Squad's territory."

"It is, but there's a lot more contraband in these ships than drugs."

"I don't suppose you could be persuaded to contact this man?"

"He's called Davey Shiu if you want to ring him." Hammond said.

"Don't you think this would get a better result through friends?"

"Okay, Stone... let me have the details and I'll see what I can do."

They both looked at each other as they finished their drinks. Stone had yet another lift up on the ladder and appeared to have nothing more to talk about, while Hammond, grateful for the satisfaction of imparting his worldly knowledge, knew that his usefulness, for the time being that is, had been taken advantage of again.

Mark, instinctively sensitive to Stone's subliminal messages, stepped in as his Boss lowered his empty glass onto the table. "You haven't forgotten your meeting with Mary Carson at two-thirty, Boss," he said.

Stone suddenly looked at his watch, "Good heavens, I did forget."

"Oh... how is Mary these days?" Hammond asked.

"She's doing fine I think," Stone replied, standing up as a hint.

"Sorry, I'm forgetting, you came in our car," Hammond said.

From that point on, all was casual pleasantries. Stone had achieved his goal, faces saved, egos satisfied: just the way everyone liked it.

After driving them back to their car Hammond contemplated doing the right thing for a change and checking with the Chief Super about his call to Davey Shiu. It was sure to turn into more than one international call, and the Super was sure to find out.

He went straight to his office and knocked on the door, knowing he was in.

"Enter."

Hammond popped his head around the door, "Got a minute, Sir?"

"I have, Inspector... I haven't seen you in ages... where have you been hiding?"

"You've had my reports, Sir."

"Personal contact would be a fine thing. What is it you want?"

Hammond sat down in the chair in front of the Super's desk and explained Stone's request, and the international calls that may be involved.

"And would you be asking my permission if they were local?"

"Of course, Sir... I haven't been near the case since I sorted out that problem with Lonergan's brother, and passing on what they found at the Indian's flat."

"Yes, inspector... I'm glad you added that. As for Lonergan, the Commissioner was very grateful. There were no more complaints."

"I'm glad to hear that, Sir. Now what about the calls to Hong Kong?"

"All right, Inspector... but mind you, they better be short and to the point."

"Most definitely, Sir."

Hammond arranged his call to Davey Shiu in Hong Kong and sat patiently at his desk watching the phone as if he was expecting a call from the Palace. Half an hour had gone by, and he found himself reaching for the phone to check with the switchboard. He resisted, instead he occupied himself with the report he had started.

Then it rang and he snatched up the notes Stone gave him, "Inspector Hammond," he said, more composed.

"Sir... sorry about the delay, the lines were busy. I have your call now."

"That's all right, thank you," he said, before he heard the clicks.

There was an unusual 'Yes' on the other end.

"Inspector Hammond here" he said.

"Jack... is that you?" came the unmistakable accent of an English speaking Chinese.

"Yes, is that really you Davey. The English accent threw me there."

"Yes... I practice long time."

"Yes, Davey it has been a long time... too long, and your accent is great."

"Why the call... I can't imagine your Boss pay for pleasure?"

"You're right. I need your help, Davey... we're looking for a Malaysian man. I've just sent you a fax of his fingerprints along with his file... can you check him out for me?"

"What's his name?"

"That's just it... we don't have one. They called him 'Half Pint' in the Japanese POW Camp 3 in Malaya. That's all I have."

"It's going to be difficult but I try my best. Don't wait for me to ring."

"I know what you mean, Davey. Do your best."

Before Hammond could squeeze in a personal word, the line went dead. He sat for a moment with the phone in his hand. He wanted to say so much, but realised Davey had hung up. The Sergeant knocked on the door with a handful of papers.

"Did the fingerprints go through all right, Boss?" he asked.

"I think so," Hammond replied, shaking his head.

"Good... what did he say?"

"That must have been the quickest international call I've ever had. You'd think he was paying for it. He said he would get back to me if he found something."

"That doesn't sound very good, did he speak English?"

"Well I can't speak Chinese, can I," Hammond snapped back.

"I thought with you being in Korea you might, Boss."

"Well I don't, and he did speak English."

"He was probably trying to save you some money."

"Do you think so?"

"I'd say, unless they don't like speaking on the phone over there."

As Hammond and Sergeant Binstead debated the financial ramifications of telephone calls to the other side of the world, his phone rang, and Hammond looked surprised.

"You don't think this is him already," Hammond said, picking it up.

"I doubt it, Boss... he hasn't had time yet."

"Inspector Hammond," he answered, "Oh it's you... no I haven't heard yet. I just sent your information... I know, but they work differently to us. Okay."

"Who was that?" the Sergeant asked.

"Damn the man," Hammond let out as he hung up the phone.

"I bet I won't win a prize for knowing who that was?" the Sergeant said.

"Stone... he just wants to know if I've got anything for him."

Superintendent Stone had a long wait. It was three days before Davey Shiu contacted Hammond to tell him they think they found the man in Camp 3. Davey was not very happy about all the questions Hammond threw at him over the phone; his English was all right for everyday conversation, but no good for technical information.

"Everything on the wire, Jack," he said. "Read it and tell me if it's your man."

"What if I'm not sure, Davey?"

"Then you have to fax me new information... I must go, Jack."

"Hold on, Davey... I wanted a few words."

"No time now, Jack... send me fax. I have mean boss too."

Hammond still had the phone in his hand when the Sergeant came in.

"Don't say a word," he snapped, putting the phone back. "What's that?"

The Sergeant had the fax's Davey sent and placed them on Hammond's desk.

Hammond flicked through the half a dozen sheets, "Well it looks substantial enough," he said, "Let's hope it's him. Sit down and we'll go through them."

The summary started by identifying the fingerprints sent earlier as matching a file raised in 1960 in the name of one Kho Chiah Sek: a Malayan national held for murder in Singapore. Sek was twenty-six at the time, accused of killing Hiro Kakinuma: a Second World War Japanese soldier on release from prison.

This sounded interesting as Hammond passed each sheet to the Sergeant as he read it. On further investigation, it turned out that Kakinuma had subsequently served a fifteen-year sentence after being found guilty by a War Crimes Tribunal in 1944, for outrageous brutalities while in charge of a POW camp in Malaya, known as Camp 3.

The summary went on to point out interesting features of these interlocking, although totally separate files, which added credence to their present scenario, as well as a reasonable explanation for the time lag between 1944 and 1981.

The first interesting point was that Kho Chiah Sek was in Camp 3 at the same time as Chessman; his age would be the same as the boy befriended by Chessman, as described by Jeff Wheaton; and the Japanese officer, Hiro Kakinuma was in fact the same Commandant who crucified Chessman.

The report identified the evidence as a major part of that, which convicted him, and Kho Chiah Sek in turn, murdered him on his release, significantly in the exact same manner as Chessman. Jack thought his murder had to be the precursor to the killings in England.

It continued to highlight that Kho Chiah Sek's conviction

was looked upon lightly, due to the mitigating circumstances, and he was released from prison in 1968 on good behaviour, subsequently moving to Hong Kong where, during the two-year waiting period, he applied for papers to immigrate to England.

Under his conditions of early release he spent the next few years in a camp, during which time he was refused entry into England on the grounds of the serious nature of his criminal record; this was after due consideration of his help during the war with allied prisoners. But in 1974, the Australian Embassy proved to show more gratitude for his services to their men, accepting him as a temporary resident, where he subsequently became a citizen in 1978.

This proved to be only a slight detour from his original plan, for in 1979 he applied once again to the British Embassy, only this time as a working student. He had attained a scholarship in the Willesden Polytechnic, providing he could obtain a work permit and residents visa. He left for England that same year.

Hammond called Stone to let him know Hong Kong had found his man. Within the hour, Stone was sitting in front of Hammond's desk reading the report.

"You got all this from the Hong Kong Military Police?" Stone questioned.

"Well let's say most of it was locked away in their millions of files, I was lucky to have a good friend in Davey Shiu, who was able to sift out each separate document which, when put together, led us to the trail of this man from 1944 through to 1978."

"You mean they kept tabs on him even after he left for Australia?"

"It appears the Australian migration authorities in Canberra wanted a copy of his police record, and the file number of that transaction was left in that folder. He looked up the file and found a corresponding Canberra file name, which was easy to bring up on the computer via their new channel of communication."

Stone continued examining the last pages of the detailed report looking for anything prior to losing contact with Kho Chiah Sek, when he arrived in England. However, like all the other sources of information, the trail stopped dead.

"Well you and your Chinese friend did a good job of filling in the gaps, and corroborating our latest assumptions. However, we're still left up the creek without a paddle, regarding his whereabouts," Stone pointed out.

Hammond thought his effort was worth more than that.

"I don't agree, Stone," he asserted himself.

"Oh you don't, do you. You'd better tell me why."

Hammond started collecting the papers together and passed them over to Stone before he once again gave him the benefit of his experience.

"Well, for one thing we've got his passport details; then there's his student permit, he has to report into the Embassy regularly to maintain that; and the polytechnic he's supposed to be studying at..."

"Okay, okay," Stone cut him short, "I just wanted to know if you knew."

"There are plenty of avenues we can still explore."

"You're right, except for one little detail."

"What's that?"

"This Kho Chiah Sek's not going to wait for us to go swanning around the establishment before he strikes next, he's sure to be waiting for just the right opportunity. What we desperately need to do is narrow that field of choice down, especially when his targets are as wide apart as these are."

"You'll just have to reinforce your surveillance, that's all."

"Oh yes, and alert him, if he isn't already."

"Well don't you think he knows what's going on already?"

As soon as Stone entered his squad room, he caught sight of Mark and beckoned him into his office. He took out the report from Hong Kong and passed it to him, "Get someone to copy this lot and come straight back and we'll go through it."

"Have we got him, Boss?"

"We certainly have."

Mark turned back, "Oh... Mary rang... I left a contact number on your desk."

When Stone got through to the number, it sounded as if he was onto a switchboard and had to wait for her reply.

"Is that you, Simon?" Mary came on.

"Yes it is, I hope I'm not disturbing you"

"No... it's all right, they agreed to take a break."

"So you're in a meeting are you? What's so urgent?"

"Steve Farney's doctor rang me. I don't know why," she paused, it took ages until she continued, Stone had to prompt her, "Oh sorry, Simon," he sensed she was upset.

"What's wrong. You sound upset."

"Simon... Steve died in the early hours of this morning."

Now it was Stone's turn to be silent. His mind immediately leapt to a fifth killing.

"Simon... are you still there?"

"Yes... sorry, it came as a shock. What happened, do you know?"

"Apparently he had a bad dream early in the evening, a nightmare the doctor said, and they had to give him a sedative to relax him."

"I thought for a moment our killer got passed the surveillance."

"Oh no... for some reason, he started having convulsions which brought on a stroke, and he died. I gather it happened very quickly; he didn't suffer."

"Well you know what this means. Kho Chiah Sek has only Collins and Drake now."

"Kho who?"

"Oh sorry, Mary. With you being out of touch you don't know the latest."

"So it seems."

"I can't tell you everything that's happened over the phone, you'll just have to come in. But we've made a breakthrough. From inquiries into POW camps in Malaya, we found a prisoner who knew Chessman. He confirmed his death in the camp; a horrible one I might add, which gave us the motive we wanted. Hammond used his contacts in Hong Kong to track him down."

"Hong Kong. My, you lot have been busy. Look what happens when I leave you alone for a minute."

Stone laughed, "Anyway, we got this man's name and his history right from the camp, everything fits, Mary: his age, the reason for the gap and the motive."

"Good, I'm pleased for you. I must go; you can fill me in when I get shot of this lot. Sorry about Steve, he was the last one out of this bunch of misfits that should go this way."

Later that afternoon Mark walked into Stone's office and sat down. He looked tired; he looked as if he could do with a holiday.

Stone glanced over from the report he was still studying, "What's your problem?"

Mark placed the papers he had in front of Stone, "I've been onto the Australian Embassy all this time. I must have spoken to everyone."

"And did you get any satisfaction?"

"I don't know, Boss... you tell me."

Stone picked up the papers and checked; it was a difficult read.

"Well they confirm everything we already know right up to his address in Uxbridge, and him going to the Willesden Polytechnic." Stone read on, "I see they lost contact with him after that... what's this about his passport?"

"Oh yes, Boss. In 1980, November in fact, he used his passport as identification to purchase a van of some sort. Apparently it's a fairly normal procedure when you don't have any British collateral."

"And?" Stone said, expectantly.

"Oh yes, sorry. In the process, they always want to verify the purchaser's personal details such as date of birth and address. The one given to us was different from the current one we had in Uxbridge, this one was in Hammersmith... see," he pointed it out.

"And this is his last current address as far as they know?" Stone asked.

"Until that last date in November, it doesn't appear they've had any further contact with the man. He seems to have dropped off the planet again."

By the time they had done their research into the latest address in the Hammersmith area it was getting late. Stone stood up, walked around his desk, and looked out of his window across to the Houses of Parliament and Big Ben.

"Good heavens... is it that time already?" he said. "Time to head home, Mark; it looks like it's going to be another big day again tomorrow."

"Hammersmith is it, Boss?"

CHAPTER 21

Early morning was hardly the time to be sitting in a car in Hammersmith unless you had business in the area; there were too many busybodies eager to report you. Stone did not intend to tip his hand at this stage; the last thing he wanted was the Malayan eluding them again as he did in Uxbridge.

As far as he was concerned, the police had no idea he lived in this neighbourhood, unlike the massive media and pavement pounding in Uxbridge to locate the van. They watched quietly for a few moments until Mark became nervous.

"Are we going to wait here all day, Boss?"

"Well I'm certainly not going to rush the place. There must be a dozen ways out of there and we cannot cover them all without proper planning. Besides, if he's still there, he'll be all right for an hour or so."

"So what are we doing in the meantime?"

"Before I set up a raid, I want to know the lay of the land. We have to find out exactly where he is, how many exits there are and when he comes and goes."

"And what do you have in mind, Boss?"

"We'll play salesmen; you remember how to do that, don't you?"

"I think so, what am I selling?"

"Well it has to be something that you don't have to carry

with you."

"I could be a Bible pusher," Mark suggested.

"Where's your Bibles?"

"Okay, what about central heating?"

"Where's your brochures, they always want to see brochures?"

"All right, what do you suggest, Boss?"

"We're doing a survey on off-street parking," Stone said.

"That's good; it'll give us a chance to ask about his van."

"Exactly... now you're thinking. You do the doors below the flat, I'll do the other side, and we can work our way towards him."

"How far away, Boss?"

"Well we don't want to look as if we just went straight to his place, use your own judgement, at least half a dozen numbers."

"This is going to take all morning," he grumbled, getting out of the car.

"No it won't, stop griping and get on with it."

Not only was Stone surprised in the number of people at home this time of day, he had difficulty noting down the mysterious cars parked outside their homes all hours of the day or night. His luck suddenly changed when he knocked on the door next to the alleged suspect. A rough old man answered. He studied Stone suspiciously.

It was the mention of off-street parking that interested him. His watery eyes brightened and his nicotine stained fingers held the door ajar.

"I'm looking into complaints about cars parked in the street until late," Stone said.

He gruffly replied, "I 'ope you're goner do somefing about this lot, I can't get any sleep, I works during the night yer see."

"A night watchman?" Stone commented, pretending to take notes.

"Yeah... at the yard," he saw Stone's eyebrow raise, "Railway."

"Oh... I see. So why can't you get any sleep"

"Well it's all this traffic ain't it, coming and going they do. They should get some decent cars, instead of these old bangers."

"Hard to start are they?"

"I'll say... that blue van next door makes an awful row."

"It's not here now."

"Well it won't be, will it? He goes off in the morning, just as I gets me 'ed down, and comes back a couple o' times later before I go to work."

"What times would that be?"

"What do you want to know for?"

"Well you do want us to look into it, don't you. It's not much good the police coming round when he's out."

The old man finally took his smelly hand out of Stone's face, scratched his head and thought, "Yeah... course I do."

He gave Stone the times along with other details related to Kho Chiah Sek's activity; boxes he constantly carried to his van and people he was seen talking to, especially the black man in the upstairs flat across the street. Stone could not resist a quick glance up at the tattered net-curtains opposite, not realising he was being watched, both of them were; as a coffee coloured hand let the net slip back.

Mark reached the suspects front door just as Stone was finishing with the old man, promptly getting the door slammed in his face. After knocking several times, it was obvious no one was home, unless the occupants were choosing not to answer.

Stone walked up behind him and told him the next-door occupant gave him a list of times their man was out with his van, and this was one of them. He also mentioned the fact that the occupant of the blue van was always off-loading cardboard boxes and nudged his memory regarding the mysterious boxes in Lonergan's barn. Walking slowly back to the car. Stone told

Mark that he was sure they were being watched by a friend of the suspect, while they tried so much to look like mundane door knockers.

Driving out of the street they turned left and left again down an alley used as an entry to the rear of the houses. The car slowed, but did not stop behind Kho Chiah Sek's flat, whilst they examined the rear of the building and its possible exits. Had they turned the other way and looked down the alley of the houses opposite, they would have seen the battered old blue van they had been looking for.

Now having a good idea that their suspect was still residing at this address, from the description of the blue van and its owner, Stone's only thought was to set up a discreet surveillance to identify the man and his movements, before they finally planned the raid they hoped would end this terrible episode.

As Mark turned into Victoria Street, off the Embankment, and headed for the car park behind the Scotland Yard offices, Stone was already planning his next offensive.

On returning to the office, Stone took a big chance in thinking he read the old man correctly, by phoning him and explaining why he had called at his house, and asking if they could set up a surveillance team there to wait and watch for the blue van.

The old man told him he was probably too late, that immediately after they left, he heard the van start up and leave from the alley behind the houses opposite. Stone was furious, but continued to arrange for his men to watch the flat.

"Damn" he shouted as Mark leaned in.

"Trouble?"

"Oh... we've blown it, Mark. Or I have," he sat with his head in his hands.

"Why the sudden change. I thought we were on a good thing?"

"I've just made arrangements for surveillance from the old man's house next door, and he informed me that the van left from behind the houses across the road shortly after we left. I should have checked both sides, we may have caught him."

"How does he know?"

"During our conversation regarding off-street parking, he made a point of knowing it was the blue van by the noise it made."

"I see. So what are we going to do now?"

"We're left with no option but to continue with our plans, but modified. First, get someone down there quickly to watch his flat and his friend's across the road. Second, whoever you put in the old man's house must first get the registration of the van."

"Do you think the old man will know it?"

"He knew just about everything else. We need that number so we can alert our patrols. Who knows, we might get lucky and spot him somewhere. Finally, we'll give him twenty-four hours, and then raid the place. So set up the paperwork."

"Right, Boss, done."

By late evening, the surveillance officer had nothing to report. There was no sign of life from the friend's flat either, no lights from any windows, no vehicles parked outside or in either alleys; It appeared they had both done a bunk

Then, around nine thirty there was a development that caught Stone off-guard. A patrolling constable had spotted Kho Chiah Sek's van. The disturbing fact was the location: it was outside Ralph Collins pub.

Ralph Collins had used a pre-arranged signal, by blipping the pub Neon sign twice to notify the officers outside he suspected the killer was in his pub. When they casually walked in, Collins pointed out a suspicious looking Indian matching the description they had of the suspect. They split up and converged on him from each side, taking hold of his arms and leading him off to

Collins office where they questioned him and duly found he had good identification, which did not tally with their records.

Once they found his documents to be genuine, they had no option but to let him go and return their attention to the blue van. It was obvious the Indian had been a ruse to allow the real suspect to dump the conspicuous van right where they least expected it. Stone was furious and decided to leave Mark in charge of Collins surveillance while he dealt with the investigation of the flat in Hammersmith.

"I do hope you got Forensics onto that van straight away."

"I did, Boss... and we're interviewing Collins again. I thought from what the constable said he was a bit hasty when he triggered the neon signal."

"And did they come up with anything?"

"Not a lot, Boss. It was clean as a whistle. Forensic is checking the boxes inside now, they were all empty by the way; just like the ones at Lonergan's"

"Is there no indication what they may have contained?"

"No. Whatever it was, it didn't contaminate the cardboard. What I can't understand is, why ditch his best asset?"

"I think he realised the van's usefulness has reached its end."

"That means he's going to need new transport."

"That's a good point. Maybe he's borrowed the coloured friend's vehicle. We need to find him and that... " Stone glanced at the Indian's details. "That Narasimram individual... See if there's a connection. It's too much of a coincidence."

While Mark left with Constable Freeman to visit the Earls Court address Narasimram gave him, Stone made his way back to the Hammersmith flat.

They soon found number 212, and as the Inspector followed at a discreet distance, the Constable knocked on the door. It took a second knock before a silhouette finally appeared at the frosted glass panel.

"Who is it," the blurred image asked from behind the door.

"Is that, Mr Narasimram?" the Constable called out.

"Who wants to know?"

"Come on open the door, Sir... it's the police."

The bolts were drawn back, the lock turned and the door slowly opened and a long black haired Indian head filled the six inch gap, while the rest of his body remained behind the door, as if someone was going to attack him.

"What do you want. I've already given my statement to the police."

"Open up, Mr Narasimram," the Inspector ordered.

The door opened, revealing he was in his pyjamas: scruffy ones at that.

"What's the matter, Sir, have we disturbed your slumber, late night was it?"

"Never you mind, what do you want?"

"Well for starters you can let us in."

"Why should I, where's your warrant?"

"Mr Narasimram, we only want to check your statement?"

He stepped back, at the same time asking to see their warrant cards; he said he needed to know they were real police officers. They flashed them in front of his face and continued into the front room.

"Where do you think you're going. If you want to ask questions, you can do it out here in the hall. You haven't got my permission to search the house."

The inspector immediately spotted two empty glasses beside plates of half-eaten sandwiches on a coffee table in front of a couch. He nodded upwards to the constable behind the Indian, to search upstairs.

"Got a guest have we, Sir, that wouldn't happen to be Kho

Chiah Sek would it," the Inspector asked to divert his attention from what the constable was doing.

"Where's he going, you have no right."

The Inspector tried to grab his arm as he turned to follow the constable.

By now, he had swiftly scaled the stairs, three at a time. At the top he immediately turned into the first open door, it was a bedroom, sparsely furnished with only a double bed, small table with radio and lamp on, a second-hand chest of draws and a large travelling chest covered in clothes.

The Constable's attention was on the bed. A young Indian girl lay face down to one side, buried in her waist-length raven hair. As the other two arrived only seconds later, they found the constable transfixed.

"Cover yourself up you silly bitch," the Indian screamed out to her.

"Have you checked the other rooms," the Inspector asked the constable curtly.

"No, Sir," still not quite rid of his vision.

"Then get on with it," the Inspector was noticeably embarrassed.

Downstairs, the irate Indian was still mouthing his objections.

"Oh shut up for Christ sake," the Inspector shouted, pushing him onto the broken down old couch. "If I hear one more word out of you, other than an answer to a question, you'll wish you never heard my name," he continued, searching the room for any indication that would link him with the Malaysian.

"You can't do anything to me," he replied indignantly.

"Oh can't I... where would you like me to start. Tax audit, emigration... "

"All right, all right... you've made your point," he said, reaching down beside the arm of the couch for a bottle of scotch, and taking a swig. "What is it you want?"

"Just a little co-operation, that's all Ashish. You don't mind me using your first name do you. I get sick of these long surnames."

"Whatever... just get on with it."

"Oh anxious to get back to bed are we?"

"Leave her out of it. Do you here?"

The Inspector smiled and glanced at his notebook.

"Okay Ashish, don't get upset. Now according to your statement at Ralph Collins pub, you eventually admitted to knowing Kho Chiah Sek. Is that true?"

"I said it was, didn't I."

"Right... did this man ask you to go to the pub and impersonate him?"

"No... I just went to the pub."

"You're lying. Why would you go to a pub in another district?"

"You know everything don't you?"

"Well I know this, if you don't start telling us the truth now, I shall leave and start making some phone calls," the Inspector stressed.

The Indian looked sick as a dog; he was obviously terrified of what might happen to him if he opened his mouth.

"Okay, you know I'm a dead man don't you."

"Stop over reacting, if we catch this man, I promise you he'll go down for a long time. On the other hand, if we don't, what's he going to think now, especially if he's watching us."

"You made your point, there's no need in going on about it."

"Okay then. Tell us what happened then we'll leave you alone."

"It's Butch Mathews I know, the black man that lives across the road to this Kho Chiah Sek you keep on about. He asked Butch if he knew anyone who looked like him enough to fool the police surveillance, as he needed to get the heat off him for a couple of days. Butch brought him around here a few days ago, and he left some clothes for me to wear, telling me what to do and say if the police questioned me. I was supposed to carry on the impersonation for a couple of days, but I lost my bottle when I heard the barman talking to the police about what he'd done, and how dangerous he was; so I come clean."

"And have you any idea where this man is now?" the Inspector questioned.

"No he didn't tell me; in fact he didn't talk to me at all."

"You just said he did."

"Just to give me my instructions. He was arguing with Butch most of the time. He wasn't interested in me; he just wanted me to impersonate him."

"Could you hear what it was all about?"

"Not really, I caught a few words: Something about Butch not being able to go back to his flat, and this other fella telling him to come with him."

"Did you hear where?"

"No, but it wasn't in London."

"What makes you think that?"

"Because Butch said something like, 'I like it here, I don't like other places.'"

"That could have meant the suburbs."

"Maybe, but I don't think so. Butch is a London boy, born and bred. He'd feel lost anywhere else. The suburbs are only a car drive away: that's where he does most of his thieving. No, it's outside London."

"Very good Ashish, you've done well. Now what about this Butch, where can I find him," the Inspector asked, tying up loose ends.

"Oh no, he'll definitely kill me if I tell you."

"No he won't, we'll say we got the information from a neighbour."

"Yeah, I can see him believing that story," he looked at the Inspector's face; he wanted everything or else. "Okay... you'll find him at the Hammersmith Snooker Hall on the high street, he practically lives there."

"Very well Ashish, now that wasn't so bad, was it, you get back into that warm bed, and we'll go and see if Butch is in a talkative mood."

They left the Indian to his nuptials and crossed over to the surveillance car that had just arrived. The Inspector told the officer to stay on here until he was relieved in case they missed this Butch Mathews character.

The Inspector decided he had better phone Stone.

"Boss... I've found the coloured guy; he's in the Snooker Hall at Hammersmith. We're on our way there now."

"Great... Don't go in. Wait for me to arrive."

The Inspector and Constable Freeman were already sitting outside the hall when Stone tapped on the car window. They had a quick discussion then left, leaving the constable to watch just in case Butch decided to make a dash for it.

Apart from accustoming themselves to the Troglodyte-like environment, they strained their eyes down the long row of tables: islands of green baize highlighted by overhanging lights, capturing the swirling smoke rising towards the ceiling somewhere in the darkness. They were surprised to find so many tables busy, making their job that more difficult as they looked for a coloured man called Butch.

Stone glanced at his watch; it was eleven forty-five. It was their lunchtime by the amount of men around the long counter down one side of the room. They were stuffing their mouths with meat pies washed down by large mugs of tea.

They suddenly realised, while they remained in the shadows, they were anonymous, and then as they entered the island of light, the typically indifferent look of, 'Cop present', crossed the occupants' faces.

"Out of your territory aren't yah," the big man behind the counter called out.

"Superintendent Stone and Inspector Fraser," Stone said in response, as they presented their warrant cards for everyone to see.

"They're no good to you up here mate. I suggest you turn round quietly and go back the way you came."

"We don't want any trouble, we're not here to cop anyone; we just want to talk," Stone continued, looking around him.

"Did yah hear that mates? They just want to talk."

"All right you lot," Stone shouted above their cries. "Shut up and listen for a moment," it actually went quiet. Who was this cop with the nerve to tell them to shut up? "You've got two choices; one you let me quietly talk to someone called Butch, and it's information we want only, or I call the hit squad down here to go through this place like a dose of salts, which I'm sure the embarrassment would close this place down."

"You wouldn't dare," a voice came from out of the darkness.

"Give me your radio," Stone asked Mark, who was beginning to sweat profusely as shadowy figures began to move forward.

"This is R37, patch me into home base, over," he called, over a resounding squawk which could be heard by everyone.

"Home base, what is your request R37. Over."

The Superintendent held the radio out for everyone to hear, "Requesting full alert of SPU force location address to follow. Over. Everyone heard the crackle of the radio, all hanging on the pause.

"Message received R37, awaiting your address. Over."

The sweaty hulk in a dirty vest came out from behind the counter looking menacing; Mark instinctively covered Stone's back.

"All right, Superintendent, your bluff's working for now. Have your interview, then go. But the next time you come in here, you'd better have a good reason."

A large coloured man approached them from out of the darkness. He had the look of a child, despite his size, wearing a baseball cap, jersey and jeans. He stood in front of them still holding his snooker cue.

"Are you the man known as, Butch?" Stone questioned.

"That's me, what do you want. I haven't done anything."

"No one says you have, we just want to talk to you... alone."

"Okay," he said, "let's go over here."

He led them towards a room filled with lockers, still clutching onto his cue.

"Why don't you put the cue down, Butch," Mark asked.

"I don't put this cue down for anyone," he said aggressively, his first sign so far.

"We'd feel a lot more at ease if you put the cue down, Butch," Stone said.

"You think I'd hit you with it?" Butch said, laughing. "These are what you've got to watch," he brandished his fist in Stone's face. "My cue's far too valuable to hit anyone with, or let them pinch it."

"Okay... okay, Butch... you can hold onto your cue."

"I will, you believe it."

"Butch, let's not mince words, we know you've been helping the Malaysian Kho Chiah Sek, you were with him yesterday in your flat, and you helped him dump his van outside the Queen's Head in Hackney last night. So where have you been since then; you haven't been home."

Butch looked serious; it was obvious Kho Chiah Sek did his thinking for him.

"Who's been talking, was it that smelly Indian. I'll kill him."

"Nobody's been talking, Butch, they didn't have to," Stone started. "We've been watching Kho Chiah Sek for ages, so we know what everyone else was doing also. We know where you all live. Who you see and what you do. But he's left you all in it."

"He hasn't left me in anything, I didn't do anything."

"You mean you don't know about the four murders he's dropped you in." Butch's face almost burst with shock; his eyes popping out of his head.

"I didn't kill anyone; I just filled his boxes for him."

"Is that so," Stone said, glancing at Mark taking notes. They had him, he admitted to his association with the suspect. "Well, Butch, I'm afraid it doesn't matter if you didn't kill anyone, you were his accomplice, so that makes you as guilty as him; unless you turn evidence against him."

"What's this 'Turn evidence'," he asked.

Stone smiled at Butch and moved closer.

"Well if I tell the court that you were helpful in apprehending this suspect, the judge would look upon your action in this case more lightly; he may even dismiss the charges against you altogether."

Butch hesitated and thought for a moment, you could see his brain trying to sort everything out that Stone had just said. "Wait a minute; you said this was only going to be a talk, not any arrest or anything like that."

Stone was about to be caught by his own petard. "Who said anything about arresting you, Butch," he looked at Mark. "Did I say anything about arresting him?"

"No, Superintendent, you didn't."

"So what are you playing here, games. You think I'm thick do you."

"No, Butch, we're not playing games."

"Then why tell me about being an accomplice?"

"We're not here to arrest you; we're here to talk about what you and Kho Chiah Sek were doing. But I had to warn you that this man is a killer, and if you don't co-operate with us, you stand the chance of being convicted with him," Stone looked him in the eye. "All I want at this time is information about your activities together. If you refuse to help us... then I'll arrest you, and you'll carry the can. I don't mind."

"Okay. I just helped him fill his boxes."

"When did you first meet him?"

"Only about three weeks ago, he came into the club looking for someone to help him for a few days. He asked Barry if he knew anyone."

"Barry?" Mark questioned.

"Yeah... Barry the big fat man behind the counter. He runs the club for the owner and helps us lot out now and then; you know, with the odd job."

"Okay... so Barry meets this man and puts him onto you."

"Well not really. Barry finds the people and charges the bloke, and then pays me. Sometimes I don't even see them."

"So it was Barry who employed you?"

"Yeah."

"But you saw this one."

"Well I had to, didn't I. We packed the boxes in his flat and drove them around in his van, dropping his deliveries off."

"I see... and what actually did you pack into these boxes?"

"It was nothing illegal."

"So what was it?" Stone emphasised.

"It was knickers and things."

Stone almost burst out laughing.

"Knickers and things. Are you telling me he got you a job delivering knickers?"

"Well he didn't know what I was delivering... you won't tell him will you?"

"The point is, Butch, what did you tell him?"

"I told him it was magazines, you know porno stuff... I had to buy some to give him, as a free gift to shut him up."

"Okay, Butch, what did you two do with these knickers?"

"Kwo, that's what I called him, would bring a big van load around to his flat, and we would spend the night sorting all the same size and colour, and putting them into the same box, and he would write out a label and stick it on."

"This label wouldn't happen to be a famous brand by any chance?" Mark questioned, finding the whole thing too ridiculous for words.

"I don't know what he did."

"Okay that's fine, it's no problem. Where did you go then?" Stone asked.

"I didn't, he never took me to his customers."

"I see, well where did you go the other day, did you go and pick up the Indian?" Stone prompted him: he was getting desperate.

"No... we met him later, first we went to a warehouse to clean the van out."

"Whereabouts was that exactly?" Mark asked.

"I wasn't really looking, it was somewhere in Wandsworth, under a bridge, I could hear the trains going over us."

"Good... then what?"

Butch thought for a moment, playing with his cue. It was obvious Butch had some difficulty organising his thoughts, and the interview was difficult.

"When it got dark we took the van to the Indian's house. I waited in the van as Kwo went inside and talked to him, then they both came out and we went to the pub."

"But you didn't leave it outside straight away, did you?"

"No... we parked up the road a bit, the Indian got out and walked up to the pub and went in. About ten minutes later these cops went in and arrested him. That was our signal to park the van outside."

"How did you know they were cops?"

"We'd been watching them."

"So what happened after you left the van?"

"We separated... I came here; Barry lets a room out if you're desperate."

"We'll have to drive you home and check your place for anything on Kho."

"He didn't stay there, you won't find anything."

Stone turned him around and pointed him back towards the tables.

"It's only procedure, Butch. On the way do you think you could remember where the warehouse was if we take you there?"

"I'll try."

Before they left, Stone tactfully explained to Butch's protective friend Barry that they had not arrested him, he was just helping them with their enquiries, following that, they would return him to his home.

Barry looked at Butch, concerned for him. Butch nodded.

CHAPTER 22

It was the worst time to be cutting through traffic from Hammersmith Road, passed Fulham across the river to Wandsworth. By the time they had concluded their arduous interview and inspected the small flat Butch called home, it was late afternoon.

Eventually the congestion eased as they crossed Putney Bridge and turned right towards Wandsworth, where their second problem began. Lock-ups peppered the area all the way along the main line from Clapham Junction between the Putney and Wandsworth bridges; you could have heard the trains overhead from any one of them.

Stone attempted to steer Butch, pointing out each noticeable landmark, some he remembered others he just looked blank, with Mark patiently following their shouted instructions. 'This way, no that', until everyone became confused, beginning to think they had passed the same sign earlier.

As dusk began creeping over the city, Stone became agitated; he knew the badly light back streets would be much harder to recognise once it was dark. He decided on one more turn around the bend in the Thames between Battersea and Putney, just in case Butch had his suburbs confused.

As it turned out, on the return journey Butch started to get excited as he began to recognise more landmarks; he was seeing them from the other direction. If Kho drove to his lock-up after visiting the Indian's house, he would have used this more direct route, rather than approaching it from Hammersmith.

They were just passing under the arches of Wandsworth Bridge, leading off York Road, when Butch shouted, "We're here, stop a bit." He got out of the car and looked around, examining all the nearby archways.

They stopped at a large junction of roads, with a canal running down to the Thames a few hundred yards away; the unbelievable noise of a passing express above them on the viaduct made Stone feel much more confident as he watched Butch pace back and forth, looking for his bearings.

He frantically waved his arms at them, pointing to the right, down a small street leading towards a green area; the car followed, and Stone wound down his window as they reached him.

"It's here somewhere," Butch said, leaning through the window, almost hitting Stone, it was so dark in the car. "There, those green painted doors... to the right," He said, running off ahead of them. "Yeah, this is it; I remember this old sign here."

He was pointing to an old ban the bomb sign, amongst other fading graffiti that covered the surface of two large wooden doors. Unbeknown to them, a ghostly figure with long hair listened to the noise as Stone jiggled the large metal catch.

The occupant had prepared for such an occurrence as he quickly gathered his immediate belongings and quietly worked his way down amongst the mass of stacked boxes at the far end of the arch.

Dragging the rickety door across the cobbles gave the shadowy figure the precious seconds that separated Stone from an encounter with his suspect; he would never know how close he came, except for his acute sense of smell.

"What's up?" Mark questioned Stone's strange stance on entering.

Stone stood silhouetted against the grimy semi-circular windows that filled one wall of the large open storage area, narrowing as it passed under the arches of the viaduct.

Suddenly they were illuminated; freezing them both with shock, until Butch enthusiastically shouted out behind them, "I told you, this is his stash."

They turned to see him standing by the light switch with a broad grin on his face, oblivious to the fact that he had put an end to any element of surprise.

"Butch," Stone shouted. "What are you doing," he checked Mark. "Are you okay?"

"Yes, Boss," he said, catching his breath. "Did you hear something?"

"No, it was just as we came in, I sensed a strange smell. Not the usual musty smell you get with these places, but… " he lifted his head and sniffed the air again. "You know… as if someone had just been here before us, a body smell, that's it."

Mark was just as perplexed, trying to capture what Stone sensed.

"All I get is dampness, motor oil and… yes, now you come to mention it, a smell of… crisps. Salt and vinegar, very strong as I walk this way," Mark commented, moving to the first group of boxes.

"You mean these," Butch called out before him, holding out a large bag of crisps he pulled from a carton. "Want one?" he said, offering the bag in his hand.

"No thanks."

Stone was oblivious of their banter, examining other boxes over to one side. Empty cartons made up as if someone had been sleeping in them. When Mark arrived to see his discovery, Stone pointed out some empty crisp packets, old bedding wrapped around straw and today's newspapers.

What attracted him most of all was the candle in a broken saucer. From its black extinguished wick, a faint wisp of smoke slowly curled upwards disappearing quickly into the shadows cast by the curved ceiling.

He reached down and cupped his hand over the smoke; warmth was still radiating from the molten wax, telling him someone had snuffed it out recently. He rushed to the window on the opposite wall, with gaping holes from shattered panes and listened, but screeching brakes of a train pulling into the station nearby muffled all else.

"Someone's been here that's for sure," he said, walking back.

Mark and Butch were examining the boxes; they were full of all sorts of cheap commodities, nothing worth considering."

"Get the team down here, there might be something amongst this lot, although I very much doubt it," Stone ordered.

"The full works, Boss?"

"Of course… our mystery man could have been Kho, he may have left something, and then again it could have just been a squatter."

"The doors weren't open, Boss."

"I'm sure if we looked around this place, we'd find a dozen ways in and out. Anyway, knowing what we do so far about his activities, our suspect could have been renting the place," Stone nodded over towards Butch and his second bag of crisps.

"I did good didn't I?" he said, screwing up his pack.

"You did, Butch, we're grateful. Don't throw that bag down, where's the other?. Stone questioned, not wanting his rubbish mixed up with the suspects.

"Sorry," he said, picking it up, then the other and he stuffed them both into his pocket. "Does this mean the judge will let me off now?"

"I'll make sure all your help goes into my report."

"Great, are we going home now?"

Stone had no answer for him; he was still preoccupied with the irritating feeling he had when they first came in. In the harsh un-shaded light that was illuminating the immediate vicinity and casting deep black shadows amidst the cardboard maze created by the cartons of crisps, knickers and whatever else this titular entrepreneur was involved with, Stone was unable to shake the feeling they were not the only ones in this damp place.

He raised his hand for silence as Mark continued debating with Butch the merits of Kho's crisps. He tried to separate the thumps and hisses of the trains passing overhead, from a scuffing sound over by the large window. He followed the sound while the other two looked on in amazement at his shadowy figure tiptoeing amongst the boxes.

The further Stone entered the catacomb-like structure the darker it got, and with that darkness, came a clammy cold that began to penetrate his thin clothing. Stone stopped by a broad pillar that peeled and flaked as he touched it; years of rotting whitewash clinging to the palm of his sweaty hand.

He looked back at the pool of light and his companions as he disappeared into the shadows. If the killer was there, and he still had his Samurai, Stone would be in trouble. Minutes passed by as Stone listened, the sound was not there anymore.

He moved forward amongst the next group of boxes, instinctively finding a course between them. The gap was too narrow, and as the sides of his jacket brushed against the cardboard, it made a rasping sound. The same sound that alerted him back by the doors.

There was a lull in the activity of the trains, a gap in their arrival and departure from the nearby station. His adrenalin was rising; he could hear his own heart beating, even the distant bark of a dog over the nearby traffic on Wandsworth Road.

He stood fixed to the spot, not knowing which way to go, until he heard the sound again, just up ahead to the left. Whoever it was, they were making their way to the left-hand corner, to the right of the last window.

This puzzled Stone. If he was making for a way out of this place, why not choose one of the nearer windows, where some of the panes were completely missing.

Stone began to follow the sound again, and concentrating so, he accidentally dislodged one of the cartons, which fell to the ground with a resounding thud. This brought on a louder scuffle up ahead, and he saw for the first time the shadowy silhouette of the occupant, no more than five yards in front of him.

Stealth was no longer the game. The figure up ahead smashed through the remaining boxes and dived into a power conduit in the wall separating this lockup with the next. Stone now waved his arms frantically to get Mark's attention, while shouting his orders.

"Head him off man, through one of those broken windows in the corner."

Not aware who Stone was chasing, Mark called back, "Okay, Boss."

Stone cautiously entered a square concrete conduit about five feet high and no more than a yard wide; he assessed this after scraping his head as he entered. He bent his six feet frame and continued in a shuffling motion into the total darkness, and except for a small rectangle of light at the far end, he was blind.

From its size, he guessed it was a few hundred yards away. He also noticed red and orange lights, implying it opened up onto the rail-yard.

He knew his quarry was in the conduit with him, but could not hear or see him above the echo of his own shuffling feet, bringing his thoughts uncannily back to the first forensic report, pointing out the distinctive blood stained sneaker print.

Suddenly the patch of light he was heading for disappeared. He froze, his heart began racing again as a claustrophobic feeling gripped him. As he stared desperately into the darkness, not knowing why the rectangle of light had vanished, or if the killer had turned back on him, a small chink of light appeared changing its shape until he realised the ghostly figure he was chasing was climbing out of the conduit.

Stone shouted, identifying himself as a police officer, cautioning him to stop; that other police were waiting for him outside. Almost out of the rectangle of light by now, his silhouette plain to see, he stopped, and appeared to look back into the darkness.

"Give it up man," Stone shouted. "There's nowhere to go."

He said nothing. He turned and stepped out into the night. In that split second before he disappeared, Stone saw the outline of a longhaired man; his ethnic profile highlighted by a red reflection. He was out onto the lines and would be lost amongst the shunting carriages.

Stone reached the opening and cautiously stepped out onto a concrete slab below half a dozen steps leading up to the railway lines. Lifting his head slowly above the wall that surrounded him, he discovered he was in a pit, in the middle of the railway junction running alongside the main line that ran across the viaduct; the conduit had taken him under the lines.

Before he had a chance to look for his man there was an ear-shattering blast from a train's siren as it came out of nowhere, thundering passed him, lifting the dirt and gravel into the air, almost smothering him.

Directly behind him was the heavy crossed metal structure of a battery of signals, the answer to his distant red and orange lights.

Ahead of him, the open lines curved off out of sight towards the west. On his left, the outbound lines ran alongside a goods yard, and as he peered across to the clusters of waiting wagons, he spotted his man again. He was working his way slowly through the shadows.

Stone raced up the steps, across to the open lines and into the gap on the other side of the wagons his man was using as a cover. He gingerly made his way on a parallel course in a crouched position, checking through the wheels for any sign of his adversary's legs.

A sound above him, to his right, on the small platform between the wagons made him look upwards. He caught a fleeting glimpse of a rod-like object crashing into the side of his head: then oblivion.

Mark lifted Stone's bleeding head onto his lap, he looked ghastly in the pale green light from a signal nearby, and he feared the worst. "Come on, Boss... for Christ sake don't die on me.

When Mark crossed the lines, after a train had passed, blocking his view, Stone was already disappearing amongst the parked wagons, and by the time he did reach him, he had already been attacked and the assailant was nowhere to be seen.

"I'm okay... don't fuss," Stone said, lifting himself and grabbing for his head. "Christ, what did he hit me with?"

"This metal bar by the looks of it," Mark said, as they examined the rod.

Stone was silent, leaving his expression to say it all. It had been a long day, and all he wanted to do was get back to civilisation and a large whisky.

"I ought to attend to that head of yours, Boss."

"You can hardly do that here."

"I know... that's what I was about to say. We have a Red Cross pack in the car if you think you can get back there."

Stone flashed Mark one of his superior looks.

"I've only had a knock on my head, I'm not totally incapacitated," he cursed as he rose to his feet shakily. Then with Mark's help, Stone limped back towards the lines. "By the way...

what happened to Butch?"

"Oh hell, Boss... I forgot all about him."

They finally arrived back at the lockup to find Butch had gone.

"He could be miles away by now," Stone said, turning back to the doors. "The thought of the killer seeing him with us must have put the fear of god into him."

"We'll find him, Boss. In the meantime let me fix your head, it's bleeding onto your collar now, and we don't want to spoil that expensive suit."

Stone felt the damp spot on his neck and walked outside. He stopped with that same stillness he had when he heard the man amongst the boxes.

"What's up now?" Mark said, trying to lead him towards the car.

"Can't you hear it... that knocking sound?"

It was coming from the car. Mark walked over and peered inside. Butch's terrified white eyes peered back at him through the darkness of the window.

"Well I never," he exclaimed. "It's Butch, Boss... he's sitting in the back seat."

He opened the door and led Stone to the front seat, sitting him down as Butch began to wail how they had left him to the mercy of a maniac.

"Shut up, Butch," Stone shouted, not looking at him as he sat sideways in the front seat with his legs out on the cobbles. "I've got a terrible headache."

Butch lent forward over Stone's seat and inspected the wound on his head.

"Oh dear... Did he do that?"

"Oh please, Butch, just sit back in your seat and be quiet."

"I knew that man was dangerous, and you went off and left me."

"He could hardly cause you any harm when I was chasing him."

"He could have doubled back."

The Superintendent turned and faced him with one of his deadly stares. "He's still out there, and if you don't shut up, I'll turn you out and you can fend for yourself."

Mark continued cleaning his wound; he could see his boss had no time for Butch. He was far away still thinking about the killer.

"All done, Boss," Mark said, closing the Red Cross pack.

"How long do we have to wait for forensics?" Stone asked.

"I gather they're finishing off at the house in Hammersmith, Boss."

"Have they just got to that now?"

"Apparently we've been keeping them busy," Mark commented. As he spoke, the flashing lights of a patrol car pulled up behind.

"Is that them?" Stone asked, trying to see.

"No, Boss... I asked for a patrol car to wait for them."

"Good thinking. Head back to Hammersmith."

"Don't you think I should take you to a hospital, Boss?"

"No... I'm all right. If we're taking Butch back, we might as well have another look at the killer's house again at the same time."

The old man next door was quite active when they pulled up behind one of their other vehicles, he was arguing with a plain clothes detective waiting outside the brightly lit open doorway of the Indian's flat, shouting about them blocking his frontage.

"Can you see all this lot," he called out.

"It's okay, they're with me," Stone said.

"What do you mean; I thought you were to do with off-street parking?"

"I knew that would come back and bite you, Boss," Mark said, laughing as he continued on into the flat while Butch waited in the car, face pressed up against the window, blowing misty circles on the cold glass.

"I'm not with Parking, Sir, we're the police," he replied curtly, turning to a constable on the door. "Get him back in his house, and watch that idiot in my car."

Forensic were in the process of packing up when Stone entered the scene. Inspector Bletchley, the team leader, almost bumped into him on his way out.

"Ah... Superintendent, we're all finished here, I'll let you have my report in the morning, not much here though," he continued, examining Stone with a puzzled look on his face. "What happened to you?"

"It's too long a story to go into now."

"Looks as if you've had an argument with a dustcart," he laughed.

"Hold on, you're not finished yet," Stone replied, grabbing his elbow.

"How's that, we've covered every square inch of this place."

"Don't forget the lock-up, Inspector Fraser will brief you."

Hearing his name, Mark stepped into the hall from another room opposite, "What am I supposed to do, Boss?" he said.

"Brief DI Bletchley on the lock-up and get Butch home."

"What will you be doing, Boss?"

"I'm going to have a look around here for a bit."

The Indian's Terrace flat was an 'Up and Down', meaning he and his adjoining neighbour lived one above the other. In this case, his front door led directly into the lower flat, and his neighbour's opened onto a small hall and a flight of stairs to the upper flat.

Stone started the rounds slowly taking in the contents of each room. To his right, was the front room overlooking the tiny walled garden and street; a stark unlived-in room, smelling of damp cloth. The floor was covered with old torn lino, so thin that an imprint of the irregular floorboards could be seen showing through, caught by the light of a single naked bulb hanging from the centre of the ceiling.

An equally old couch was pushed up against a wall in the far corner, with cushions missing, exposing what was left of the inner springs. Stone squatted down beside the black grate fireplace surrounded by what once must have been beautifully decorated tiles, only now a group of shattered remnants. A few fragments of burnt paper lying to one side had caught his attention. He examined them carefully with his pen and found they were the outside edges of notepaper, probably an exercise book, minus any markings.

The grate itself was empty, and he hoped Inspector Bletchley had found something burnt in haste and bagged it for further investigation. Stone made a note in his diary to check that later as he placed the fragment in a bag of his own. On leaving the room he made one last three-sixty degree scan, noticing the powder trail left by the fingerprint men.

In the meantime, Mark had returned to the room he was in previously. This was further down where the stairs next door crossed the ceiling. It appeared to be the main living area, with a large table and chairs, television, cheap carpet and another couch to one side.

His attention returned to the table that was reminiscent of the one in Uxbridge; covered with thick felt and rolls of cloth. Pins were everywhere, stuck into the felt as if put there for easy access; a tin full of sewing bobbins lay to one side and an open bag of half eaten crisps; the same type Butch munched into at the lock-up.

In a corner by the television was a pile of paper rolls looking like patterns, which confirmed their suspicion, when they found his flat in Uxbridge; that he was in the garment trade. Stone thought it strange there was no sewing machine.

Most of the flat was a mess. The kitchen, toilet and small bathroom was filthy, and the absence of any food was baffling.

All Stone could see were breakfast dishes and a mass of fast-food containers spilling over a waste bin.

Mark walked in, looking tired, "Any luck in here, Boss?"

"No... This place is a pig sty, I don't suppose Butch's place is much better," he said, as they headed for the cool fresh air of the street.

"Actually, he's got it quite nice," Mark said.

"Maybe that's why they call him Butch."

After grabbing a sandwich or two from the all night vending machine and brewing a couple of Mark's steaming specials, they settled down in front of the white board, staring at the mass of notations. Stone started rubbing his head. He had forgotten his injury, but now the headache was back.

"Don't you think you should go and have an X-ray, Boss?"

"No... I'll be all right."

"You could have a fracture after a blow like that"

"Okay... damn it. I'll go to the hospital tomorrow."

"I'll make sure you do," Mark said.

They returned their attention to the board. Like the case itself, it had become a mess, with erratic notations everywhere.

"It's a lot different now to what it was a few weeks ago," Stone commented, trying to sip his tea, giving up and taking a bite out of his sandwich instead.

"You're right there, Boss, actually I have to clean it up a bit, things have changed a lot; it's taken on a mind of its own."

"Go on... say it. It's nothing like my original concept."

"We've progressed, Boss."

"You think so. He's still out there. I bet Hammond would have him locked up by now if this was still his case."

"I still think our way is more efficient than his."

The Superintendent rested back on the bench in front of the board, still staring at it. "You know it was different in those days, you didn't get promotions on passing exams; you had to have experience, especially if you were in charge of a lot of personnel in different work roles. I'm not saying nothing was achieved by taking the exams, just that first-hand experience was more practical then."

"We still need training, Boss, that's why I follow your lead."

"Good, I'm glad to hear you think like that."

"Now can we get down to our overview, Boss. I do have to go soon."

"Sorry, I often forget you lot have other lives besides the Met."

"We do, believe it or not.

"All right, point taken... leave the board until the morning."

"Thanks, Boss, I'll make an early start. Oh... that reminds me, Inspector Hammond called earlier; he said he'd pop round later for a drink."

"And you told him I'd be here until late?" Stone said, disinterested.

"Afraid so, I didn't know then you were going to get knocked on the head. Anyway it'll do you good, get out to the pub and chin-wag about old times."

"I don't chin-wag about old times," Stone claimed indignantly, as if the comment had inferred he was an old man.

"Sorry, Boss. Can I go?"

Stone stood up, stretched his arms as he stared at the board, "Okay, Mark, get off to the girlfriend or whatever, but remember I want to see this board in shape in the morning, this is the last move... I can feel it."

"What are you going to do now?" Mark asked, grabbing his coat.

"I'm going to sit down, try and relax and focus my attention on what questions I'm going to throw at Hammond. He's a good sounding board," he chuckled. "Not unlike Mary, by I could do with her foresight right now. I'm sure Hammond will have a good idea what this maniac is going to do next as well."

CHAPTER 23

Inspector Hammond stood silhouetted in the doorway watching Stone, who had his back to him staring out into the darkness through his large window.

"Thought I'd find you here," he said.

Stone was looking out towards the dark majestic towers of Westminster Abbey and beyond to the Houses of Parliament, identified by the illuminated face of Big Ben; moonlike against the starry office lights either side of the shimmering Thames. Below, in the inky darkness, the only sign of life in this metropolis was the continuous chain of red and white criss-crossing lights from London's evening traffic.

"And what brings you here, Inspector?" Stone answered indifferently, without turning round; he had no need to, by now the voice was familiar to him.

"Oh it's Inspector now is it, Sir?" Hammond replied.

"For heaven's sake, Jack, what do you want. Or are you here to gloat, say, 'I told you so', as you have on so many occasions."

"That's not true, and you know it," Hammond said, walking over to Stone's side of the desk, sitting in his deep reclining chair between the two windows, managing a sideways glance without moving his head.

Stone kept moving his position, "You say that now."

"I meant it... I just came over to congratulate you, and take you for a drink."

"After all that he got away."

"But you're closing in."

"At what cost."

"Inspector Fraser told me about your confrontation. Why aren't you at the hospital getting your head seen to?"

"Oh you're right... I need my head seen to. Why I didn't call for back up and surround the place before I went in, I don't know."

"You should take more notice of the Inspector. He would have followed the book. Not like us old ones. I would have done just the same."

Stone turned to face him for the first time, "Would you, Jack?"

Hammond laughed, "You know I would."

Stone returned to the window, "Do you remember, Jack, just across the road and around the corner... the old Scotland Yard?" he said.

"I certainly do. I spent a couple of years there in my early days."

"So did I, Jack, we must have just missed each other... again."

"Those were the days."

"You're right, Jack. And the Thames... it's always fascinated me."

"I suppose you're right, looking at it like that, makes you want to take stock of your life," he said, walking over to the window.

"That's it, Jack. You're exactly right," Stone agreed.

"Looks like Fraser was right after all."

"What do you mean?"

"You've given up, haven't you. Why did you want my case in the first place? It was just another notch to you, another rung on the ladder," Hammond goaded him.

Stone spun round; the light from the squad room caught his angry face, along with the three-inch long plaster above his left temple and the yellow discoloured bruise that was beginning to spread down his cheek. Hammond looked shocked.

"My God man you look terrible."

"I know, Jack... I just got carried away."

"You mean you just got drawn into a trap."

"I didn't, Jack... he was trying to get away... he didn't want a confrontation."

"You didn't know that. What if he was drawing you into a trap, and was waiting for you with that Samurai of his... then what?"

"Don't go on, I've got a big enough headache," Stone said with a grimace.

"That's just it, Stone, you've allowed him to do just that. Now you're sitting here feeling sorry for yourself looking out of your window, wondering where he is. While all the time he's probably preparing for his next victim, he's been playing you all the time; a half educated Malayan."

"I wish this last one hadn't been your case, Jack. I'm a good cop, despite your innuendoes, but I've been saddled with the notion that you've been out-thinking me all the time; instead of getting on with my job. I've allowed myself to wonder what you would have done when I had to make a decision. I couldn't see it before, but I can now, quite clearly. So it's no longer, Jack or Stone, it's Inspector and Superintendent, and when I want your advice in future I'll ask for it in just the same way I do the others; no special old buddy stuff."

"Bravo Sto... Superintendent, that's fine with me, Sir. Why don't we forget about magnificent scenes and get on with the job in hand?"

Stone looked surprised.

"What about your Boss. Although I imagine he has as much sway as I do."

"I just took some overdue leave, Sir, so I'm at your disposal, free of charge."

"Do I have a choice?" they looked at each other in the half-light and knew.

"As far as I'm concerned, Sir, there's only one objective, however it's done."

"So what were you saying about this half educated Malayan man, Inspector?"

"Sorry, Sir, I know you've had a traumatic experience tonight, but I didn't think that's the reason behind your mood. I had to shake you out of this death-wish."

"Well... where do we go from here?" Stone said, switching on the lights.

Inspector Hammond could see he was a lot worse than he first caught a glimpse of, although still a greenish shade, the bruise on the side of his face was spreading.

Hammond continued, "What I was going to say was, this man's not as elusive as you may think, unless you're hell bent on turning over every stone: no pun intended."

"Don't you think I've explored all other possibilities?"

"I know, Sir."

"Oh stop calling me, Sir, you sound ridiculous," Stone said.

"What I mean is, he will in fact hand himself over, if we let him."

"I don't follow."

"Look... all we've done so far, and I include myself in this, is draw him away from his original mission. Our good detective work in trying to understand this man, find out who he is and what his motives are for continuing this monstrous course, have only driven him off line and further away from detection."

"Tell me about it," Stone rang his hands out in front.

"So let's play the game his way, and follow his lead."

"You're still not making sense, Jack."

"What I mean is, his actions have already been ordained for him, and he's blindly following a need for justification. If we make it too hard for him he could just give up, or drag us around until we do."

"I see what you're getting at now. You mean we should be concentrating on his future victims, not running ourselves ragged looking for him."

"Exactly... except we don't have to wait, we can draw him to us now, using his own passionate hatred for these people."

"He wouldn't fall for an old trick like that," Stone scoffed.

"Want to bet. Look he's obsessed, so he isn't in control of what he's doing. He's simply fulfilling a destiny mapped out for him back at that camp, all those years ago. And so long as he has a breath in his body he'll continue executing these men until they're all gone."

"Poor old Steve beat him to it?"

"He won't distinguish. To him they're all just images in this role of judge and executioner; names given to him by Chessman; they're faceless. In fact, I'd go so far as to say he doesn't even know what it's all about any more."

Stone stood up again, walked over to his glass wall overlooking the squad room, stared at the large white board, barely visible on the far wall, then swung back.

"That's all very well, Jack," he said, "but it doesn't answer our immediate problem; we can't afford to wait until he's ready."

"That's what I'm saying, Stone. We have to get inside his head and think like he is, try and forecast his next move in this game he's playing."

"See... you think this is all a game yourself."

"Of course I do, just as you suspected yourself, according to Fraser. He said you didn't believe he used the Indian dupe just to leave the van outside the pub."

"That's true, but I don't know why."

"It's called a 'gut feeling' Stone, the thing you're always

accusing me of having, the difference is I trust mine, and you're scared of yours"

"You're right of course: I've always envied you for that."

"Then for once let go, do what your instinct is telling you. He's testing your weakness; he's trying to spread you out thinly across London, making you think he's going to strike here, there and everywhere."

"When in fact he's going for the Major."

"Now you're thinking, Stone. It's the Major he's after next, not Collins. It makes sense. He can't do anything about Steve now, he's already used Collins as bate to get you buzzing about, setting up more surveillance. And when he's ready he'll hop on the next train to Harrogate, unless he's managed to get another vehicle."

"What's to say he's not there already?"

"No... don't think like that," Hammond raised his voice. "Think like him, he's not finished with you yet. You spoiled his plans, as I did in Uxbridge, and what did he do, he thought, 'I'll teach them a lesson,' and left so many clues we're still chasing them down. That's what he's good at, leaving clues that lead nowhere, but take up time and manpower."

"I can see it all now, Jack, but how does he know he's running us ragged?"

"That's right, think like him, that didn't occur to you before. The only way he could know that is by watching us, and that's his mistake... that's how we'll get him."

"So if he's watching us, we can do the same to him and keep him busy."

A giant smile crossed Hammond's face.

"Exactly. Now let's go and get a drink and formulate a plan, all this has made me thirsty, I don't know about you?"

"Lead me to it," Stone said, in a better frame of mind.

Hammond checked his watch, "First, we're going to the hospital."

Luckily, Stone's head injury turned out to be superficial. There were no fractures or underlying problems: just a deep gash that needed stitching and an almighty bruise.

The convivial atmosphere of the Met's local pub, enforced by a constant flow of Watney's with a whisky chaser, did wonders for both their dispositions. Wedged tightly into a corner stall, with high protective sidewalls, they felt secure in discussing what really should have taken place in the confines of the Yard.

The outcome, despite their condition, was that Major Drake was going to be the next victim in Harrogate. On previous performance, they knew Kho Chiah Sek always did his homework. He meticulously checked out every aspect of his target: the location, the victim's premises and the times people came and went.

Then there was the opportunity. In each case, he was able to lure the victim to a secluded place or take advantage of the local surroundings: as he did with Lieutenant Lonergan. In each case all this took time.

"You have to make him think you have taken his bait," Hammond said.

"I know," Stone replied. "Mark has instructions to maintain the surveillance on Collins, the flat in Hammersmith and the warehouse in Wandsworth, but what about Major Drake. We have to cover him as well."

"All we need is one operative... you and I will do the rest."

"But how are we going to draw him in without him knowing?"

"We need to work that out with the Major."

The following day Stone rang the Major to inform him of developments and outline their sketchy plans for duping the killer. He had not taken into account the Major's experience in strategy; a skill attained in his second military life after the fiasco in Singapore. Like Lonergan, he was a regular.

He had given the problem some thought in his assessment that Stone would eventually call upon his assistance, and he came up with the perfect scheme. He had an Army Reunion party coming up and they had arranged everything except the venue.

"Why don't we have it at my place, Superintendent; it's big enough. As you said earlier, my situation means he has to do his foul deed there anyway. I'm sure a few soldiers wouldn't deter him. He's mad enough."

"It may even suit him, Major. You know what they say, 'Safety in numbers. He may even see the confusion as a good cover."

The Major laughed, "There'll be plenty of that, Superintendent."

Hammond arranged to call in on Stone later in the morning. When Stone told him of the Major's suggestion, he agreed it was just what they were looking for. However, he did have reservations; only Stone and himself, Mark and Sergeant Binstead should be involved.

"How are we going to pull this off with only four officers?" Stone said.

"I spent all night thinking about this regardless of the venue," Hammond said. "The only way this is going to succeed is the fewer that know about it the better."

"But it's going to be a big operation."

"No it's not. Think about it. Mark and my Sergeant can be in charge of the imaginary surveillance, leaving you and me to deal with Kho Chiah Sek."

"I suppose it will work."

"Of course, it will. Our lads will keep Kho's spies busy all right."

"Leaving us to get on with our job," Stone said.

Hammond had brought the Sergeant with him and he was bringing himself up to date with Mark's latest information on the board.

"That looks a lot better, Mark," Stone said, walking over. "Let's have some lunch and you can brief Inspector Hammond."

The Sergeant glanced at Hammond and he nodded his head.

When Stone chose one of the secluded booths, the stage was set as he began briefing Mark and the Sergeant on the latest move in the case. Neither wanted to interrupt and just sat quietly eating their lunch. Hammond did the same, happy to let Stone take the lead.

Stone explained the need for secrecy. He then made sure Mark and the Sergeant was to keep up the surveillance on the key sites while he and Hammond unfolded their scheme to trap Kho Chiah Sek in the act of killing the Major.

"You lay out the detail, Jack." Stone said, getting on with his lunch.

"Are you sure?"

"Yes, Jack... carry on."

"Okay. The plan is for the Major to have his reunion party at his house and for the Superintendent and I to go in with the caterers: details can be worked out later. Kho is sure to have someone watching each location while he is in Harrogate, so you two need to be making a lot of activity... that's your job."

"Excuse me, Boss," the Sergeant spoke up, "Where will you and the Superintendent be while we're doing this?"

"I told you... in Harrogate," Hammond said.

The confusion was setting in already.

Mark jumped in, "I know what he means... surely Kho's spies will be looking out for you two. I mean... you are his main adversaries."

"They're right, Jack," Stone said.

Hammond thought for a moment, "Yes... I hadn't taken that into account."

"We can't be in two places at once, Jack," Stone added.

"Yes you can," the Sergeant interrupted. "There's a police helicopter stationed at Westminster. A car could rush you from Collins' pub down to the river where the Thames police could be waiting to take you to the helicopter."

"That's excellent, Sergeant," Hammond said. "He only needs to see us at one location. We can make a quick commotion and leave."

Stone looked enthusiastic, "Done... make all the arrangements."

"There's just one thing, Boss," Mark said hesitantly, "How is Kho going to know about the party. He might have his own plans."

"He's right, Jack."

"All right," Hammond said, "It's just a detail."

"That's an awful lot of details to tie up, Jack."

Hammond brought out his notebook and thumbed through the first few pages until he found what he wanted, "If you lot had given me a chance I was going to bring you up to date on my last discussion with the Major."

"Sorry, Jack," Stone continued. "I think this bump on the head has blurred my memory... you carry on."

By now, Mark had ordered drinks in and Hammond took a long gulp of his, "Okay. From what you told me of your discussion with the Major, I couldn't sleep knowing everything hinged on him understanding our plan. It was one thing him saying he did, but I just had to be sure." He took another drink, and then returned to his notes. "My main aim for ringing him was to check on the situation in Harrogate, and he told me he had already organised everything, all he had to do is send out the invitations. Oh, and another thing that will please that sceptical mind of yours: his daughter has noticed a strange car parked regularly near their house."

"I hope she didn't frighten him off?"

"No... if you recall, there's a green area opposite the Major's house and apparently this individual takes his dog there for a walk every day."

"How long has that been going on?" Stone questioned.

"She said she spotted him a few days ago... so we can only assume he's one of Kho's spies. And that's good; it will work in our favour. I arranged with her to accidentally drop an invitation card when she's posting them; they conveniently have a box within eyesight of where he's parked."

Stone took Hammond's pause to be the end of his brief.

"What about the caterers?"

"I told you... the Major had everything organised," Hammond said.

Mark spoke up, "I don't know, and I'm sure the Sergeant doesn't."

"Neither of you are involved in that part of the plan, but I'll fill you in if you want," he said, finishing his drink. "We have arranged to go in with the caterers... they just have to be informed of the date and this new change of arrival in a helicopter. If it's all right with you Superintendent I'll ring the Major this afternoon along with the final date. Can we settle that now... the caterers need three days?"

"Stone took out his diary, "Well it has to be a weekend and the next one is four days away. Is that enough time?"

"It has to be. If you two start turning over each venue tomorrow; and keep it going until Friday... we'll go into Collins place in the evening."

"So I'll organise the helicopter for Friday evening, Boss?" the Sergeant said.

"That's right. Keep them on standby; we can radio them when ready."

When they arrived back at Stone's squad room Hammond made his call. The Major's daughter answered; her father was resting and she hoped she could answer any questions Hammond might have. He informed her that the plan was on for this weekend. She was to send out the invitations immediately, discreetly dropping one by the box and inform the caterers to start preparing.

Hammond spent the rest of the afternoon with Stone organising the plan that was to take affect the following morning. No one would miss him: he was on holiday.

Later that afternoon the Major's daughter rang Stone's number. She had done what Hammond asked her and after returning to the house, she watched the man leave his car with the dog, walk up to the box and under the pretext of adjusting the dogs leash, he picked up the card, read it and dropped it in the box.
Stone turned to Hammond and said, "We've got him, Jack."

CHAPTER 24

Stone walked into Ralph Collins' pub, after a routine check around his surveillance sites before joining the Inspector to take their helicopter trip. All was quiet; there was no sighting of the suspect yet. Maybe the reason was inside, he thought, as he joined his friend sitting away from the main drinkers. The Inspector's attention was on a suspicious looking Asian.

"He's over by the dart board, leaning against the bar," Hammond said, taking a sip of his beer. "He knows I'm here watching him, I'm sure it's our man. You see how he's pretending to watch the darts, but really his eyes are all over. I knew without looking, when you arrived, he picked you up straight away."

"Well I hope something happens quickly," Stone said impatiently, looking at his watch. "We're due at the heliport in fifteen minutes."

"Why don't I get you a drink, beer okay. We can't have him seeing what a mess he made of you, and then we'll see what he does when I go up to the bar."

"Beer will be fine, I'll keep my eye on you, and him; and for your information I have just spent the best part of an embarrassing hour with one of the female constables, having my face made up... see."

Hammond glanced at Stone and nodded his head in approval

before he slowly zigzagged his way through the milling crowd between him and the suspect.

Hammond's move proved that the Asian was frantically scanning the area, attempting to keep Stone and Hammond in view at all times. Their separation seemed to confuse him, posing him a dilemma on which one he should watch.

Instead of going for Stone's drink directly, Hammond aimed for an opening further down the bar nearer the Asian. He spotted the change straight away and casually made his way to the toilet in the far corner.

Stone watched what was going down and worked his way across to the front entrance, ready to rush outside if needed. He snatched the opportunity behind a pillar to radio the team outside to be alert.

Hammond followed a few yards behind, but when he opened the inner door the urinal was empty. He banged open the toilet doors one by one; they were empty also. He couldn't have just vanished, Hammond thought. Then he saw it, a small open window above a cupboard holding a cistern.

He rushed back out into the bar, hastily looking for Stone, then noticing him by the door, gave him the sign of a slit throat, and nodded his head to one side indicating he'd skipped. Stone was out into the street within seconds, just in time to see two of his men chasing another down the dimly lit cobbled back lane.

"Missed him," Hammond gasped, catching up to Stone outside.

By now, the running figures had already disappeared into another back alley and were gone, except for the sound of running feet echoing down the lane.

"Their chasing him," Stone said, out of breath. "I don' hold out much hope, he had too much of a head start and he obviously knows this place like the back of his hand."

"See what I said about careful planning," Hammond added,

sucking in deep breaths. "He had everything worked out for such a contingency. I was only seconds behind him. He must have gone in earlier and set-up his escape route."

"Are you sure it was our man, or just a drug dealer thinking his patch had been rumbled," Stone questioned, slightly out of breath.

"Oh you may well be right, but one thing I am sure of, if it wasn't him you can bet he or one of his cronies was watching everything. So find out what's happened to your men, and then we can make our way to the waiting helicopter. At least he can't follow us there."

It was never on the cards that they would catch the suspect this easily. Each time they came close to him, he managed to slip away like a ghost in the night.

Stone was sure he was going to draw this out to the ultimate end, and in all probability, there would be more deaths to account for. His two exhausted men returned after the chase to confirm they had lost him amongst the labyrinth of back alleys.

They were convinced he had fallen into their scenario. Satisfied they were giving him the impression that Stone's elite squad was running about chasing their tails as they left for the heliport on the Thames South Bank.

After an uneventful evening flight, the helicopter landed at the Leeming RAF base where a car was waiting to take them to a motel. Hardly a word passed between them during the flight, and even less in the car. They were both pondering on the possibility that their adversary would be waiting for them, and that their encounter in the pub was yet another of his grand demonstrations of his cunning.

Collins was secure, if not by the police that surrounded the pub, then by his own defence: strategies to alert him to an intruder and his faithful wartime Browning automatic.

Early mornings in Yorkshire at this time of the year were much different to those in London. The Thames valley was a sheltered area that, other than its fair share of rain, was far milder than most parts of England. The motel was just a few miles from the town centre on the nearside of the river Nidd. The whole area was cloaked in a shroud of chilling dampness, as Stone rubbed the condensation from his window to see what the day had in store before going down for breakfast.

As he entered the room, he could see Hammond already seated.

"I don't know about you, but I had a rough night," Stone said.

"I know what you mean," Hammond replied groggily. "I couldn't settle down after that helicopter ride, I hate the things."

"They don't bother me, it's all this uncertainty," Stone said, looking down at Hammond's English breakfast of bacon and eggs, with fried bread on the side; it was still bubbling and wet, "I don't know how you can eat all that."

The girl came over to take Stone's order, "I think I'll just have a continental breakfast and coffee please," he said, resting on his elbow.

"We just do English," she informed, flicking a piece of hair from her face.

"What about some toast, you can do toast I assume?"

"Yes, of course," she grunted indignantly. She looked down at Hammond pushing his bacon about. "I'll bring two servings, with jam shall I?"

"That'll be fine"

She dashed off; they could hear her loud cries to the chef from where they sat in the small front room of a converted house.

"Why on earth did you book us in here?" Stone asked. "What was wrong with a hotel. We don't even have a car.

"I didn't, the catering man arranged it, it's free; he probably owns the place."

"What time are we meeting him?" he asked again, just as the girl arrived."

"That's more like it," the Inspector said, eyeing the 'door steps'."

"I thought you may be hungry," she replied, setting it down in front of them, with extra pots of tea and coffee. "Oh by the way, my father said he will be here in about three quarters of an hour."

"Your father?" Stone questioned, still half asleep.

"Yes... he's the caterer," she replied, and left.

"You were right, Jack, as usual," Stone said, diving into the toast.

Feeling a lot better and back in their rooms gathering their overnight gear together, the phone rang in Hammond's room, his door was open and Stone popped his head round to listen, it was a call from the desk telling him the caterers' van had arrived.

Standing outside was a Mercedes mini-bus with plenty of room for the caterers and a large hot and cold storage area at the rear. It was early Saturday morning and the two men and an older woman had instructions to drop the police officers off at the Major's while they discuss his requirements for that evening.

The woman in her fifties turned round in her front seat, "Today's exercise is for your benefit gentlemen, but I would appreciate as much information as you are allowed to tell me for my staff's sake. I don't want them involved in this."

"What did the Major tell you?" Stone asked her.

"Not much, just that you're special police and that the party is set up to catch someone you expect may try and infiltrate the group."

"That's enough," Hammond exclaimed loudly."

"There's not going to be any danger is there?" she continued.

"No... not at all, it's not that type of operation," Stone said.

"We're here," the driver called out. "What do you want to do?"

Hammond checked his window while Stone checked the other.

"Is there some way you can drive up close to the side door?" Hammond asked, noticing a grey car parked over the road by the trees. "I wonder if that's our dog walking character," he whispered to Stone.

"Do you want me to go across and ask?. Stone said, regaining his humour.

"How about I drive the bus right round to the back, Sir," the driver suggested.

"That'll be great if you can."

The man nodded and continued.

"No problem, we've been here before, there's plenty of room. His garage is further back than most, so we can drive up in front of it."

Major Drake's daughter was there to greet them; they could see her father watching from the French windows, as the bus neatly reversed into a niche by the back door, narrowly missing a group of dustbins.

"This is an awful lot of fuss to go to just for a reunion party," the daughter said, as they alighted from the bus and Stone and Hammond quickly dashed inside through the open door. She followed them, still waiting for an answer.

"Better safe than sorry, Miss Drake," Hammond said.

"Why... you don't expect any trouble do you?"

"No, Miss," Stone replied.

He took hold of her arm and led her through into the sitting room. Apparently, she was unaware of the staged affair. The Major thought it would be better if she arranged to see her friend, and stay over, as things usually got a bit rowdy.

"You just get off to your friend and we'll look after the Major for you," Stone assured her. Her bag was already packed and standing at the foot of the stairs.

She half accepted his reply; "Oh very well, maybe I'll see you later?"

"I'm sure you will," Stone replied with a smile.

She left the caterers pretending they were organising for the party later while Stone introduced Hammond to the Major in his conservatory. He was sitting by the window looking out over the garden; or as it turned out, watching his daughter trying to manoeuvre her car around the caterers' Mercedes.

"Is everything going off to plan gentlemen?" he said, turning round.

"Everything's fine, Major," Stone replied.

"This is Inspector Hammond."

Hammond was surprised for the moment; he thought he was the General. "Ah... you turned up the Army connection with Lieutenant Lonergan."

Hammond glanced at Stone, he hardly expected him to lay praise on another party, least of all himself. "How do you do, Major, I only had the one case, and it turned out to be the mess Colonel Lonergan's men were in."

"Yes I heard about that, we lost touch you know. Then the General had that book launching party and we all discovered each other again, except poor old Steve Farney. Is he any better by the way?"

"I'm afraid Steve died recently, Sir," Stone answered.

"Oh dear... I am sorry. Not another casualty I hope?"

"No, Sir. It was natural causes."

"Well... it comes to us all," he paused and looked down into his lap, then looked up sharply again and continued. "The team's almost gone now. The sad thing is no one will ever remember them... they won't even know the sacrifice they made, like a lot in their situation; just a bunch of unknown soldiers."

"And we mustn't forget Chessman," Stone said. "He's the cause of all this."

"Yes..." the Major appeared particularly distant. "What's the agenda?"

Stone walked back over towards the large dining room being prepared for the party and closed the door for fear the caterers may hear him.

"Well hopefully the caterers have managed to get us in here without being noticed, that is of course if the person in the car across the road is who we think he is. So all we need to do now is lay low until party time."

"That's good, the trap is set then... I'm ready for him. As for it being a party, I don't know about that. I'm afraid, if you're not familiar with regular battalion reunions, some of our rituals could surprise you."

"Don't be too ready to play a part, Sir," Hammond urged. "We don't want you to get involved if it can be avoided. We need you where we can watch you."

"Ah but, Inspector, can you?" he said manipulating his reclining chair so he could point out his gun collection on the wall to his left. "Take your pick, if you want," he said. "If I am the target, we shall most definitely come to face each other at some time or other. In that event, I shall be prepared. He patted the small automatic under his blanket.

"We'd rather you didn't provoke him with a weapon, Sir," Stone said.

"Superintendent, you told me this man used a Samurai to torture his victims, if not to eventually kill them. In this instance, I doubt if he will follow that same procedure, therefore it's reasonable to assume he will combine both into one or two well-placed strokes, which won't do much for my disposition. In that event, I intend to keep him out of Samurai range."

"We can't stop you, but we would prefer it if you played a low profile during the festivities, Sir," Stone recommended.

The Major chuckled to himself.

"Do you really think I could get up to any of those Army battalion reunion shenanigans, Superintendent?"

They both laughed and agreed not. They left him to start their rounds of surveillance and check out the guest room prepared for them to rest up before the show, and then change into their disguise as part of the catering staff.

"I don't know about you, Jack, but I'm bushed," Stone said as he yawned.

"We're off now," the caterer said. "I think we've taken enough time to organise the details. Do you want me to do anything particular when I leave?"

"Such as what?" Hammond asked.

"Well draw attention to ourselves."

"Don't you think that great big Mercedes will do that?"

"Sorry... of course it will. I haven't done this sort of thing before."

"And you're not expected to," Stone said. "We just wanted you to smuggle us in, that's all. So get going, and do what you normally do for tonight.

Secreted behind the net curtains they watched the bus head into the road and drive off towards the town centre. A few seconds later, the small grey car followed.

"We should have had a car standing by to follow him," Stone muttered.

"Let things run their course. Slowly, slowly catchy monkey," Hammond said. "Something I learnt in Korea.

They agreed to take two-hour rests, which meant two before lunch and two after, bringing both of them together around five, when they could have some tea and prepare for the enormous task of watching everything that was to follow that night. Each of them dropped in on the Major during his shift, making conversation and discovering how active a life this man had had during his service years.

He lived several lifetimes compared to them: well at least Stone. He was not alone, his faithful valet from the Army days joined him when they retired, and Stone spent some time with him questioning what sort of duties he had.

It was apparent he worshipped the man and would do anything to protect him, as Stone found out when he mentioned the firearm the major proposed using if he had to. The valet said he would, without hesitation, and was an excellent shot, despite his condition. However, he would watch the Major like a hawk, and head off any danger that would threaten him. When Stone told him what Kho Chiah Sek had done to his victims, he smiled; he and the Major had plenty of experience, and were prepared.

The caterers were punctual, as the clock in the study chimed seven. Bringing with them all their baskets and heated containers, and taking over the proceedings of the household.

Stone and Hammond tried to keep out of their way, as difficult as it was, and still maintain some form of effective surveillance, with everyone passing in and out of the house preparing for the night's celebration.

Then the lull that descended on the house snapped them out of their passive numbness; most of the caterers had left in the bus, leaving just the smartly groomed servers, in their immaculate starched white shirt and jacket, black trousers and bow tie, putting the final touches to the main table.

While they decanted bottles of wine, the first of the guests arrived and the two watchdogs changed into their caterer attire also before making one more circuit of the house, popping in to see if the Major was ready.

By eight o'clock, the full complement of officers was standing in the dining room with their ration of toasting port facing Colonel Cockcroft, the master of ceremonies. A crescendo of rah-rah's and banging of feet on the parquet floor heralded the start of the rituals, followed by the removal of the magnificent Persian carpet for the occasion.

Due to the Major's condition, his valet moved his chair to the opening of the grand hall as the officer's stood to attention and raised their glasses. Unable to join in the festivities, they at least carried him to his seat next to the Colonel and following another round of toasts, the usual anecdotes of past battles and more toasts, the Major returned to the peace of his conservatory.

After dinner the games started, progressing to a wilder state as more drinks flowed while Stone and Hammond deliberately left the officers to celebrate their reunion without knowing the real reason for the gathering. They were losing control realising the Major was content to let the reunion continue until it had run its course.

Later that evening, one of the officers, in his magnificent red jacket and black trousers, sporting a gold stripe, interrupted Stone and Hammond as they were leaving the kitchen with a fresh supply of drinks; his face was white with shock.

"I say, there's a dead man outside in the bushes," he spluttered.

His condition prompted them to think he was drunk; mistaking one of his colleagues who had passed out in the shrubbery.

"Are you sure your friend hasn't just passed out, Sir?" Stone remarked, steadying the young soldier as he swayed back and forth.

"I know what I saw man, and he isn't my friend. He's one of you chaps."

Hammond looked at Stone; the same notion must have crossed both their minds at the same time. They placed their trays on a nearby table and rushed outside; the officer following closely as others joined them.

"There you are, he's just behind those bushes there," the officer said, pointing from behind, while Stone was trying to keep the others from trampling the scene.

They squeezed passed two Rhododendron shrubs, bathed in light from the open door, and noticed two deep drag trails from the path.

"Poor chap, what's happened to him?" the staggering officer called out.

"Please, Sir, go inside, leave this to us," Stone said, escorting him back. "The rest of you also, will you please gather in the main room."

"I think I have the authority here," stated the Colonel, looking bristly.

Stone showed him his warrant card, he looked blank.

"Good god man, what are the police doing here?"

"Colonel, it's a long story, and not over by any means yet, could you please use your authority over your men and get them into some form of order until we get this sorted out?" Stone asked politely, herding them back into the house with his arms outstretched, leaving Hammond to see to the dead man.

"Right... most definitely, leave it to me, Superintendent."

Before Stone put a foot out of the kitchen door to return to the crime scene, he bumped into Hammond rushing back into the house.

"He's one of the caterers... he's been garrotted."

"I checked everyone... I've been doing that all night," Stone replied.

"I know... so have I, but he's taken the man's jacket."

They moved swiftly through the guests. Those who had no idea of what was going on were still playing their games, while the others that did, stand mesmerised.

"Colonel," Stone called out, "You must get these men under control; the Major's life is at stake. At the same time can you please post men at all the exits, including the windows, we have an intruder in the house who's hell bent on killing the Major."

"Where is he. Do you know?" the Colonel asked, more resolute.

"He can only be with the Major, that's where we're going now. But if he isn't, and any of your men come across him, please tell them to be careful."

"My men know how to handle themselves, drunk or not."

"He's probably armed with a sword," Stone warned him.

"Right, Superintendent, leave it to us. They're good men; they can look after themselves in enemy territory. You get on and find the Major."

"And do stop anyone following us," Hammond called out as they left.

They both reached behind their backs under their uniforms for the automatic they were carrying. They checked the clips once again, and then rushed to the end of the room to the conservatory. Without hesitation, Hammond opened the doors as Stone covered him.

The room was in darkness, except for the two figures clearly silhouetted by the French windows, in the soft garden lights adorning the trees and paths.

"Shut the door gentlemen, I've been expecting you," an Asian voice corrupted with a metropolitan accent spoke calmly from the shadows.

It was an educated voice, although it could be no other by the planning that went into each of his missions. It was calm, not affected by the traumatic event.

Since the only source of light was behind the killer who was standing over the Major in his chair, and a glint of bright steel poised at his throat, Stone attempted to move forward, expecting to hide his movement in the shadows.

"Stay where you are, Superintendent," he ordered. "I can see your reflections in the glass of the French doors, it would only take a flick of this blade and the Major would be minus his head."

Stone stopped dead in his tracks, still poised on his next step.

"Do as he says gentleman. As infirmed as I am, I still have a fondness for this head," the Major pleaded, appearing to give the impression he was scared and frail, certainly not the image they had of him when he told them he could fend off all comers with the small automatic under his blanket.

Stone wondered whether he still had it, or that Kho had searched him. It was obvious that, under the circumstances, their weapons were useless.

"Now Superintendent Stone and Inspector Hammond; I know you're both carrying automatics, so let's be sensible and place them on the table in front," there was a pause. "Oh... you think you can beat me to the draw do you. Probably you have them pointing at me now, with the idea of using them in the dark. I assure you... I shall have this head off before you pull the trigger."

"Don't do anything hasty," Hammond shouted. "I'm moving forward with my gun in the air," he placed it carefully on the table, making sure Kho heard it touch the wood.

"Very good, Inspector... now you, Superintendent."

Stone reluctantly did the same.

"Now gentlemen, step back to where you were... and if you're crafty enough to have another weapon on you, remember... the hand is quicker than the eye."

"We have no other weapons, so you can relax," Hammond said. "There's no need to have that blade on the Major."

"You're not in a position to demand anything."

"I wasn't. If you won't relax then at least let us put a light on and see what's going on, for your sake as well as ours."

He did not debate the request. He told the Major to switch on the lamp over the small table and be careful about it. They watched the two melded figures move over to their right. The Major reached up for the switch.

The light came on, and although it radiated a soft restricted glow, sending harsh shadows dancing around the walls and ceiling, it still blinded them for a moment. They caught a fleeting image of Kho standing behind the Major before he turned his head and faced the windows.

The Major looked grave, but as resolute as anyone could with a razor sharp blade at his throat. Kho, although unmistakably Asian, looked surprisingly refined.

This man, with his light coffee coloured completion, white teeth and shoulder length raven black hair, tied back behind his neck with a cord, did not look as if he had spent his childhood fighting for scraps left by the Japanese.

"How did you know we were here?" Stone asked.

"I didn't, one up for you, Superintendent, you certainly fooled me in London. I thought you were all running around in circles, until I looked through the kitchen window and saw you both filling your trays with drinks. Those uniforms suit you."

"Then why did you enter the house with all these soldiers about, you must have known you would be caught?"

"Superintendent, my success to date has been entirely due to my lack of personal concern. My only objective was to make these men pay for what they did, and if that means a swift death for the Major at my own expense, then so be it."

"But that's not what you really want, is it?" Hammond questioned, as Stone edged forward. "You want him to suffer like you made the others suffer, don't you. A quick death wouldn't suit your purpose."

That agitated Kho, and a trickle of blood ran down the Major's neck onto his white collar, as he tensed his grip on the weapon's hilt.

"Don't attempt anything, Superintendent or I'll do it. I've nothing to lose now," he shouted out nervously, mirrored against the darkness of the multi-paned French doors he could see all that was going on behind him, yet Stone could only see down to his chest from where he was; it was enough to see the decorated hilt of the Samurai's small companion.

"Why did you have to kill that man, he did you no harm?" Stone goaded.

"I had to, he would have cried out."

"But the fact that he was missed, alerted us to your presence anyway," Hammond said, hoping to stall him long enough to find a way out of this.

It was obvious by Kho's shifting posture, that he was uncomfortable with them to one side, with the small table between them. It meant he had to switch his concentration from the Major to see what they were doing.

"Come around here where I can see you both," he ordered, "and be careful."

"Why don't you move round to face us?" Hammond replied.

"Oh yes... you would like that, an opportunity to catch me off guard. Besides, moving to your left will take you further away from your guns.

They moved around him slowly, and the glow from the lamp that was highlighting his face changed him: catching the pockmarks from his cheekbones to the line of his sharp chin. Sweat was now glistening on his brow.

Stone still clung to the hope that an opportunity to grab a gun may present itself later, and he had to be within easy reach. As for Hammond, he edged his way in the opposite direction, looking as furtive as possible, hoping to draw Kho's attention.

"Don't separate, do you think I'm stupid. Both on one side," he shouted.

Hammond looked at Stone and realising his motive, stepped over to his side still playing his game, attempting to distract Kho. As they drew alongside him, giving them an opportunity to see beyond the shadowy reflections on his face, a new realisation suddenly gripped Stone.

"Narasimram... What are you doing here?" he exclaimed.

His question puzzled Hammond. He never met the Indian dupe.

"What's going on here?" Hammond finally spoke out.

"Let me introduce you to the Indian dupe we actually had in custody," Stone said curtly. "Can you believe we didn't check his prints?"

"So what happened to Kho?" Hammond said.

"Kho Chiah Sek doesn't exist anymore. He never left Australia," the Indian said. "I killed him and took his identity. He relaxed for the first time, even managed a smile. "I can see Superintendent you're having difficulty with that. You're wondering where along the chain of events our identities changed."

CHAPTER 25

Narasimram's revelation was devastating. What had they been doing all this time. How did they come up with all the incriminating evidence. And the fingerprints that lead them to Kho in the first place. All these thoughts were rushing through their minds and he looked delighted in their confusion.

Hammond was the first to say something, still not quite believing his statement. He felt as though he had returned to a conversation after missing the middle: the part that contained all the important stuff.

"I think you owe us an explanation, but before you do, why don't you release the blade from the Major's throat, you must be getting tired. And another thing, whatever happened to the Major's valet?"

"He's over there," the Major said. "Behind the curtains."

Hammond made a move as if to see, but was stopped in his tracks as Narasimram unsheathed the other small blade and pointed it in his direction.

"There's no need, I assure you he's beyond help now," he threatened.

"He just cut him down where he stood, it wasn't necessary," the Major pointed out to his detriment, as he felt the pressure on the blade increase.

Narasimram thought for a moment, he was not ready to kill

the Major yet. Had he been able to accomplish the deed on his terms, his venue, things would have been different. Without any hope of escape, his only satisfaction would be to show this so called brilliantly famous police force, how he ran rings around them. Then, to their surprise, he removed the blade from the Major's neck and rested it on his shoulder, while returning the other blade to its sheath.

"So you want an explanation do you?" he started, "it's quite simple really. Back in the seventies, I killed several men and felt it prudent that I leave the country for a while, although the authorities had no idea what was going on. I had friends in Australia, so I decided to take an extended holiday; let things cool off for a while. They introduced me to an Asian club, where I met Kho, who was interested in my English background because he had arranged to join a school in London sometime in the future. I gathered he was waiting for clearance from the emigration people. We became very close... lovers in fact."

"Yet we found you with an Indian girl at Earls Court," Stone said.

"My sexual preferences aren't under discussion. Let us just say, I got on well with Kho, and we were good for each other; we were able to confide our innermost secrets. That's when I discovered his tormenting experience with the Army." He pressed the back of the blade against the Major's shoulder forcefully, frightening him and the others. It was strong enough to have cut deeply, had it been the other way round.

"Don't let your anger do anything silly," Hammond shouted.

"These sorry excuses of men; you saw them out there, riding about on each other's backs. They're monsters, vile perverts; forcing young men to their gladiatorial delights, shattering two lives, mine and Kho's... so they had to pay. But Kho was sick of it all. His passion had waned after his wait for the Japanese

Commandant to vent all those years pent-up emotion, by executing him the same way he did his friend Chessman. After his mistreatment at the hands of the Hong Kong police, he was finished. So I told him he had to seek vengeance against the Special Forces that left Chessman to be tortured. But he couldn't do it, so I had to take over."

"We were under the impression that was his idea," Hammond said, trying to draw his attention away from Stone, who was attempting to inch his way very slowly towards the corner of the small table and the guns.

"No... his revenge against the Japanese Commandant drove all thoughts of the real criminals out of his mind, regardless of my prompting. I didn't need him anymore."

"But why should Kho's problems interest you?" Hammond asked again, keeping his attention focused on him; staring intently into his eyes.

"Oh... didn't I tell you, I kill soldiers. I like killing soldiers."

"Why soldiers in particular?" the Major asked.

"I suppose it goes back to my father, he was a soldier in India, where he met my mother and they had me. Right up till I was ten it was good having a British soldier for a father; it was like being rich and part of the elite set."

Peculiarly Stone was satisfied in that remark. It put credence to his earlier assumption that this man was not born of low caste, with a British soldier as a father.

"What was his rank?" the Major asked.

"You see, to them rank is all important, it's a class thing... them and us. My father was a Sergeant Major. You can keep your officers, he ran the show."

Hammond interrupted to regain his attention.

"So what happened when you were ten that was to change your life?"

"I don't know, except my father started to drink heavily, and stay out late."

"That wouldn't be enough to hate soldiers," Hammond continued.

"Consequently my mother was very unhappy; they used to fight a lot. He then started to abuse me sexually; he said it was time I started to learn about these things. My mother tried to stop him, but he just beat her each time she interfered."

"How long did that go on?" the Major asked, trying to sound sympathetic, "You could have complained to the Chaplin."

"No we couldn't, not an Indian woman, they had no rights. It didn't matter anyway, his drunkenness was reported and he was sent back to England. Then things got worse. He drank more, womanised more, anything to distract him from his demons."

"And you never found out what that was?" Hammond asked.

"No. Finally, he went too far. One night he burst into our billet with five other drunken men, who got hold of me and tied me to a chair. I thought they were going to abuse me again, but he had something else on his mind. My mother was screaming at him. He laughed at her and stripped her naked so the other five men could rape her in front of me.

"Whenever I tried to close my eyes, one of them would prise them back open, forcing me to see what vile things they were doing to her. A few days later, when I returned from school I found her dead: she had slit her wrists and bled to death. I vowed I would make them pay. It took me a while, but I did it. I killed them all one by one, and I made them know why; Like the Japanese Commandant, I cut their genitals off."

"And how did you finally kill them, or did you leave them to bleed to death like your mother," Hammond prompted.

"Why like my ancestors did to men like that, I garrotted them."

"The way you garrotted Chessman's colleagues?" the Major asked.

A mad grimace crossed his face.

"Why not... nice touch, don't you think. I copied what the Japanese Commandant did to Chessman first, and then added my touch."

"What surprises me is; why didn't this come out when we investigated your history? Hammond continued, noticing Stone was now very near his gun.

"Probably because it all happened on Army property, you know how you people like to bury your own mess," He said, returning the blade to the Major's neck.

"Hold on," Hammond interrupted, trying to distract him. "What you say is all very well, but you couldn't be in two places at the same time. If you played the part of the Indian dupe, then who was Kho and how did we get his fingerprints?"

"Why Kho of course," he said, breaking into a laugh that bordered on the hysterical.

The questions were serving the purpose of taking his mind off killing the Major, but at the same time, they were also changing his mental state. The Inspector had no idea which was worse: a devious killer or a raving lunatic.

Although the Major was becoming uncomfortable with the blade resting against his throat, he was attempting to talk him round, or at least divert his attention from Stone.

"It appears to me you have good grounds for mitigating circumstances. It would be a pity if you spoilt that now by accidentally cutting my throat."

He loosened his grip on the Samurai, "I assure you, Major, your throat will not be cut accidentally... it will be on purpose, and very soon if you don't shut up."

He continued staring at Hammond, who by chance had incited in him, the urge to bare his soul. "To answer your question Inspector; it's so simple, I'm surprised you didn't realise it earlier." He unfolded his dire machination to the absolute confusion of

Stone and Hammond, changing their whole outlook on this case as it unfolded.

"After I got back to England, using Kho's identity, I reverted to using my own to get at my assets, but used the name Allen Dumbleton generally to get my flats and other things. When I realised my anonymity had been blown in Uxbridge, I decided to fall back on Kho's papers, at the same time leaving material at the flat with his fingerprints on."

"So that's why the flat was full of evidence, when your previous crime scenes were very clean," Hammond said, "I knew there was something wrong."

"Yes... well it worked didn't it, long enough for me to get set up again somewhere else. I knew Kho's identity would catch up with me, so enter another Kho."

"Butch's friend," Hammond said, nodding his head and smiling.

"Yes, poor old Butch, a nice boy but stupid. My worst problem was finding someone I could shape to fit the scenario I had started, without getting suspicious. Anyway, you know the rest. I quickly reorganised my little garment fraud, not much to speak of really, but it paid the rent. I got the new Kho to start a trail for you to follow, while I decided on my next victim, which looked very much like it was going to be Ralph Collins."

His tale was finished, he had satisfied his ego, ensuring they learned the truth or his blood lust would have gone unheeded, and his flashing eyes said it all. Moving towards this moment, ready or not, Stone had to do something before the lunatic took a new breath.

He needed a diversion, as the pressure on the blade at the Major's neck brought forth a new bead of blood, glistening bright red as it trickled down his throat. Stone focused his singular attention on the gun nearest to him on the table.

In that split second of Narasimram's heightened paranoia, Stone and Hammond instinctively reacted at the same time. It was an adrenalin surge, one minded focus and sheer expectation compressed into one desperate moment.

His last glimpse of Hammond from the corner of his eye was of his attempt to distract the lunatic with his own sideways movement. It worked. Narasimram was distracted from the Major and forced to choose which target to direct his vicious blade. They had underestimated his agility.

As graceful as a ballet dancer, he swung round on the ball of his foot, from behind Major Drake to confront Stone: his choice of attack. Hammond was too far to his right to pose a threat, at least not until he had struck his fatal blow.

As best as Hammond tried to regain his balance and intercept, he knew he was too late as the long blade of the Samurai glinted, catching the light from the small lamp, sweeping upwards into the darkness and outwards to its apogee before it began its deathly downward arc towards Stone.

At first Stone terrifyingly lost sight of it until it swept back into the arc of light. He could now see every line of the engraving on the broad blade as it sped in his direction, transfixing him, travelling faster than he could think.

In that split second Stone realised he had lost. He had extended his reach too far to regain his balance, and he found himself instinctively closing his eyes, sensing the scratching of desperate fingers against his sleeve as Hammond reached out for him. Then a sharp crack rang out, like a whip snapping at the air, followed by the clatter of steel striking bare floorboards.

Major Drake had taken the moment he had patiently waited for. As soon as the blade left his throat for a new target, he fired his small automatic from under his blanket; he knew he could not miss: Narasimram was leaning across him.

As the Major examined the hole in his blanket, Hammond was the first to speak, "I have to admit, Major... that was a crack shot." There was no need to examine Narasimram; the bullet had penetrated his left side under his lower rib and entered his heart.

"It should be, Inspector, I still practice every week."

There was no time for further explanation. The door burst open and the Major's comrades in arms stumbled through. Like a gallant charge, they entered as one; led by their Colonel in Chief.

"What in God's name is going on in here," the Colonel shouted, at the head of his drunken soldiers, all staring at the body on the floor.

Hammond, the least traumatised of the group, ushered them out with outstretched arms. "This is a police matter, Colonel, as I've already said. I would appreciate it if you would collect your men together."

"What about the Major... is he all right?"

"He's fine, Colonel... now I need everyone ready for questioning."

"Come on, Inspector," he responded. "What fit state are they to answer any questions... look at them."

"Tomorrow, Colonel, they won't remember a thing of this night, better we struggle with them as they are now."

"Oh... very well, I'll do my best."

As soon as the Colonel had marched his men out of the room to sober them up, Hammond turned back to the scene. The Major had stopped examining the hole in his blanket and was placing his gun on the small table alongside theirs.

Stone was still trying to come to terms with the event; staring at the lifeless body of Narasimram, lying face down in front of him. The deadly Samurai sword, that Stone came so near to feeling, stood upright in the wooden floorboards where it had fallen from his assailant's hand, still swaying slowly from the recoil.

"What a fiasco," Hammond exclaimed, picking up the phone to call the local police, as Stone slowly returned to the present.

"God... that was close," he uttered. "Too close"

"The locals are on their way," Hammond said, replacing the receiver. "How are you feeling. Not too good I bet."

"Actually I feel quite exhilarated," Stone said. "What about the, Major?"

They both looked towards the old man who had saved the day. He was still in the same position. "It's all right," he said. "I'm not dead."

Hammond moved over to inspect the body of the Major's valet: his first opportunity.

"Why did he have to kill him like that?" the Major said, turning round in his chair to see him lying behind the curtains. "He didn't do anything, except try and protect me."

"You can't fathom the mind of a maniac like that," Stone commented.

"I suppose I shall have to see how the Colonel's getting on with his men," Hammond said, standing up from the valet's body.

He picked up his gun, handed Stone his and sauntered off to the grand hall.

Although it was hardly necessary for forensic to be there, the Yorkshire CID spared nothing in their enthusiasm. With a garrotted caterer, a valet with his throat cut and another shot by the Major, Inspector Carrington was making the most of his brush with Scotland Yard.

"Is someone going to tell me what all this is about?" he asked, looking in their direction, not knowing who was in charge. "I know a Superintendent had the courtesy to inform my Boss of the operation," Stone raised his finger without speaking. "But I don't think even he was expecting such carnage."

"Neither was I, Inspector," Stone stated.

Stone turned to Hammond as he returned to the crime scene, after handing over the gathering of statements to an eager sergeant.

"Jack, would you like to run through what today was all about with the Inspector while I see how that lot are getting on?"

"Sure I'd be happy to," he replied, taking the Inspector's arm and leading him over to where a doctor was examining Narasimram. "You see, Inspector, the reason we came to Yorkshire goes back to the surrender of Singapore..."

EPILOGUE

Superintendent Stone and Inspector Hammond took their places in the Coroners court; they said nothing, observing the Silence Order as indicated on several signs throughout the large wood-panelled room.

Hammond allowed his eyes to scan the unusual number of participants, also interested in the inquest of Ashish Narasimram: alias Kho Chiah Sek, Allan Dumbleton and so on. He was a man of many faces: Indian, Australian or Englishman, he certainly had no relatives or friends to speak of; no one to stand on his behalf, to explain the mitigating circumstances that he willingly imparted in every detail before his death.

The inquest concentrated on the man duly killed in self-defence whilst committing a crime: one of many. A case one would have thought was 'open and shut', at the least. Nonetheless, here they were along with all these strangers.

Stone was quite resolved, whereas Hammond was restless.

"You do know we're going to have to pay for this," Hammond said.

WHO GOES THERE?
CHARLES BEAGLEY
BLOOD BROTHERS
CHARLES BEAGLEY
THE SHERWOOD FOREST MAN
CHARLES BEAGLEY
Write On Read On
Charles Beagley

About the Author

As a child in the London blitz, Charles Beagley distracted himself from the horror of his family's situation by making up stories or drawing. His eventual training was at Art School, which equipped him for the many years he spent working in advertising and design. He lived in London initially, did two years National Services in the RAF, worked in Ireland and Belgium and then set up a Design Consultancy back in England for twenty years.

He married and had two sons whose futures concerned him as things were grim economically in 1982 England. He jumped at the opportunity to move his family to Australia when he was offered a managerial position in design. During his years in England, his writing developed as he wrote promotional text and an occasional short story.

Since coming to Australia he has honed his skills, writing many fictional stories, mainly mysteries.

Carter's Boys is one such novel that mixes fact with fiction and war time espionage.

OTHER TITLES BY CHARLES BEAGLEY

Blood Brothers
It takes a plane crash to bring two cultures together.

Who Goes There?
The "Troubles" in Ulster is a place where only villans and heroes survive.

The Sherwood Forest Man
The skeleton that revealed more than its ancient origin.

Cult Wars

In war, man reverts to his beliefs and they can prove far worse than imagined.

An Eye for an Eye?

The sequel to Who Goes There?
When vengeance is all that's left.

The Blue Pen

Six individuals come in contact with a magical blue pen that changes their lives forever.